DISTURBING THE UNIVERSE

Wagner's Musikdrama

DAVID VERNON

CR
Candle Row
Press

First edition September 2021

Interior layout by miblart.com
Cover photograph by vlue/DepositPhotos

ISBN:
978-1-5272-9924-5 (paperback)
978-1-5272-9923-8 (ebook)

Published by Candle Row Press

To

Karita Mattila

—in friendship, love and admiration

Contents

PART THREE: THE LATER WORKS

APPENDIXES

Acknowledgements

Although this book is dedicated to one very special artist in particular, opera in general, and especially Wagner's, requires a legion of forces for it to succeed: singers, players, designers, technicians, producers, administrators and a whole host of other talents. Those on stage get the glory and the glamour, but so many others are needed, and without them we cannot enjoy the immense riches of this vast and complex medium. To all those who help create this extraordinary art form: my eternal thanks.

Like composing, writing is a solitary activity. But like opera — or musikdrama! — publishing is a group effort, and I am grateful to the many literary and non-literary forces which have helped shape this book and bring it to its final form.

Special final thanks are due to my amazing editor, Elyse Lyon, who sees what I cannot see and always knows what I am trying to say. Any errors are, of course, my own.

Glyndebourne and Grenades

Richard Wagner was not an opera composer; he was a music-dramatist. Wagner perceived that music, especially symphonic music, could do more than simply accompany singers on the opera house stage. It could also tell difficult stories about complex individuals. It could minutely examine characters' minds, motivations, moods — even their souls. It could debate politics, theology and metaphysics. It could not only sound frightening or captivating, violent or beautiful, but could take listeners on vast intellectual, emotional and spiritual journeys, deep into subjects normally reserved for poets, priests or philosophers. Music, Wagner saw, could work in such a dramatically dialectical way that it could approach Aeschylus, Shakespeare and Schopenhauer for theatrical flexibility, expressive profundity and cerebral sophistication.

Think of opera today and, alas, music is not often the first thing that comes to mind, let alone intellectual activity. We still tend to imagine evening gowns and dinner jackets;

champagne and cummerbunds; divas and debutantes; ruby and gold horseshoe auditoriums; gourmet hampers from Fortnum & Mason on the lawns at Glyndebourne. In a word: 'posh'. In two words: 'elitist entertainment'. Wagner's own attempt — the Bayreuth Festival — to get away from this ghastly and snobbish state of affairs itself almost immediately became the leading event on Germany's social calendar: a gossip factory, a rumour mill, a symbol of conservatism and a place to be *seen*.

It might, therefore, surprise some people that Wagner not only stood on the barricades of the Dresden revolution but helped make hand grenades to lob at the police. He wrote numerous seditious pamphlets arguing for the destruction of contemporary society, the toppling of monarchies, an end to property ownership and, yes, the abolition of opera houses, those facilities of middle-class divertissement. Human nature being human nature, unable to know what is good for itself, the revolution failed, of course. But Wagner's musical and dramatic bombs did not fizzle and fade away into the status quo. His musikdramas* persist today as violent, energetic, explosive expressions of radical, world-shattering fervour and social commitment, dynamically arguing for a different and better future for all. Richard Wagner, poster boy for fascists and plaything for rich playboys, is, in fact, the ultimate anarchist.

To come into contact with Wagner's art is to experience deep sensual pleasure, profound emotional feeling, complex intellectual debate and otherworldly spiritual illumination. Wagner is a lover, a scholar, a shaman and a sorcerer. He is

---

*   I've chosen to use the German spelling *Musikdrama* rather than the English *music drama*; to my mind, the English translation does not capture the full sense of the original term. This book argues that Wagner created something exceptional, if not unique, and the term's use is therefore appropriate. To avoid the infelicities introduced by using German capitalization and pluralization in an English-language context, I've treated it as an English word — *musikdrama/musikdramas* — rather than employing *Musikdrama/Musikdramen*.

a truth-seeker and a myth-maker, a prophet and a historian, a doctor and a cleric. Wagner's art is a library, a brothel and a church. It is a sunrise and a snowstorm, a vista and a labyrinth, an island and a road. It exposes malice and humiliates pain. It charts reality through a dissection of fantasy. It refuses to stand still, its internal energy reaching into infinity, but its precision and dexterity avert loss of control. Wagner is a juggler and a magician, an acrobat and a scientist, an engineer and an artist. His art destroys the false boundaries of convention and declares eternal emancipation. Wagner's musikdramas decline to play by the rules or observe any of the social graces. Propriety, modesty and decorum are alien to their spirit and foreign to their understanding.

What is it that makes Wagner's art so endlessly powerful? So influential, seductive and repellent? So simultaneously creative and destructive? So disruptive and divisive? And where did it come from?

છે.

Beethoven, Berlioz and others had developed the symphony to an unprecedented level of intense and erudite expression. But Wagner knew that such intricacy and subtlety could be applied to the world of opera, where composers too often wrote orchestral music to order, by prescription, or simply to show off. They flaunted shallow musical effects to dazzle audiences, who themselves were often there only to be seen or, at best, mildly entertained. Opera libretti, too, were seldom better than fourth rate: they didn't need to be good, because no one was paying attention, or because it was necessary merely to get the flimsy characters from situation A to situation B with a minimum of fuss in time for the next flamboyant aria or multifarious ensemble. The orchestral music didn't need to engage with the action on stage; it just needed to parade and amuse.

Wagner knew that things could be better: that the erudition of the symphony, the string quartet and the piano sonata — the holy trinity of classical musical form — could be brought to the opera house, as could the power and poetry of the great dramatists. Some opera masters, especially Gluck, Mozart, Beethoven, Weber and Bellini, had come close, but, for Wagner, much as he admired those geniuses, even their radical innovations had congealed into conventions, customs which had stuck and, worse, become deep rooted in the culture of Europe's musical theatre. The virtuoso singing, sensational stage pyrotechnics and futile plots of the opera house were, to Wagner's sensibility, hollow, meaningless, directionless. They were a wasted opportunity. Stage effect and bravura vocal technique Wagner would certainly cultivate, but only for the overall effect of the drama, not simply for their own sake.

Wagner sought, on the one hand, to cultivate the sophistication of the non-musical elements of opera (text, acting, lighting and so on), asserting all the arts to be ineludibly equal and united. Yet on the other hand, and at the same time, he strove to heighten the refinement of the musical component, eventually seeing music as the most important and powerful element of emotional-intellectual expression. It is this apparent contradiction — unity and superiority — which is the key to Wagner's distinctiveness and originality, the paradox wherein lies how he was different to what had gone before and which would be the prototype for the many who would follow. Strauss, Janáček, Schoenberg, Bartók, Prokofiev, Berg, Britten and countless others would, in their very idiosyncratic ways, follow Wagner not only in expanding the orchestral component to opera but also by cultivating the seriousness and quality of the libretti they set and the overall intellectual and artistic experience of their works.

Wagner never contradicted his earlier view of aesthetic parity but developed beyond it, turning his works into complex syntheses in which music, drama, text, and so forth could not be easily separated. They would truly work together, music creating drama by the power of its own articulation, drama becoming impossible to entirely detach from the music. The boundaries between the arts became porous, fluid, intricate, and although music was the mainspring, the principal motivator, it existed only to amplify and enrich the other elements, to drive the drama and its dialectical finesse.

Although Wagner himself had problems with the term *musikdrama*, the distinction between this and opera is a crucial one to make, since the musikdrama, as Wagner advanced it over the course of his stage career, functions in a fundamentally different way to traditional opera. It is not merely a fussy attempt at Wagnerian (or Wagnerite) pomposity and self-importance, nor a desire by Wagner and his devotees to stand apart from and above the shambolic unsophistication of the opera house, its gaudy, glitzy stage and wearily attendant social bubble.

Many people, quite reasonably, dislike Wagner because of the noise he makes — or rather, the sound, since noise, in terms of loudness, is only a small part of his art. Yet Wagner cannot be judged on sound alone. He requires us to invest our time in everything that the sound is endeavouring to do, in terms of emotional drama, philosophical debate, political ideation and so on. Even in an audio-only experience of Wagner, we cannot, or should not, ignore the extra-musical elements, not least because those elements are very often created by, and discussed in, the music alone. To truly appreciate the music, then, we have to comprehend and explore what it is saying both within and beyond itself.

Wagner and the musikdrama are constantly exploiting and cultivating the possibilities of music as a potent, and often very subtle, means of expression. Wagner's vast symphonic networks are not only powerful in absolute terms — their sheer size makes for an immensely forceful sonic engine — but also in the elasticity, delicacy and intricacy of their articulation. By one of his greatest works — *Götterdämmerung* — this orchestra is working incredibly hard, every bar, every note seeming to talk to every other bar and every other note, a garrulous and effusive analytical tool of extraordinary facility and complex communicative power. Wagner demands much from us in terms of time and attention, not only in the length and gravity of his works but also the 'homework' we need to do to get the most out of them, scrutinizing musico-dramatic interaction, poetic text, characterization, stage design, philosophical debate, political deliberation, and so forth.

It is not that the music is not powerful, interesting or beautiful enough without these additional elements, nor that we are fetishizing them, but that they are a vital feature of the musical argument and expression. To ignore them, to consider the music only on its own terms or in isolation, is to undermine both the potential and purpose of Wagner's music as well as to misapprehend Wagner's revolutionary new genre: the musikdrama. While this book does not intend to be a crib sheet for this musical and extra-musical homework, it does hope to unlock and explore some of the exquisite networks and astonishing mazes which Wagner created through his radical development of opera into musikdrama.

❧

This book does not aim at biography. There are countless volumes, and the excellent resources of the internet, devoted to the life of Richard Wagner. Many are admirable; some are overwhelmed by the complexity of their subject; others are controversial — either due to disproportionate hatred or excessive praise. Like Wagner himself, Wagnerian biography has proved a contentious arena. But this book does not seek to explore Wagner the man, except on the few occasions where his life and his art most obviously overlapped and interacted. A complete understanding of his works, like that of any artist's, is possible only through a thorough comprehension of the life, its times and circumstances. But considering Wagner's biography is not absolutely essential in order to appreciate most of the relevant qualities and deep layers to his art. Indeed, with Wagner in particular, biography has often tended to distort an accurate recognition of his artistic brilliance.

No book on Wagner should ignore or believe itself above the many objectionable aspects to Wagner's life and personality. We need to accept, address and explore his failings and shortcomings, not only to complete the picture but also to grasp the wider background and potential objectives of his art. Many of these facets have been affected by events which followed Wagner's life. Consideration needs to be given to such shifting contexts and perspectives, while at the same time, we must maintain our condemnation of his racism and other prejudices, only some of which can be understood as part of the socio-cultural milieu in which he lived. Racism is always racism, prejudice always prejudice.

Wagner was a deeply compassionate and often very affable man, but he was also a virulent racist. He not only wrote articles which we quite rightly find abhorrent, but he also helped — unwittingly or otherwise — foster an environment which led to some of the most appalling activities in human history. While it is true his life and music were posthumously hijacked by poisonous individuals and contagious forces, to entirely absolve Wagner from blame seems both dangerous and unnecessary.

The function and existence of Wagner's own attitudes within his works is strongly debated. It is possible to argue for prejudice occasionally existing in an oblique way, often in a manner indirect enough that it is now almost impossible to discern — much as topical Reformation jokes in Shakespeare are now lost to us. But it has to be said that such instances are exceptionally rare, and many have argued that they do not even exist, implicitly or otherwise. Unfortunately, this book, given its scope and limitations, will be able to address only some of these occurrences, though the reader is encouraged to probe further in the scholarship mentioned in the bibliographical appendix (see Guide to Further Reading).

If this is convenient, it is also hopefully fair to the works themselves, which exist as pedagogic monuments to love and redemption and as dynamic, living appeals for the obliteration of hatred and violence. There are a huge number of important, fascinating and challenging books and articles exploring both sides of the discussion regarding, most especially, Wagner's disgusting anti-Semitism. But this book is a consideration of how his musikdramas operate, and therefore, while it does not ignore his viewpoints, it can only examine them intermittently. To do otherwise would risk undermining the truly redemptive aspect to Wagner's own strange life: the works themselves.

That said, a brief contemplation of Wagner's biography, for readers both familiar and unfamiliar with the journey of his life, is appropriate for this introduction, both to contextualize and to comprehend the creative force behind the works under consideration. It cannot possibly hope to cover even all the main events of this extraordinary individual's extraordinary life, but some pointers may prove useful.

Wagner was born on 22 May 1813, in Leipzig. Verdi would be born five months later. Haydn had been dead for four years; Weber, Beethoven and Schubert had only thirteen, fourteen and fifteen years to live. And Wagner died on 13 February 1883, in Venice. His great successors, Mahler and Strauss, were already twenty-two and eighteen. Brahms was nearly fifty, Schoenberg just eight. Such was the span of Wagner's life: the greater part of the nineteenth century. The times in which he lived were dominated by colossal political, economic, social and cultural changes, and art both reflected and cultivated these impulses. Wagner's life and art would be no exception; indeed, in many ways, they were the paradigm.

Questions over his paternity have persisted, and while this might offer some explanation for the many orphaned or fatherless characters in his works, we should also consider that step- and indefinite parentage was widespread in Europe and elsewhere in the nineteenth century. Moreover, it is an expedient and stimulating operatic/narrative device, familiar to many, so we do not need to overemphasize these possibly enigmatic origins to his uniquely captivating stories.

Wagner's education was fairly normal, as was his introduction to music, though music played much less of a role in his early life than for many of his peers in the pantheon of great composers. Wagner was a relatively slow student, initially, but was possessed with an uncommon imagination. Together, work, ingenuity, determination and this fertile inventiveness would unite to create his revolutionary and extraordinary art. But it took time. We also need to consider the exact nature of the art he would create. It, as we outlined above, needed more than just musical talents, which are often and easily nurtured from a very young age. Wagner had to take time to become a great poet, dramatist, librettist, musical theorist, dramaturge, stage designer — and, eventually, opera house architect — as well as political agitator and voracious consumer of vast philosophical tomes. This could not be achieved in either the nursery or schoolroom.

The need for all these dynamic elements for his art to develop meant that for most of his life, Wagner was deeply frustrated. His imagination and artistic reach very much exceeded what he — or the opera world — was, at that point, capable of grasping. So there were years, decades even, of dissatisfaction and poverty, both for him and his long-suffering first wife, Minna. Jobs in opera houses, when they existed, were insufficient for his vast ingenuity and ambition. But they did help him foster the ingredients he needed for his revolution, both in terms of the basic skills of conducting, orchestration, dramaturgy, and so on as well as the negative aspect of seeing what was done poorly and badly needed improvement. Being a witness to deficiency cultivated in Wagner the tools of development.

By the 1840s, he had several operatic works to his name, of which three have survived and are occasionally performed, though Wagner later dismissed them as apprentice works: *Die Feen*, *Das Liebesverbot* and *Rienzi*. Although there is much musico-dramatic interest in this early trio, Wagner was perhaps right to largely disown them, not least because truly Wagnerian art does not really begin until 1841 and *Der fliegende Holländer* — the work with which, for this reason, this book starts. The decade which began with the Dutchman would also see Wagner write *Tannhäuser* and *Lohengrin*, continuing the direction of the musikdrama, as well as begin sketches for his grandest project: *Der Ring des Nibelungen*, which would take quarter of a century to complete.

This period was dominated not only by Wagner's musico-dramatic advancements but by his socio-political activities, meaning that, as this book argues, we should be cautious about separating his socialist and revolutionary principles from those in his art. They were very often the same thing, springing from the same source and seeking the same objectives. The annexation of Wagner by dangerous forces of the political right, up to and including those in our own societies, should never blind us to the much more radical, liberal and uncompromising aspects of his art. This is not to suggest he never held more conservative views or that his opinions didn't shift back and forth over time, but to deny Wagner revolutionary status in his life, politics and art is to misunderstand all three of them.

In Dresden in the later 1840s, he was literally on the barricades as revolution swept both the city and wider continent. His own experiences of penury and rejection, especially in Paris, had fostered his own sense of the injustice at the heart of contemporary society, which was being made worse, not better, by the twin forces of the industrial and capitalist revolutions of the eighteenth and then nineteenth centuries. The destruction to human lives as well as to the natural world (so important in many of his musikdramas, especially the *Ring* and *Parsifal*) was something that deeply concerned him and motivated many of the features of his dramas, which need to be considered as ecological, socio-economic and political warnings and indictments as well as works of art.

Although posterity has tended to enjoy seeing Wagner as a megalomaniac, a power-crazy and autocratic genius, we should understand that he lived in an age of revolution and that, as an artist, it is only right that he might consider his art to be a vital component of that transformation. From today's perspective, it might seem absurd that opera would seek to change the world, but Wagner very commendably believed in the life-changing potential of art and artists. This was something nineteenth-century Romanticism promoted and which was then more widely recognized in the twentieth century, despite — perhaps even because of — the fractures, paradoxes and incongruities of modernism and postmodernism. Art was not to be a polite and supplementary component to society but a profound, far-reaching and altering force that would shape and reshape civilisation.

Wagner's involvement in the uprisings of 1848–9 — ironically, at a time when he had found some permanent work as the Royal Saxon Court Conductor — led immediately to his exile from the German states, something which would last for over a decade. These were not idle years. On the contrary, they were his most productive and significant. Initially, there was the formulation and formalization of the elements of musikdrama fashioned in *Oper und Drama*, Wagner's theoretical work from 1851. Then, flowing from this, the first parts of the *Ring* — *Das Rheingold* and *Die Walküre* — before the first two acts of *Siegfried*. He then broke off the *Ring* to write *Tristan und Isolde* and *Die Meistersinger*.

During most of this time, he faced extreme difficulties: personal, domestic, financial and professional. None of these new works had been performed or had the possibility of being properly produced. *Tristan* went through countless rehearsals but was then deemed unplayable and abandoned. A revival of *Tannhäuser* in Paris in 1861 was mounted but ended up being ridiculed and roundly mocked. Wagner drove on, creating work after work which revolutionized both opera and music (and, eventually, many other art forms too).

Then, by the early years of the 1860s, his professional fortunes began to change, and his personal life acquired a deeper and more meaningful dynamic than it had thitherto attained, which was to become a crucial feature of his later years. Wagner's marriage to Minna finally collapsed (it had never been strong) and, in 1863, he committed himself to Cosima von Bülow, née Liszt, the composer's daughter and then wife of the virtuoso pianist and conductor Hans von

Bülow. (Bülow would, with boundless magnanimity, conduct the world premieres of both *Tristan* and *Meistersinger*, placing his veneration of the composer above any personal resentment or sadness, though he also recognized his former wife's greater happiness with Wagner.)

For all Cosima's importance to him, it was perhaps an even greater event than enduring and mutual love which truly saved Wagner. On 10 March 1864, King Ludwig II of Bavaria ascended the throne. A fanatical devotee of Wagner's works — especially *Lohengrin* — he would not only rescue the composer from domestic exile but would bankroll and advocate the production of Wagner's works and, to top it all, fund the construction of a building and associated festival with which to promote them.

Initially, however, Wagner could not be found. He was, after all, still a political outcast and wanted man, on the run from the police as well as innumerable creditors. Eventually, the king's messengers tracked Wagner down and convinced him they were not bailiffs or law enforcement agents but envoys from his biggest fan, who demanded an audience with his hero. It was the miracle from heaven Wagner had always dreamt of.

At a stroke, his fortunes — financial and artistic — were transformed. If this were in an opera, it would be deemed unrealistic, mere fantasy plotting, the laziest kind of deus ex machina. In the years that followed, first *Tristan* (1865), then *Meistersinger* (1868), *Rheingold* (1869) and *Walküre* (1870) were staged in top-notch professional productions. The *Ring* was finally completed: first *Siegfried* in 1871 and then *Götterdämmerung*, the final touch to the score being added on 21 November 1874, over twenty-six years since the initial prose sketches had been penned. Meanwhile, the Bayreuth Festspielhaus was constructed as a technically and personally suitable venue for the groundbreaking new work. The first complete *Ring* was staged in the summer of 1876.

The final years of Wagner's life were mainly devoted to his expanding family — children Isolde (1865), Eva (1867) and Siegfried (1869) — and to administering Bayreuth, writing some questionable theoretical and political tracts, and, of course, undertaking the composition of his final stage work, *Parsifal*, first presented at the second Bayreuth Festival in 1882. He planned no more musikdramas, believing he had taken them as far as he could, but intended instead to develop the symphony further with one-movement works, unfolding and unfurling in a single span. Alas, time and death intervened: Richard Wagner died in Venice in 1883, much mourned as the most famous composer in the world.

Wagner died in luxury, courted and grieved by kings ('Wagner's body belongs to me!' screamed Ludwig from the north). But Wagner had endured as a revolutionary to the end, even as he enjoyed the material and regal attentions which he considered merely his due. He still believed not only in the need for socio-political developments but in the power of his art to beget those changes.

Absurd as it might sound, Wagner also wished for a time when his art would no longer be necessary. Art could effect revolution, and then it would be redundant. There was, after all, no art in Eden. In the period of (relative) personal, domestic and financial serenity of his later years, he begrudged more than a little the time he needed to spend alone composing; he wanted to be with his wife and children. But he knew his art held important and revolutionary possibilities that society required. Whatever megalomaniacal spin might be put on this, he was surely right that change was needed. And however inflated Wagner's ego, he had honest and sincere expectations for a healthier, happier, fairer world, ones which never went away. Wagner's anti-Semitism colours and distorts this, of course, but we should be wary of simply amalgamating Wagner's hateful attitudes with the exterminatory policies of the Third Reich.

Today, we might consider Wagner's hopes for societal change through art not only conceited but fanciful. But this is to consider, as most of us do these days, Wagner's works only in their aesthetic capacity, which is to say their largely musical form. As we outlined above, however, Wagner's works cannot be isolated as purely musical works of art. Their poetic, dramatic, political, philosophical and ultimately moral components are conveyed by and through the music. Moreover, aesthetic, ethical and metaphysical categories in Wagner, as in all great art, overlap and are fundamentally indivisible aspects of the same thing: a kind of holy trinity of art.

For many, such questions pertaining to art might seem, at best, an unhelpful distraction or, at worst, a monstrous indulgence. When billions fight daily for something to eat and drink, what is the point of discussing opera's role in bringing about socio-economic change? But this is to see opera only as the social vulgarity and decadent parasite Wagner despised. In this regard, Wagner's vision of opera houses as egalitarian institutions for the promotion of social change has probably regressed, if anything. (There is always a neat irony when attending the revolutionary *Ring* in London's *Royal* Opera House...) Opera houses and summer opera festivals, whatever positive and admirable programmes are inaugurated to make them more accessible and inclusive, remain largely the preserve of those with the financial outlay to attend (as well as the leisure time, which is essentially the same thing), a playground for the wealthy or pastime for the bourgeoisie.

When we focus on Wagner's works, however, as this book intends to, things are different. The musikdramas remain — and will always remain — shocking, challenging and potentially transformative works of art, offering the possibility of hope and opportunity for redemption to individuals and their wider societies. The harmonies of *Tristan* will always be alarming because of the assault, and demands, they make on our expected ways of hearing music. We cannot become acclimatized to them. *Die Walküre*'s incest will always be scandalous because of our (understandable) socio-genetic customs and expectations. And, partly as a result of these shockwaves, both works will forever retain a power to assert the claims of love over all else, especially power and socio-cultural propriety — to take only two examples from the countless ones available to us in Wagner.

Mozart's revolutions and confrontations can sometimes be lost beneath the elegance and refinement so much of his music wears. It can be noticeably dark and stormy (the great C and D minor piano concertos; G minor String Quintet; *Don Giovanni*; the Requiem), though Mozart typically presents a stylish façade. But Mozart's grace is both a mask and a weapon, a tool of subtle power and instrument of concealment and change. Wagner is, on the other hand, much more obvious — infamously so, so that almost daily one hears habitually ill-informed platitudes about his 'bombastic' and 'aggressive' music. To anyone familiar with his art, Wagner is very much more than the manic dynamics of the Ride of the Valkyries or the furious anvils on the way down to Nibelheim. The preludes to *Lohengrin* and *Parsifal* are, for the most part, extended expressions of peace and calm. It is a weird, empty and futile distinction, but Wagner's works are probably more full of 'quiet' than 'boisterous' music. Moreover, when Wagner *is* violent or bombastic or overbearing, he is so for good reason, not to brag or to subjugate us but because of what his art demands. Wagner is always motivated by musico-dramatic considerations. The entry of the gods into Valhalla at the end of *Das Rheingold* is pompous and ostentatious for a purpose: to expose the grandiloquence of the gods.

Wagner's art, like Mozart's, is an art of interrogation and revolution. It perpetually seeks change through its restless, uneasy desire for the new — both internally, as a self-renewing art, and externally, as a force for transformation in society. Wagner's art could never be an art of relaxation, even if it might be one of occasional leisure for its users. Listening to Wagner (or reading this book) will not effect or achieve social change, political instability or economic upheaval. But radical art is, paradoxically, more patient, more enduring and subtler than the more recognizable socio-political revolutions of history. Wagner's art, perhaps like its consumers, is particularly patient, even as it urges change: it persists in radical determination, always rejuvenating its powers.

Wagner's works send you to odd places: near, far and familiar. He makes the peculiar seem normal, reminds you why peculiarity is the norm and alerts you to the uniqueness and idiosyncrasy of everything and everyone. Attitudes to Wagner's musikdramas change, of course, over time: cultural perceptions alter, deepen, weaken and revolve. We change, too, especially if we experience particular works of art across our entire lives. As powerful and transformative art, Wagner's musikdramas will likely adjust us over time, as well as amending our attitudes to love, power, society and death. The works are themselves long because they need a long time to work out and articulate their intricate musico-dramatic arguments. Wagner's art is 'difficult' in terms of its length as well as its complexities and ambiguities. Often this is used, directly or indirectly, as a justification for avoiding it. But life is (we hope) long and sufficiently extensive to encompass complexity.

Wagner's scoring has a walloping magnificence, subtle beauty and thrilling power which means his music, per se, will always be the first and last of our attraction to him — even an addiction, like a dangerous narcotic or perilous first sip of wine that takes us into another world. But it is the other things he does that keep us so enthralled. Like Shakespeare, Wagner asks questions but does not provide easy, or any, answers — to social problems, metaphysical quandaries or ethical dilemmas. Both these supreme dramatists employ their art to expose, probe and quiz, cross-examining belief, perspective and judgement, and in so doing both celebrate and condemn the eternal human condition. They leave ghosts, too; traces not of themselves but of their meanings, which are not fixed or stable but always changing. Over time, there are more and more cracks to be found in the artefacts of human creation, but these are not the flaws of imperfection but rather the crevices of genius, the rifts and clefts which make landscapes, faces and great art so continually fascinating. They are fissures which we are invited to fill — with reflection, interpretation and reinterpretation.

Wagner's musikdramas are, as this book seeks to show, agitated and agitating works of art: restless, disconcerted, frantic; exciting, protesting, campaigning. Like all revolutionary art, Wagner's retains its power to outrage, provoke and confront because of the nature of its conception, execution and reception. Revolutionary art does not mellow over time, even as further revolutions and advances are made around and/ or after it. To stay only within western classical music, and to name only some of the most obvious examples, Monteverdi's *L'Orfeo*, Bach's *48 Preludes and Fugues*, Haydn's symphonies, Mozart's *Marriage of Figaro*, Beethoven's sonatas and quartets, Stravinsky's *Rite of Spring* and Schoenberg's op. 31 *Variations* — all remain radical compositions, cutting edge and brand new, forever contemporary because of what they were and still are asserting. They do not become harmonized or softened by time; on the contrary, they constantly renew their strength and force, like shark teeth.

Wagner's musikdramas writhe, defiantly, in this category: edgy, intense and unstable, relentlessly reconditioning their capacity to question, confront and surprise. Like other radical art, Wagner's works constantly urge us to revise and reconsider not only our assessments of them in isolation but also in relation to the art which came before and after as well, altering our perceptions of both art and history. Wagner's creations are a cosmos in themselves, but they are also an intense and vibrant feature of our own world. Like supernovae, Wagner's musikdramas explode in violence and beauty, enlivening and enriching existence. Like black holes, too, they distort the fabric of space-time, their gravity troubling our complacency and stability — disturbing the universe.

Bayreuth: Theatre, Temple, Prison

Put 'Bayreuth opera house' into an image search engine and a remarkable sight will appear on the screen before you: a baroque masterpiece of theatre architecture. Elaborate and highly decorated, it is a golden gem-box of lights, jewels, ornaments and crystals, rich in detail and opulent in impression. It is a luxurious, princely pageant, full of ceremony, ornately painted and sumptuously presented.

Richard Wagner found it absolutely hideous. For this is not his opera house, but Bayreuth's earlier, eighteenth-century Margravial Opera House. When scouting Germany for locations to put on his *Der Ring des Nibelungen*, the quiet little town of Bayreuth in northern Bavaria had appealed to him. But its rococo theatre was everything he hated: a bourgeois fantasy world, an anti-democratic tiered horseshoe, its trinkets and adornments a distraction from the stage. Revolutionary art needed a revolutionary theatre. The purpose-built Festspielhaus in Bayreuth was that theatre, and it remains, in terms of function and dedication, arguably the finest opera house in the world. Everything is built for and geared towards the realization of Wagner's works. If you want quaint little theatres that resemble wedding cakes or auditoria that look like palace drawing rooms, Bayreuth is not for you.

Wagner had always known that *Der Ring des Nibelungen* was beyond the stage and orchestral capacities of the theatres available at the time. A new space was needed, one that was not only physically capable of but ideologically suited to the task. Early plans for a temporary structure that would be — along with the score — burnt to the ground after the final conflagration of *Götterdämmerung* were eventually left behind. This is a slight shame: there would have been a splendidly modernist, even postmodernist, symbolism to the act of burning the both the house and the score in the very bonfire that closed the stage work.

Nevertheless, much of the revolutionary spirit lived on in the design and construction of the theatre, as well as in the festival attached to it. Bayreuth was chosen to be far from other cultural institutions (and the often interfering enthusiasm of King Ludwig down in Munich) to avoid conflict or competition, and a suitable plot was eventually found there, on the now-famous Green Hill. Wagner was keen that the event be special, a proper festival, not simply part of the routine of everyday life. This was to be not after-work amusement but life- and world-changing art. A summer festival afforded the best opportunity for this: pilgrims (the term is not inaccurate) could journey and shake off the cares of the world. Our work and leisure schedules have altered considerably since Wagner's time, but this vision still largely holds true.

Bayreuth is not quite in the middle of nowhere, but neither is it at the centre of a major city, where one might dine at fashionable eateries or ride the metro home afterwards. To attend Bayreuth in Wagner's time, as now, required a certain amount of planning and devotion, just as the composer intended. He was quite specific. In his preface to a new edition of the *Nibelungen* poems in 1863, he mentions the horror of people attending the theatre after a busy day at the shop, office or laboratory for mere relaxation or entertainment. His works were not created for the mere post-work merriment of solicitors or bank clerks.

For mere recreation, no doubt, certain composers' works were ideal, since they were, to Wagner's sensibility, mindless entertainments without significance or integrity beyond being superficial distractions before the tedium of the next day's labours. Such labour was itself a futile and oppressive contemporary construct that Wagner despised and which the *Ring* goes some way to denounce: the endless toil of the Nibelungs under Alberich's capitalist rod condemns the drudgery of modern office workers as much as it does that of those workers' brothers in the factory. Wagner knew Kafka before Kafka existed.

No, what was needed was a summer festival in a suitable town with a custom-made theatre, one not only technically and physically up to the job but also democratically designed for the purpose. For this last aspect, Wagner was principally concerned with the auditorium and its seating plan. Since the marvellously democratic Greeks, Wagner argued, with their fan-shaped seating, theatres had become unjust, reactionary venues of vanity, division and mediocrity. Not only were the seats hierarchically tiered away from the stage action and sound, but the horseshoe shape meant many could not see everything that was taking place on the boards. If an artist has gone to the trouble of creating world-changing art, they might quite reasonably expect people to be able to experience all of it. The curved, tight crescent design also meant, of course, that people tended to look at each other across the way as part of social or mating rituals (splendidly captured in Zola and Flaubert), making the opera house not a centre of sacred art but a schmoozing circus or flirting zoo.

Wagner did away with this first by designing the Bayreuth auditorium as a fan, with as little rake as possible, resurrecting the Greek theatre, and then by also placing the house in darkness. The first gave unobstructed sight lines to everyone, no matter where they sat. Why should someone who could not afford a better ticket be unable to see what was happening, be potentially unable to experience the life-changing art? The second occurred partly by accident. Wagner was keen to place the theatre in considerably dimmed light so that attention was focused on the stage action, but technical hitches at the first Bayreuth Festival in 1876 meant that it was even darker than he had expected. But he liked the impression, and it stayed. Today, of course, most theatres and opera houses plunge their attendees into obscurity and anonymity when the drama starts. Flirting doubtless still occurs, but at least it is out of sight.

One problem the opera house has which the straight theatre doesn't, in terms of lighting, is that the musicians need (bless them) to be able to read their scores and see their conductor, for which some illumination is required. To resolve this difficulty, Wagner created one of Bayreuth's masterstrokes. Indeed, in many ways, the whole Festspielhaus is constructed around it, since it also has vital acoustic purposes: the hallowed sunken area for the players.

Normally, the musicians and the bandmaster exist in a visible way between audience and stage — many maestros insisting that they be *very* visible. Not only was this for Wagner a further distraction, but it generated too much brightness, disrupting the delicate optical and scenic effects he intended. Hard, he reasoned, to begin *Das Rheingold*, the birth of the world, amid garish bright lights. Wagner's orchestra, especially for the *Ring*, was also a huge apparatus and had the potential to drown out the singers and their crucial words — for Wagner's new art meant that what they said was as important as how they sang it.

The submerged, 'invisible' orchestra pit was a key feature of Wagner's musikdrama-haus design, and it solved both problems. It was created not to diminish the role of the orchestra but to enhance its ability to blend with the voices on stage and to unobtrusively transport the audience into the world of the dramas. The Wagnerian orchestra, as this book will see, is a great locomotive, a 747 of sound; but it is also a vehicle capable of immense subtlety, and nowhere can this be achieved with finer consequence than in the sunken pit of Bayreuth. Here texture, mixture and rapture are merged in a fragile and highly refined acoustic equilibrium.

Bayreuth's buried pit is a thing of wonder, a miraculous void. The opulence of Wagner's scoring, with its dense and complex textures, needs a colossal orchestra, but this can overwhelm the performers if not handled carefully. Bayreuth's sunken pit is able to moderate the volume, dampening the overall sound, but without loss of detail or texture. This is crucial for the tremendously subtle and precise orchestral impressions Wagner wanted, especially in the two works most associated with Bayreuth: *Parsifal* and the *Ring*. The Festspielhaus was built for the *Ring*'s intricate aural dynamics; but *Parsifal* was written for the Festspielhaus, and here, where the orchestral quality is much more diaphanous and transparent, Wagner exploits the hidden players to combine and control textures of the most fragile sensitivity. *Parsifal* is best heard at Bayreuth.

The pit hovers between stage and seating, partially covered by a cowl, then extends deep beneath the boards, making conditions for those playing down in the chasm for long hours at a time often extremely taxing. Working at Bayreuth entails a devotion and pious self-sacrifice to match that of the spiritual pilgrims above. The musicians are arranged in a manner different to most opera houses — again, to meet the particular requirements of the works the building was created for. Nine rows descend over half a dozen subterranean levels, each sinking further into the abyss. Violins are at the top, the first desks on the right, followed by violas, cellos (flanked by double basses), woodwinds (flanked by harps) and then, at the very bottom, completely under the stage, the deep sonorities of the brass and percussionists — who, if they did not suffer from claustrophobia before Bayreuth, might need some help after the summer is over. Difficult as the conditions are — hot, airless, awkward, dark — it does create the effect Wagner wanted, and for this, musicians are prepared to experience physical discomfort and a far-from-ideal playing environment.

The hood above the conductor and strings and the sound damper above the brass and woodwind help to manage, focus, blend and balance the sound of the orchestra before it is sent out into the auditorium. The Bayreuth sound has a particular richness, a mellifluous and refined excellence, possible nowhere else. In the auditorium, the reverberation time is long, ideal for the rich and weighty resonances Wagner creates. Although many people have complained that only Wagner is performed at Bayreuth (failing to understand that it is not a regular opera house or festival), it is unlikely that the sound of many repertory operas would work in the Festspielhaus: the glorious lighter textures of Monteverdi, Handel, Gluck or Mozart would simply be lost. Bayreuth is in the lucky position, too, of only having to accommodate this one sound — every other opera house has to be able to put on the whole repertoire.

The auditorium, and building in general, is characterized by a range of details ignoring beauty or comfort but all geared towards the perfect acoustic for complex orchestral sounds and for enhancing remarkable voices. The Festspielhaus is, despite its brick shell and some recent modifications, essentially a wooden construction. Beneath the timber seating is an empty space: a resonator. Above the audience is a wooden roof from which hangs a sailcloth: a reflector. Rows of hollow wooden columns support the structure, forming an uneven surface along the sides of the auditorium that disperses the energy of the sound. Just as the music is mixed to perfection in the cocktail shaker of the pit, it is held, tempered and clarified in the tumbler of the auditorium.

Looking at the stage, the audience is faced by a double proscenium (and six parallel pairs of prosceniums receding into the theatre, formed by the wooden pillars of structural support). This helps create a distancing effect, enhancing the illusionary impression of transport and otherworldliness Wagner wanted to create, especially for the *Ring*. Added to this is the extremely deep stage of Bayreuth, as well as its superb and constantly modernized backstage and technical facilities. Most opera houses in Wagner's time, and many of our own, struggle to accommodate the immense demands of Wagner's works — again, particularly the *Ring* — but Bayreuth was designed with them in mind and can solve their staging problems much more easily than anywhere else. Indeed, it relishes the challenge. Wagner knew every facet and requirement of the opera house from a lifetime of either working in it or writing for it, and Bayreuth is an enduring, living testimony to this expertise.

The building was inaugurated on 22 May 1872, the composer's fifty-ninth birthday, in a soggy ceremony hastily removed to the Margravial theatre for a celebratory performance of Beethoven's Ninth conducted by Wagner. Funding for both the structure and the first festival was provided — intermittently — by King Ludwig and various local and national governments, as well as by societies and groups of supporters. It was these latter assemblages which helped foster, with some assistance from the composer, of course, the obsessive aspect to Bayreuth, the notion of religious zeal and holy rite, turning the Festspielhaus into a temple and the festival into a site of pilgrimage for disciples from across the decades and across the world.

It is certainly true that, despite magnificent playing, productions and amenities elsewhere, Bayreuth is *the* centre for experiencing Wagner. As we outlined above, there are very particular qualities to the building, as well as to the already high levels of Wagnerian knowledge held by most of the participants, which make this so. Moreover, attending in the twenty-first century is a good deal easier than it used to be, making this unique and special place more widely accessible than probably at any time since its birth. Greater numbers of Wagner, opera and music fans can now undertake their hajj to this holy place to worship at the shrine. This is unquestionably a good thing, not least because more diverse audiences will (one hopes) foster more diverse ideas and productions (not that Bayreuth has ever been short of either).

But there has always been something a little precarious, a little fanatical, about the festival and its temple. Veneration easily slips to unthinking devotion and blind allegiance. In the years after Wagner's death, when his widow Cosima took over the running of the festival, productions became stifled, inert in their bogus preservation of their master's apparent wishes (itself a false notion; Wagner believed in the constant evolution of his art). Thus with Cosima was born the dishonest and dangerous notion of the composer's intentions, which continues to inhibit, hinder, suffocate and generally impair Wagner's works. Wagner attracts the sharpest minds and most innovative of directors, as well as some of the most open-minded, imaginative audiences. But Wagner also appeals to a certain kind of individual desperate to cling to a past and a conception of Wagner (and opera) which never existed. This, of course, is something the works themselves address and interrogate with a ferocity which might startle some of the more conservative members of the audience if they ever bothered to pay attention.

At Bayreuth, this congealed into something far nastier than mere dull opera productions or lazy audiences. The exploration and cross-examination of German myth and history in Wagner's work was something which naturally appealed to malign forces desperate to evoke a non-existent fairy-tale past in order to manipulate and control the future. The annexation of Bayreuth and its festival by the Third Reich was, for some, the natural and deserved outcome for the anti-Semite Wagner. But Wagner, despite perhaps enjoying the attention, would have been unlikely to have enjoyed the way the Nazis restrained his art, confining his culture in order to serve politics. Wagner's art, especially the *Ring*, was created in order to powerfully and radically change society for the better, to usher in a new age of liberty and autonomy, not to be a mechanism appropriated to promote a period of unparalleled subjugation, violence and murder.

No one turned Bayreuth into more of a temple than the Führer; no one worshipped at the shrine of Wagner more than the vulgar and deluded Nazi dictator. But he turned it into a prison, too, for few people have so stubbornly, perversely and gravely failed to understand the depth, dynamism and variety of meanings in Wagner's work quite like Adolf Hitler, who ordered dull productions with his duller mind. With ignorance and the blind faith of stupidity, he turned a theatre of art into a temple of futility and then a prison of evil and disgrace, aided — of course — by many internal forces within Bayreuth itself.

Many valuable and poignant books have been written on this shameful episode of Bayreuth's history, and the reader is urged to consult them, alongside the appropriate works of scholarship on the Third Reich. Frederic Spotts's biography of the festival is a useful point of departure on this harrowing object lesson from history about how praise and adoration can so quickly curdle into extremism and thence disaster. Bayreuth, however, was lucky that it was founded on strong principles which could one day return. The gossips and intrigues of the Wagner clan are for books beyond this one; some of their story, especially since the Second World War, is amusing and occasionally interesting. But Bayreuth is a centre of art, and it is the art with which this chapter wants to end. The resurrection of the festival in 1951 by the composer's grandson Wieland was a miracle many might not have expected, given not only the ruination of Germany in general but the indictment of Bayreuth in particular. Productions before Wieland were reverential to the point of mummification — and, with their creaking, dilapidated sets, liable to be just as dangerous. Wieland stripped the festival and its art of its political trappings by presenting fresh, innovative, simplified (but not simplistic) stagings, focusing on light and the inner truths of the musikdramas.

Under Wieland's direction, *Parsifal* was reborn as the traumatic, meditative and profound study of spirituality Wagner had created. The *Ring* resurfaced, along with the other works, as dynamic drama which could speak to new audiences and societies, taking them in fresh directions, thinking, engaging and reengaging with art, culture and a new kind of politics. Wagner's works were not holy fossils, the sacred relics of a crumbling temple. These artefacts were living, breathing works of art which needed constant repair and invigoration so that they could truly exist in the vibrant form in which they had been created.

Fashions and successes would come and go. Wolfgang, Wieland's brother and successor, was in some ways more conservative than his sibling but could be radical when he wanted — not least when he invited Pierre Boulez and Patrice Chéreau to stage the centenary *Ring* at Bayreuth in 1976, with magnificent, shocking and epoch-making consequences. Peter Hall's fairy-tale *Ring* of the mid-eighties was rather insipid by comparison, an inert fabrication. But Harry Kupfer's 'end of history' *Nibelungen* teratology in 1989 seemed a suitable, thought-provoking (and often dazzling) way for the festival to begin to say farewell to its tumultuous century of entombment, conflict, destruction, renaissance, innovation and modernization.

In the third century of Bayreuth's existence, it continues as a centre for self-motivated, outward-looking, energetic and challenging culture, but one always aware of its heritage, both good and evil. Its productions still command the most attention, and often this is with good reason. In the twenty-first century, some exceptional directors have sought to examine the peculiar and tainted history of Bayreuth itself through absorbing, often meta-theatrical and occasionally surreal productions, of which Stefan Herheim's 2008 *Parsifal* has perhaps been both the most inspired and the most significant. Not only was it able to narrate and quiz both Bayreuth's and Germany's history in the twentieth century, but it did so in a way which energetically enhanced *Parsifal's* own immanent narrative as well. It was active, organic, exciting and engaging theatre. Herheim's production benefited especially from Bayreuth's *Werkstatt* ('workshop') concept, in which productions develop year on year, nurturing a healthy flexibility and preventing stasis or rot from setting in — to either the musikdramas themselves or the wider cultural contexts in which they are presented.

Bayreuth not only is comfortable with interrogating its own history but wants to go further, restoring its founder's works to their place as investigative, progressive and persuasive agents of spiritual scrutiny and emotional-intellectual consideration. The prison has been demolished, the temple deconsecrated; but the theatre has been raised to even greater heights as a beacon of artistic endeavour and creative potential.

Table of Wagner's Completed Stage Works

Dating Wagner can be a tricky activity. Not only were these dramas gestated over a very extended period of time, but they were also occasionally revised, and a long gap often existed between the work's completion and its eventual premiere. Therefore, to simplify matters, this table gives both the year of completion of the entire work and the date of its world premiere. The three 'apprentice' works are included, though they are only mentioned in passing in this book.

Title of Work	Year Completed	Date of Premiere
Die Feen	1834	29 June 1888
Das Liebesverbot	1836	29 March 1836
Rienzi	1840	20 October 1842
Der fliegende Holländer	1841	2 January 1843
Tannhäuser	1845	19 October 1845
Lohengrin	1848	28 August 1850
Das Rheingold	1854	22 September 1869
Die Walküre	1856	26 June 1870
Tristan und Isolde	1859	10 June 1865
Die Meistersinger	1867	21 June 1868
Siegfried	1871	16 August 1876
Götterdämmerung	1874	17 August 1876
Parsifal	1882	26 July 1882

PART ONE

THE EARLY CANON

Chapter One

Navigating the Future:
Der fliegende Holländer

During the summer of 1839, a small German merchant ship was travelling from the Baltic port of Pillau to London. As it began its journey across the North Sea, it encountered a ferocious storm. The captain and his half-dozen shipmates battled the elements, arduously trying to keep the vessel afloat, while below deck lay prostrate and queasy three passengers: a gigantic Newfoundland dog named Robber; a young German actress named Minna; and a young German musician named Richard Wagner. They were on the run, fugitives escaping Wagner's creditors in Riga, where he had been forging his career as a conductor-composer, with fluctuating degrees of success, while his wife, too, found some modest acclaim on the stages of Königsberg.

Paris, centre of the operatic world, was their destination: here would be the conquest and respect (as well as money) that was his due. A triumphant return to Germany was assuredly guaranteed. As it was, of course, the Paris years (1839–42) would be marked by devastating poverty and humiliation (Wagner once having to pawn not just his wedding ring but the *ticket* for the wedding ring). Socially, linguistically and artistically, he would be the wrong man in the wrong town, despite some often very thoughtful assistance from leading figures, like his compatriot Meyerbeer. In the French capital, however, he would manage — when not writing absurd novelettes about Beethoven and impoverished artists or undergoing the indignity of hack arrangement work of other people's music — to complete his final 'apprentice' opera, *Rienzi*, the finishing touches to which would be inked in a debtors' prison, and the first of his canonical works: *Der fliegende Holländer*.

The idea of a dark opera loosely based on a satirical prose work, *Memoirs of Herr von Schnabelewopski* (1834), the poet Heinrich Heine's version of the Dutchman legend, had been evolving in Wagner's mind for some time prior to his dangerous, illegal, penniless and passportless sea crossing. The death-defying journey itself had been preceded by weeks of outlandish events straight out of a contemporary adventure novel by Alexandre Dumas or Walter Scott. The Richard-Minna-Robber trio loitered in smugglers' drinking dens, illicitly ran across borders in the dead of night, had their absconding stagecoach crash and overturn, evaded the harbour police by crouching in a small boat, prayed their hound would not bark as he was hoisted on board the ship in a rope basket, and then finally underwent the torture of being concealed below deck as the customs inspectors examined the craft. And then when they thought they were free, sailing towards Paris and victory, the storm struck.

The boat's captain was forced to navigate the treacherous southern seaboard of Norway, desperately seeking a harbour along the rocky coast. Overcoming his seasickness, Wagner was up on deck, surveying the magnificent terror of the wind and waves as it pummelled them ever more hazardously towards the jutting rocks. Eventually they entered the quiet sanctuary of an inlet and the little fishing village of Sandvika. Wagner would later relate how, as the six sailors attended to the ship, casting the anchor and wrapping away the sails, they sang, their transitory cadenced cries resonating back from the colossal granite bulwarks of the fjord. Wagner, with good reason, claimed it was one of the happiest moments of his life.

Wagner's explanations of the origin and gestation of his works need to be taken with not just a pinch but several shovelfuls of salt: his musico-dramatic imagination and creative licence often collaborate to produce fanciful beginnings far from the mundane ordinariness and routine banalities of most artistic labour. But he really did suffer such a sea voyage (which would continue, post-Norway, in stormy waters and as they negotiated precarious sandbanks all the way to the safe mouth of the Thames), and in all likelihood he did hear the mariners singing at various points. Certainly the relief after the event, not to mention the glorious natural fjord setting, would have inspired anyone, let alone a creative mind like Wagner's. Thus, the project which he had been chewing over was given grand impetus, and peerless inventive sanction, by the real-world episodes en route to Paris.

Wagner had enquired with his hosts on ship about the innumerable versions of the Flying Dutchman legend: which did they know, fear, recount, sing about? Any account would have appealed further to his growing passion for the tale of a captain condemned to sail the seas forever, a fate that must have felt extraordinarily real during the interminable anguish and spectacle of his own very recent experiences being tossed about the various eastern arms of the Atlantic Ocean.

During his spell in Paris, usually alone and always without money, Wagner would befriend a number of similarly impecunious and unsuccessful artists, writers, agitators and shufflers who helped introduce him to various political, philosophical and mythical ideas (some of which would filter into *Tannhäuser* and *Lohengrin*). One of their number, Dresden-born art student Ernst Kietz, creator of the earliest known portrait of the composer, an enchanting pencil sketch, was to be of incalculable help in creating a better environment in which Wagner could work. Convinced of the composer's genius, Kietz sold his own belongings to furnish Wagner with funds while he worked on *Der fliegende Holländer*. He wrote the music rapidly, taking only a couple of months in the late summer of 1841 for the sketches and finishing the complete score in the autumn, to which he appropriately (and accurately) appended:

> Paris: 5 November 1841. In darkness and misery.
> Per aspera ad astra. God grant it!

Through adversity to the stars: he had no soles to his shoes, was deeply depressed, and despised all things French or Parisian. But he had completed the work which in many ways defines what he would achieve in music and drama. When the time came to depart Paris for Dresden in the spring of 1842, with the cautious prospect of premieres for *Rienzi* and *Holländer* in the offing, Kietz came to see the Wagners off, pressing his last five-franc note into his friend Richard's hand, the German composer in tears. They remained lifelong friends, and Wagner repaid all his financial debts to Kietz as soon as he could. But the breathing space Kietz gave Wagner to compose the opera he really wanted to, unchained from any immediate economic concerns or aesthetic obligations, is surely something that neither Wagner, nor music, can reimburse.

In the leviathanic brotherhood of Wagner, *Der fliegende Holländer* is the smallest of the group, but fierce and brooding, its might and majesty far outweighing its more diminutive size. Like all Wagner's post-apprentice dramas, *Der fliegende Holländer* has its own particular sound-colour, its own specific verbal flavour. Here, as everywhere, Wagner wrote his own libretto, and while it is not first-rate dramatic verse, it is absolutely suited to its purpose. And the *Dutchman* reeks of the sea, the tang and taste of salt and brine flavouring its astonishingly intense sonic and poetic personality, the howl of wind and gale reverberating across its three interlocked acts. (Originally and innovatively conceived to run continuously, it is still performed — and surely weakened — in Wagner's three-act version, which he wrote for opera houses perhaps unable to cope with his modernizations. As a single act, its status as an embryonic musikdrama, symphonic in style and scope, is more readily apparent.) And yet, for all its vibrancy, all its ruddiness of substance and spirit, it is also a complex, profound and extremely shrewd piece of musical theatre focused around the idea of emancipation through love, which would govern all Wagner's works, up to and including *Parsifal*.

Its overture crashes into life, the wind and rain roaring straight into your face, with frantic and frenzied strings — a hectic oblivion — before the Dutchman's theme rises up on horns without delay: intrepid, insolent, unflinching. The score is determined, electrified and driven both from without (the Norwegian storm) and within (the Dutchman's soul), its disconcerting squall eventually dissipating into stillness and fragmented spluttering in the depths of the orchestra. This lull is continued as Senta's quiet theme emerges on the woodwind like the sun through clouds, its solace and geniality offering peace before the storm smashes in once again, something it will repeatedly do each time a theme tries to establish itself in this violent concoction of scene-setting, tone-painting and metaphorical musical landscaping.

The internal psychological and emotional states of characters we have yet to meet are vividly conveyed to us in the overture, though it is going too far to claim these are leitmotifs such as Wagner would go on to generate most fruitfully and abundantly in his four-opera cycle *Der Ring des Nibelungen*, where they bestow unity on the vast fifteen-hour network of the drama, among many other applications. In *Der fliegende Holländer*, the organization of underlying motifs fully unifying the musikdrama has not yet been developed, nor indeed has the musikdrama itself, and establishing the identity of certain themes is not straightforward (or even possible and desirable). That said, the capacious horn refrain at the opening of the overture and the sweet interlude on woodwind are, as we've seen, largely associated with the Dutchman and Senta respectively, since this music appears whenever they are on stage or mentioned in the text. However, these themes can't be classified with the characters specifically. Senta's theme might also represent her love and longing, as well as the more multifaceted impulses of her emergent yearning to be the Dutchman's salvation, as well as his less clear-cut aspiration to be hers.

Moreover, these themes are not developed to the extraordinary extent they are in the *Ring*, where more concise, succinct musical ideas (whether relating to characters, objects, events or emotions) are given huge range to expand, invert and adapt according to theatrical situation, methodically elaborating across the vast canvas of the drama. In *Der fliegende Holländer*, the Dutchman's and Senta's themes remain the same musically, despite the immense dramatic development these characters undergo over the course of the opera. Nonetheless, Wagner is beginning to develop his musico-dramatic principles of recurrence and reminiscence, not least in the way he structures both the overture and other large areas of the score around themes such as the Dutchman's and Senta's, where they work in a much more complex, intricate and elegant way than mere signposts or musical placards.

Wagner later liked to claim that all the music for *Der fliegende Holländer* developed from the sprouting seed of Senta's Ballad in act 2, perhaps in a retroactive bid to make the opera a burgeoning musikdrama, systematically composed as a refined amplification of a handful of nascent themes. This is perhaps overstating the case, but in *Der fliegende Holländer*, Wagner does go further than his contemporaries, who composed opera as a series of separate numbers and recitatives, and towards the 'infinite melody' and through-composed realm of his later works, with their highly sophisticated musico-dramatic structures. The temperamental tone and compelling advances of this extraordinary work announce something very new. If not precisely the symphonic musikdrama as Wagner would later conceive it, it is something in close and unruly proximity.

Senta's Ballad is, however, very important — organizing and implementing many aspects of the opera's musico-dramatic logistics — and Wagner's assertion of this passage as the kernel of the work does have some rationale. It begins with the same brisk trembling strings as the overture and with the horn call of the Dutchman, initially below in the bass, then up in Senta's vocal line, containing alarming fluctuations between major and minor keys, while also promulgating the Redemption motif that persists elsewhere. It is here that we learn the remaining elements of the Dutchman's story not conveyed to us already, and Wagner carefully interweaves them with Senta's growing realization that the Dutchman's release and her liberation from loneliness are not only connected but perhaps the same thing. The conflation between the Dutchman's tale and her fate, although there in the text, is primarily communicated to us via the music, by music's superior ability to combine and coalesce disparate strands. (It is not for nothing, after all, that the centre of the opera is a musical form, a ballad.)

Such aspects to the opera have been borne out, and emphasized, by various stagings of the work. Harry Kupfer's 1978 production at Bayreuth staged the entire work in Senta's imagination, as her dream, essentially making the whole opera Senta's Ballad — a wonderful conception, plausible and sympathetic, that was effectively executed and corresponded with most of Wagner's own text. Taking a psychologically demanding drama and thrusting it even further into one character's mind and subsequent mental disintegration was a gamble, but one that paid off abundantly. Set in an age-old and suffocating Norwegian fishing community of the nineteenth century, it portrayed Senta as a sensitive, daydreaming, perhaps slightly hysterical young woman yearning to disentangle herself from the oppressive, narrow-minded society in which she finds herself, with its subdued, wretched women and wearisome, uninspiring men. In the Dutchman legend, she finds an opportunity and an agency for escape, projecting onto it her fantasy of unqualified self-sacrifice and the passage to liberty.

During a staged overture, Kupfer set the second act's spinning scene amid a furious storm, the worker-women frightened and huddled together. Lightning strikes, and a familiar picture of the Dutchman falls to the floor. Snatching it up, Senta is seized by her delusions and clasps the painting, which remains in her arms until the end of the opera. Hallucination and reality, rapture and dejection, turbulence and composure then mix in agonizingly swift succession, the suitor her father brings folding into both a fantasy Dutchman and a real one, Senta's trance-like state splitting, merging and confusing the figures. Her agitated imagination compels reality to keep up with her extortionate demands, which it cannot do. Her make-believe wedding in the third act sees her guests devoured by the ghostly crew of the Dutchman's ship, before Erik's reminders of her promises to him further undermine the fragile boundary in her head between fantasy and reality. Her only escape is suicide, jumping from a high window in delirious and ecstatic exaltation, believing she is saving the Dutchman, and herself, by shadowing him into infinity.

Senta in *Der fliegende Holländer* is only the latest (and far from last) in a long line of psychologically unbalanced women on the opera stage, though the exact degree of her disturbance and fancy is often left up to the determination of stage directors, of which Kupfer is naturally one of the most extreme. Whatever the degree of her mental unevenness, Senta has a courage and strength that will come to demarcate many of Wagner's women. Elizabeth (*Tannhäuser*), Elsa (*Lohengrin*), Isolde (*Tristan und Isolde*), Sieglinde and Brünnhilde (*Ring*), Kundry (*Parsifal*) and even, to some extent, Eva (*Meistersinger*) are all formidable individuals who, though often mocked by audiences and critics for following their men into silent expiry or transfigured annihilation, confront and revolutionize the societies of which they are a part.

There is a neat twist in *Der fliegende Holländer*. Senta challenges the culture by which she feels stifled, acting on the claims of love. Ironically, she does this with a suitor her father provides. Daland, meanwhile, is unaware of the emotional and fantastical hinterland his daughter has generated around the stranger he unwittingly brings home. Erik the huntsman would seem to be the figure a determined and audacious woman would usually, under the restrictions of the time, elope with, defying the practices of a close-knit fishing community by running away with a labourer of the land rather than of the sea. But Wagner makes Erik a slightly dull and needy chap, caring but dreary. Moreover, Senta's relationship with a wild and romantic seafaring hero is positively endorsed — indeed (unsuspectingly) coordinated — by her own father, whereas in conventional opera he would be the obstacle the drama seeks to overcome. This, after all, is a celebration of the sea, its power, fright, majesty and possibility: Daland monetizes it; Senta utilizes it as a dominion for passionate fulfilment.

This most sea-centered of great operas, at least prior to Britten's great Napoleonic maritime drama *Billy Budd* (1951), experienced several developmental changes along the way, but these nevertheless help highlight Senta's centrality to the work. Wagner's escapades off the Norwegian coast in 1839 seem to have persuaded him to switch the drama from its initially drafted Scottish setting to Norway, renaming Donald *Daland* and Anna *Senta* in the process. There is no essential difference in the blustery atmosphere and craggy localities on either side of the North Sea. The Dutchman himself remains the same, drifting anywhere the world over (like Ulysses or Ahasuerus, the immortal wandering Jew, a figure with whom Wagner strongly identified and would return to again and again in characters like Wotan in the *Ring* and *Parsifal*'s Kundry). And yet, amid these modifications, there is something fitting about Norway as the final chosen setting for *Holländer*: Senta is a character in keeping with and closely anticipating the resilient but restrained Norwegian women Henrik Ibsen would create later in the century. Nora in *A Doll's House* (1879) and the eponymous Hedda Gabler (1890) are, like Senta, women with a personal sense of autonomy (and logic), which is held secret or unconscious until it erupts into new purposes and processes that seek to overcome their lack of satisfaction in the male-dominated society which encloses and asphyxiates them.

To some, the emancipation-redemption motif that directs Wagner's works is little more than a gesture: at best a vacant idea, at worst a dangerous flight from reality. It might be easy, too, to present Senta as experiencing some form of celebrity crush, a film star infatuation with fatal repercussions. Indeed, this is something the Dutchman himself sometimes seems to believe, his desperation demanding he doubt her love. During their central duet and first meeting, over darkly textured strings, he enquires:

> Will you not disagree with your father's choice?
> What he promised — may it hold valid?
> Could you surrender yourself to me forever
> and give your hand to a stranger?
> After a tormented life, shall I find
> in your true love my long-sought peace?

Senta replies with a quirky, bright and lively accompaniment on the brass that might be honest feeling or juvenile fixation (or both), in addition to some conveniently re-exploitative domestic obligation to her father. In this, her dreams and duties are expediently wed:

> Whoever you are, and whatever the doom
> cruel fate may ordain for you –
> whatever destiny awaits me,
> I will always be obedient to my father!

Whatever her sense of filial responsibility, Senta seems to know what she is doing and letting herself in for, as well as the jeopardies that might be in store for her. There is always a danger, with Wagner's women, of their falling prey to what Nietzsche ridiculed as a refined form of parasitism wherein male figures manipulate feminine good nature, vulnerability and naïveté in order to nestle down and abuse another soul, another body. Yet here Nietzsche — and others, even perhaps the Dutchman and Senta themselves — betray their own prejudices and expectations, finding it incomprehensible that two people in stuffy, strait-laced nineteenth-century society might expose their souls and commit through love to each other.

If Senta is an instrument for both her father's and the Dutchman's greed and desires, a marginalized victim mistreated by patriarchal whim, she can also, and perhaps more powerfully, be regarded as her own agent. She chooses to embrace the Dutchman before this also becomes her father's wish; she opposes and discounts the convention and convenience of a marriage with Erik. Her empowerment is complex, without a doubt, but it is there, structured, reinforced and emboldened by the ambivalent music Wagner gives her: both sensual and sweet, knowing and innocent, hypnotic and becalming.

Erik, standing — as the spinning women do — for orthodox ideas of affection, marriage and desire, is given a traditional cavatina with regular forms and rhythms at the climax of the opera, when he anxiously tries to evoke in Senta pastoral images of their relationship, all blossoms and dales and the soft memories of conventional sweethearts' love:

> Senta, oh Senta, do you deny it?
> Do you no longer wish to remember the day
> when you called me to you in the valley?
> When I courageously took numberless risks
> to win for you highland flowers?

In the context of *Der fliegende Holländer*, these 'risks' seem negligible, even ridiculous, not least as Erik here fretfully tries to recapture Senta's heart. What is more, perhaps he should be regarded, both dramatically and musically, as the jailer, detaining Senta in his prison of predictability with the familiar controlling emotional-verbal tools of the abuser.

The Dutchman himself does not set her free, but merely produces some of the conditions through which she can liberate herself. In her Ballad, Senta — before she has met the Dutchman — establishes her own sense of destiny and identity. Furthermore, the ballad is her own, an old-fashioned style of verse narration she usurps and forces everyone else to circumnavigate. She becomes the principal vehicle of the drama, a co-creator with Wagner of the opera in which she is to be found, navigating her own bold course whatever the choppy vagaries of those around her, and resembling other world-redeeming figures, from Christ to Karl Marx.

In his 2013 production for Zurich Opera, Andreas Homoki focused on the monetary-colonial aspects of the drama, making it a capitalist thriller. Concentrating on the historical surroundings rather than mythical folklore, this *Holländer* was set in the very dry-land offices of the maritime company which entrepreneur Daland owns, his wealth deriving from the late nineteenth-century exploitation of Africa. The nautical aspect to the story was largely confined to the music and imagination (and all the more powerful for that, absolutely present through its absence), so the sailors became clerks and financiers, the spinning women office secretaries. The Dutchman, with his tattoos and face paint, had appropriated the culture of the Europeans' imperial conquests, going semi-native on his sea journeys (perhaps undertaken for the Dutch East India Company or whatever Daland's megacorporation is). This Dutchman was eager to reject the corrupt private enterprise and abuses of his own society and reintegrate elsewhere — even, in this production, snubbing Senta in consequence, compelling her own very violent suicide, which she executes with the hunting rifle she has viciously snatched from Erik. Here the pressures and miscarriages of mercantile development jar with and excite the needs of personal fulfilment, Daland's avarice taken to its logical and damning conclusion, his own daughter the debris of vulture commerce.

Der fliegende Holländer is not necessarily a socialist entreaty, though Wagner's own left-wing and subversive politics in this direction, especially in the 1840s, are well-known — and works like *Lohengrin* and *Der Ring des Nibelungen* make a very clear case for socialism. Nevertheless, it is evident that Wagner saw, and Homoki made explicit, Senta as a casualty of the brutal world the nineteenth century fostered, with industrialization and imperial subjugation on a massive scale. People's lives were being made — if they were lucky — arid, sterile, hollow and mechanized, and — if they were not — worthless and dangerous, by the relentless thrust of the industrial/capitalist revolution, and to condemn it was not to be blindly seduced by the myth of a (non-existent) rustic idyll in the recent past.

Women in particular had suffered immensely throughout history, not least via the twin labours of work and childbirth, but contemporary changes were, if anything, worsening their circumstances and quality of life. Although many of Wagner's views on women were essentially of his time, he was also progressive in seeing, in his stage works, the potential for women to remedy many of the socio-political, fiscal and environmental problems created by male-dominated societies. Without their energy and emancipation, the status quo would merely persist. And, as we have come to discover for ourselves, issues of gender, race, human rights, workers' rights, ecology, politics and economics are interrelated, closely bound by their own intricate and vindictive histories.

If these issues might seem detached from the sedate and cushy world of the opera house, this was precisely Wagner's point. Both life and art had become separated, particularized, and this was reflected in the dismal, conformist stage compositions available to them, giving citizens shoddy, soporific and meaningless thrills, perpetuating division and inequality — something visible in the stage works themselves and, in even more banal fashion, in the hierarchical seating design of theatres. Wagner perceived that people's lives should and could be enriched by a challenging art which tackled the imperative and inter-reliant issues of identity, society and destiny. He envisaged art as necessitating and facilitating change and his art in particular as being a fundamental part of this process. And if this seemed megalomaniacal, it only proved Wagner's point about the life/art divorce which had befallen civilisation.

Although many of these ideas about art and society would only find their apotheosis in *Der Ring des Nibelungen*, as well as Wagner's design and erection of the Bayreuth theatre and the accompanying establishment of its festival, they are also distinctly present in his three post-apprentice, pre-*Ring* works: *Holländer*, *Tannhäuser* and *Lohengrin*. All three showcase outsiders challenging the existing state of affairs of stagnant but damaging societies, and the musico-dramatic spheres Wagner creates strikingly exhibit his often exasperated plea for change.

This is not least the case in the first of these to be written. The exterior worlds of *Der fliegende Holländer*, the public realms of Daland, Erik, the sailors and spinners, are allotted traditional forms and harmonies, ostensibly secure in their practices and conventions. The interior worlds of the imagination, of Senta and the Dutchman, as well as the socio-political hope contained therein, are awarded more challenging music, with disruptive rhythms and patterns — the disturbances needed to forge the future. The far-reaching advances of *Der fliegende Holländer* have often been overlooked, or at least underplayed, compared to the even more pervasive dramatic and musical innovations of *Der Ring* and *Tristan und Isolde*. Composing *Holländer* amid poverty and neglect in Paris, Wagner knew as well as anyone the need for revolution, in society as well as art. His music conveys that urgency to us, imploring change and an end to the bourgeois complacency and exploitative socio-economics of the age. 'Die Frist ist um', sings the Dutchman in his great first-act monologue: 'The time is up'.

Chapter Two

Cupid and the Skull:
Tannhäuser

Wagner knew rejection. Despite — and because of — his arrogance, genius, self-assurance, egoism and conviction, he knew what it meant to be spurned, scorned and unwanted. He knew the despair and loneliness of isolation — from his own wife, from his own country, from his audiences and peers. Since its first appearance in Dresden in 1845, the various versions of *Tannhäuser* became progressively darker, more obsessively agitated and desolate, with some superficial opulence, as their hero is further isolated from his culture and himself. *Tannhäuser* is a consideration of how an extraordinary artist journeys to a wintry private kingdom of isolation and insanity after daring to challenge his deluded, smug and self-righteous civilisation.

Tannhäuser presents a disconcerting, disturbing view of human society — and the malicious judgement of God — whatever the potential redemption ambiguously presented, both musically and theatrically, at the drama's close. To the very end of his own life, Wagner felt dissatisfied with the work, claiming to 'still owe the world' a *Tannhäuser*. Yet the very imperfect nature of this work, its incomplete, in-progress and occasionally unsettled temperament, help convey its themes of inadequacy, uncertainty, faith, doubt and love. If Wagner is the black sheep of composers, *Tannhäuser* is the most troublesome of all his works: the outsider, the pest, the reclusive stranger.

In writing *Tannhäuser*, Wagner combined tales of antique fourteenth-century songwriting contests (known as *Sängerkrieg* and performed by *Minnesänger*) with the mythology of Venus and her enchanted subterranean realm, the Venusberg. This gives *Tannhäuser* a vivid surreality: both historical and mythical, real and illusionary, it is art that is simultaneously fixed and fluid. Such distinctions, inevitably intermingled and played against each other, are matched by the work's ostensibly central dichotomies of sex/salvation, saint/sinner, body/soul — contrasts whose naivety *Tannhäuser* soon exposes as not only untrue but dishonest and damaging. Although Wagner presents us with two highly contrasted settings — Venusberg and Wartburg — they do not represent mere dramatic boundaries or prospective life choices. For Wagner, obsessive sex and fanatical piety were both equally false and therefore equally detrimental. As ever, he took what he wanted from religion (myths, symbols, profundities, truths — though not 'the truth' in its theological sense), and here the notions of a pagan sex cult and an essentially bourgeois spirituality serve as a stage — tangible, emotional, metaphysical — for Tannhäuser's inner conflicts and consequent segregation.

The struggles he faces, apparently between fleshly and spiritual love, might be replaced by any number of human afflictions, addictions and their apparent opposites: alcoholism, drug abuse, gluttony, dieting, materialism, avarice, revelry, irresponsibility, frivolity, voyeurism, promiscuity, pornography, gambling. (This last vice last may well be especially pertinent since, when he awakes in the Venusberg, some of Tannhäuser's first words lament that he can no longer tell the difference between day and night: the Venusberg might be conceived as a Las Vegas casino.)

Productions of *Tannhäuser* have presented these vices in various ways, making, for instance, the singer-knight an opera star, Venusberg the scene of his endless shows and dependence on performance, and depicting him eager for privacy and withdrawal, by act 3 exhausted but bored with operatic retirement and longing for the adoration of the crowd. Whatever 'vice' the Venusberg represents, and whatever 'virtue' the Wartburg correspondingly signifies, *Tannhäuser* is not interested in either sin or salvation — the 'good' or 'bad' paths we choose, forsake or renounce. It is concerned with the struggle, the discord, solitude and captivity such conflicts entail, and the relationship of individuals to themselves and their surroundings.

Indeed, such isolation is connected to society's collective tendency to reject or disapprove of sexual rebellion/licence, binding itself up in hypocrisy and insincerity to preserve itself — its status, its wealth, or its so-called values. Tannhäuser's truth-telling about sex and passion in the song contest disrupts the conveniently oblique and inoffensive language about love the courtly minstrels acclaim. *Tannhäuser* knows that excessive indulgences are harmful, that internal conflict is damaging and injurious. But it also knows that social pretence and cultural duplicity are more destructive. Society's inability to cope or deal with candour, honesty, directness — its need to cloister everything with rules, conventions and euphemisms — is exposed by the truths Tannhäuser refuses to soften, even as he knows certain elements of those realities harm himself.

To some extent, Tannhäuser is that youthful stereotype: the angry adolescent first realizing the hypocrisy of the grown-up world around him, the interminable deception of the adult sphere. And it is this deceit, among other things, that has damaged Tannhäuser, compelling him towards the delights of the Venusberg, cursed as depravities by his society. Forbidden fruit has become the target of an illicit infatuation he can neither face nor fight. The Wartburg is, in some respects, a closed, two-faced system that contains the Venusberg as a (physically, spiritually and psychologically) submerged aspect of itself, a proscribed but exploited realm — like the brothel-Venusberg attached to the factory-Wartburg in Sebastian Baumgarten's 2011 Bayreuth production. Here, the Venusberg is an open secret not fit for conversation in polite society, but functions to both appease and motivate, subdue and incense, humanity.

Tobias Kratzer's 2019 Bayreuth *Tannhäuser* also focused on this societal component, diverging from the sometimes misleading sacred/profane dichotomy, by representing the Venusberg as a hippie commune, its members living in a camper van and on their wits. Here, the Wartburg is the Bayreuth Festival itself, the pilgrims the audience, the minstrel-knights the performers, Tannhäuser the wayward star. Here it is the audience that is staid and tradition bound, disingenuously embracing Wagner's pioneering art but rejecting innovative interpretation, rather than the culture of the opera house itself. Bayreuth has been, and continues to be, host to some of the most challenging of productions, not least in the twentieth-first century, with creations (such as Stefan Herheim's 2008 *Parsifal* and Barrie Kosky's 2017 *Meistersinger*, as well as the aforementioned Kratzer *Tannhäuser*) that meta-theatrically interrogate the historicities of Wagner, Germany and

Bayreuth itself. As ever with Wagner, a complex combination of provenance, performance, reception, history, mythology and reality enter into discussion, debate and skirmish, collaborating and cohabiting in often alarming ways but always inviting us to enquire what the works might mean, just as the song contest in *Tannhäuser* asks what love means.

Like Shakespeare's Coriolanus or Timon of Athens, Tannhäuser is an isolated outsider, rejected by his society for refusing to play the hypocrisy game. As such, Wagner makes him wait until the third act — despite being onstage nearly all the way through — to obtain his own music. It only then, during his most severe crisis, that he is able to understand that neither Venusberg nor Wartburg are to be his salvation. In fact, as a singer-artist, his redemption has been obvious from the start: music.

Wagner's characters, especially in *Der Ring des Nibelungen*, are likely to have their own musical identities. Siegfried's, prophesied in both orchestral and vocal terms in *Die Walküre* and used throughout *Siegfried* and *Götterdämmerung* in a range of guises and manipulations, is a broad and noble motif that nonetheless contains the poignancy of what might have been. Wotan, chief of the gods, is primarily associated with the threatening, controlling Spear motif and the expansive, majestic Valhalla one, again both considerably modified and customized throughout the *Ring* according to dramatic/emotional need. Moments after the overture to *Der fliegende Holländer* has launched the opera (and, in many ways, Wagner's career and true identity as a music-dramatist) into life, the Dutchman's motif and its wildly distinctive sonic cosmos are musically instituted, allowing Wagner to inaugurate the intricate chemistry between straightforward ideas and their complex contexts.

Tannhäuser has no such aural personality for the first two acts of the drama that bears his name. Elizabeth, Venus, the Pilgrims — all have characteristic evocations in the score. This is especially true in the overture, which in many ways represents the alternating worlds into and out of which the hero is to be thrown. *Tannhäuser* parades into existence with an overture of stunning vitality, deep emotional agony, and rousing spiritual muscle. It begins with a passage of unflustered dignity on winds with the Pilgrims' Hymn before sad and wounded lower strings anticipate the anguished personality of Tannhäuser to come, their musical torment corrupting the orchestra's splendour before it recovers to imposingly reaffirm the Hymn, now attended by vigorous, throbbing violins. This develops into the sparkling rapidity of the Venusberg music: harmonically dangerous, opulently orchestrated, relentlessly repeated with rhythmic carnal energy. But there is an emptiness to much of the music's erotic drive: it seems to portray despondency and frustration with coerced labour and toil rather than any truly satisfying sensual union. The music slows down, and a solo clarinet seductively petitions further pleasure. This serene interlude builds to reprise the Hymn, seemingly in triumph, before descending again into the Venusberg music, and the curtain rises on a ballet scene of frenzied, turbulent desire and cackling castanets.

This opening scene, with Tannhäuser's unconvincing attempts to thank Venus and move on, is characterized by a mechanical song to love that we know to be routine and meaningless — he's telling Venus what he thinks she wants hear. A song to love will carry more depth and significance when Tannhäuser shocks the stolid Wartburgians with his apostrophe to sexual love in act 2 — asserting his defiance of yet another world he feels excluded from — but it will remain music that is not his but the Venusberg's. In the opening Venusberg scene, Tannhäuser seeks tranquillity (and individuality), desperately, automatically trying to extract himself from the frenetic sensual-musical world that is dominating him. He knows the alternative to Venus is someone else's rules, someone else's music: the Wartburg's realm of courtly love, chaste sobriety and formulaic games.

Within this inflexible orthodoxy, Wagner presents the fascinating, appealing and multifaceted character of Elizabeth. No saintly virgin, she is a touching, if occasionally perplexed, figure of great integrity and goodness, as her music shows. We witness Elizabeth's exhilaration at seeing Tannhäuser again together with her sorrow at his long absence. She confronts the daunting, frightening institution of the Wartburg: amid the nonchalant vastness of the great Hall of Song and its prudish, demure society, she has the strength of character to intervene, break ranks, in order to prevent violence and persecution being enacted on her alienated Tannhäuser. She is a flexible and reasonable human being, an anxious, excited lover as well as a devout attendant, emancipating Madonna, and self-sacrificing paramour. It is her complexity that helps give the lie to *Tannhäuser*'s being merely about the tussle between sex and salvation. She understands Tannhäuser's internal and social ostracism, his search for an identity. She cannot herself abandon her community — like Ellen in Britten's *Peter Grimes* (1945), she also has no need to — but she still grasps the pain and exclusion of the outcast.

The way Elizabeth musically and dramatically rises above Wartburg conventionality — literally so in her heaven-bound departure — helps Tannhäuser realize his own aural identity and with it his own salvation, since he is redeemed not in human or divine terms but musical/aesthetic ones. Tannhäuser never becomes part of Wartburg society, a culture Wagner impeccably portrays with unadventurous, square music: he surpasses and transfigures it. This is a drama about time, backwards and forwards: it is a stage work about waiting, about anticipating, about anguished memory. Elizabeth must wait for Tannhäuser, both for his return from the Venusberg and then for his accompaniment of her into otherworldly grace; Tannhäuser must wait to locate his true identity and, in so doing, eclipse the dull, dishonest worlds of Venusberg and Wartburg, progressing into redemptive honour via the art of music (but not the fraudulent, fabricated music of song contests). Tannhäuser is not dithering — or agonizing — between sexual gluttony and complacent respectability: he despises both because neither are truly him. Erotic gourmandising irks him as much as duplicitous piety.

The magnificent prelude to act 3 captures the weariness of Tannhäuser's quest for himself. Superficially labelled 'Tannhäuser's Pilgrimage', it is to some degree a musical travel diary of his trek to Rome, his self-flagellation, penance and papal rejection. But it is indubitably more complex and mysterious than this. The orchestra state Tannhäuser's memory of the pilgrims and render the labyrinthine, excruciating paths — physical and psychological — he still has to negotiate.

Orchestras in Wagner, of course, have a tendency to know characters far better than they know themselves. But in *Tannhäuser*, the orchestra is not an omniscient narrator, as it will become in *Der Ring*, but the multifaceted reverberation of Tannhäuser's soul. To an extent, this is because Wagner has not yet fully developed the extraordinary depth of orchestral and leitmotivic facility that characterizes his great cycle of musikdramas. However, it is also because he wants to present *Tannhäuser* through Tannhäuser's mind: the work's musical memory is closely conjoined to the hero's own conscious reminiscences and fluctuating, preoccupied recollections.

In the act 3 prelude, horns vaguely propagandize the Pilgrims' Hymn and alternating woodwind seem to sorrowfully advocate Elizabeth's plea from the end of act 2. All is devout and dutiful before the exhaustion of Tannhäuser's journey to Rome (and back) is drawn on alienated strings. Ominous brass vehemently announce the Pope's curse and his cold-hearted refutation of clemency. Yet the events of Tannhäuser's pilgrimage are indeterminately presented: they are veiled, distorted, indistinct, frustrating the very notion of depiction and disclosure. As the prelude progresses, musico-dramatic associations become looser, more absent, inexplicable and unexplained. All is anonymity, obscurity, inscrutability. We will need Tannhäuser's Rome Narration to reveal the music's meaning and significance. Anticipating the tormented journey of *Parsifal's* own third-act prelude, in *Tannhäuser's*, Wagner presents a haunted, oppressed soul's excursion into madness and disintegration.

Although neither Wolfram nor Elizabeth totally abandons him, Tannhäuser is nevertheless utterly alone, coerced into becoming a self-blaming victim full of sexual shame and disappointment, cursed as a sinner, failure and pariah by the very society that once celebrated him. Tannhäuser is a damaged and ravaged protagonist, a complicated and distrait anti-hero, and Wagner fiddled and fidgeted with him over the decades, making him more and more wayward, erratic and unpredictable. He is, by turns, optimistic narcissist, death-pursuing outcast, impetuous dilettante, disruptive insurgent and self-hating paragon. His purgatorial pilgrimage, as depicted in the act 3 prelude, shows us his ordeals, his effort and his determination, thorough to his abasement, his degradation and his denunciation. He will finally elucidate his journey later in the act, in his Rome Narration, after his return home and as he searches for a despairing, pitiful return to the Venusberg.

Wagner's art of continuity and transition, his rejection of both artificial vocal exhibition and a chain of separate, neatly organized prescribed items, mirrors his subjects' rejection of the normal, the conventional, the everyday. His dramas require the complex interaction between musical ideas not only to express their dramatic density but also to provide the environment for their extension and ultimately the resolution to their conflict and ambiguity. The acute antagonism between the splendid, imposing Pilgrims' Hymn and the overexcited, lavish, precarious Venusberg music helps foster the polarized world of the drama, as well as being the location for modulations and equivocal evolutions.

The old-fashioned Wartburg song contest of act 2 at the centre of the drama is presented as a series of purposefully anachronistic self-contained arias (as is Wolfram's Song to the Evening Star in act 3), which Wagner's art spurns (and will reject further as his career progressed). The intentionally backward-sounding and archaically structured Wartburg is contrasted with the revolutionary developments of the Venusberg, with its musical cross references, rhythmic autonomies and harmonic asymmetries, as well as the highly reactive way the orchestral writing responds to the text.

By the time Tannhäuser narrates his Rome journey to Wolfram in the third act, he is done in, wiped out, dejected, and has reached a hazardous emotional threshold where there is a danger he has gone genuinely insane. Confrontational and inflammatory, he is a nomad meandering through a dead topography. David Alden's challenging, stark, insightful 1995 Munich production featured a landscape strewn with reproachful, jeering icons and the disintegrating remains of a ruined society. Elizabeth, herself now departed and near death, was vividly interpreted not as a patient, hopeful saint but as a similarly disturbed wanderer, grasping absentmindedly at deteriorating musical scores, thus shrewdly drawing attention not only to Elizabeth's role in Tannhäuser's deliverance but music's too.

Tannhäuser's Rome Narration is an unbroken dramatic recitative which keenly anticipates the method of Wagner's later musikdramas. Here the disposition of the vocal line changes as the text communicates sequentially Tannhäuser's repentant frame of mind at the start of his pilgrimage through his remembrance of Elizabeth, his contrition and ultimately the Pope's unsympathetic rejection. Acerbically imitating the callousness and hardheartedness of the Pope, the spokesman of God on earth, Tannhäuser is broken, finished, sarcastic and spent. He is accompanied by an immensely powerful orchestral commentary with a shifting, mobile density that carries the weight of the dramatic argument and which looks forward to the momentous innovations of *Tristan* and the *Ring*. Musically, the end of the Narration is close to anarchy and collapse: there is no dominant key, no sustained thematic material. Sounds scurry and whizz hither and thither with Tannhäuser's haphazard, unstable memories. The Pope's dismissal itself is escorted by a hostile sonic splinter: dark, ugly, ruthless.

In the so-called Paris and Vienna versions Wagner made of *Tannhäuser* in 1861 and 1875, the hero yearns not merely for salvation or atonement, as he had in earlier editions, but for death itself — absence, annihilation, nothingness. There is now a real anguish, wretchedness and desperation to Tannhäuser, an existential peril and appalling suffering, in which he meets with Tristan and (*Parsifal's*) Amfortas, waiting for death. Gone are the shimmer, gleam and strut of his earlier outbursts to sexual love in the Wartburg song contest. He is panicky, agitated, and uncompromisingly depicted in music of great distress and in shards of electric grief. His long voyage has burnt forwards, but he has travelled nowhere. Tramping with little hope, waiting shattered and drained for an impossible deliverance: this is Richard Wagner as Samuel Beckett.

But if act 3 of *Tannhäuser* is Beckett before Beckett, it is also Wagner before Wagner. Part of Wagner's dissatisfaction with the work was that he was trying to write *Tristan* and *Parsifal* before he was ready, musically or dramatically. In fact, in *Tannhäuser*, he achieves something to stand proudly next to both those later masterpieces, forming a stunning triptych of dread, suffering and psychosis.

Although necessarily severe, such perspectives on *Tannhäuser* do not cast it as mere misery-*oper*. Expectancy is contained within the despondency, as many directors have envisaged. Götz Friedrich's subversive 1972 *Tannhäuser* at Bayreuth, breaking from while also developing the abstract, mystical dominion of Wieland Wagner's post-war productions, wanted to combine symbolism with a human story. Here was a character-artist (perhaps Wagner himself) in search of his identity, labouring against an unsympathetic civilisation. This *Tannhäuser* was a struggle against isolation and exclusion, which Christendom (if not Christ) and capitalism cultivated, the artist-citizen exquisitely alone and caught in the delicate lines between triumph, survival and catastrophe. Friedrich sought a narrative realism which is undoubtedly at the heart of this harsh journey, secularizing the religiosity, making redemption and deliverance something everyone has to win for themselves, with hope and solidarity rather than the parasitic benefits of capital or nepotism.

In Wagner's drama, it is only when Tannhäuser has reached his nadir — banished from normal human society, rejected by formal religion, and at the anxious, fractured end of his Rome Narration — that he is able to discover his true identity through musical underworldliness and otherworldliness which, to an extent, transcend unresolved textual questions on the exact nature of his redemption. Tannhäuser expires in reprieve and exaltation, partly through Elizabeth's sacrifice but also through the restorative power of music — not religion. Music, which gave Tannhäuser memory, also grants him death and a release from the opposing worlds that have haunted him. Salvation lies not with compulsive physical pleasure, celestial devotion, or even the harmonies and frictions of competitive singing but with authentic, stimulating, evolving and perhaps revolutionary art. Wagner's work tells of expectation and deliverance, of liberation and renovation that is possible through the redemptive power of art — an art which we can all experience, partake in, be redeemed by. We are all, in this sense, active co-creators with the composer.

Like another great unfinished and arguably unfinishable work, Schoenberg's *Moses und Aron* (1932), *Tannhäuser* expresses the incomplete, inconclusive and inexplicable nature of all art, which constantly needs reinterpretation for its own renewal and meaning. Whatever stylistic and dramatic inconsistencies exist between the various versions of *Tannhäuser*, as well as the vexing global debt Wagner felt in regard to it, the number of *Tannhäuser*s that exist is suggestive of the metaphors at work within the drama concerning music, memory, self-determination, rigidity and regeneration. For Wagner, *Tannhäuser* was always a work in progress, the definitive edition simply the most recent version. Art is never complete, it is always ongoing: searching, restless, inquisitive, hopeful.

Chapter Three

The Revolutionary Question: *Lohengrin*

Lohengrin is a fairy tale gone wrong, a love story without a happy ending, a romance which collapses as its lovers implode amid the pressures of their partnership. Two lonely hearts, yearning for love amid their isolation, are given a shot at bliss and squander it, their dreams of happiness marooned on the island of despair. Their relationship is largely predicated on silence; on the essentially unspoken devotion they claim for each other. Yet no relationship can exist on feeling alone. It must journey from the delight of adoration and buzz of the unknown into the full realities of love: admiration, communication, exploration, with boundaries but not barriers.

In *Lohengrin*, Wagner asks us to interrogate love and ask what it means to us, what our own terms for its existence and success are, how it is born, cultivated or destroyed. Elsa is a true revolutionary, seeking love as collaboration and companionship, based on mutual values and considerations, not status or station — which is why she feels the honest obligation to ask who Lohengrin is in the first place, in order to truly and profoundly love her husband.

There has tended to be more than a whiff of misogyny when interpreting *Lohengrin*: female frivolity and inquisitiveness gain a catastrophic advantage over marital harmony, destroying a holy union, for which Elsa is accordingly — and harshly — penalized. Yet the mysterious knight, too, arguably has his share of culpability: his exorbitant demand for anonymity provokes her necessary, faithful and unavoidable questions. For his part, Lohengrin aches to escape his divine and heightened nature, to love and be loved for himself, not for where he comes from or for his special standing, which would produce mere worship or adulation.

Like Lohengrin, *Lohengrin* wants to break free of its generic operatic armour but is not quite able — not entirely ready to take the radical step towards musikdrama and the (relative) autonomy of a groundbreaking new musical form. It is these tensions — internally between love and duty, externally between musikdrama and Romantic opera — which Wagner exploits so magnificently in *Lohengrin*, producing a hybrid artwork in the best sense, where emotional and religious, progressive and regressive, elements combine to stunning effect.

For this, his saddest work, Wagner wrote music of exquisite beauty. There is a fragile, ethereal light and ecstatic harmony to much of the opera's score. Right from the start, the act 1 prelude ushers in a new sound-world of enchanting brilliance and shimmering, otherworldly space. Lofty violins interspersed with flutes begin a divinely prolonged orchestral upsurge, the extended crescendo expanding to a glorious culmination before relaxing back to its initial whisper. Wagner takes us into the seductive sphere of *Lohengrin* with music that is clean, bright and continuously mesmerizing — and that will return at key positions in the drama. The prelude is monothematic (unlike the conflicts of the *Holländer* and *Tannhäuser* overtures). Its beauty is based on its distinctive, meticulous timbre and the way it is able to simultaneously convey both the sensual and spiritual, its continuous elaborations hypnotically transporting the listener into the realm of the Grail which it both signifies and embodies, while never being dour or austere. This is to be a love story, after all.

Yet beneath the entrancing exterior and delicate silver-blue colours of *Lohengrin* are deep socio-political and psychological undercurrents, as well as complex, forbidding and sometimes hostile truths. This is a lyrical opera with a malignant core, where the murky alcoves of the second act pull, twist and distort characters and their fates with an atomic force of magic and manipulation. Act 2 opens with malevolence and a sinister *Siegfried*-like despondency, creating the gloomy space for the villain Ortrud to chillingly probe human fragility. Whatever the mythical or old-fashioned components to the work, it is absolutely vital in its cynical conception of human behaviour, as well as the dark arts at work in political intrigue — the result of thwarted or unsated ambition. Telramund is a thug and a bitter, grievous bully, but Ortrud, though also resentful, is in addition a very skilled (and cynical) civic operator, and she is given music of an extremely advanced, inflected kind — anticipating the fragmented, adaptable outlines of the Ring motif which dominates and, to an extent, shapes *Der Ring des Nibelungen*. Ortrud's music is ominous, agitated and harmonically troublesome, the vocal lines unshackled from traditional phrase frameworks, bequeathing the words (and their import) greater immediacy and power, as well as the ability to creepily reintegrate into a range of musico-dramatic contexts. *Lohengrin* is no mere medieval fantasy world of naïve strings and noble processions, however much some would like it to be.

Although Ortrud represents the old pagan world, her musical sphere is progressive: she characterizes the modern demolition of the established order (be it political or Christian, categories heavily intertwined) which Wagner wished to overthrow. He wrote *Lohengrin* at a time of revolution in Europe, during which he even joined the barricades in Dresden in 1848 (an activity which led directly to his long exile and required Liszt to organize *Lohengrin*'s premiere in Weimar in 1850). Ortrud, then, is curiously close to Elsa in her revolutionary status, the sorceress's music a dangerous subversion of the time-honoured arrangements and comportments of operatic tradition.

Lohengrin himself is radical, embodying love and truth as liberation (Wagner conceives of the Grail in a secular light) even as he himself is bound up in the restrictive power struggles of society. Lohengrin wants to be appreciated through love, as an individual, without needing to divulge his identity. But he takes an unnecessary and obstreperous course to attain this ambition: imposing, with the Forbidden Question, not only a symbol of the irreconcilability of the realms between which he is torn but a literal obstacle that is opposed to the truthful, all-embracing love Elsa knows to be the only one worth having.

Lohengrin is wounded, largely by his own narcissism and self-absorption, a self-love that should not be regarded as wholly or even partially negative. It is connected to his status as an artist, a modernizing personality, capable of transforming his society but always (and tragically) destined to remain outside of it — something Wagner knew only too well at the time before, during and after the composition of *Lohengrin*. The artist wishes, not unreasonably, to be known, understood and accepted unreservedly through feeling, but is denied this sincerity and fidelity by the fickle world. He must, therefore, address and love himself, in tragic solitude.

Nikolaus Lehnhoff's stunning abstract-militarist *Lohengrin* for Baden-Baden in 2006 portrayed the swan knight in the third act as a singer-songwriter, on his wedding night in open waistcoat and shirtsleeves at the piano, pencil in hand, composing the bridal music we hear. Hovering about him, Elsa was a mixture of boredom, frustration and admiration, and we were compelled to ask, with her, if this artist would free himself of his art (which is also part of his identity) and love her. For *Lohengrin* is Elsa's catastrophe too. She *must* ask the forbidden question *because* she loves Lohengrin; fully loving him is not possible without asking it. Yet this will destroy him, his identity, his ability as an artist, and — ultimately — their love. Irony is piled upon tragedy.

The realm of the Grail, synonymous with the timeless realm of art, appeals to freedom, but its denizens have self-absorbed traits which prevent attachment and a truly genuine association in this world. Although his deeply fulfilling relationship with Cosima Liszt would eventually disabuse Wagner of the pessimism expressed in this view of artistic life, at the time of writing *Lohengrin*, he certainly felt its cynical gloom — trapped in an unhappy marriage with someone who, admirable though she was, could not understand her husband's genius and revolutionary mission.

Lohengrin's tragedy is that Lohengrin and Elsa are complementary figures, isolated and longing for love, the one the unconscious of the other, striving for candour and transcendence in a world which will not allow it and which ultimately corrupts even their view of each other. They journey towards each other, Elsa travelling up, Lohengrin down, before the traumatic necessity of their separation, which anticipates the exquisite sonic desolation of the imposed partition between the lover-twins Siegmund and Sieglinde in *Die Walküre*. Just as

Siegmund's realization that Sieglinde cannot accompany him to Valhalla generates music of horrific beauty, *Lohengrin* ends with a remarkable and rapturous sorrow.

Wagner developed *Lohengrin*, as he did many of his works, from the mythologies and literature of ancient Greece, pre-Christian and medieval Europe, Norse saga and German epic. He imagined — as his earlier operas had also begun to do — an original and genuine human-dramatic total artwork (*Gesamtkunstwerk*) with sweeping social, political and cultural reforms that amounted to revolution and rebirth, a true renaissance of humanity. The artifice of absolute musical forms, negligible orchestral garnishes to ostentatious vocal declamation and recitative: these were alien to the spirit of authenticity and gravity he wanted to inaugurate. Drama, text, music, motivation and scenic effect were to be united.

The libretto to *Siegfrieds Tod*, contemporaneous with *Lohengrin*, likewise conveys Wagner's artistic quandary, caught between grand opera and musikdrama. Although the first of the four *Ring* libretti to be written (Wagner at each step realizing he needed to tell more of the story), *Siegfrieds Tod* was eventually the final instalment of the cycle and the last to be set to music, so that the ostensible orthodoxy of its libretto would be swept away by the revolutionary nature of the music and the music's relationship to the libretto. Wagner came to realize that although all the arts in a Gesamtkunstwerk are equal, some are more equal than others. Moreover, he had not yet acquired a fitting musical patois for *Siegfrieds Tod/Götterdämmerung* — it would need not only the developments and innovations of the first three *Ring* dramas (*Rheingold*, *Walküre*, *Siegfried*) but the modernizations of *Tristan und Isolde* as well.

Lohengrin was also a part of this progress. Indeed, the far-reaching and uncompromising nature of *Lohengrin*'s musical language and structures urge that it be conceived as a musikdrama, where the orchestra in particular is not only responding to the text and stage action but helping create it, in terms of atmosphere as well as its direction and implications. We have the remnants of recitative, aria, ensemble and chorus, plus calls to arms, revenge duets, parades, marches and montages so familiar from grand opera. Yet such gallant edifices and staid configurations are breaking down, crumbling under the tremendous stresses Wagner's art exerts in its desire to reforge and retell. Similarly, the work's narrative seeks to explore, then undermine, an outdated, restrictive religiosity and archaic notions of love. New formulas, where music and text are combined in complex and extended new ways, are being developed, fusions that will find their ultimate expression in *Das Rheingold* and *Die Walküre*.

In *Lohengrin*, Elsa's bridal procession is twice disturbed (first by Ortrud, then Telramund) at the end of act 2. (In Peter Konwitschny's 2007 Copenhagen production, set in a school classroom, naughty imp Ortrud superbly and spitefully stepped on Little-Miss-Perfect Elsa's train, arresting her progress.) Wagner is here following a common operatic practice of ceremonial processions being melodramatically interrupted. But Wagner enlarges the possibilities, conceiving the convention on a vastly broader scale. The disruptions' tension and tremor not only motivate the conflicts of the principals on stage but also provoke and permit the colossal choral dynamism Wagner creates. The chorus is here especially outstanding, reaching new heights of expressive possibility, even for Wagner (always an exceptional composer for grouped voices). The writing is intricate and vigorous, its rhythms and textures both instinctive and alarming, effortless and contrived, variously coalescing with the solo lines of the cast, intermingling with their socio-emotional disputes. Elsa tends to be pitched above the group, the differentiated bride-bridge towards revolution and liberation. It is a scene of immense theatrical power. Utilizing convention for his own progressive purposes, Wagner shows himself the master of hybridity and fusion, networking his work with an array of musico-dramatic techniques to cast shadows and doubts — just as the scene requires.

Together with pioneering choral writing and compelling choral–solo interactions, Wagner weaves an orchestral backcloth of considerable complexity, detail and command. As well as restructuring opera's form, Wagner makes the orchestra work in a new way, in order to function as an at once subtle and immensely powerful commentator, analyst and interrogator of the intellectual and dramatic discussions which are occurring. In *Lohengrin*, instrumental divisions seem relatively straightforward and are designed for the requirements of character and plot but also allow for intricate orchestral conflicts, confessions and reconfigurations. Apportioned, sometimes even alienated, sound-worlds are generated. Thus violins sing the music of the Holy Grail; Elsa is given elegant but often fidgety woodwind, the king regal, occasionally baffled brass, Ortrud her menacing concoction of wind, strings and timpani rolls (which anticipates Fafner's sinister lethargy in the prelude to act 2 of *Siegfried*). By separating the orchestra into different and dynamic parts, rather than having it exist as some attendant homogenous mass, Wagner countenances new directions and combinations, new capacities and possibilities. These not only provide a range of textures and shrewd effects but allow text, voice and action to be accorded even greater depth and intensity, combined with a vitality towards socio-political or philosophical argumentation, the latter granted a freedom and flexibility on a par with music's.

When Elsa sings of her dream in act 1 ('Einsam in trüben Tagen') and when Lohengrin narrates his history and origin towards the end of act 3 ('In fernem Land'), both passages open in a predictable manner, balanced and organized: the rigid formality required for public address. Then, as their stories progress, they surrender to less stringently ordered forms, their emotions disrupting the music into looser structures. The fantastic and fantastical nature of their tales is exhibited in, perhaps even generated by, the impulsive emancipation of their music. These two episodes — Elsa's Dream and Lohengrin's Narration — are, fore and aft, the lovers' yearning for liberty, for autonomy from their social, political and religious confinements. Elsa's is all optimism and anticipation; Lohengrin's, following the event, couched in sadness, since he must now return to his divine prison. That it is music which carries much of the burden of communication is imperative: words are (to some extent) hampered by their communal availability and thus a liability, hindered by their essential directness. Paradoxically, the subtler, more equivocal sphere of music is necessary to convey the truth and sincerity of love and revolution.

Between hope and sorrow lies reality. The act 3 prelude depicts the wedding feast and opens with a flurry of eager and enthusiastic notes, first on strings, then wind. A raucous tune on the brass is bellowed out, followed by the celebrated wedding march. It is all the prelude to doom and the ironically happy music to the world's shortest marriage. The beatification and vulgarization of the wedding march in nuptials from Victorian times to today (as well as its muddle-headed transformation from being exit, 'going-to-bed' music in the opera to entrance music in our churches) conceals the incongruously cheerful nature of the music, its profoundly unfortunate merriness and joviality.

Wagner makes the ceremony (the shift from feast to bridal chamber) into a brief scene, a reduction where most opera composers would expand. Traditionally, such a scene would involve the extended, privately aired misgivings of one (or both) of the couple amid the clamour and customs of a civic event. Wagner, master of transition and extension, instead has Elsa's uncertainties naturally develop in an expertly long-drawn-out interchange, alone with her new husband, with an exemplary management of the unbroken melodic-musical discourse that is one of the chief features of musikdrama. The semi-public ritual scene accompanying the newlyweds to their conjugal night is thus merely a prologue following the festive act 3 prelude, an introduction to the key drama which Wagner wants centre stage and uncluttered by convention or superfluous staff.

Left on stage — the chorus and bridal cavalcade having departed to gently evaporating flute, harp and strings — Lohengrin and Elsa are alone for the very first time. (In his brilliantly inventive and now infamous 'lab rats' production for Bayreuth in 2010, Hans Neuenfels had the couple immediately isolated on their first meeting in act 1, one of the many experiments and incarcerations in this playful and poignant staging.) Forced now to speak, to communicate, and now outside the public roles and conditions they have hitherto been both imprisoned and incubated by, it is not long before anxiety, breakdown and calamity occur.

Along with infinite melody, the other defining (if not entirely original) Wagnerian feature is the leitmotif, the recurrent theme or themes throughout a work and their distinctive association with a particular character, object, event or emotion. It is the leitmotif itself, of course, which permits and encourages a continuous musical discourse in the first place, and in *Lohengrin*, both are given a vital importance and are fundamental to this prolonged wedding night scene, the first and only time that Elsa and Lohengrin are alone together, but which has been prophesied and foreshadowed throughout the drama via the leitmotivic technique. The crucial leitmotif employed here is the so-called Forbidden Question, those enquiries concerning Lohengrin's name and origin which Elsa is prohibited from making.

Wagner would most dazzlingly and resourcefully exploit the leitmotif technique in the *Ring*, where short, pithy musical ideas are capable of immeasurable transformation (as well as forming a complex structural occupation for the entire work). However, in *Lohengrin*, Wagner is well on the way to developing this method, even if, in this earlier work, motifs are more generally complete themes, well developed and therefore less able to metamorphose and mutate, and accordingly serve less subtle descriptive and theatrical functions. Nonetheless, as with *Lohengrin's* Forbidden Question, they can, even in this stage of their evolution, entertain huge dramatic sovereignty, travelling from mere reminiscence towards a theatrically driven utilization of (as well as a degree of transformation to) the thematic material.

The Forbidden Question motif is first heard in act 1, scene 3, to Lohengrin's words 'Nie sollst du mich befragen' — 'Never shall you ask me' — as he lays out the terms of his commitment to both Elsa and, in a wider context, to the people of Brabant. Elsa barely acknowledges the dictate (she is 'almost unconscious' in Wagner's stage directions), and Lohengrin is forced to, somewhat petulantly, reiterate his conditions. Here the orchestra sound the first of many constant and repeated reminders of this uncompromising order to Elsa never to probe his name or origin. Its most dramatic application, prior to its actual and consequential vocal utterance by Elsa in the bridal chamber, is its recurrence at the very end of the second act: the twin interruptions to the wedding pageant seemingly neutralized, the procession continues amidst the bright world of C major sanguinity. Suddenly, Ortrud raises her arm in a gesture of triumph, and the callous F minor of the Forbidden Question screams out on trumpets and trombones. Far from being Lohengrin's jurisdiction or instrument of control, the Forbidden Question (and its connotations) is, in *Lohengrin's* second act, constantly abused as a manipulative, Machiavellian tool by Ortrud, who is closely associated to its motif, her key being primarily F sharp minor (itself the relative minor key of Lohengrin's A major).

For the swan knight, the Forbidden Question is as much an impediment to his own love and happiness as it is to Elsa's. Lohengrin wants to escape his divinity, the burden of the religious and the political spheres in their many permutations. But it is convenient for society to maintain him, along with his myths and structures (just as it is expedient to have him lead them into battle). Too often, as we saw earlier, Elsa is misleadingly portrayed as a nosy, intrusive woman, the butt of jokes about asking questions that, to outsiders, can seem easy to avoid or simply to not be concerned by. Likewise, Lohengrin — whatever his many attractive and positive qualities — is more typically regarded as, and reduced to, a furtive martinet, a perverse weirdo with something to hide, unreasonably keeping his past and identity from the spouse he claims to love. But *Lohengrin* is more complex than such readings will allow.

Immediately after he has decreed the Forbidden Question and (at the second time of asking) secured Elsa's commitment to faithful silence, Lohengrin speaks three words. These words are so universal and commonplace as to be very often a cliché, a slogan, despite the gravity and import of their message and meaning. We utter them constantly and unremarkably, yet they retain the power to transform lives forever. Lohengrin, at this moment in the opera that bears his name, speaks these three words just once: 'Ich liebe dich' — 'I love you'. It is, in fact, the only occasion on which they are spoken in post-apprentice Wagner, the only instance in over forty hours of music and drama about love, passion, desire and redemption. Why?

In many ways, the phrase is ill-suited to Wagner, his characters and their situations. They are far too involved for the trite banalities of lovers' exchanges. Tristan and Isolde are concerned with being and nothingness, with death and exalted metaphysics; Siegmund and Sieglinde with the world-changing possibilities of their illicit union. Tannhäuser and Venus, even if they felt it, simply haven't the time to articulate it. For any of these pairings to utter the straightforward words 'I love you' would risk undermining the vastness of their missions, the limitless potential their love confers, just as Wagner's musikdramas conferred incalculable possibility on art (and, directly and indirectly, on politics and wider world history). In many ways, the characters don't need to speak these words: the significances they contain are self-evident to themselves and conveyed emotionally to us through Wagner's music. What, then, makes Lohengrin and Elsa different? Why does Wagner allow his swan knight this sole instance of the most ubiquitous phrase of feeling known?

Lohengrin hovers between the operatic past and operatic future (both in Wagner's career and more generally), as well as between myth and history, and Lohengrin himself hangs between competing realms. His music, and that of the Grail, rhythmically and harmonically shimmers like sunshine: bright but static, stable but inert. The phrase 'I love you' seems caught, too, between the world of courtly love and chivalrous conduct (which, after all, is the reason Lohengrin has just materialized in the opera, to fight for Elsa's honour) and the more candid, outspoken, free love of the future, which Wagner was impatient to see realized in his own life and society.

For Lohengrin, 'I love you' is both a ribbon and a bind: a decoration of the honest, faithful feeling which he maintains for Elsa and a hindrance preventing him from journeying fully to her and escaping the limited, limiting realm of the Grail. 'I love you', for Lohengrin and for us, is something that can be spoken routinely, meeting expectation and obligation but carrying little meaning. Yet it is also something spontaneous, uninhibited, crammed with a range of emotional connotations, extraordinary consequences and life-altering prospects. Love, like art — especially Wagner's art — can change the world.

Like Elizabeth in *Tannhäuser*, Elsa has tended to be considered by scholars, directors and audiences as a feudal throwback, a medieval regression of passé passivity and meekness. Yet, like Elizabeth, she drives the drama, exhilarating in love and goodness, confronting the formidable, alarming institutions around her. Her intricacy and need to break rank confer on her modernity. Her concern for Lohengrin, her desire for their love to be complete, is not merely touching but radical. She understands his internal conflict, his own search for a new identity amid his vaulted status, which serves only to ostracize him. Yet Elsa will not submit to the knight's requirement for blind compliance and, musically, she never acquiesces either, instead hovering around Lohengrin's A major in her own A flat.

When he finally takes his leave of Elsa, Lohengrin gives his wife three items, partially for her brother's use, should he return, but also as farewell gifts and tokens of love. These three objects — horn, sword and ring — will come to govern and structure Wagner's next project and grand, world-changing achievement: *Der Ring des Nibelungen*. As Lohengrin passes them to his wife, as he sees her for the last time, it is as if Wagner is bidding farewell to his own past, passing the future on to Elsa, the true and inspiring revolutionary of *Lohengrin*, the woman who lives for love, who will not be bound by convention, and who knows that to ask her husband who he is is a necessary and modern, not forbidden and antiquated, question.

In many ways, *Lohengrin* is an appetizer to the modern musikdrama Wagner created most completely in *Das Rheingold*. It offers some of the tastes and textures of the world to come but nonetheless is not the whole meal. Although this is partly a matter of the composer's not yet being ready to produce musikdrama, it is not mere hesitancy or uncertainty on Wagner's part, nor is it a desire to stay within the sphere of safe operatic traditions. *Lohengrin* is expressly designed to be tantalizingly caught between the future and the past, glancing backwards while provocatively glimpsing the challenges and benefits to come. Musically, dramatically and politically, *Lohengrin* is the revolutionary prelude to the *Ring*.

PART TWO

THE RING

Chapter Four

The Infinite Web:
Der Ring des Nibelungen

Richard Wagner's *Der Ring des Nibelungen*, written between 1848 and 1874, is a tragic symphonic vortex packed with connective alchemy and motivic weavings. Foreshadowing, reflecting, revealing — the music of the *Ring* moves up, down, backwards, forwards, sideways in an alluring web of associations and a neural aural network of infinite intersections. An epic cycle of four musikdramas uniting orchestral complexity with theatrical irascibility, the *Ring* invites enquiry into the nature, history and future of our species. It gazes to the past by reviving the principles of Greek drama and the political-psychological subtlety of Shakespeare, while simultaneously forging modernity with an intricate musico-poetic synthesis. The *Ring* unveils panoramas on a vast range of historical, social and philosophical landscapes, while also taking us deep inside the heads and hearts of its characters, exposing their inner lives, their darkest fears and profoundest hopes, whether for good or ill. Its ethics, too, are immeasurable and disturbing, our attitudes to behaviour shifting as the cycle, and our own lives, progresses — for the *Ring* needs a lifelong engagement to do it justice.

This colossal project took over a quarter of a century to complete, with a long gap in the middle to realize two equally revolutionary and multifaceted enterprises, *Tristan und Isolde* in 1859 and *Die Meistersinger von Nürnberg* in 1867. Wagner conferred unity on this enormous scheme through his series of leitmotifs: short musical ideas, infinitely developed across the cosmic arc of the drama. Although not Wagner's absolute invention — Handel, Gluck and Mozart had all used forms of musico-dramatic reminiscence akin to the leitmotif — no one had cultivated the technique with such extraordinary dexterity, intensity and possibility. But if it is the music that is the main reason we go back, again and again, to this work, its text, its drama, its influences and its sources are absolutely crucial to understanding how the sound of the *Ring* functions — indeed, they cannot be separated from it.

When Wagner first drafted the libretto for the *Ring* in the late 1840s, the anonymous medieval epic poem the *Nibelungenlied* (*c.*1200) was well-established in the cultural life of Germany. It was becoming a standard text in schools, a 'national epic' for the nurturing of young minds, an emblem in the struggle for German unity, as well as a creative curiosity for poets and composers. Written in Middle High German, its key event is the death of Siegfried, and that is likely the seed from which the whole *Ring* project began. But Wagner became increasingly concerned with telling the whole story of how this tragic episode occurred. To do this, he turned to Germanic literature located in Norse and Icelandic myth: the *Thidriks Saga of Bern*, the *Prose Edda*, the *Poetic Edda*, and the *Völsunga Saga*, all from around the thirteenth century, and all containing tales of castle-building gods aided by giants and the exploits of dragon-slaying heroes, with the familiar blend of fame, fortune, intrigue, betrayal and destruction.

Put simply, these latter sources comprise the dramatic material for the first three works of the *Ring* — *Rheingold*, *Walküre*, *Siegfried* — while the *Nibelungenlied* furnishes *Götterdämmerung*. This helps explain, in part, the structural and stylistic differences between the final part the *Ring* and its earlier instalments. *Götterdämmerung* was also the first text to be written, before many of the other influences on the *Ring* had fully marinated in Wagner's mind. As we will see, these differences, though very real and enthralling, do not damage or undermine the integrity and unity of the whole. Indeed, they actively heighten its tensions, paradoxes and complexities: surely something all great art aspires to encompass.

Immersing himself in these myths and epics not only gave Wagner the raw dramatic material for his project but enabled him to begin to see the overall configuration and character of his endeavour, though these would hugely expand as well as darken over time. Whatever the poetic and narrative qualities of his Germanic sources, Wagner was always a keen psychologist, an exceptionally gifted communicator of the intricacies and contradictions of the mind, and in these myths, there was too much surface and not sufficient depth. So, for his *Ring*, he looked back to those he regarded as the first and finest literary analysts of human behaviour and mental mechanisms: the Greeks. Here were the destructive relationships; the confrontations; the familial sagas and fallings-out; the precarious and yet inescapable memories; the piercing, pungent command of conscious, semiconscious and unconscious processes. Here were all the poignancy, dignity, muddle and confusion which make up human life.

For the Greeks, the concept of the tetralogy was essential: Aeschylus and Euripides, masters of the form, tended to write a series of three tragedies with a concluding satyr play. (Aeschylus's remarkable *Oresteia*, from 458 BC, is the only extant trilogy from ancient Greece and was a huge influence on Wagner, not least in its examination of family conflict, the complexity of inheritance, the battle between old and new orders, and the false binary between good and evil. Its satyr postscript, *Proteus*, survives only as a single line.) For his own purposes, the composer inverted the Hellenic four-part arrangement, putting a preliminary evening, as he called it — *Rheingold* — before the three days of *Walküre*, *Siegfried*, and *Götterdämmerung*, but the ethos was the same: an immersive, large-scale, all-embracing *event*, something that occupied one's life and was a break from the conventional and the mundane.

Crucially, the Greeks also considered their dramas as being fundamentally sacred in character, to be celebrated at a special and distinctive festival, a religious ritual open for all that was set apart from the daily grind. Wagner, too, wanted his new work to be exceptional, unique, differentiated, to become a life-enhancing and rejuvenating aspect of reality, a courageous celebration of existence unburdened by guilt or routine. The Bayreuth Festival, founded to stage the *Ring*, which eventually evolved into today's institution, with its byzantine booking systems, corporate sponsorships and celebrity endorsements, might not seem to be the open, hallowed religious festival the Greeks or Wagner had in mind, but the past is not as pure as we may imagine. For all its problems and intermittent crudity, the festival still realizes a distinctive magical ambience. Not only the specially built theatre but Bayreuth's location, on a Green Hill out of town, and timing, for a few short weeks in the summer, help foster that atmosphere of an event, an occasion: the ritual, the rite. For those worshipping the creed of Wagner, Bayreuth remains a holy pilgrimage and as transformative a journey as time-travelling to the Theatre of Dionysus in the shadow of the Acropolis, bustling under the festival sun of twenty-five centuries ago.

To go with the meat and veg of Germanic myth and Greek drama, Wagner added a further ingredient to the cooking pot of the *Ring*, lending it even greater colour, texture, spice and flavour: contemporary philosophy, which also helped magnify not only the size, scope and direction of the cycle but its essential complexity. In the 1840s, Ludwig Feuerbach was one of the most contentious and idiosyncratic philosophical voices in Germany, appealing to the revolutionary principles Wagner was expounding, politically as well as in the realms of music and drama. For Feuerbach, God was merely a projection of human desires and needs, a fabricated outlet created in order to cope with the problems of life — and death — but which ultimately had divided humankind against itself through asserting our own sinful inadequacy against the meaningless perfection of the divine. In Feuerbach's philosophy, removing God allows for a celebration of love, which is the true essence of human nature. Only in our contacts with others, not with God, do we generate our emotions, our ethics, our systems, our awareness of responsibility, generosity and exultation. Such a world view had radical implications for the structure of society: an ending to age-old prejudices and inherent injustices, most of which we are still trying to overcome.

The optimism Wagner took from Feuerbach became clouded in the 1850s, both by the failure of actual revolutions of 1848–9 and by his first reading of Arthur Schopenhauer in 1854, which would not only influence the *Ring* but interrupt its creation, directly instigating the necessary intermediary composition of *Tristan* and then *Meistersinger*. First, there was Schopenhauer's pessimism (something Wagner's own personal and artistic disappointments at the time made him greatly receptive to). Pain in this world was a result of the 'will to live', something which one had to deny in the manner of Buddhist renunciation and the illusionary nature of human life (a religious world view which deeply influenced Schopenhauer's own thought). Love/sex was the ultimate expression of this will — something both Schopenhauer and Wagner agreed on, even if they disagreed as to consequences. For the philosopher, it was a destructive force; for the composer, a creative energy. Although Wagner would take what he wanted from Schopenhauer, picking and choosing ideas which appealed to him, as he did with German myth, Norse saga, and Christianity, Schopenhauer's aesthetics regarding music would radically alter the composer's attitude to the relative structures of his operas, now fundamentally differentiated as musikdramas.

Schopenhauer raised music over and above other media, something which undermined Wagner's own speculative musings on the direction of opera, developed in his extended theoretical essay *Oper und Drama* (1851). These principles had argued for the essential unity and equality of the arts, especially between words and music in opera, and had governed the construction of the whole *Ring* libretto, plus the entire musikdrama of *Das Rheingold* and the first act of *Die Walküre* (perhaps the greatest execution of his revolutionary codes). But Schopenhauer persuaded Wagner that music matters more.

This might seem obvious to us: we return to Wagner for his music. But for the composer-librettist, his texts carried significant weight, and this was no precious, pretentious attitude of a wannabe poet: musico-dramatic unity was fundamental to his conception of the *Ring*. Over time, however, music — primarily orchestral music — began to dominate. The richness and complexity of Wagner's instrumental sound even in *Rheingold* might make this occasionally hard to discern, but as the composition of the *Ring*'s music wore on, the orchestra took on a more powerful structural and aesthetic role. This seems appropriate since, in some ways, the libretto of the *Ring* is its most political aspect, whereas music is its emotional and metaphysical core, music being better-suited to such subtle communications. Over time, as Wagner's political hopes were dashed (though not relinquished), the security and assurances of metaphysics took on a greater importance, something the non-verbal orchestral ending to the whole work is able to convey. This is not to say the *Ring* is not an astonishingly powerful political document, even a compelling manifesto for socialism, but is only to emphasize the pronounced weight of philosophy on its bearing, especially in its final completed form.

Wagner's discovery of Schopenhauer helps explain many of the changes and inconsistencies to the libretto, which went through half a dozen endings — variously known as the 'Feuerbach Ending', 'Schopenhauer Ending', and so on — but which seem to actually enhance, not emasculate, the overall *Ring*. To expect flawless consistency (whatever that might mean) from any work of art, not least one written over a quarter of a century, is perhaps to miss the point and to overlook some of the aesthetic, intellectual and emotional benefits of incongruity. (The details, deviations and consequent shifts in meaning attached to these various modifications are fascinating and demand extended attention which is sadly beyond the scope of this book, though recommended reading is included in an appendix.)

The libretto to the *Ring*, famously, was written backwards, then the music forwards. If this summation is a little crude, the double span captures something of the convolution of the task, the immensity of Wagner's labours. He began his long journey with the proverbial first step: a prose draft scenario, *The Nibelung-Myth: As Sketch for a Drama*, dated 4 October 1848. He wrote an essay, of dubious quality, about his project, and worked up his poem, *Siegfrieds Tod* ('Siegfried's Death'), even writing some music for it, but this was never included in the final *Ring* (and also sounds entirely different to everything we have). As he went on, however, Wagner felt he was only telling the end of the story. Everything was theatrically loaded with an extremely potent back-history, but it was all compressed into a vessel unable to contain the density of its material.

Thus the *Ring* became a pair of operas, with the earlier story of Siegfried to be told in a prequel: *Der junge Siegfried* ('The Young Siegfried'). But this was not enough: the story of Brünnhilde, woken to life only in the second half of the last act of *Der junge Siegfried*, necessitated a work of its own: *Die Walküre*. Although this third opera told much of her father Wotan's story, Wagner felt the chief of the gods demanded more than three dramas presenting simply the consequences of his actions. We needed to see the beginning, the initial deeds and crimes (or at least some of them; there is an even remoter backstory which comes out in the narration at various points). So a fourth and final part was added: *Der Raub: Vorspiel* ('The Theft: Prelude'), which, as its name suggested, was an introductory work, though still substantial in size, and was later renamed *Das Rheingold*, as *Siegfrieds Tod* was retitled *Götterdämmerung* and *Der junge Siegfried* rechristened simply *Siegfried*.

Seen this way, with each newly conceived drama generating the need for years and years' more work of musical composition, it must have been a daunting prospect, bordering on insanity. But its magnitude does match the content of the works themselves: their vastness of conception and eventual execution are fully justified and borne out through the truly cosmic musikdramas we have. After the formation of the four libretti 'backwards', the music was then composed 'forwards', starting at the beginning with *Rheingold* in 1853, followed by *Walküre* and the first two acts of *Siegfried*, before Wagner broke off in 1857, leaving his hero in the forest, in order to create *Tristan* and *Meistersinger*, the impact of Schopenhauer necessitating the hiatus. When he resumed *Siegfried* in 1869, he had developed and strengthened his skills as a composer and wrote with heightened sophistication and dexterous intricacy, finally concluding *Götterdämmerung* on 21 November 1874.

The text of the *Ring* has been much mocked, especially by those experiencing poor-quality translations of the work or by those reading it in German and either forgetting it is over a century and a half old or that it is based on medieval myth and legend. In truth it is a startlingly contemporary text, dynamic and evocative. Despite its difficult and long-drawn-out parturition, it is a beautifully constructed poetic drama, approaching, if not quite attaining, the achievements of Aeschylus and Shakespeare — but then, for all its qualities, this is still a libretto, and it is not designed to be read in isolation from its music. The *Ring* text is pungent, poignant, vigorous and biting; lyrical, pugnacious and inimitable. It not only presents scenes of violence, primal conflict and unfathomable love, it does so with language that is very often raw, then unexpectedly warm, full of sincerity and humanity and even a little humour. Reckless, tender, terse, fertile and inventive, the *Ring*'s libretti merit and reward close attention — before, during and after their immersion in the music.

One aspect of the libretti which is much talked about, usually in derisive terms, is the amount of repetition in narration across the four works, something which arose largely because of the way the dramas were constructed, Wagner working backwards as his conception broadened. When reading the texts, there is indeed a certain amount of reiteration and restatement. However, not only can this be seen as part of the narrative methodology of the *Ring*, reminding us of the previous days' events, but it serves as part of the work's complex relationship with, and understanding of, time and history. When we hear about past events in the light of present ones, the past changes its meaning. This, of course, is one of the primary functions of the music, especially the leitmotif, in a musikdrama, but — to an extent — the same process occurs within the text; it is simply amplified exponentially by the music.

Such a gigantic expansion of the drama from one to four works had altered not only its overall shape, as well as its temperament and outlook, but also the relative importance of its characters. The work had started off as a paean to a hero — Siegfried — and a delineation of the appalling tragedy of his death. As the work expanded, however, two other figures came to be given even greater importance: Wotan and Brünnhilde. Each absorbed three of the four works and encompass the longest roles for male and female voice in the operatic repertoire. They dominate the *Ring* in ways subtle and blatant, indirect and deliberate, offering perhaps the deepest and most fascinating characters in all of Wagner.

Nevertheless, everyone in the *Ring* is of interest. There are really no minor characters, certainly not in any qualitative sense, since, like Shakespeare, Wagner is able to give intensity and elusiveness to every role he creates. If Fasolt and Froh from *Rheingold* or *Götterdämmerung*'s Gunther and Gutrune seem a little shallow, a little bland on the page, they are given music of immense interest and engagement, though its simplicity often beguiles us into believing they have nothing to say or no meaning in the wider drama. Yet just as objects in this work — sword, apple, helmet, the Ring itself — have rich inner lives, highly developed connotations and interactions, so, too, each character is a mesmeric, hypnotizing admixture of exterior and interior, public need and private vulnerability, tight-lipped intangibility and exposed honesty.

In the same way that narrative cannot be simply reduced to plot, character in the *Ring* cannot be diminished to people being merely who they are or what they say. The events and emotions of the drama alter them, especially in our minds, long after we leave the theatre, shelve the CDs or close the app. We care even about slighter characters whom we are initially coerced to see as relatively phony, cardboard figures: hollowness has its own pain, its own anger and curiosity, not least when such characters are emblematic of certain political traits, behavioural attitudes or psychological postures. Consider the gods of *Rheingold* during *Götterdämmerung* and they take on a strange new import: less pompous, more complex; less grandiose, more sensitive — more *human*.

The more significant characters seem to exist as several different people over the long course of the drama (one of them, Wotan, even takes on a new form and a new name as the Wanderer in *Siegfried*). The *Ring* libretto was expanded, after all, not just to see more of the story but to see how characters developed and changed over time: sometimes maturing, sometimes regressing, often both together in a bewildering but very authentic mélange of chaotic humanity. Here Wagner had not only the implements of text and stage, words, gestures, actions: he had music, a vast toolkit of melodic and harmonic utensils to enrich and augment his drama, conveying its subtlest sentiments and grandest statements. The characters of the *Ring* are granted music which integrates and reintegrates them with other music, other characters, other events and other emotions. This bequeaths a staggering depth and complexity by association, as well as a new individual significance, to characters' peculiar and fluctuating dramas as part of the whole vast network Wagner created. For it is, of course, in the music of the *Ring* that Wagner truly triumphed.

The sonic and symphonic expansions of Beethoven and Berlioz are one of the key musical hinterlands to the *Ring*, as are Wagner's own substantial advancements in his earlier works. However progressive the *Ring* was, it certainly didn't come from nowhere, either internally or externally, and it was not for nothing that Wagner chose Beethoven's Ninth Symphony as the work with which to inaugurate and consecrate the Bayreuth Festspielhaus when construction started on a home for the *Ring* in 1872. Beethoven's stormy drama was the culmination of a series of symphonic and orchestral expansions in sound and design, topped by the inclusion of text and voices in its finale: an ur-musikdrama.

Wagner inherited from Beethoven, and others, a symphonic enormousness which was both highly expressive and exceedingly flexible and developed it even further, creating not only vast new dramas but new possibilities for the orchestra, which would lead to the various and extraordinary sound-worlds of Bruckner, Mahler, Strauss, Webern, Debussy, Schoenberg, Messiaen and countless others. It is not fanciful to conceive of the *Ring* as a sixteen-hour symphony rather than an opera or even a musikdrama. Indeed, we might wish to see its structure in classical symphonic terms, opening with a Rhenish allegro followed by a lyrical, adulterous adagio and the *Siegfried*-scherzo before the nightfall climax of *Götterdämmerung*. Whatever the architecturally symphonic features of the new work, as well as the communicative orchestral potency which matches anything in Beethoven, Berlioz or Liszt, the *Ring* could be discreet when it needed to be. Passages of it have an extraordinary chamber- and lieder-like quality to them. Extended sequences of soft rapture and expectation enhance the overall dramatic eminence of the

Ring, an obvious necessity in a sixteen-hour drama, as well as giving the lie to the persistent lazy stereotype of Wagner's music as somehow a constant barrage of noisy nuisance.

The *Ring* begins, after all, in the prelude to *Das Rheingold*, with the birth of the world, a sound of inexpressible tenderness and tranquil organic growth quietly filling the air, unobtrusively pervading our souls and softly occupying our hearts. The creation of the world in Haydn's *Die Schöpfung* and, later, Beethoven's Ninth Symphony had been, respectively, in tempestuous C minor and turbulent D minor. Wagner's was in warm, low E flat, barely audible down on the lower strings.

This simplicity was to govern both the method and the design of the entire work, for the vast musical architecture of the *Ring* is constructed from a small number of short, basic themes — leitmotifs — which enter into a vast series of symphonic developments and contrapuntal affiliations as the drama progresses. These ideas, starting with the basic rising major chord, 'Nature', which opens the whole work, melodically or harmonically grow, invert, split or otherwise transmute, spawning an infinity of organic connections from their initial embryonic or definitive forms. They can amalgamate with each other, forming composite motifs, conspiring to expose unfathomable secrets or reveal graver truths.

The score to the *Ring* is an interior trellis of translucent filaments endlessly entangled to create an eloquent labyrinth of intense drama. It is fertile, abundant, propagating an unbroken emotional-intellectual system of intricate dialectical arrangements. Motifs are also organized, appropriately for the *Ring*, into families, each spawning various and variant new areas of sound. Characters, concepts, objects, events and emotions are contrasted in the grid of pain, moulded from simple pliable musical ideas to complete, reshape or interlace in associative magic, thickening perspectives on time and eluding fixity. Words and dramatic action are enriched, augmented, in this work which journeys with liquid insinuation through restatement and reproduction in organizational remembrance, altering the relative burdens between the past, present and future.

Such is the scope and complexity of the *Ring* that it spawns an infinitude of discussion and debate. Meanings and denotations change across the cycle, across successive generations and according to personal interpretation, inclination or sensitivity. Connotations, suggestions and memories for one individual will never be the same for someone else. In addition, the very luxuriant, fertile prolixity of the musico-dramatic technique and its associated structure mean that almost any moment can be isolated and endlessly deliberated in its relative association to either another moment or the wider structure of the network, with all the musical, dramatic, emotional, psychological and philosophical implications that might result.

Wagner's *Ring* is a human-made artefact that resembles the true complexity of the planet, from the socio-personal density of a city to the ecological intricacy of a coral reef or biodiversity of a rainforest. And these are not frivolous examples, for the world of the *Ring* is a combination of the human and natural worlds, in all their majesty and convolution, as well as their dramatic, chaotic and often detrimental interaction. Just as music is at once the most artificial and most natural of art forms, the *Ring* unites and divides the human and natural worlds in both conception and execution. Individuals, spouses, siblings, families and whole societies are presented amid a range of landscapes (aquatic, arboreal, mountainous) and lifestyles, variously interacting with nature: urban, nomadic, autonomous.

The tensions and connections between nature and the world, as well as Wagner's overall general technique, can be seen in the way the Nature motif, which opens *Rheingold*, speeds up to morph into the motif of the Rhine or is inverted from major to minor and slowed down to create the murky motif of Erda, the earth goddess. She herself generates a dynasty of motifs, such as those of (tragic) heroic humanity and the world's boundless sadness, both associated especially with Siegmund and Brünnhilde and then later Siegfried. Even abject Gunther is related to this heroic motif in his piteous and pathetic way, his claims to gallantry almost ironically asserted in the especially craven world of *Götterdämmerung*. And nature can also create the tools of heroism: the Sword motif, a symbol of intrepid love and valour in action, derives ultimately from the basic Nature motif and then itself breeds a whole strain of interconnected musico-dramatic themes.

More drastically, the original Nature motif can be turned on its head, suggesting its own inverse, as when it becomes the falling motif of the Twilight of the Gods, which permeates *Götterdämmerung* but is first heard in *Rheingold*. Thus the motif and its inversion both bookend and prophesize the entire *Ring*: life-giving evolution modifies to become destructive death. Even with such basic modifications to simple material, a wealth of musico-dramatic possibilities is generated. And each time an alteration occurs, or has another added to it, or is presented in a new dramatic situation, the motifs become even more complex and profound in their potential. Huge books would be needed to map out the nearly infinite links, conversions and musico-dramatic associations in the *Ring*, but the essentially uncomplicated method Wagner employs is fundamentally the same whatever takes place.

Leitmotifs are not simple musical signposts — forests rustling, birds fluttering, fire flickering through the score whenever a character sings about or encounters them. This might happen, but Wagner and the *Ring* are more interested in telling us why that bird is important or what that forest suggests in the evolving context of the drama. Leitmotifs are fundamentally about relationships, good or bad, generative or destructive: the connections between a chemical substance in a riverbed and a piece of jewellery; between a fortress and a spear; between a hero and a sword; between a giant's lust and a dragon's greed; between a flowing river and a rainbow bridge; between elation and despair; between love and distress; between envy, celebration and dissatisfaction. For instance, the motif of the Rhinemaidens' joy in their gold is distorted into the Nibelungs' misery in working that same cruel, enticing element as slaves. Accompanied by the sound of their anvils, in *Das Rheingold*, we hear the latter's subjugated pain, an agony infinitely amplified when we also know the jubilant origins of their woeful music and the way in which it shows how nature can be corrupted by humanity, twisted, deformed and abused for our own selfish, satanic purposes.

The motif of the Ring itself, one of the key symbols of the drama, arises in the first scene as Alberich steals nature's gold and then (it is intimated) forges a ring of power from it. The Ring motif is a violent chromatic sound: nasty, injurious, discordant; full of friction, dissent and disagreement. Its hostile, groping, disturbing noise can be felt throughout the *Ring*, since it generates a whole broken family of dark, bitter and scheming motifs which infect and drive the drama. We have space to discuss just two. The Ring's maker, Alberich, has a brother, Mime, closely associated with the Ring's ominous harmonics and creeping, displaced resentments, and his rancorous, twitchy music governs large areas of the score to *Siegfried* as he connives to manipulate his foster child, Siegfried, into obtaining the Ring. Hagen, Alberich's ill-gotten progeny and the principal villain of *Götterdämmerung*, is also musically and dramatically associated with the Ring motif, since it is its sinister influence he conspires to acquire at any cost. Consequently, the Ring motif's music contaminates and distorts virtually the entire sound-world of *Götterdämmerung*: menacing, corrosive and almost absolute, it takes the combined energies of several motifs to defeat it by the drama's end.

Fluid, merciless and contagious, the Ring motif is an excellent example of how Wagner's musical techniques are able to disclose the nefarious, inevitable and inescapable forces at work in the world, as well as how they are all closely interrelated. They are gloomy energies, monstrously corrupted: ruthless, unstoppable, overwhelming. Wagner's gift was to exhibit this in music that is not only continuously enthralling but exquisite and even beautiful, however sinister it also turns out to be. Emotions, like ethics, are never uncomplicated in the *Ring*.

More straightforwardly attractive music — primarily that of nature and love — is also unquestionably a great and vital part of the *Ring*. The symbol of love stands in direct antagonism to symbols of power: Alberich's Ring and Wotan's spear. Indeed, it is the abandonment of love which leads directly to the forging of the Ring itself, as well as to the socio-economic, political (and later personal) entanglements Wotan involves himself in, since he essentially barters away love (in the form of Freia, goddess of love) in order to remunerate the builders for his vanity construction project, Valhalla. This motif of Love's Renunciation pervades the four dramas, since it sets the whole cycle in motion, and to an extent the entire *Ring* is an attempt to reacquire love and its life-giving potential.

The more affirmative, energetic features of love's functioning in the world can be seen with the first part of Freia's rising, swift and lithe Love motif. It reappears in various places throughout the *Ring*, as the thrills and sensuality of love are imagined or experienced by a range of characters, but it always remains the same: no new motifs are created from it. However, the motif of Love has a second part to it. Often misleadingly labelled 'Flight', since the characters associated with it are habitually fleeing the forces threatening love, this segment of the Love motif conveys the ephemeral, potentially transitory perils of love, existing in the harsh, frightening world of the *Ring*. But the delicate, sensitive and endless variations this part of the motif undergoes show not only the dangers of love but its compassion and commitment, too, particularly when associated with the incestuous twins Siegmund and Sieglinde in *Die Walküre*, and then later with their son, Siegfried, and Brünnhilde. In these pairs of lovers, standing in defiance to the callous cosmos of the *Ring*, the second part of the Love motif goes through a number of transformations, showing Siegmund and Sieglinde to be companions in sorrow, whom love will unite, or Siegfried and Brünnhilde as resolute lovers, fighting for the valiant, superhuman prerogatives of love.

Accordingly, the first part of the Love motif represents love's opulent bliss, the second, love's kindness, confidence and vulnerability. The first is unchanging, static; the second, infinitely variable. When, in *Das Rheingold*, the clumsy, ungainly giant Fasolt forlornly sings of his love for Freia, imagining a simple married life together, he is accompanied for a few seconds by a sad and sensuous oboe playing both portions of the love theme. Perhaps only the oboe is capable of achieving so simply both the erotic and despondent aspects of Fasolt's hope. He is after not just sex but domestic contentment and tenderness as well. As we will see in the next chapter, this tiny instant is one of the most important, subtle and beautiful moments in the entire *Ring*.

Despite the darkness, then, positive connections are possible, and the ingenuity of the affirmative, constructive forces inherent to music (and, by implication, everything else) are put on constant, if sometimes veiled, display in the *Ring*. Love can reproduce not only sexually but emotionally, generating a proliferation of hope amid the shadows. And love is arguably the strongest ultimate momentum in the drama, whatever the vigorous, virulent might of power and wickedness, eventually overcoming death and transcending malevolence in *Götterdämmerung*'s huge, final, wordless contrapuntal culmination and benediction.

Here, in some of the most rudimentary musico-dramatic components and transformations of the *Ring*, we see many of its larger-scale psychological, political and even ecological ideas. And, again, it is about relationships: the perverted bonds between the obscure magical potentiality of nature and its brutal exploitation; between umbrage and power; between love, death and grief; between growth and deterioration. Many of these occur in the first part, *Das Rheingold*, but the connections and complications endure throughout the *Ring*. They deepen in subtlety and complexity, taking on new musical forms as they explore and realize new dramatic happenings, requiring ever more dexterity from Wagner and acuity from the listener. The *Ring*'s sweeping symphonic tapestries, especially in *Siegfried* and *Götterdämmerung*, are crowded and highly particularized, rich in motivic interweaving and layers of past dramatic action, with the inscrutable associations produced from several hours of constant propagation and interaction.

But amid the density, Wagner also shows the basic simplicity of the *Ring* — how, for example, midway through the second act of *Siegfried*, nature and avarice can be straightforwardly traced back musically and dramatically to the *Ring*'s first few minutes. In this way, the music of the *Ring*, and the accompanying connections in time, history and ethics, moves backwards as well as forwards, its circularity and infinity matching the complications of its own production. To understand, appreciate and enjoy the *Ring*, we need intellectual curiosity and generosity regarding its diversity, as well as respect, or patience, for its intensity.

Wagner's orchestra in the *Ring* is titanic. For *Götterdämmerung*, the composer claimed he really required a pair of orchestras to express everything he intended. The scope and complexity of the *Ring* necessitated unusual means to give expression to his vision, and the size of the ensemble is obligatory not only for the absolute generation of immense sound but the huge range of textures the work demands, as well as the more modest deployments of individual instruments or diminutive groups and alliances. Not only did Wagner exploit the sonic and interactive possibilities of each instrument but he tremendously expanded the forces needed, which still place inordinate demands on opera houses.

The brass section alone requires three trumpets and three trombones, a bass trumpet and contrabass trombone. The *Ring* asks for eight horns, with four of them doubling as an instrument the composer invented: the Wagner tuba. This looks like an elongated French horn and produces just the characteristic smooth, noble and silky tone Wagner wanted for one of the *Ring*'s grandest aristocratic themes, the Valhalla motif. Its mellifluousness additionally has something uncanny about it, however, lending eeriness to Valhalla and Wotan. This strangeness is exploited fully when the full quartet of Wagner tubas announce the sinister expansiveness of the Fate motif and its associations with Siegmund's impending death in *Die Walküre*.

The woodwind section is also expanded, and generously expended, throughout the *Ring*, but one of the most fascinating and touching uses Wagner yields from this department is when it sounds a motif generally heard on the brass. The gentler, more forlorn tones of the oboe give a wholly different suggestion to the Sword motif when it is heard on this instrument rather than on its more familiar bass trumpet.

The strings are immense: sixty-four players are needed, even before we add the six harps required by *Das Rheingold*, fabricating the rich red-carpet texture Wagner is known for. The opening hurricane of *Die Walküre* is an awesome application of the full corpus of strings, but, again, it is their arrangement into particular clusters, constructing elaborate, competing networks of tension and exploration, which is perhaps most enthralling. When, again in *Walküre*, the violins perform the Magic Fire music which ends the work, they are implementing an intense and extremely swift figuration almost unattainable as written by even the finest player (as Wagner well knew). The blazing, sparkling, fiery effect of over thirty violinists contending to outshine one another is one of the *Ring's* great marvels and a dazzling conclusion to its second part — and creates the very impression of fire that Wagner required. The demands on the sextet of harpists at the end of *Rheingold*, as they create the illusion of the rainbow bridge to Valhalla, might be best summed up by the fact that their six individual parts inhabit so many lines in the score that they have to be consigned to a remote appendix at the back.

The timpani and percussion of the *Ring* are, contrary to the popular fancy of Wagner's sound-world, actually used fairly frugally. Ominous beats on the drum, the fretful throb of a soon-to-be-broken heart, accompany the Annunciation of Death in *Die Walküre*; a cymbal glistens and gleams as the gold of the Rhine; the glockenspiel gives a silvery shimmer to the Forest Murmurs of *Siegfried*, and a lone stroke on a triangle ends the second act of that work, an isolated, defiant *ping* amid the vast thicket of the Wagnerian orchestra.

Where, then, does all this music, all this drama, leave meaning? Does the *Ring* mean anything beyond its astounding collection of noises, gestures and scenic backdrops? It is surely obvious that multiple, even potentially infinite, interpretations and understandings of the *Ring* are possible, each shifting, engaging and reengaging with others over time. We have seen how the words *subtle* and *complex*, as well as their cognates and synonyms, have reappeared again and again in this chapter. Wagner's *Ring* is no easy read or experience. For many, it will remain simply a musical masterpiece, a symphonic celebration. If the *Ring*'s assessments of power, fascism and abuse prove too much for some, be they malignant or benign individuals, such people can always disappear into the rich, measureless sound-world Wagner created. This does his wider idea an essential disservice but is perhaps to be expected, given the sheer quality of his music.

Wagner himself must have had several meanings in his head, which changed as the project moved forwards, evolving and fluctuating as truly great works of art do, regardless of their scale. We have seen how Wagner's conception of the *Ring* moved backwards in its expansive, embryonic stage, sanctioning deeper perspectives on character, time and history. Then, when writing the music, the internal and external forces of — among other things — insurrection, exile, theoretical essays, Schopenhauer, *Tristan*, Cosima von Bülow and King Ludwig II helped further reshape and reforge the *Ring*, adjusting its form and content as well as its meanings and potential connotations.

Given the *Ring* was conceived when the youthful Wagner was in thrall to a literal revolution, it is clear that a revolutionary interpretation is not only reasonable but perhaps necessary. By the time of its completion, Wagner was twenty-six years older, more pessimistic but not entirely disillusioned with the prospect of global change. His fawning on monarchs and settling down into domestic harmony, amid the accruements of Bayreuth and his new villa, Wahnfried, constituted, he considered, not a movement to the right but the indispensable and appropriate compensations that were his due. The *Ring*, and Wagner, remained certain of the need for upheaval and hopeful about the potential for the former to realize it. The *Ring* is Wagner's most overtly political work, and although its study of power relations and decision-making can be interpreted in a range of possible ways, as well as reattached to other concerns, politics is likely to remain the *Ring*'s principal means of clarification.

However political the *Ring* is, its psychological, philosophical and ecological depths cannot be ignored — and, indeed, are a vital element to the political content. They can also, perhaps, be detached from it to a degree, authorized to be used in exploring the vast range of emotional, spiritual, metaphysical and environmental components to this extraordinary work. But, as should be apparent from the musico-dramatic organization of the *Ring*, any attempts to wholly isolate these readings from the political sphere, at least in the general sense, are probably doomed to failure. A 'Green *Ring*', surveying the biological and conservationist concerns of the drama, would necessarily have to engage with the way political decisions and actions plunder and desecrate nature. Putting the *Ring* on the psychiatrist's couch would mean engagement either with internal or domestic politics or the psychological mechanisms at work in the minds of leaders, administrators and elected or unelected officials.

The religious and/or philosophical concerns of the *Ring* are perhaps more obviously associated with its political ideation, as well as its potential ideologies. A socialist *Ring* would seek to return the world to a harmonious simplicity from a situation in which it is besmirched by church and state. Indeed, exactly as Wagner began writing the *Ring*, he was also preparing sketches for a drama, *Jesus von Nazareth* (1849), which probed the democratic and egalitarian ideals Jesus promoted in the gospels and which were later distorted. For Wagner, religion and politics were largely the same thing, as they had been for Shakespeare and the Greeks, both in their works and societies, and few truly great composers — perhaps only Bach, Haydn, Beethoven, Schoenberg and Messiaen — have engaged with theological and spiritual discussion in music to the extent Wagner did.

In philosophical terms, the *Ring* asserts a range of competing influences — Rousseau, Kant, Hegel, Feuerbach, Schopenhauer, Proudhon — and their attachment to, or utilization by, political points of view and dogmas is readily apparent. The *Ring*'s more abstract and universal qualities have frequently been emphasized in readings during or immediately after periods of political catastrophe or social anxiety. There were several attempts to depoliticize the *Ring* following the Second World War, both in performance and theory, foregrounding its archetypal elements, as well as its employment of myth, readings which resurfaced at the uneasy turn of the millennium. Other analyses have sought to further expand our understanding of the more metaphysical concerns of the *Ring* and the way it explores the nature of reality, cause and effect, time, space and memory.

Interpretations addressing the position of women in the *Ring* have rightly flourished in the twenty-first century. Wagner's reworking and expansion of the drama not only provided Brünnhilde with a more central role but made her story and development less attached to Siegfried's fate. In the final version of the *Ring*, Brünnhilde is not defined by her love for Siegfried but has her own existence, her own moral and spiritual development, and a bravery and intellectual understanding far in advance of every other character. In Brünnhilde, Wagner was developing the type of powerful revolutionary woman he had created in Senta, Elizabeth and Elsa and, with the Valkyrie, perhaps realized his ultimate statement of not only feminine but human power, compassion and intelligence.

Interpretation of the *Ring*, or any stage drama, can probably fall into three interrelated groups: theoretical, personal and directorial. The last is the arena where most people are likely to come into contact with the work, though the former two, since the very beginnings of the *Ring*, have demonstrably contributed an immense, precious treasure of challenging, subjective and fascinating analyses and elucidations. Personal perspectives are, in part, shaped by engaging with such material, as well as with the huge range of stage productions, either as they appear in the opera houses of the world or as permanent video memorializations. Their importance might seem obvious but cannot be overstated, given the way Wagner conceived and then implemented his project. To experience the *Ring*, we need to experience it in full.

The *Ring* demands interpretation in part because of its sheer size — why create something this massive if not for a purpose? — but its dimensions not only magnify the number of meanings but make each one of them more elusive. Some of the best interpretations of the *Ring* upset and dislocate existing orthodoxies. They explore and even highlight the obstinate, embarrassing or problematic little nooks and crannies of the work, not necessarily caring for overall aesthetic or intellectual unity. The *Ring* was meant to be literally unsettling to the society it was first thrust upon. Arguably, its meaning should always be interpreted as such, as insubordinate and disconcerting, whatever the established conventions that need overturning — or, at the very least, offending.

Ask for two words to sum up the *Ring* and *love* and *power* probably spring most easily to mind, the two concepts battling it out, independently and collectively, resisting, entwining and competing over sixteen violent, tender hours. Neither love nor power is straightforward, and each exists in an enormous range of guises: sex, kindness, friendship; deception, violation, manipulation; strength, responsibility, sympathy; teasing, supporting, cajoling. Love and power are common to all humanity, in and at any age, so the truths and meanings in the *Ring* will continue to inform our species' perspectives on perhaps its two dominant topics for as long as we remain as we are.

Whether we will choose, collectively or individually, to heed the *Ring*'s warnings or forsake love in the pursuit of power is another matter. Part of the 'message' of the *Ring*, embedded in its explorations of love and power, seems to be that meaning now must come from within ourselves, the work's internal dialectics transferring across to us. A world not only lacking the guiding structures and hope of traditional religious institutions and practice but also encompassing societies interminably broken and forever alienated can perhaps only be reconstituted by our own personal engagements with art in general and the *Ring* in particular. We might then seek to rebuild civilisation from there. Wagner's artwork of the future *is* the future.

As we indicated at the beginning, these private perspectives on the *Ring* will alter over the course of our lives — just as our attitudes to a Bach cantata, Beethoven quartet or Mahler symphony will shift as we experience and re-experience these works. What is more, the process is two-way: just as we change our understanding of art, our experience of art changes us over time. Life and art intensify each other. Our stance on the *Ring* will be different depending on whether our lives are, or have been, full or void of love, work, play, narcissism, altruism, tragedy, privilege, anger, addiction, empathy, abuse, exuberance and suspicion. Most likely our lives will contain all of the above, enriching and disturbing our approach to this ultimate attempt to represent in art the complete human experience: all its beauty, all its ugliness, its sadness and its joy.

This chapter has argued for the essential unity of Wagner's largest work, exploring the gargantuan organizational structures which govern and fuse the *Ring*. However, the *Ring* is composed of four separate dramas, each with a sound-world that is almost miraculously distinctive, given how they share their musical and dramatic material. The following four chapters will seek to characterize each of these works in their idiosyncratic way, scrutinizing how they exploit their mutual musico-dramatic ingredients to assert their individuality amid their collective existence, forging unity through diversity — surely the only motto for the *Ring*.

Chapter Five

Tech, Toil and Tenderness: *Das Rheingold*

The *Ring* begins in the depths of the river Rhine, and *Das Rheingold* opens with the sound of the past, a phantom drone from the farthest reaches of time and space, a ghostly hum from the bottommost point of the orchestra, deep down on the double basses. The primary low E flat on these lower strings sounds like sonar, a haunting pulse of energy which grows and grows before being joined by the bassoons in B flat. Two quartets of horns gradually elaborate this primal chord with the ascending arpeggio of the Nature motif, further amplified and developed into the flowing motion of the Rhine by the strings. It is calm, unbroken and magnificent.

The source and destiny of all existence are shown to us in the *Rheingold* prelude. A primordial enigma in eternal E flat, time hangs immutable, suspended in sonic space, the mass and weight of the planet prearranged for melodious transmutations:

defined, expanding, surging, swelling. This is the nativity of
the world, the very performance and achievement of creation.
Cells and sounds double and replicate, copying, augmenting,
multiplying, before discharging into the primeval calls of the
daughters of nature, the Rhinemaidens' welcome to the waters:

> Weia! Waga!
> Billow, you wave,
> Surge to the cradle!
> Wagalaweia!
> Wallala, weiala weia!

Their call is folksy, an alliance of word, song and atmosphere.
Immediate, expedient, the unmoral damsels of the Rhine
float and swim on stage, dreaming past and through the self-
renewing motives of nature, forever repairing, replenishing.

Yet inside the origins and innocence lie the germs of
perversion: potentiality shifting to the malevolent minor.
The miraculous, hypnotic spell of the prelude, prolonged by
the Rhinemaidens' song, is, ultimately, broken. Just as the
fundamental elements of sound and harmony are programmed
to mutate, to fluctuate and morph elsewhere, so the
Rhinemaidens, their ecosystem, and the gold they guard cannot
remain chaste and untouched for long. After barely a minute of
carefree bathing, they encounter Alberich the dwarf, who enters
on uneasy cellos, clunking against the smooth syncopations
of the Rhine. Alberich's angry and annoyed tumbles on the
rocks prefigure the unhappy fall of both mankind and the
environment, nature's factory of creation turned from kernel
to corruption. It is a jagged precedent for time-bound man as
author-designer to destiny and destruction.

Wagner was keen not to simply retell old stories in the *Ring*,
insipidly reprocessing time-worn sagas and legends. As with
his earlier dramas and their sources, he wanted to exploit and

develop their literary material for his own purposes, to realize his own ideas and ideals: new myths for a new age. The gods of the Icelandic *Edda*, and others, were added to the Germanic *Nibelungenlied* as representatives of the weary, crumbling world Wagner saw around him. Like his almost exact contemporaries Darwin, Dickens and Marx, Wagner abhorred the ecological disaster of the Industrial Revolution and its attendant socio-economic calamities; he was also dismayed by the failure of the 1848–9 insurgencies.

Developing his source material, Wagner depicted the Ring of the Nibelung as not only a perverted source of wealth and power but one curiously bound to love and nature: Alberich must reject love and nature to attain wealth and power. His dismissal by the Rhinemaidens, and the disasters which ensue, causes not one but two curses — first on love, to gain power; then on the Ring itself, when this power is taken from him under duress. The despoilment of nature by humanity not only violates the natural order but creates a cycle of violence, a yoke on freedom, a burden on existence which constantly seeks sovereignty but merely tightens the noose.

The Rhinemaidens' behaviour is complex. On the one hand, they are simply blameless creatures of nature, beyond morality or originating before it, their mischievous, coquettish harassment of Alberich doubtless driven by boredom. And yet there seems to be something more than this. Anthony Burgess played on this in his 1961 novel *The Worm and the Ring*, a sardonic retelling of Wagner's cycle, in which one Albert Rich, a schoolboy, is teased by three of his female classmates. Here, the Rhinemaidens are more knowing, crueller — not yet enacting adult malice but on the way there, and with plenty of spite. On stage, in Patrice Chéreau's legendary 1976 *Ring* at Bayreuth, the world was already stained as the drama began. A huge hydroelectric dam had been built on the Rhine, and the Rhinemaidens were nineteenth-century courtesans: no longer naïve, but cogs in the industrial-commercial-sexual nexus. Peter Hall (Bayreuth, 1983) restored their innocence by removing their clothes, as did Keith Warner in London in 2004, the nymphs hastily dressing when Alberich appeared.

Directors and audiences have to decide just how innocent the Rhinemaidens are, how far we can excuse or ignore their potentially repugnant goading of Alberich, which has such devastating consequences. A degree of chauvinism has always surrounded interpretations of the Rhinemaidens, as it has Eve, so that masculine flaws and ruinations can be conveniently placed on the malicious, enticing, merciless and wayward shoulders of women, who lead men astray with their temptations and inducements.

Although for some it is appealing to place responsibility for the *Ring*'s catastrophes on the Rhinemaidens' initial behaviour, the music seems to stress otherwise, to underscore their innocence in both moral and sexual terms. If they are not identical with nature, they are clearly closely aligned with it. Wagner asks us to explore the maidens' conduct, to negotiate within ourselves how far we condemn or acquit them. But even if we try to explain away their actions by accusing them, in the victim-blaming verbiage of modern misogyny, of dressing or acting provocatively and so forth, Alberich is still the villain, the rapist of nature, his actions disgraceful and beyond the possibility of exoneration.

Alberich's ur-crimes (cursing love, stealing the gold and forging the Ring) join those even earlier violations committed by Wotan, about which the Norns will finally give us the whole story in the prologue to *Götterdämmerung*. Where

Wotan's misdeeds occur in history, or in the *Ring*, is in a sense a deliberate mystery, a curious paradox of twinned time; yet they are not just historical but mythical and archetypal, perhaps transpiring adrift, amid the mesmerizing sounds of the *Rheingold* prelude. This double time scheme is consciously confusing, especially since we learn the god's complete story only after he has left the stage (though parts of it emerge over the course of the preceding dramas), the ultimate consequences of his actions to be played out in the Wotan-less machinations and climaxes of *Götterdämmerung*.

The disruptive chronology not only disorientates but helps emphasize the cycle of defilement, the endless succession of hope, rebirth and desolation which has always characterized human existence. Harry Kupfer's 1988 production of the *Ring* at Bayreuth began at the end, briefly staging the final moments of *Götterdämmerung* before dissolving into the *Rheingold* prelude. It was a peculiar but probing prelude to the prelude. It helped to highlight, from the very outset, the never-ending cycle of (destructive) human activity, forcing us to engage with and own up to our actions, our perpetual harm to the planet and each other. Kupfer's *Ring* managed to be both timeless and timely, connecting with contemporary fears about a post-Chernobyl nuclear holocaust and the grubby activities of corrupt politicians and gangsters while also asserting the mythic, elemental nature of the drama. It was simultaneously modern and antediluvian, catastrophic but strangely optimistic.

In the prologue to *Götterdämmerung*, the Norns tell us how the god, like the dwarf, transgressed nature — by sipping from the fountain of wisdom and fashioning a spear of authority by ravaging the World Ash Tree. Indeed, Wotan is referred to in the *Ring* as 'Light Alberich', the god's conduct merely a milder, arguably more hypocritical, form of the dwarf's desecrations. Wotan is, of course, the dishonest, torn and worn politician, a type modern but unchanged since time immemorial. He is shiny, smooth, all smoke and mirrors, doing dodgy deals in the shadows and wearing clean white shirts in the sun. Magniloquent, sanctimonious, incongruously unctuous and essentially phony, with hubris born of inner self-righteousness, he is a grandiose, then awkwardly self-effacing, Machiavel, placing expediency over morality. Wotan himself and countless commentators since have tried to explain away the chief of the gods' conduct as the necessary compromises of democratic politics. But this lets him off the hook, not least for his initial sins, which were a power grab, like Alberich's — and like Adam's in the Garden of Eden, transgressing a law in order to gain knowledge of good and evil (i.e., everything).

Wotan's subsequent behaviour, as we resume his story in scene 2 of *Das Rheingold*, shows the god repeatedly failing to face up to the aftereffects of his actions, always claiming to be constrained by laws and treaties but really bound by his own desire never to relinquish power. His peevish appeals are the present-day squeals of democratically elected criminals the world over, claiming that they were only doing what they thought was right, for the best, and knowing they were doing wrong yet unable to confess to it. Wotan, in fairness, will achieve insight and some redemption — he has the luxury of several operas in which to do so. But, in *Das Rheingold*, he remains unredeemed, cantankerous, arrogant and aloof.

The transition from scene 1, Alberich's theft, to scene 2, our first meeting with Wotan, is a majestic metamorphosis from the hostile, antagonistic, grappling motif of the Ring to the broad, regal one of Valhalla, the music most associated with Wotan (along with that of his spear). The methodology of musikdrama, as developed by Wagner, shows wonderfully the link between Valhalla and the Ring, the musico-dramatic bond between Wotan and Alberich, between 'good' politics and 'bad' politics, the dangerous and entangling connection between government and criminality, lawmaking and lawbreaking.

If Alberich's renunciation of love — though, crucially, not sex — for power is entirely base and unethical, Wotan's contains at least the (deluded) desire of good intentions. Alberich's Ring is an object of power, Wotan's spear one of rule and rules, envisioned as bringing stability through responsibility. Alberich's enslavement of his own race (which problematizes the notion of Alberich as a Jewish stereotype) is mirrored by Wotan's passive subjugation of the world through the orders and commands of his supposedly harmonious harpoon. The Ring motif is an unusual mixture of a minor scale descending then ascending, of outward and inward pain, suffering given and received. This is the unceasing cycle of despair it both represents and initiates. The Spear motif, like that of Alberich's curse on the Ring, is one of overlays and intersections: C major and A minor, indicating the intended good and inevitable despair at the heart of Wotan's world order. Like many a popular politician, Wotan's success lies in his confidence, but Wagner binds the Spear motif with grief declining towards misery.

Both Wotan and Alberich are assisted in their misdoings (and misery) by adjuncts and technology: Loge and Mime; the magic fire and the magic Tarnhelm. In Norse mythology, Loge (Loki) is the god of fire and a trickster, and Wagner saw his potential to be a slippery adviser to the chief of the gods. A devious, untrustworthy but very useful aide, Loge has cunning, insight and an amoral intelligence which breed resentment and grudging respect from those around him. He is, in fact, a demigod, and as such stands somewhat apart from the other deities — literally so at *Das Rheingold*'s end, when he does not join them in Valhalla but keeps his nonchalant distance.

This makes Loge both an insider and an outsider, and accordingly, the minor gods tend to have misgivings about him and his ways. He has an objectivity they envy as much as they distrust it. His neutrality also makes him a threat: who else has he advised — or will he advise — as well? Indeed, Loge has no

allegiances and will happily assist anyone. He provides advice to
Fasolt that the Ring itself has more value than all of the gold:
impartial, accurate information which seals the lovelorn giant's
almost immediate doom. The gods are also perhaps jealous of
the easy access Loge has to the big boss, since Wotan is wise
enough to know he needs Loge's ability and acumen. The
disinterested, unbiased fire god will find a means to disentangle
his chief's problems, even if it is ultimately ruinous, which is
not Loge's liability. His independence and individuality make
him useful but also unaccountable. Loge is Wotan's missing
eye, his intelligence gatherer, a lethal mixture of weirdly neutral
data harvester, detached philosopher and pyromaniac anarchist.
Every government has one. Every government will come to
regret hiring them.

Alberich's brother Mime is ferociously oppressed, like
his fellow Nibelungs, but his skills as a craftsman afford
him a little more freedom in the industrialized hellhole of
Nibelheim, though he remains both physically vanquished and
economically exploited. In *Das Rheingold*, Mime manufactures
the Tarnhelm, the helmet of invisibility, a piece of technology
to match Loge's magic fire (the music for them is, perhaps
inevitably, closely related). The magic fire and magic Tarnhelm,
as technology, are part of the shadowy and unknowable realm
which surrounds (and now pervades) human life. Which
of us truly understands how our smartphones work or the
swathes of data produced by them, gobbled up by Big Tech
and anyone who wants it and is willing to pay? Our work and
our play are continuously monitored in secret, often in the
guise of 'productivity' or our own 'protection'. Both Wotan and
Alberich need (and argue for) similar powers — the powers of
the priest or secret police and the current power of constant
mass surveillance.

The basic flickering, chromatic motif of Loge and his
symbol, his magic fire, will generate not only Wotan's cloak

of anonymity as the Wanderer in *Siegfried* but the associated technological motif of the Tarnhelm. In the third scene of *Das Rheingold*, when Wotan and Loge have journeyed to subterranean Nibelheim, the Magic Fire segment of Loge's motif is presented on six subdued horns, now upturned into the minor and without the original motif's dancing configuration. It is an odious, intoxicating sound, full of mystery and malignance. The technology — the Tarnhelm — described by this sound enables invisibility, a chilling, ancient capability given new meanings in the internet age, and holds a fearful power in the *Ring*, eventually becoming a critical piece of equipment for Hagen's conspiracies in *Götterdämmerung*.

The Tarnhelm's baleful resonance colours and structures most of the third scene of *Das Rheingold*, its ominous, enigmatic dread and terror permeating the lord of the Ring's dark, concealed underground domain, in which Alberich is a silent fascist manipulating the world. Alberich's self-satisfaction and delight with the device will prove his undoing: showing off his gadget's capacity leads to his capture, as befalls many an overconfident computer hacker or vainglorious fraudster unable to resist flaunting their talents and tech. But even when he is stripped of the Tarnhelm and Ring, these objects' unscrupulous control lingers on, the cursed effects of the technology Alberich and Mime have unleashed persisting, like atomic radiation and other poisons.

In many ways, *Das Rheingold* is a miniature version of the *Ring*. Like the *Ring*, it is in four parts, and each scene in *Rheingold* might correspond to a drama in the wider cycle. Thus the Rhinemaidens' scene with Alberich is the ultimate origin of the action, *Rheingold* itself; the Valhalla scene mirrors the manoeuvrings of Wotan in *Walküre*; the fourth scene foresees the eventually destructive consequences of Wotan's actions in *Götterdämmerung*. In this admittedly fanciful scheme, the third, Nibelheim, scene of *Rheingold* echoes and anticipates

Siegfried. Although *Siegfried* will escape its claustrophobic first two acts to the relative freedom of the mountain heights, it initially shares Nibelheim's cavern world, its mixture of nature and machinery, and the presence of Mime, the skilled smith and protoscientist.

Several twenty-first century productions of the *Ring* have set Nibelheim in some sort of laboratory where science, knowledge and technology are engineered for evil ends. In Keith Warner's 2004 *Rheingold* at Covent Garden, Nibelheim was a grimy, white-tiled chamber of horrors for observation, dissection and all manner of macabre, unspeakable experiments. Alberich was a stereotypical mad professor. He was also agitated, smutty, sarcastic and entirely at home in his morgue-cum-research-facility, assisted by a hectic, trembling Mime and visited by elegantly sinister Victorian illusionist Loge. For Copenhagen in 2006, Kasper Holten's *Ring* journeyed through the twentieth century, setting Nibelheim in a possible Los Alamos, Alberich and Mime evoking the white-coated perpetrators of the Manhattan Project, with Loge a sleazy tabloid reporter, complete with oily comb-over. Increasingly, on stage, such laboratories are taking on less of the appearance of boffins' workrooms, with smoking test tubes and the usual array of menacing scientific contraptions, and are beginning to resemble nondescript data-processing centres, with their racks of servers and air conditioners, Alberich and Mime bland media magnates and internet entrepreneurs.

The instruments of power and control which Wotan and Alberich employ, whether in the figures of Loge or Mime, and their disturbing expertise have, as we have seen, both their modern and antique equivalents. Wagner's perspicacity and faculties of political-technological foresight were remarkable but, perhaps, not surprising. As an astonishingly adept and versatile man of the theatre, eventually designing and building his own very specialized opera house at Bayreuth, Wagner was aware of both technology and the powers of illusion (and, like most people in the rapidly changing world of the nineteenth century, he had an ambivalent attitude to science). As a committed political agitator in the 1840s, he knew how to both manufacture hand grenades and write seditious pamphlets. Had he not been committed to musical revolution, he might have been a formidable political force. As it is, his art demarcates and investigates his own particular doctrines and dogmas.

Wotan is an indictment and manifestation of Wagner's own era, as well as of those before him and our own. He is an accusation and an impeachment, a summons for change, while also conveying an acceptance of the invariable nature of the politician's character and the business of governance. Narcissism, pride, self-admiration and self-absorption: Wotan is a very familiar figure. A mixture of ego and impotence, he encounters the paradoxes of power — aspiration and capacity, strength and helplessness — better than many who have desired authority (which they tend to call duty, while forgetting accountability). But he abuses his position to hide his previous misconduct. He steals the Ring and the gold in order to pay off a debt he should never have incurred, which he brought upon himself by (literally) mortgaging away love and life, in the form of Freia, to pay for a new house. Valhalla is a vanity project, born of smugness and conceit, the wish for comfort curdling into the desire for status and splendour, and his feeling that he has 'earned' it is merely proof of his delusional self-importance.

This complacency and self-assurance derives from the initial self-righteous sense of responsibility Wotan imposes on the world. There is a glimmer of goodness in what he wished — to allow different beings and races to coexist via the *Pax Wotana* of his treaties — but the arrogance of his imposition, plus his violation of nature to achieve it, negates that virtue. Unable, or unwilling, to acknowledge his original crime, Wotan becomes increasingly ensnared in further delinquencies and dilemmas,

which we see played out first in *Das Rheingold* and then in
the later dramas of the *Ring*. Wotan's burdens become more
personal, the god more grief-stricken, as the cycle wears on.
He might have been able to prevent much of the abuse and
suffering, at least for himself, had he not involved himself in the
contractual noose with the giants, but this was the inevitable
stale harvest of his continued hunger for power. Just as his
contracts have enslaved him, his vanity has incarcerated him
in his own castle.

There is a vivid surrealism to the ending of *Das Rheingold*,
with its brilliantly ostentatious — and ultimately empty —
grandeur, the gods swaggering into their fortress and, in due
course, their doom. By *Die Walküre*, Wotan will begin to
comprehend how he has perpetrated exactly the offences his
own system of ethics was intended to avert. He comes to see
how love and power interact. He recognizes the futility of his
authority, the worthlessness of his lordly grandeur, and the
shame of his self-aggrandizement. By *Siegfried*, he testifies to his
own transience and limitations, abdicating his power to wander
anonymously. By *Götterdämmerung*, he is gone, enduring only
as a living ghost.

If we are angry with Wotan, as we are angry at our
politicians, we should also pity and weep for him. If we are
to maintain our own humanity, our own sense of dignity
and moral-emotional balance, we should uphold our belief in
the possibility of redemption, of the potential for offenders
to reform through self-acknowledgement of their own
wrongdoing. Recovery and release come predominantly (and
necessarily) from within, but they can be aided by assistance
and compassion from without.

First Wotan must stop clutching power and its cognates,
by this means unblocking a conduit to his own deliverance.
To some extent, Wotan leaves it to everyone else to clear up
the mess he has caused — an inescapable accusation when

politicians resign (and when, though apparently retired, their influence continues to be felt, for good or ill). But Wotan also (optimistically, if naïvely) believes in the categorical difference his hero grandson Siegfried will represent: a new cohort, independent of his misdemeanours. We will not meet that hero, Siegfried, until part three of the *Ring*, in his eponymous musikdrama. But there exists, even in *Das Rheingold*, a hero for Wotan to observe and potentially learn from, were he better able to overcome the constraints of his self-love. This hero is an implausible, even incredible, one, but one who stands out amid the dazzling, stark, unfriendly first drama Wagner created for the *Ring*.

As we saw in the previous chapter, the genesis of the *Ring* was a complex one, especially that of the libretto's composition, which travelled back in time from *Götterdämmerung* to the world of *Das Rheingold*. As a consequence, this drama was the one for which Wagner began to write music when he was most in thrall to the principles he laid down in *Oper und Drama* (1851). He did not necessarily renounce these codes in later parts of the *Ring* — in truth, he went beyond them — but in *Das Rheingold*, the musico-poetic fusion he had argued for is most readily apparent (though perhaps better executed in the lyrical synthesis of *Die Walküre*'s first act).

In the musikdrama of *Das Rheingold*, the vocal line was to be unambiguously shaped in order to convey the mood and meaning of the text, without the limitations of established musical phrases or verbal rhymes. Wagner's innovative vocal line was to be an accurate manifestation of the drama: not only its verbal inflections and the meaning of the text but its emotional substance too. The music and verse would be seamlessly tailored by Wagner to disclose the relationships between often closely associated but disparate elements: sorrow and joy, love and pain, Ring and spear, and so on. Modulations and modifications like this were possible given the subtlety and nuance the leitmotif system afforded the musikdrama, a flexibility and complexity hitherto unavailable.

In *Das Rheingold*, there is an abruptness, aloofness, and more prosaic quality to some of the musical ideas. Yet if this strict desire to match the vocal line with the delineations of the text results in some intermittent musical sterility, surely this only strengthens the barren, frigid and loveless world of *Das Rheingold*. The musico-poetic perfections of *Walküre*'s first act marry with the more emotional tone of the *Ring*'s second part, as human beings enter into the world of the drama — along with mutual, reciprocated love.

Yet amid the gleaming frostiness of *Das Rheingold*, with its glamorous, empty gods, inaccessible Rhinemaidens, and vindictive or subjugated dwarfs, there lives a hero. Hope and warmth endure in improbable places.

The *Ring*'s first hero is perhaps an unlikely one. Awkward, galumphing giant Fasolt does not meet our conventional expectations of heroism, either inside or outside the *Ring*. The two giants, Fasolt and Fafner, are large, hairy demi-monsters — grotesque, ugly, their hands calloused, rough and worn through labour — and, by their own admission, they are uncouth and uncivilized. We want our heroes to be cleaner-cut than this. *Der Ring des Nibelungen*, over the coming days, will show us a pair of more predictable masculine adventurers — Siegmund and Siegfried, whose very names speak of victory and bravery, success and fearlessness — as well as female champions of love, honour and a new kind of power: Sieglinde and Brünnhilde. But in the second scene of *Das Rheingold*, all their feats and proclamations of valiant, world-shattering heroic love are prefaced in an inelegant, graceless ogre.

When we first encounter Fasolt and Fafner, they are legitimately seeking the payment which has been previously agreed upon for their construction work: the lovely Freia. They enter *Das Rheingold* with plain, steady music, as secure as the foundations to their unimpeachable building projects. Fasolt frankly, if a little petulantly, requests settlement of the unpaid bill. Wotan tries to renege on their deal and find a substitute payment (Alberich's hoard), but there is a snag: Fasolt has fallen in love with Freia.

His brother, Fafner, is by far the smarter of the two, as well as being the more ruthless, the more hardnosed: he represents the heartless, unsentimental and utilitarian side of commerce and enterprise which exploits human feelings or needs for its own reward. Fafner instinctively sees the merit of utilizing the goddess of love for capital gains, which is why he is more than happy to exchange her for actual treasure as soon as the opportunity arises. Fasolt, on the other hand, is really on only the operations side of the brothers' castle-building business. Fasolt, we might imagine, has done most of the heavy lifting work in building Valhalla, as well as perhaps some of the more skilled craftwork, while Fafner has organized things, arranging the logistics and dealing with the bureaucracy involved in fortress assembling — which perhaps might be even greater when your client is the CEO of the gods. (One resourceful North American opera company once sold in its gift shop T-shirts emblazoned with a corporate logo for Fasolt & Fafner: General Contractors and bearing the witty slogan 'Fees Negotiable!')

Fafner is selfish, insensitive, pragmatic: when the time comes, he will happily sit on his capital, doing nothing with it, no matter what damage it does or the privations it causes others. He reproaches his brother for his self-pitying lamentations over Wotan's broken pledge and the giants' gruelling toil, intuitively knowing the value of Freia as a bargaining tool: the gods need her; he does not, except as an instrument of market and exchange. But Fasolt has seen a greater prize than money or gold: love. He truly loves Freia, and the sincerity of this feeling is unambiguously communicated to us through Wagner's music.

Although the giants are cumbersome and oversized, it is crucial that stage directors and designers do not make them a joke, a cartoon, a mere caricature. We need to see the giants, or at least one of them, as demonstrative beings, capable of love and emotion, able to rationally imagine a conjugal prospect together with a wife, living in domestic bliss. This is the marital ideal Fricka, goddess of marriage, argues for with her husband, Wotan, as surely being valuable enough in itself, sufficient for their happiness without any additional power. (Fricka, existing in mutual misery within a loveless union to Wotan, is a more fascinating character than is sometimes supposed. Guardian of custom and the social confines of wedlock, she is obviously reactionary and an enemy to the future, but portrayed well, she has a persuasiveness that disrupts our casual dismissal of her obsolete orthodoxy.)

Fasolt yearns for Freia not merely as an object of lust or sexual gratification, though these aspects are not absent from his feelings, but as a potential mate, a partner with whom to share his hitherto miserable existence. He is not simply a horny (in both the amorous and anatomical senses) beast. He is aware of what love is, perhaps in a rather unsophisticated way, in a manner easy for the louche and lazy gods to mock, but it is a genuine, unpretentious feeling, a modest if artless appreciation of love, an understanding which many characters in the *Ring* might do well to heed. And the authenticity of Fasolt's feeling is conveyed to us not by his melancholy words of hope but through music, music which cannot be undermined by any directorial whim or other mockery of the giant. In fact, the music's effectiveness only increases the more Fasolt is lampooned.

The two giants' motif is, as we have said, stable and straightforward: it is not going to alter much; in truth, it is hard to know how it could. It is solid, dependable, unwavering — exactly like these bulky brutes and their construction trade, as well as Fafner's subsequent move into an appalling early form of wealth management or investment consolidation. Indeed, when we re-encounter Fafner disguised as a dragon in act 2 of *Siegfried*, the orchestral prelude to that act is principally formed out of the giants' heavy, banal music, monstrously slowed down and contrapuntally interwoven with the Curse motif, while Fafner sleeps, guarding the Ring, Tarnhelm and massive stockpile of gold.

But the giants' music is not the only music associated with Fasolt. When he sings to Wotan about his aspiration of domestic harmony with Freia, his vocal line is accompanied by Freia's Love motif on the oboe. As we saw in the previous chapter, Freia's Love motif has two segments, the first representing the sexual, sensual aspects to love and the second characterizing its compassion, confidence and vulnerability. The first is unchanging and static; the second, infinitely variable. Crucially, when Fasolt sings forlornly of his love for Freia, both sections of the Love motif are heard on an oboe in almost unutterably exquisite tones, its sound floating up from the orchestra to join Fasolt's words. His love is real, honest, full of sorrow and hope. He is mocked — by his brother, by the gods, by quite a few directors and countless audiences of the *Ring*. But he should not be made fun of by anyone, for his love is not only sincere but important. This ridicule corresponds, to a certain extent, with the Rhinemaidens' sarcastic jeering of the obnoxious, ostracized dwarf Alberich in the opening scene of *Das Rheingold*, and the shattering consequences of that scorn will be matched and developed in the mistreatment of Fasolt. Whatever Fasolt's and Alberich's failings, poking fun at the less fortunate or unsightly is clearly not only nasty in itself but highly detrimental.

The derision so many heap on Fasolt's love for Freia, both inside and outside the drama, is doubtless partly explained by class condescension. How can this creature, this labourer, this blue-collar pleb, possibly know what love is, especially the kind of cultured, refined love *we* know about, read about, write about? We go to the opera, the theatre, read poetry and novels, and have a much more distinguished awareness of what love really is. This manual worker cannot conceivably know about it. He is a lustful, crude giant, incapable of the finer feelings. Wagner knew the snobbery of his own time, the insincerity, duplicity and hurtfulness of class attitudes, the contempt and arrogance towards the so-called lower orders. This remains, unchanged, in our own societies, as haughty, lazy and mean as ever it was.

But Wagner had anticipated, and to an extent trounced, such smug mindsets through the haunting oboe which accompanies Fasolt's lament. This music guarantees the authenticity of his love by being a restatement in the definitive major form of both segments of the Love motif, without change or corruption. It is not ironized by inversion or burlesqued through exaggerated, mawkish strings. It is a simple, skinny, flexible and desperately yearning sound, and it asserts Fasolt's place as an immortal hero, an innovative hero, an unforgettable figure of the future where the claims of love triumph over those of money or power. That beautiful, alien and deeply moving oboe stands not only for love but as a rebuke to those closed, narrow-minded mentalities that have condemned or derided innumerable generations of lovers for crossing class boundaries, for knowing that love matters more than wealth, status, position or power.

The force of this extraordinary and tiny moment amid the politics and power moves of *Das Rheingold*, among the vastness of the *Ring*, is often overlooked. But it is immensely compelling. The unexpected character and station of the lover-hero, and the strange isolated potency of the oboe's magical sadness, attest Fasolt's memorable significance in the bitter, violent dramas to come. He is shortly to become the first victim of the Ring's curse, felled by his brother's greedy, acquisitive hand. But before his unfortunate demise, he asserts the ultimate goal of the *Ring's* long journey: the victory of love.

Fasolt's love might be unrequited, even unrequired in the hard-headed, bland, monetized world of *Das Rheingold*, but it is an honest testimony to his feelings as well and to his own honourable, diligent labour, which is due its reward. Fasolt is not attractive in any conventional sense, and he is estranged from his own brother, who fits more easily and comfortably into the gods' hierarchical and supercilious society. Fasolt is a weirdo, an annoyance, who must be silenced, ridiculed or eradicated. And thus he swiftly is: Fafner senses his brother's weakness, abuses and then suppresses it.

In the loveless world of *Das Rheingold*, Fasolt stands apart as a romantic revolutionary, a hero asserting the value and values of love above the interests of power or capital. He may be gauche and improper, not least by the hypocritical standards of the gods, but he is honest, genuine, principled, with the sparkle of decency within him. His is a light all too quickly snuffed out — a pattern to be followed throughout the dramas to come.

Chapter Six

The Hurt Nexus:
Die Walküre

Whereas the preliminary evening of the *Ring* began with the soft, steady birth of the world, the gradual entry of instruments, and the undulating course of the river Rhine, its first day opens with a violent tempest and a thunderstorm of sound from the full mass of the orchestra. This is a ferocious burst of strength, energy and dynamic symphonic writing, a massive demonstration of the power of the Wagnerian orchestra, all recurring loops and trembling threads, with an agitated current on the lower strings. The music is quivering, frantic, panicky, but oddly static, staying suspended in D minor, unable to find an escape from the howling whirlwind of fright and confusion in which it finds itself. But the magnificently disturbed state of the orchestra is not merely an exhibition of its own power or a symphonic representation of severe weather. The storm is, like most of

Wagner's vast atmospheric panoramas, as much psychological as meteorological.

A man is on the run, pursued by his invisible enemies, and the disturbing, turbulent world Wagner conjures up at the beginning of *Die Walküre* is a tremendous musical description of this man's state of mind. Over the course of the act to come, we gradually learn about his catastrophic and wretched life as he unburdens himself of his tragic tale to an unknown woman who gives him refuge from hurricanes without and within. Yet, as he tells his story, the orchestra frequently play music familiar from the previous evening, sounds associated with Wotan. It becomes clear that the chief of the gods has been manipulating the pitiful passage of this man's life in an attempt to free himself from his own attachments and restraints. (During the storm, Donner's thunder from *Rheingold* is also heard as Wotan engages the other gods in action.)

In *Rheingold*, we encountered gods, dwarfs, giants, their skirmishes for power, and the undermining of divine rule both by the external acquisition of control by Alberich and the internal deception of Wotan by himself. The leader of the gods has been able to limit the power of the former only through the latter process, stealing the dwarf's stolen gold to meet his own obligations and in the process loosening that malign strength further, its presence now immobilized but fixed in the world. In order to try and preserve (or restore) his own power, Wotan has ensnared himself in further dingy compromises and delusions, arguing that he needs an unbound hero oblivious to the dark past and free from the political-psychological shackles the god is caught in. The lost and hunted man in the storm is to be that hero's father.

❧

We saw in the previous chapter how, with one glorious, lonesome exception, *Das Rheingold* is a cruel, empty world of false charm, appropriated (and re-appropriated) wealth, and violations of one sort or another. Debt and desecration just about sum it up. Musically, too, we saw how it has a wonderfully frigid sound, interspersed with glamorous, clamorous noises. Unlike Wotan, it meets its responsibilities — to the principles of *Oper und Drama* (1851) which Wagner had laid down as the 'artwork of the future', but with a certain infertility in regard to some of the musical movement and motivation (which, happily, only contribute to the overall sound-world of the drama).

But, for the *Ring*'s first day, freedom reigns within the rules. The first act of *Die Walküre* is not only the most perfect execution of Wagner's new principles but is the beginning of their rapid and extraordinary development. This is the very centre of Wagner's career, the intersection of his many musical and dramatic roads. In act 1 of *Die Walküre*, word stresses are protected and the melodic lines record every shade and subtlety while the music proceeds in a much more uninhibited and spontaneous way than was possible (or desired) in *Das Rheingold*. By the second and third acts, the unconditional unity of text and music is beginning to be overtaken by the orchestra, thus redeploying music as the absolute master of the musikdrama.

Part of this emphasis on music can be explained by Wagner's growth as a composer, as well as by his discovery of Schopenhauer's aesthetics and metaphysics, which would reorganize the relative balance of the musikdrama (and lead to the epoch-making insurgencies of *Tristan und Isolde*). Yet it was also entirely part of the progression of the *Ring* cycle itself. On this first day, not only humans but love, sincere and shared love, enter the unsettled cosmos of the drama. And it is fitting that a more flexible, abandoned symphonic style is there to meet them.

The gods from *Das Rheingold* that we re-encounter — Wotan and Fricka — are more human, too (though not necessarily more humane). We witness the global political vexations of this incompatible operatic power couple turn more personal, their show of force and composure crumbling inside as they each try to maintain dignity and self-control amid the chaos. Fricka sticks to the principles of her career, maintaining values that have given her a semi-independent existence alongside the presidency of her powerful husband. For his part, Wotan is now compelled to bring his favourite daughter into the fray and in so doing lose her forever.

Walküre's first act, however, is about the human twins Siegmund and Sieglinde, and their act has a sovereignty and self-determination that sets it apart from the rest of the *Ring*. It is probably the only act of the cycle that can be experienced independently, its narrative a self-contained drama, whatever the additional musico-dramatic tentacles which reach from it. It radiates warmth, freshness and genuine feeling amid the dark world of the *Ring*. Fasolt's love for Freia, for all its sad meaning and significance, was fantasy. Brünnhilde and Siegfried's great confederacy will be indisputable but more forced than the authenticity of the Völsung twins' absolute compassion and desire for each other. This is also, of course, the only union in the *Ring* which is productive: Siegfried will be the vigorous crop of their illicit joy.

The symphonic cyclone which drives Siegmund into first the house and then the arms of his sister is a bravura approach to begin the first day proper of the *Ring*. It is arresting, gripping and entirely spellbinding. But it soon subsides as Siegmund collapses, exhausted, in this stranger's hut. From then on, the first act exists almost as an interlude, an island of respite from the violence of the *Ring*, seemingly protected from the squalls and wickedness which rage beyond. There is danger within, of course, in the form of Hunding, Sieglinde's legal husband, who will darken the proceedings, making up the threesome of astonishing voices which govern this extraordinary act. His presence is a black one, but it is soon removed to allow the twins to discover one another in the relative freedom of the night.

Walküre's first act — a chamber play on acid — is beautifully structured to give the twins an initial meeting alone before their reunion is interrupted and then resumed when the drugged Hunding goes off to bed. This first contact establishes not only their bond but our attachment to them and their plight: the one a hounded fugitive, the other an imprisoned wife in a brutal and loveless marriage. Wagner, in the first minutes of the *Ring*'s first day, isolates their love within the universe to give the twins a few moments of infinite tranquillity and tenderness before the entrance of Hunding and then the ecstasy of the twins' end-of-act coupling.

Let us examine this more closely. At the end of the prelude, when the storm wanes in the orchestra, Siegmund unknowingly enters the hut of his sister, crumpling to the floor, shattered. He begs for water, and the concerned Sieglinde passes some to this mysterious man. The strings dance like their eyes: sensual, nervous, embarrassed. But as he drinks and then returns the vessel, an unaccompanied cello is the only sound we hear. The rest of the massive orchestra is silent, on standby. This lone cello line carries Siegmund's exhausted theme upwards to meet the other low strings and his lover-sister's eyes. All the power and dissent, penalty and mercy which are to follow in *Die Walküre* and the rest of the *Ring* cease to matter. For these few moments, a single string is allowed voice, alone amid the immense ocean of the Wagner orchestra. We share in the stillness, in the infinite beauty of this pause where the rough engine of time has stopped.

This solitary cello proceeds to sing of spring and a burning affection — music which will return in triumph later in the act. There is a vernal freshness to the atmosphere, just the lonely sound of love, a truthful love without the sultry air of *Tristan*. It is still an illegitimate love, a forbidden fruit, but its insubordination of the bourgeois brutality of Hunding and Fricka (a curious additional power couple in this drama) is a forceful and defiant statement of the *Ring*'s true ethics. There are many competing centres of the *Ring*, and many of them are in *Die Walküre*: Wotan's encircling of Brünnhilde's rock by Loge's fire, leaving his daughter in suspended sleep. Or beforehand, in act 2, when he narrates to her the story of his woe. Or is it even earlier, in the first act, when the sword is retrieved from the tree and the Völsung twins flee together into the moonlight of a springtide night? But surely it is here, when Siegmund and Sieglinde gaze into each other's eyes for the first time, attended only by that single cello. Its gentleness will turn to bleak agony amid the miserable experiences to come, but for now it affords warmth like that of the fire by which they sit.

The nascent lovers exchange a few words, Siegmund beginning to divest himself of his tale, before a severe, unyielding fanfare announces Hunding's homecoming and the return of reality to the *Ring*. Once the initial awkwardness of the unexpected guest on the hearth with his wife has passed, he permits Siegmund to resume his story. They hear how he was separated from his sister during childhood: he had returned to their forest home one day to find his sibling abducted and their mother slain. More recently, he has fought with the relatives of a girl coerced into wedlock and is now evading them. It becomes apparent that Hunding is one of those relatives, from whom Siegmund was fleeing when we first met him. The Völsung seems cornered. But so absurdly bound is his curt, stern host to society's conventions and rules that he cannot even kill, there and then, the enemy of his own people. The laws of hospitality mean he must wait until morning — not only exposing the ridiculous boundaries of conservative culture but affording the lovers a night together. It's all they will need.

Hunding, however, should not be simply dismissed as a dull mass of leaden custom and weary orthodoxy. After all, civilisations are based on a certain civility, even if these customs can grow stale and even aggressive, as have the marriages between Wotan and Fricka, Hunding and Sieglinde. The best vocal actors, if their directors and conductors let them, imbue Hunding with a certain sarcastic wit, a caustic tongue to go with his massive, black bass, for he can be more than simply a bluff, gruff simpleton, Fricka's tool. The goddess of marriage, too, needs to be shown as more than a petty, pedantic misery-maker, a tiresome termagant: we need to see some of her own pain, her own desperation amid the frustration, just as we need to observe some humour in Hunding, some flicker of humanity beneath the enormous voice.

Dramatically, Hunding is easily dealt with. A figure from tradition, he can be silenced by the conventional draught of a drugged drink, leaving the stage free to return to the lovers with whom we had begun to become so emotionally and musically involved. While Sieglinde is away dealing with her inconvenient spouse, Siegmund, alone and unarmed, ponders his situation. He recalls how his father promised him a sword, which Siegmund would find in his deepest distress, and then sees it before him, lodged in the strange trunk which forms the centre of Hunding's hut. His sister slips back into the room and tells her brother how a peculiar man — Wotan, of course — appeared at the wedding banquet of her forced marriage to Hunding, embedding this blade to the hilt in the tree. She has longed for a hero to come and liberate both the weapon and her. That hero is now in front of her: her long-lost brother and soon-to-be lover. Adultery and incest are to be conjoined in an act of defiance and rebellion, shattering the comfy conformity of the world. The truest love and noblest passion of the *Ring*, and of all Wagner, will be the most illicit, the most perverse, the most shocking.

Siegmund sings of the exit of winter and arrival of spring. Bleak storms have dissipated before the Maytime which now appears in their lives, gentle breezes blow through the woods and meadows with the sweet songs of the birds, every subtlety indicated in the vocal line of Wagner's brave new musico-poetic fusion. The hidden kernels of their devotion are now free to germinate, and the lovers sing of a rapturous range of natural and passionate images, the pictures mingling as the orchestra and voices mount in higher and higher transports of love, fondness and delight.

'You are the spring for which I have yearned', sings Sieglinde, her interstellar soprano matching the heroic lunar light of her tenor brother. The music gleefully explodes into their release, the two freed to face the future unrestrained and together, aided by the opportune gift of the sword, Nothung ('Need'). The lyrical warmth and euphoria which end *Die Walküre*'s first act are unmatched anywhere else in Wagner's output, the twin voices rising above a superbly sympathetic orchestra, the instruments exquisite in their elegant support of these magnificent, genial lovers.

Many composers, after the heady scream of ecstasy which ends the first part of the drama, might have found it musically and theatrically a hard act to follow. Not Wagner. With his usual shrewdness regarding both audience psychology and dramatic intensity, he lets the Völsung twins have their time alone in the background, fleeing and fornicating unseen after the prelude to act 2 has first — and with tremendous, exhilarating power — signalled their courageous, disastrous flight. This then symphonically develops into music which has been hitherto only hinted at in the *Ring*. It is some of the most famous music ever written: the notorious, disreputable, staggering and stupendous theme of the ride of the Valkyries.

Wotan and Brünnhilde appear, she the Valkyrie of the title and her father's energetic favourite daughter — and, in her astonishing vocal entry, 'Hojotoho!', it is not difficult to see why. She has a vigour, a momentum, of which any parent would be proud. The amiable scene between father and daughter, prior to the fractious one between husband and wife, is brief but important in establishing the close bond between Brünnhilde and her father, making its severance the more heartbreaking as the drama unfolds.

It is also a brief prelude to the long and tender narration Wotan painfully imparts to his child, which forms the structural weight of the whole work. But before this affectionate scene, the 'old storm, the old strife!' — as the god ungraciously, but perhaps understandably, refers to his wife Fricka, guardian of marriage and its related social customs. As we said above, Fricka should be performed with more sorrow and despair than she often is, since she provides, after all, an opportunity to complicate and deepen the perspectives, as well as to assert something more solid than the ceaselessly fluctuating values and feelings we have been observing. She is also, of course, horrifically *right*, however annoying it is to us (and Wotan) that she is. We believe in the Völsungs; we know they have the moral victory. But Fricka's assertions — convincingly made with some absolutely imperious and resplendent sounds — cannot simply be the cantankerous old strains of sour convention. To be dramatically powerful, they must contain a considerable degree of legitimacy. Not only are adultery and incest immoral, but Wotan's belief that Siegmund is a 'free hero' is pure nonsense: he has been controlled by the god throughout.

Fricka lays bare, as only a spouse can, her husband's self-deception, and he surrenders to her demands almost in relief:

he has embroiled himself in a quagmire of deals and deceit, to which he has now had to add the offence of emboldening incest and adultery. Wotan, energetic dallier though that he is (a liaison with Erda, the earth goddess, produced Brünnhilde), has some moral standards. His renunciation of power, although an abdication cultivated by his wife, is a liberation. But freedom and self-knowledge come with a price: that of his cherished daughter. In the ephemeral scene which opens this act, where Wotan instructed Brünnhilde to defend Siegmund, Wotan has already planted in her the seed which will blossom into her own understanding of the precious value of love, first during the Annunciation of Death scene later in the act and then in her awakening in act 3 of *Siegfried*.

The fertile soil which nurtures this comprehension of love is provided unwittingly by Wotan in the extended, intimate scene after the confrontation with Fricka. It starts with harsh, then poignant strings announcing anguish and despondency: the inexplicable bleak, black tenderness in which *Walküre* specializes. Wotan exposes his weary consciousness to his daughter, telling her — and us — of his endless transgressions. Although we already know of them (they are essentially the plot of *Rheingold*), this is no mere repetition. It allows those events to be instilled with regret, dignity and tragedy. Musikdrama, after all, is not merely about storyline unfurling as stage action. It is about psychology, metaphysics and orchestral interaction, here communicating, as only the vast network of leitmotifs can, the complexity and intricacy of Wotan's predicament. Constantly imbricating motifs — subtle, grand and broken — pervade the solemn air around him and his daughter. We hear of Valhalla, the Ring, Erda, each motif entering and amalgamating as the narration wears on, Wotan's spirit troubled, then angry, then empty, before filling with despair. His act 2 monologue has an encumbrance, a burden of remorse, new to this character. He is confessing, beginning to relieve himself of his umbrage and iniquity.

It is testimony to Wagner's exceptional management of immense stretches of music that this scene never wanes or sags but is a constant and fascinating landscape of Wotan's mind. Wagner's art has reached some of its finest potential, now not only able to sustain a mood for a scene but shifting temper and tension in an instant while maintaining the overall span. The scene is vast, anticipating the narrations of Waltraute in *Götterdämmerung* as well as of King Marke in *Tristan* and Gurnemanz in *Parsifal*, but none of those can match the grandeur and despair of Wotan's lament. The orchestra not only relentlessly employ the array of leitmotifs but shift in texture: thick, thin, dense, emaciated, despairing, violent. Wotan's soul is shown as an organic, unstable and kaleidoscopic monster of affliction and disappointment.

Wotan lets go of all suffering in his daughter's presence. Pride and adoration might make some fathers hide such histories in shame from their children. But Wotan's love allows him to admit and acknowledge his past to his treasured child. Her own father's father confessor, Brünnhilde also receives his command to fight for Fricka, to protect her laws and not defend Siegmund. But as his priest, she is also his counsel, and Brünnhilde advises Wotan to act to save Siegmund, since she knows he truly loves him, whatever Fricka, or Wotan, has said. He refuses. It is too late.

The emotional impact of this scene is immense, its probing psychology revealing the full power and profundity of Wagner's art. Its orchestral tapestry is densely woven and beautifully shaped, lending a sublime inexorability to the tragic expansion of the tale. It proceeds to the tragic climax of the act, to the place in the forest where Brünnhilde announces to Siegmund his impending death in battle and where his love moves her to disobey her father, acting as she believes Wotan genuinely wishes. Brünnhilde is powerless to defend Siegmund, however, and he falls to Hunding's spear after his father shatters his sword. The compelling scene between Siegmund and Brünnhilde is one to which we will return, partly because of its colossal dramatic force but also because it allows us to continue the emotional arc between Brünnhilde and Wotan which, along with that of Siegmund and Sieglinde, dominates *Die Walküre*.

The third act opens with the pugnacious infamy of the Valkyries and their ride, as they gather corpses for Valhalla, before they desert, then protect, then re-desert Brünnhilde and Sieglinde, dispersed by the machine-gun strings of Wotan's approaching wrath. Sieglinde and her unborn child, the future Siegfried, have been safely despatched, but not before Sieglinde's ecstatic cry 'O hehrstes Wunder' ('O, utmost miracle!') as she praises Brünnhilde to the accompaniment of the Redemption motif — Wagner's conception of unalloyed, unfettered humanity — which will not be heard again until the very end of *Götterdämmerung*.

The stage is now free for the tragic final meeting between Wotan and his daughter, the gigantic scene of farewell which is concluded by a devastating valediction and the gift of magic fire. Between this scene and the long narration of act 2, father and daughter have disobeyed and defied, violated and contravened each other, flouting their own senses of duty, love and truth. But the sympathy and close bond between them still exists. In fact, it is stronger, and Wotan's farewell to his daughter, though immensely poignant, is also an act of love, one generated by Wotan's own inimitable and unenviable jumble of compassion and despair. His removal of her godhead is a further act of affection which will allow her to experience the full power of the emotion which so moved her when she witnessed it between Siegmund and Sieglinde.

The extent of Wotan's love creates, of course, its equal and opposite fury. His sense of betrayal, compounded by his knowledge that Brünnhilde had acted as he truly wanted, is a violent awareness of the futility of his own divine project. When he walks away from his daughter in the drama's final moments, he is relinquishing his own being: he will return only (though at some length) as the Wanderer in *Siegfried*. In this final confrontation, Brünnhilde's appeals to Wotan's heart only provoke his anger, his inner knowledge of his own failure. This is all portrayed in emotionally fraught musical passages of limitless hopelessness and engaging poignancy, abundant in fertile scoring and orchestral details which not only capture the characters' pain but send our own feelings into an emotional firestorm. Leitmotifs and jagged chords are flung about in rage, bitter and fragmented, then stunningly entwined more gently into the score, the textures softening as choking asperity subsides towards the inevitable sentence Brünnhilde is to receive.

It is here that both parties are able, through the cathartic process of their monumental clash, to reveal their profoundest, most affirmative feelings, the music transporting them and us into a realm of sanctified leave-taking and grand departure. It is a hallowed scene of consecrated parting, the music alerting us not only to Brünnhilde's heroism, courage, endurance and determination but also her own sadness, matching her father's deep pain as he bids the principal virtuous force of his life goodbye. It is music of forgiveness, compassion and clemency, building and building to its ultimate climax of heartbroken farewell before subsiding into Wotan's overwhelming words 'The radiant pair of eyes which often I smiled upon', its gentleness shored up by a blanket of comfort from the orchestra, enfolding us, as Brünnhilde, in its tender embrace, strings and woodwind each working in different ways to console and reassure as the music drifts towards its unavoidable leave-taking. Trumpets and trombones herald that their time is up; strings glide in, soothing the immeasurable pain as Wotan kisses his daughter's godhead away.

The god, preparing to renounce his own identity as well, summons his old adviser and technical wizard, the fire god Loge, with massive sonorities from the darkest brass. The sparkling, dancing figuration of the Magic Fire music begins, and for several minutes the orchestra sweep around and envelop Brünnhilde's rock, building, ebbing and flowing, fusing and interspersing with subtle motifs in an extraordinary orchestral display of almost overpowering emotional force and sonic beauty. It is one of Wagner's grandest conclusions, full of majestic brass and far-reaching strings, lines floating in and developing away, around and around the rock on which Brünnhilde now lies sleeping. Lastly, as the god gazes one final time at his beloved daughter, and with the dappling Magic Fire motif prevailing, the Fate motif (a tiny two-chord alteration) is heard, but now held fixed in the key in which the drama ends, suspended along with Brünnhilde in her magic sleep.

The final scene of *Die Walküre* is a musico-dramatic tableau we never want to end, which we want unceasingly to be repeated, both for its musical force and its dramatic meaning. We want Wotan and Brünnhilde to be together for that little bit longer. We don't want them to have to say goodbye. It is the ultimate departure because it so faithfully conveys the agony of farewell, the enduring desire to prolong even something as painful as this.

This scene has, understandably, inspired a wealth of stimulating, often confrontational, ideas, as well as having encouraged some of the finest stage and lighting effects from directors and their design teams. Wieland Wagner's conceptions of the *Ring* between 1951 and 1965 involved a circular acting area, often a rotating disc, inspired by the Greek amphitheatre and encouraging the generally Hellenistic, apolitical and mythological atmosphere Wagner's grandson wanted. For the end of *Walküre*, this immense space enabled a vast and towering inferno to surround Brünnhilde, an imposing barrier for all but the most courageous hero.

Götz Friedrich's 1974 *Ring* for Covent Garden was a fusion of antiquity with the nineteenth and twentieth centuries, a theatrical time machine interrelating alternative perspectives, though never arguing for dramatic unity across the four works. When Wotan left Brünnhilde atop the flame-girdled mountain, he walked to the front of the stage, challenging the audience themselves to defy his spear and claim his daughter.

For Bayreuth's centenary *Ring* in 1976, Patrice Chéreau's groundbreaking exercise in reactionary revolution, *Walküre's* third act occurred in a disturbing, phantasmagoric graveyard colonized by Valkyries who were savage and ungodly messengers of death, its walls parting to reveal the glacier on which Brünnhilde was to lie. In truth, the mountain merely looked like an underdeveloped Matterhorn, and the tense majesty of farewell was emasculated. In later years, this scene was modified so that Wotan and Brünnhilde's parting took place in the imposing ruins of a chapel, modelled on Böcklin's moody painting *Isle of the Dead*. A triumph of Bayreuth's *Werkstatt* ('workshop') concept, where productions progress from year to year, the scene now had all the tragic grandeur the music demands: Wotan laid his daughter down to sleep at dusk, Loge's magic fire taking over from the setting sun as the first day of the *Ring* ended.

Ruth Berghaus's remarkable Frankfurt *Ring* in 1985 continued her lively, Brechtian engagement with *Parsifal* in 1982, removing the need for coherent narrative and instead focusing on the theatrical signs inherent to the drama. For Berghaus, the *Ring* was a dark playground, a maze of participation and performance, so Brünnhilde and Wotan frolicked onto a nursery-stage at the beginning of *Walküre's* second act, a mischievous presentation of childhood play which made the pathos of their farewell even more moving by the end, as Brünnhilde was sentenced to a future of very human domesticity, enthroned on a kitchen chair. Berghaus's amused recreation was matched by the extraordinary depth of her psychological penetration and exploratory forensic analysis.

At Bayreuth a few years later, in 1988, Harry Kupfer memorably sealed Wotan's daughter in a red laser cube, the crimson light and mist an astonishing contrast to the desolate magnificence of his gloomy 'highway of history'. Kupfer's *Ring* was a dark parable of power, of moral, intellectual, emotional and ecological dread, with bleak, uncompromising sets and a ruthless atmosphere throughout. The laser beams which formed Brünnhilde's magic fire were not just a protection for her but a beacon of optimism in an otherwise merciless world.

In the new century, the scene has continued to offer a place for catharsis and hope. Keith Warner's *Ring* for Covent Garden in 2004 had, prior to *Die Walküre's* final act, been characterized by an obstacle course of stage paraphernalia and scenic clutter, a gallimaufry of discarded props and incongruous symbolic objects. But suddenly, all this was swept away by a spinning white wall, clearing a space for Wotan and Brünnhilde to fight and to forgive, the god's daughter eventually surrounded by a very real cleansing conflagration.

For all the power and radiance which closes *Die Walküre*, there is perhaps an even more moving passage, its poignancy hidden away amid the tragedy and chaos of the second act. It is the so-called Annunciation of Death scene. After her extended meeting with her father, Brünnhilde meets Siegmund before battle, and this is the crucial point where the Wotan/ Brünnhilde and Siegmund/Sieglinde storylines rendezvous. The scene is decisive in Brünnhilde's progression towards humanity (in both the non-divine and charitable senses). It is the effect on her of Siegmund's display of feeling for Sieglinde which is at the critical heart of *Die Walküre*'s dramatic narrative, the crisis of Brünnhilde's realization of what love is and means which drives her to disobey her father. It will ultimately remove her divinity but bequeath her humanity — in the world of the *Ring*, a far more valuable possession.

The scene is sublimely introduced by the four Wagner tubas as they announce an ominous and spectral expansion of the Fate motif, the music metamorphosing and intensifying in a typically Wagnerian fusion of grandeur and sadness. Brünnhilde enters to tell Siegmund that he is to follow her to Valhalla, the eternal abode of heroes, having been called there by Wotan. He asks whether he will be welcomed warmly there by a woman (meaning his beloved Sieglinde). Brünnhilde replies, accompanied by celestial harps, that many maidens will be there and she herself will serve him drink.

Siegmund responds graciously, as the music begins to build and build, mixing tension, sadness and affection: But will Siegmund be able to embrace his Sieglinde there? Nothing else matters to him but this. The music, as he asks this question, is of inexpressible wonder: in this question, the entire future of humanity lies. If Siegmund cannot be with his beloved, then all the pleasures of paradise will not suffice. It is this moment, ultimately an augmentation of the twins' first gentle and kind-hearted meeting in act 1, where their eyes met to a solo cello, which is the true centre of *Der Ring des Nibelungen*. All the love and suffering of the *Ring* centres on this moment, and

Wagner's music is an unadulterated expression of tender feeling, an instant of infinite anxiety, anguish and yet total and overwhelming love.

Brünnhilde's reply, the orchestra immediately switching to the callous minor, is negative: 'She must still breathe earthly air'. Siegmund is defiant and to the point: then he rejects heaven and all it contains. Paradise is nothing without Sieglinde. Although Brünnhilde is initially dumbfounded that anyone might decline eternal life, gradually she begins to realize what is so powerful, so valuable, to him that he will forsake Valhalla for it: love. He cares not for death, not in any stoic Greek way but because love matters more.

Although Fricka was earlier correct in her assessment of the essential fiction in her husband's belief that he was creating a free hero — he has, after all, been manipulating events throughout — Siegmund here vindicates Wotan by acting in a way neither the god nor his wife could have foreseen. He asserts his own world-shattering activity and progressive agency by rejecting the promised gifts of Valhalla and everything it stands for.

Siegmund, foreshadowed by abject Fasolt and his lonely oboe and followed by the more garish heroics of Siegfried, is the true central revolutionary hero of the *Ring*. Siegmund's rejection of paradise for love is the ultimate manifestation of revolutionary thought, feeling and action combined. It is a conscious expression of double humanity: an unqualified refutation of the divine and a powerful proclamation of compassion. Such is the force of Siegmund's declaration of love that it is sufficient to convince the chief god's daughter, who will begin her own courageous journey towards a new form of being, an emboldened identity within humanity.

The second act of *Die Walküre* is a vast span, with a complex narrative and three couplings (Fricka–Wotan, Wotan–Brünnhilde, Brünnhilde–Siegmund) of immense philosophical, political, psychological and emotional power. It contains music of astonishing intricacy, density and freedom of intellectual-emotional expression, able to move between thoughts and moods with lightning speed and skill. It begins with the animated companionship and joyful camaraderie between a father and his daughter; it ends with the murder of a son by that same father. In between, it has perhaps Wagner's sincerest, purest expression of human love.

We earlier argued that the ethical, emotional centre of the *Ring* is the weary, then compassionate solo cello line when Siegmund and Sieglinde first gaze into each other's eyes. That is so, but when Siegmund asks whether he will embrace Sieglinde in paradise, that moment has been extended, deepened, the twins' love given an appalling power unequalled anywhere else in Wagner's vast sequence of musikdramas. 'Umfängt Siegmund Sieglinde dort?' The exquisite sonic desolation of the moment — in truth the very last moment before the inevitable imposed partition between the lovers, the music rising and swelling in overwhelming beauty — is one of horrific splendour. It is, accordingly, the true tragic centre of the *Ring*, the juncture of all its avenues of love and pain. It is the hurt nexus.

Chapter Seven

Subverting the Fairy Tale: *Siegfried*

After the emotional maelstrom of *Die Walküre*, the dark, dark comedy of *Siegfried*. A work of enormous, malevolent power and strength, *Siegfried* begins in the obscurity of a cave before journeying to the forest and finally the sunlit hope of the mountain heights. The *Ring's* second day is a ghostly, sinister and sardonic work of light and shade which anticipates the gloomy humour of Alban Berg's *Wozzeck*, Anton Bruckner's vast orchestral landscapes, and the ironic, magisterial symphonies of Gustav Mahler. For all the murkiness, it is one of Wagner's most distinctive and enthralling scores, with an instrumental palette both exploding with flamboyant colours and exploring the infinite shades of black, brown and grey. It is a musikdrama dominated by male voices, before being seized by the vivid vocal pyrotechnics of a roused soprano.

In many ways, *Siegfried* is a folk or fairy tale straight out of the Brothers Grimm. With its simple narrative arc, it is an adventure and a coming-of-age story containing bears, riddles, dragons, stolen treasure, talking birds and sleeping beauties, as well as confrontations with a father and an evil stepmother — for Mime is, as he himself says, both a maternal and paternal figure to the orphaned Siegfried. Add to this familiar figures (one-eyed strangers, scheming brothers, virginal heroines) and geographically memorable locations (a mysterious, womblike cave, a liminal forest, a spacious mountaintop), and the stage is set for a traditional and transitional rite-of-passage yarn for a hero: Siegfried.

Yet *Siegfried* is in constant negotiation with itself about both the eminence of its protagonist and the narrative genre in which he is to be found. It develops and disrupts its fairy-tale traits and questions the positive standing of its hero. The quest and discovery elements, among other features, assert the recognizable topography and structure of fairy tales, but this hero is both better and worse than we expect, his encompassing fiction both more surreal and more realistic. Wagner problematizes the status and surroundings of the hero, challenging us to enquire what heroism means to us and where we think we will find it. This, the scherzo of the 'Ring Symphony', is a mercurial, unpredictable and seditious creature of shifting certainties and volatile values. If modernity stresses complexity and ambiguity, then both Siegfried and *Siegfried* are some of Wagner's most modern creations.

Part of the complication of *Siegfried* arises from the convolutions of its creation. On the one hand, its hero was demoted from his position as the tragic prince dominating a pair of operas to a latecomer in a cycle of four. On the other, its composition was halted for a decade as Wagner turned to writing first *Tristan und Isolde* and then *Die Meistersinger von Nürnberg*, leaving his young hero in the lonely places of the forest at the end of act 2. But such significant changes in both the conception and execution of *Siegfried* reaped unexpected benefits. Not only was the hero made much more interesting by becoming one of three highly contrasted figures (alongside Wotan and Brünnhilde) but in musico-dramatic terms, the developments of *Tristan* and *Meistersinger* enhanced the sonic geography of the third part of the *Ring*.

Siegfried has a fascinating orchestral panorama, full of fluctuating light and shade, with an expertly judged employment of unusual vocal combinations: lower voices blended with distinctive instrumental mixtures and a striking delayed use of higher vocal pitches. The icy dazzle of *Rheingold*, shadowed by the black warmth of *Walküre*, is followed in *Siegfried* by a sound texture that cannot be easily characterized: it is constantly on the move. It is certainly dark, yet not only is that darkness repeatedly punctured by light but its gloom is not uniform, the result of very particular arrangements in the score.

Wagner's organization of orchestral ratios is meticulous in *Siegfried*, as are the idiosyncratic uses of particular areas of instrumental colouring. In the first act, especially in the opening and closing confrontations between Mime and Siegfried, the violins have very little to do compared to the other strings. Violas, cellos and basses, along with tubas and bassoons, give a wonderfully solemn and sombre tone to the drama. It is a dusky, opaque tapestry of infinite subtlety that makes the two tenor voices of Mime and his foster son Siegfried sound not only higher but lighter in relative terms against this murky orchestral backcloth, allowing Wagner to exploit the tenor voice's potential for histrionic farcicality as Mime squeals and conspires, contrasted with impulsive and energetic Siegfried.

Both roles need exceptional understanding of rhythm, since it is the pace and beat in the score which also balances and energizes the subdued orchestral colouring. However gloomy things might be, that gloom does not linger for long, and these two characters are both — for different reasons — restless individuals. Curious, too: Mime in the sense of strange; Siegfried, inquisitive. Mime is a conspiratorial, resentful figure of frustration and revulsion; Siegfried a youth, aggravated in his own way but keen to learn to (literally) forge a way free.

Mime is usually accompanied by those eternal orchestral bridesmaids, the violas. Hovering between the more alluring ends of the string market — below the singing violins and above the grave cellos — the violas have not often been allotted such an important role in the instrumental topography. But in *Siegfried*, especially in the first act, they are given heightened prominence, communicating the sneaky opacity of Mime, both in terms of his malevolent intrigue and his ambiguous heroism: whenever Siegfried (or Alberich or the Wanderer) misbehave or taunt Mime, we feel slightly sorrier for the dwarf than we otherwise might.

Mime has a pluckiness, a certain peculiar valour, which modern audiences have often warmed to. This is, in part, due to Siegfried's divided status in modern terms: we no longer exalt the brawny superman figure in the same way, nor do we care for his coarseness and bullying of a diminished personality. Mime has been, we know from *Rheingold*, ruthlessly terrorized and maltreated by his brother Alberich, and we can easily — and quite naturally — side emotionally and morally with the outsider/underdog. Moreover, Mime has a mad charm which is hard to resist. His insane triumphant screams of 'Mime is king!' at the very end of act 1, with some extraordinary auxiliary orchestral noise, form an unforgettable musico-dramatic portrayal of vexation, lunacy and vindictive glee. Mime is a clever, petty, opportunistic and rather nasty piece of work, pathetic both as a ridiculous and a pitiful figure. As such, he is a magnificent musico-dramatic creation who should remarkably, if perversely, rule any scene he finds himself in.

Against the bizarre obstinacy and malign craft of Mime, the tainted heroics of Siegfried. Early on in the musikdrama which bears his name, Siegfried has a particularly accented music, with harmonies crushed and contracted to express his irritation and impetuosity. But his sound is able to evolve at speed, reflecting his growth (and occasional maturity) throughout the entire opera and in each act. Together with Siegfried's vigour and animation, handed such exceptional demands in the great Forging Song, there is a lyrical quality essential for his contemplations of his mother and nature, as well as his passionate scene with Brünnhilde. These subtler, more mature elements arise as his music progresses in the first act, achieving its natural, harmonious maturity as he reforges the sword and is able to free himself from the encroaching chromatism of Mime.

As with Mime, however, this character is not as straightforward as we would like him to be. Siegfried is not a clear-cut strapping romantic idol. He has a more complex and humane inner life than do heroes in fairy tales, offset by his victimization and self-centredness, which destabilize, and eventually destroy, any claim to his perfection. Siegfried, even in the first act alone, is tender, violent, vulnerable, probing, indifferent, entirely ordinary and absolutely superhuman, and Wagner's music reflects these growing pains and unstable traits.

In *Siegfried*'s first act, the lugubrious orchestral shades, dynamic pulses and high-energy hostilities between Mime and Siegfried are counterpoised and separated by a central episode which is both grander and more deliberately traditional, musically and dramatically. Enter the Wanderer. This mysterious figure is identified, of course, as Wotan himself, now in semi-retirement from ruling the world, hoping his 'free hero' will be able to resolve the problems the god has created. The Wanderer's music, both from his bass baritone and the orchestra, has the dignity and nobility we recall from *Das Rheingold*, as well as some of the fragility and sense of culpability from *Die Walküre*. The Wanderer's appearance adjusts the sound-world of *Siegfried*, bringing with horns and cellos a glow and stateliness to the bickering foster family's strange little forest grotto. The score is still dark, since the Wanderer himself is pained and helpless, but the god's presence allows the embers of the music to burn a little brighter, affording a little warmth to the gloom, which will be fully ignited by the hearth and sparks of the forging scene which comes next.

The Wanderer–Mime scene is one of the most intriguingly artificial and reactionary in the *Ring*, the more so for the supple and progressive episodes which surround it. And this is no accident. It asserts the fairy-tale notions of riddles, questions and answers — especially from enigmatic strangers — familiar from countless tellings and retellings of these stories over time, and in so doing, it begs us to interrogate our own accounts of (and attitudes to) events thus far in the *Ring*. The trope of the three riddles is as old as stories and is a deliberate trick to isolate and quiz convention and methods of storytelling. By drawing on antique narrative devices, in addition to utilizing as the substance of the questions the very plot and characters of the earlier *Ring* dramas, Wagner is able to cross-examine the relationship between past and present, romance and realism. The riddles of the scene are the riddles of the *Ring* too. Moreover, by employing the architecture and toolkit of the leitmotif, which sounds so strongly and evocatively in this scene especially, Wagner explores, by the leitmotif's very nature, the intricate associations between characters, objects, events and emotions. Wagner asks us to reconsider the future by reviewing the past in the present.

For all the consciously archaic ruses and imposing tone quality to the scene, interpolated most obviously by Mime's persistent nervous energy, the back-and-forth Q & A has a rich absurdity to it. It is a black comedy anticipating Samuel Beckett's *Endgame*, *Happy Days* and *Waiting for Godot*. (The scene, for the Wanderer at any rate, is very much *Waiting for Götterdämmerung*.) *Siegfried*, not least in its first act, is a very self-aware work, alive to its own place in both the *Ring* and wider musico-dramatic history. It looks back only to get a better view of what lies ahead, shaping the future by applying and exploiting the past. The victorious, thrilling and sublime ending to the opening act, as Siegfried reforges the sword and Mime finalizes his plan to murder Siegfried once the boy has slain the dragon, is not only the stuff of adventure and youthful escapades but is symbolic of the way *Siegfried* (and the *Ring*, and Wagner) created and recreated the future of an art form.

Much of the Forging Song's power comes from its simplicity, both in musical and dramatic terms — complicated by a sense of its own eventual futility in the overall *Ring* — and Mime's contrapuntal plotting. It is one of Wagner's grandest creations, an arc of sound which emanates from the cave to fill the score with a light and muscle not yet fully experienced in *Siegfried*. It is well-regulated and skilfully paced, with interruptions and pauses, sometimes for the practical business of smelting and hammering, as well as for the conniving (and cooking) of Mime. It grows, then subsides in power, ebbing and flowing in scheming and steelwork, with episodes of extreme sonic strength and agitated rhythmic vitality loosening to eruptions of ferocious opulence and clouded joy: Siegfried's freshly minted but destructive maturity; Mime's misplaced, screaming confidence in his own newfound supremacy. Mime is king only within the sad prison-realm of his own twisted soul; Siegfried has found his vocation as a hero, but it is one which will ultimately lead to his own death.

Staging the scene is an opportunity for some thrilling theatrical effects, just as it is an immensely difficult sequence for the tenor playing Siegfried. Not only does he have to cope with some extremely demanding vocal music but his actions are tellingly arduous and very specific in Wagner's stage directions. The realism of the episode, in terms of stage action and character portrayal, is key to establishing Siegfried's heroic status as an adroit, talented champion, as well as both balancing and confusing the more romantic/fairy-tale aspects of the drama. Wagner's details regarding little hammers, files, anvils and flasks have a Zola-like veracity to them, and although they obviously don't need to be followed to every last rivet and gesture, their very intricacy helps establish our disbelief in the extraordinary new skills of this sulky bully boy. (Mime, we remember, is a master craftsman, but even he is still unable to reforge the sword; Siegfried, revealingly, can, mainly through an application of inborn, natural strength.)

If we don't believe in Siegfried's fortitude and fearlessness during this scene, the subtlety of his demise is undermined. Wagner has preprogrammed Siegfried's vulnerability and death into the musico-dramatic fabric of the score. These are an inherent part of who Siegfried is and what he sounds like; there is an innate wistfulness to even the broadest statements of his theme. Consequently, directorial attempts to present an ironically heroic Siegfried in this scene play a dangerous game with disrupting the internal fatefulness already at work. It's not that we can't find the episode a little bit absurd. Indeed, we need to, since the drama plays on the relationship between comedy and tragedy, reality and surreality. But we should be overwhelmed by it, too, staggered and satisfied by the brand-new capacities of the orphan boy becoming something extraordinary. Wagner telescopes several years' worth of childhood and adolescence into the electrifying first act of *Siegfried*, and we should thrill at its simultaneous speed and plausibility, as well as by what emerges at its end: a new sword, and someone to wield it.

Fafner, the giant-turned-dragon, has been a background but persistent presence so far in *Siegfried*. His ominous theme is rarely far from the music, haunting both the rear of the score and the back of Mime's mind, occasionally coming to the foreground on the tubas, with all their stygian iniquity, and when Mime experiences various forms of serpentine nightmare throughout the act.

The prelude to act 1 was as dark and secretive as anything Wagner wrote: a ruminating, anxious masterpiece for timpani, bassoons and subterranean strings, weaving a variety of themes before settling on the Nibelungs' hammering rhythm, which gradually developed into the first scene depicting the skilful smith Mime's thwarted attempts to reforge the sword himself. The prelude to act 2 is similarly opaque and gloomy, utilizing similar material to its precursor in act 1 but with more focus on the Curse and Ring motifs as we edge closer to their dramatic location: the dragon's lair in the forest. Fafner himself structures the prelude in one of the most quietly awe-inspiring of all Wagner's motivic transformations. The motif of the Giants, so loud and strident in scene 2 of *Rheingold*, is simply slowed down, some elements of the original motif deteriorating, in order to represent the lethargic, brooding presence of Fafner, now (via the Tarnhelm) in dragon form, as he sits on the Ring and treasure, doing nothing with them but fostering his own festering greed.

Act 2's instrumental tenebrosity continues when the first scene opens in the predawn darkness of the forest, the site for a final stage confrontation between Licht-Alberich (aka Wotan, aka the Wanderer) and Schwarz-Alberich himself. The first act remained entombed in the cradle-cave, albeit ending in the sparks of the Forging Song and promise of independence. Now the second act is outdoors, in the relative freedom of the forest. Here, unlike in the cave, day is sure to come. Indeed, it does. But it is a dappled light, hope and meaning confused by the shifting luminosity of sun, shade and score. The forest is a new realm of autonomy, but it has its own restrictions, its own puzzles and dangerous, porous boundaries. It is a liminal, transitional space for Siegfried to continue his development, something reflected in the score as the higher strings and woodwind begin to take over from the heavy brass, cellos and basses. Gradually, the music is releasing itself from its burdens, emancipations which will not survive long beyond *Siegfried* but whose radiant, valiant truths are incandescent.

The end-of-night scene between Alberich and Wotan forms a dawn prologue to Siegfried's evolution. The dwarf expresses his continuing need for the Ring, and the peripatetic god voices both his resigned disinterestedness and desire for his story to end. As the Wanderer furtively disappears from the stage and Alberich hides, Siegfried and Mime enter with the sunrise, squabbling as usual but with a brighter feel as the day dawns and a more natural light occupies the score, compared to the fiery illumination which ended act 1. Mime soon leaves Siegfried on his own and hides, like his brother, and the score further relaxes, expanding to bask in the gradually warming sunlight of a forest morning. Siegfried here is able to reveal himself as a child of nature, like Parsifal. He is genuine, innocent and naïve, responsive to the animal world, though with a more positive relationship with the avian community than his *Bühnenweihfestspiel* successor, speaking to the birds rather than putting arrows through their necks.

This charming scene is one of Wagner's finest portraits of nature: it flows and eases with all the graceful magic of Beethoven's Pastoral Symphony. Yet, like that work, it is also no mere tone painting but a reflection of feeling, of an internal psychology, as Siegfried prepares to meet his first major challenge. Here the hero reflects on the absence of his parents — something else he shares with Parsifal — continuing on his own some of the discussions he had with his unnatural father in the opening scene of act 1. His status as an orphan and his relationship with nature are linked, the one providing a reassurance and arena for growth and development which the other could not bestow.

Siegfried identifies with the life-enhancing properties of nature and is at home in the forest because he is not only a heroic figure but a life- and love-giving force of nature. Mime, Alberich, Fafner, Erda, the Wanderer and, to an extent, Brünnhilde maintain more complex relationships with nature: shunning it, inverting it, destroying it, manipulating it, restlessly or furtively moving through it. The Wanderer is itinerant, edgy. Erda an admonishing, unnerving cosmological force personifying the earth but curiously constricted: pessimistic, evasive, distant. (Her motif, after all, is a simple inversion of the Nature motif from the major to minor, slowed down.) Fafner, Alberich and Mime use the forest as cover for nefarious activities. Brünnhilde, on an inaccessible rock, is imprisoned both by isolation and magic fire, the latter a debasement of a natural force. Alone with the drama's voice of nature — the Woodbird, whose music is closely related to the Rhinemaidens' — Siegfried has a close and comfortable rapport with the natural world. It is the site for his profoundest feelings so far, as he develops his earlier inquisitiveness about his origins into more nuanced sentiments about his mother, which will also affect his scene with Brünnhilde.

Where other characters cynically stage-manage nature for their own clandestine ends, Siegfried utilizes it playfully. In order to try to communicate with the Woodbird, he fashions a pipe from the reeds by a spring before considering his own horn as a better instrument. This is the sound which rouses Fafner from his slumbers. Siegfried might not be cunning or an intellectual, but he has a natural intelligence and instinctiveness which further mark him a hero. (His reforging of Nothung is as much down to natural strength as any learnt skill.) Simple, guileless and straightforward, Siegfried's introspection makes him a more sympathetic character, as well as preventing him from being merely the stereotypical dragon-slayer-and-maiden-winner from fairy tales. His heroism is, then, defined frequently by his activity rather than identity, though they are clearly interrelated: it is his native audacity which provides him with the potential to kill Fafner and gain the (apparent) rewards.

There is nothing savage about Siegfried in his relationship with nature. He plays games with bears and reeds as he does with woodbirds. His slaughtering of Fafner is an entirely daring and instinctive action, part of an adventurous day out rather than any strategy or even real purpose beyond its inherent amusement and diversion. We might consider elements of his behaviour reckless and directionless, especially when he is — not unreasonably — portrayed as a moody teenager with an attitude problem, but in the musikdrama which bears his name, we need to embrace his fearless freedom to a considerable extent.

One of the *Ring*'s supreme dramatic ironies is that Siegfried's first heroic deed is the one that essentially signs his own death warrant. He doesn't know this, but we most certainly do, our enjoyment of Siegfried's sportive derring-do undermined by our knowledge that gaining the Ring is the very last thing anyone should do. Fafner's death is an extraordinary realization of music's subtle power to communicate the paradoxes and incongruities at the heart of Siegfried's valiant, intrepid mission.

The Siegfried motif is fleetingly heard on the orchestra's principal horn, not in its usual heroic form but ever so slightly diminished. Siegfried has now passed into the sinister world of the Ring — and into all the malevolent maturity this will mean for his life. His innocent motif, unbeknown to him, has been immediately corrupted into the form it will have in *Götterdämmerung* and which will also control the awful majesty of his funeral march, which precedes the final scene of the *Ring*.

Directors of *Siegfried*, and commentators, have sometimes seemed to excessively focus on the dragon, fetishizing either its importance or triviality, significance or irrelevance in the wider drama. It can certainly be argued to lie at the drama's structural and thematic core, as its killing is the first heroic deed of the protagonist and the turning point of the *Ring* towards the tetralogy's further (and final) tragic developments. Undoubtedly, as with the other fairy-tale or folkloric elements, there are a range of cultural, psychological, political and socio-economic meanings buried deep, or not so deep, inside the universal tropes of the dragon and its treasure. Fafner can easily be regarded, especially given the revolutionary origins of Wagner's own drama, as a capitalist hoarder, or more precisely a rentier, living off his income from property/securities. A miserable existence, of course, not only exploiting others but creating a passive, sluggish survival for the 'investor'. Fafner, in *Siegfried*, is feared, despite his passivity and idle nature, because he has power — the power of capital.

Productions which have removed the dragon permit Fafner to be more obviously a tabula rasa for the director (and then spectator) to complete with their own apprehensions, attitudes and expectations. Other productions have been even subtler. For Bayreuth in 1976, Patrice Chéreau's radical conservatism was especially mischievous when it came to Fafner, asserting artificiality by having a gigantic toy dragon pulled around on conspicuous wheels by very visible stagehands. All this took place in a defoliated copse rather than a romantic, iridescent forest. The Woodbird was no longer a free agency of nature but imprisoned in a wooden box: a caged, mechanical pet and product rather than a wild creature. For Chéreau, the trick to *Siegfried*, and the whole *Ring*, was to playfully, dangerously, assert more orthodox fairy-tale elements and then undermine them. We get a forest and a dragon and a talking bird, but not quite in the way we expect. It was a brilliant understanding of the way Wagner conceived of *Siegfried* in particular: an extension, then destabilization of fairy tale into the dark realities of modernity. (Here, too, we might take a moment to reflect on the sad fate of the first Fafner, at the Bayreuth premiere in 1876. The dragon prop was manufactured in England and shipped in pieces. The tail arrived first, then the body, and finally the head sans neck, which — according to some reports — ended up in Beirut.)

Siegfried's assassination of the dragon-giant Fafner cautiously links him to the folk tales of Jack the Giant Slayer. This Cornish legend, which also has parallels to Welsh, Breton and Norse mythology, features a farmer's son who initially slaughters a crop-eating giant before embarking on numerous colossus-killing exploits. Notably, in relation to *Siegfried*, Jack collects various trophies from his giant-slaying activities, including a cap of knowledge and cloak of invisibility, clearly identifiable with the *Ring*'s Tarnhelm, which will be put to such devastating uses in *Götterdämmerung*. Later in his adventures, Jack meets an old man who directs him to an enchanted castle where a duke's daughter is imprisoned. He rescues her and lives, in the time-worn phrase, happily ever after. Clearly, the Wanderer, Brünnhilde and rock surrounded by magic fire are identifiable here, with Wagner (consciously or otherwise) adjusting them for his own purposes, especially by extending the folk tropes to make his hero a more rebellious and insubordinate figure. Furthermore, in Wagner, Siegfried gets the girl but they do not, ultimately, live happily ever after (even if Wagner's brilliantly equivocal final music in *Götterdämmerung* does give them an ambiguous, contested glorification).

Siegfried's accidental tasting of Fafner's blood, which enables him to at last understand the Woodbird's mixture of warning (about Mime) and then exhortation (to Brünnhilde's rock), is not only a classic fairy-tale decoration in itself but a potent portent of potions to come. In *Götterdämmerung*, he will not only swear a blood-brotherhood with Hagen's credulous instrument Gunther but will be given a forgetfulness/love potion by Gunther's equally gullible sister, Gutrune. If we wish to mock such convenient devices, these narrative tools have more complex structural and representative qualities than mere plot development. They denote the psychological, political and mystical forces at work within the world. Their very obviosity and artificiality draw attention to the need to interpret their meaning and symbolic attributes.

It might have been theatrically expedient for Wagner to have Siegfried immediately dash off, per the Woodbird's instructions, to find Brünnhilde on her mountain. But Wagner was a more astute dramatist than this, and he inserts a remarkable double scene. First, a fizzing curiosity between Alberich and Mime as they bicker and wrangle over how they will gain the Ring from Siegfried. This brief interlude contains probably the most modern-sounding and extraordinary music in the whole *Ring*. It possesses jazz-like syncopations and a gloriously bizarre combination of woodwind instruments: clarinets and bassoons jumping and squawking as the brothers constantly try to outdo or put down one other. It is a wonderful comic prelude to the darker scene it morphs into: a final confrontation between foster father and foster son, where the former tries to poison the latter (another malevolent liquid) but is exposed by his own inexplicable self-promotion. Siegfried's stabbing of Mime is rarely pretty and can be fairly horrific, with some troubled wickedness from the orchestra, but few mourn the dwarf's passing, at least at this moment, as the journey of the hero reaches a new stage.

Siegfried is now free to take his treasures and follow his new friend, the Woodbird, to his culminating adventure in the final act (though with some surprises still in store). The day and Siegfried's maturity have slowly been progressing throughout the second act, and here, as it ends, it has a resplendence and a cheerfulness entirely absent from the score to this point, even during the optimistic fires of the Forging Song. As Siegfried dashes about collecting his things and the Woodbird circles, its soprano incarnation giving a new brightness to the vocal line, the text talks of love and a new kind of fire: that which ardently burns in passionate human hearts.

The closing forest scenes of the second act were where Wagner broke off the *Ring* to compose *Tristan* and *Meistersinger*. Although, as we have indicated, there is nothing sedate or humdrum about act 2 — in its dynamic, enthralling light and shade, it is a kind of Schubert on steroids — when he returned to the *Ring* in the late 1860s, he did so with an orchestral vehicle of unmatched power, complexity and dramatic force. The prelude to act 3 of *Siegfried* is one of Wagner's most exceptional creations: a dense, deluxe, embellished and intricate masterstroke of contrapuntal criss-crossing which will now dominate the rest of the *Ring*. It is not to devalue the earlier parts of either *Siegfried* or the *Ring* — we have clearly delineated their immense qualities — to acclaim the enormous quantum leap of this music. It is an injection of fierce, unstoppable amphetamines into an already highly intoxicated score.

Technically, it is a symphonic progression of several distinct and integrated motifs; in practice, a whirlwind of sonic possibility and aggressive orchestral power, motifs flung about as they display the Wanderer's disturbed, angry state of mind as he rides to meet with Erda and confront his fate. Indeed, this Riding motif, commandeered by Wotan from the Valkyries, governs much of the prelude and gives it not only its texture but its metrical vitality. To this pounding rhythm is added an accelerated form of Erda's brooding motif amalgamating with the theme of the Need of the Gods. Next enters the brass with the Spear motif, monstrously cultivated, and its assertion of Wotan's controlling power before two motifs (Erda's and that of the Twilight of the Gods) are first fused, then furiously amplified. Behind all this hurried, startling elaboration, the Wanderer's motif is massively expanded on the brass, before the whole sweeping sequence climaxes with the sinister motif of the Power of the Ring, slamming everything else into brutal submission before abating into the quieter descending chords of Sleep from which both Erda, and later Brünnhilde, will soon be awoken.

The prelude to act 3 is a blazing, merciless proclamation of musico-dramatic supremacy, the genius of its conception exceeded only by the astounding virtuosity of its execution. The skill of its motivic interweaving is a breathless statement of Wagner's powers, now reaching their greatest height. Its psychological, philosophical and theatrical landscapes are strikingly depicted with immense musical command, as we prepare to see, on stage at least, the chief of the gods for the last time. The orchestra is now functioning at a supreme level of contrapuntal-emotional-intellectual brilliance, conjuring images and ideas from across the preceding hours in a roaring, far-reaching network of musical sorcery. It is almost as if the motifs, simmering unobtrusively for over a decade as Wagner worked elsewhere, have boiled over, contemptibly and wrathfully overheating in a thunderstorm of fury.

As the vehemence begins to subside, the tone-colour shifts immediately from flashes and intensity to the pallid grey sparsity of the oblique, evasive Erda. The mood, in this final meeting, is tense and equivocal, full of rage and circumvention, but it also serves, like so many of Wagner's early scenes in his third acts, as a prologue to something else. Here, it delays and anticipates, with bravura suspense, not only the long-awaited encounter between Wotan and his hero Siegfried but Siegfried's own confrontation with destiny on Brünnhilde's rock.

Productions of *Siegfried* have often made much of this subtle scene between Erda and the Wanderer. Kasper Holten's 2006 *Ring* in Copenhagen was a fairly comic conception overall: he had the Wanderer visit Neidhöhle in act 2 as a tedious continental tourist, complete with camera, thermos and tweeds — but, as often in Holten's work, what was conceived in comedy was poignantly developed to tragedy. For the Erda–Wanderer scene, the earth goddess, once a grand duchess, was now bedridden, deteriorating in a nursing home, hooked up to tubes and propped up by pillows. It was a powerful and tragic elaboration on the comedy. So, too, was the strange and tender sight of Wotan and Erda sharing a bottle of vintage champagne. A wistful reminder of better days, it was a pensive comment on decay and insignificance, brilliantly exploiting not only the alcohol leitmotif which was present throughout Holten's *Ring* — the Wanderer had a hip flask of whisky to pep himself up from time to time — but also the interplay between calamity and humour so vital to *Siegfried*.

Wagner's *Siegfried* is a compelling geographical, emotional and developmental journey for its hero with a persuasive and relatively uncomplicated narrative arc (especially compared to *Götterdämmerung*'s byzantine manoeuvrings). This qualified simplicity, however, is consistently destabilized by musico-dramatic interruptions or postponements. These disturbances are principally the Wanderer's attempts to obviate or influence events, in a frantic mixture of the satiric and tragic. He can stall things, but he is powerless to prevent their occurrence. As he himself is aware, the Wanderer is by now a disillusioned, fatalistic figure, almost a caricature of his former self but never quite that: he preserves the essential grandeur he has always managed to maintain.

Thus, after the great Wanderer–Erda scene, narrative drive and narrative impediment, past and future, old world and new world convene as Wotan and his grandson's paths finally cross, a tempestuous conference which will lead to yet another astonishing first encounter, between Siegfried and Brünnhilde. The vast personal, cosmological and theatrical configurations of the *Ring* are aligning in the final act of the drama's penultimate day.

Wagner's peer in dramatic complexity, Mozart, does not discuss ageing to any significant degree in his operas; his premature death perhaps prevented this. We see old people in Mozart's stage works, but not the pain and processes of becoming older, declining and depreciating. Wagner, on the other hand, is distinguished by the way he repeatedly examines the tragic capture of time, especially in individuals like the Dutchman and Hans Sachs and through multiple figures in *Parsifal*: Kundry, Amfortas, Titurel, Gurnemanz, and Parsifal himself are all, in different ways, victims of time's dictatorial regime. Wotan was promoted to a central figure of the *Ring* when its four libretti were fashioned, his complex and evolving character then further developed in the music as Wagner himself aged over the quarter century of its composition. Wotan is seen growing old and, to some extent, wise over the course of three musikdramas — as well as being a powerfully present musical spectre in the fourth. He has seen himself apparently become more and more unimportant as the cycle progresses, his authority and hegemony slipping away.

Kasper Holten's Copenhagen production of the *Ring*, discussed above, moved through the twentieth century: *Rheingold* started in the roaring '20s but edged towards the catastrophes of the 1930s; then came the conservative 1950s of *Walküre*. The cycle ended with a brutal Balkan-like civil war in a 1990s *Götterdämmerung*. *Siegfried*, in this chronology, was part of the liberal revolutions of the 1960s, Siegfried a student radical in double denim with an anorak and a rucksack. As itinerant as his backpacking grandson, the Wanderer was clearly not enjoying his retirement travels, however. Siegfried drank bottled water; Wotan sat with never-ending beers and unending sarcasm. Wotan was a tired figure from the older generation, eventually giving way to the changing mores of the decade and the energy of its youth, breaking his own spear before Siegfried could shatter it with his sword. It was an unexpected and tragic self-realization of impotence and irrelevance.

In Wagner's *Siegfried*, Wotan has, as the Wanderer says, in repugnance and wrath hurled his ownership of the world to the Nibelungs' envy, his legacy left to the intrepid son of Siegmund and Sieglinde. As the scene shifts from Erda–Wanderer to Wanderer–Siegfried, the musical weight begins to lift, taking Wotan's burden, as Siegfried's presence is felt in the orchestra and he then approaches on stage. For the first time in *Siegfried*, perhaps even the whole *Ring*, Wotan's music begins to profess a certain relaxed rapture, a visionary relief at his own approaching end as he hands over to the unknowing Siegfried the destiny of the drama. Siegfried himself generates a degree of bitterness delectably mixed with paternal pride as Wotan encounters his impulsive, big-headed and gloriously innocent grandson. Questions and counter-questions are traded back and forth to the sound of impatient notes, these as agitated to get past this tiresome old man as Siegfried is.

It is the victorious reversal of Wotan's and Siegfried's respective weapons' potency which not only frees the way for our hero to climb the mountain to Brünnhilde but opens the floodgates to a grand symphonic sweep as he does so. Reforged, the sword which Wotan's spear shattered in *Die Walküre* now splinters that very jaded javelin, removing Wotan's authority as well as most, if not all, his divinity and eliminating the (false) barrier to Siegfried's destiny. False, because Wotan knows he cannot stop the hero, nor does he want to: the spear/sword clash is merely symbolic, energizing the final act's drama. (Holten's having the Wanderer break his own spear was thus in keeping with the god's will.)

The Wanderer, in Wagner's terse stage direction, 'suddenly disappears in complete darkness', and the music rushes into the orchestral interlude of Siegfried's ascent. Any of the doubt and darkness the score has hitherto held is swept away with bright and gleaming orchestral writing, fusing Siegfried's heroic motif with that of the magic fire. After this huge symphonic tone poem, where the hero breaches the vast wall of flames, the music suddenly begins to thin out as Siegfried reaches the summit, plus his fate and fortune.

At this point, the slender high string line Wagner asks for is a masterstroke of surprise and evocation. The light and space of the mountain heights is wonderfully conveyed to us, still and cool, as far from not only the scorching noises we have just heard on our way up the peak but also the dark, clandestine malevolence we've experienced over most of this vast musikdrama. Siegfried's arrival at the mountaintop is a kind of rebirth from the womb and tomb of the earlier acts, a revitalization which anticipates Brünnhilde's own imminent reawakening.

Wotan's daughter's regeneration, her own effective resurrection, is handled with supreme care and dramatic pacing, with more of the delays and theatrical deferrals in which Wagner, and *Siegfried*, have specialized. When it does occur, however, Brünnhilde's awakening is a beautifully judged and tender moment of bliss and brilliance. The orchestra three times, and with solemn, almost ceremonial deliberation, proclaim her. This has the grave dignity and spare ecstasy of a religious rite — ironic, and poignant, given her now non-divine status — and Brünnhilde meets the occasion by hailing the sun, light and day to which she has been reborn.

If the Woodbird's soprano voice gave some bright hope to the end of act 2, Brünnhilde's equivalent in act 3 outshines that light like a supernova does a candle. Cave and forest, their darkness and ambiguity, are sonically expunged from the musikdrama as Brünnhilde awakens on the mountain, a beacon. From here the score is largely variations on radiance as the new couple move towards their musical and dramatic self-identification and unity. Brünnhilde, understandably, has her doubts and fears. Her self-theologizing can even grate slightly if handled wrong, not least if Siegfried is made to seem overly impatient rather than joyfully expectant.

Brünnhilde's hesitations are, in fact, one further manifestation of Wagner's shrewd juxtaposition of romance and reality in *Siegfried*, his interrogation and manipulation of the fairy-tale structure and motifs. Brünnhilde is one of Wagner's strongest, most intelligent female roles in a whole squad of smart, brave women. It is credible, therefore, that she will have instinctive fears and hesitations about not only her new life, with its new status, but the new man who will, in essence, replace her father as the principal figure of her existence (just as Siegfried intuitively identifies Brünnhilde with his mother). This need not be messy or sniggering Freudian psychoanalysis but is rather the characteristic demonstration and collocation of fear and sexuality which myth, folk and fairy tale explore.

It is easy to see how Brünnhilde reminds us of the classic sleeping beauty from fairy and folk tales, but with crucial developments and changes to the various extant versions —

like the way her magic fire replaces Dornröschen's roses. The Brothers Grimm saw how Sleeping Beauty's story was traceable to an early Germanic story and was also seen in the Old Norse sagas and poems like the *Poetic Edda*, though they added key elements, like her awakening with a kiss. The clearest evolution Wagner contributes, however, is the agency he awards Brünnhilde. In earlier versions of the fairy tale, she is a naïve, malleable character: passive, bland and uninspiring. For Wagner, his great heroine needed to assert her own future. Unlike Fafner, who awakes to his own demise, or Erda, who awakes to nihilism and evasion, Brünnhilde awakes to her own strength and subversive action. In *Siegfried*, she continues the dissident activity of *Die Walküre* which led to her excommunication and imprisonment on the rock. One further crucial change Wagner makes is where the sleeping beauty tales end with the traditional 'lived happily ever after'. Such a simplistically contented final future is not to be the ultimate destiny of Brünnhilde and Siegfried — though, in *Siegfried* at least, they are to be temporarily assigned a happy ending.

As Brünnhilde's qualms are quelled, the drama moves to the exquisite, delightful tranquillity of an idyll. Her enchanting words 'Ewig war ich, ewig bin ich' — 'I always was, I always am' — confirm Brünnhilde's yearning bliss, Siegfried's ardent proclamations of love met with her own. Their love, in both the words and the music, takes on the uninhibited vehemence of *Tristan*'s second act, but without the chromatic hesitancy. The drama is now in free fall towards its beaming C major conclusion of 'luminous love' and 'laughing death' as the orchestra barely manages to keep up with the lovers, and the work ends in a final burst of dazzling, drunken happiness.

Siegfried urges us to play along with its fairy and folk tale elements, to revel in the adventures and exploits of the hero. Wagner wants us to believe in his protagonist so that Siegfried, and then Brünnhilde, and then the musikdrama, can first interrogate and then subvert their conventional casing. The exterior paraphernalia — forests, dragons, giants, sleeping beauties — are a peripheral and outward mask for the inner action of the opera, the complex and intricate musikdrama. Not only is the hero of *Siegfried* a more multifaceted, sensitive and probing figure than his folkloric equivalents but his bride is infinitely more advanced and revolutionary than the passive counterparts found in fairy tales. For all his depth, however, Siegfried remains both less intelligent and less human than Brünnhilde. His declarations of love when he meets Brünnhilde are no doubt honest, but we know they are also vigorous fearlessness, an enamoured young man fixating on the first woman he has ever met.

Brünnhilde, on the other hand, is highly conscious of the gift of humanity she has been given — hence not only her theologizing on first waking but the attendant hesitation with her would-be suitor. Her initial indecision is an indicator of her love and humanity, not a mark of its doubt. Like Elsa in *Lohengrin*, Brünnhilde is a modern and radical hero who wants more certainty in the surety of her love. Because of this delaying step, when she comes to acknowledge and declare it, her love is both stronger and more real than Siegfried's. Ultimately, this will prove fatal, since, in *Götterdämmerung*, Brünnhilde will not give up Siegfried's token of love — the Ring itself — because of everything it represents to her.

Siegfried's true hero is not Siegfried but Brünnhilde. Brünnhilde, like Elsa, is not prepared to simply accept the kiss of the prince and live happily ever after. That is only possible in fairy tales, and *Siegfried* — and the *Ring* (and *Lohengrin*) — is not a fairy tale but a progressive musikdrama, alive to the more pressing and dangerous realities of human existence, as well as the treacherously passive toleration of the past which needs to change. Productions which fetishize the fairy-tale components, making *Siegfried* a picture postcard of mawkish Disneyfication, miss the revolutionary nature of the drama. Yet, at the other end, directors who completely eliminate the fairy tale deny the work the brilliant coup of sabotage from within. Wagner's dazzling trick in *Siegfried* is to give his drama the appearance of a fairy tale so that he can broaden, destabilize and then overthrow the genre, and everything it represents, from the inside. The subversive *Siegfried* is a musikdrama Trojan horse.

Chapter Eight

The Illusion of Time:
Götterdämmerung

G*ötterdämmerung* is a sumptuous and seductive experience, a black hole of beauty, dragging you down into its dark and mighty depths. It warps space and time, its gravity denying light liberty, its energy creating miracles and mirages, wonders and confusions. So much matter in one place. It exposes naïveté and cruelty as it interacts with other phenomena, distorting and projecting past, present and future. Cosmic, elastic and local, it plays on our fears and beliefs, perverting our assumptions — of opera, of drama, of musical possibility. It asks us to accept contradiction, inviting infamy and awe, before disclosing the malleable truth of its own paradoxes.

Götterdämmerung is a remarkable achievement. To return to musico-dramatic material he had begun over twenty years earlier was an immense, daunting and invigorating challenge even for Wagner. A work begun amid the fires of relative youth and political passions of revolution, it now stood apart, remote, alone in size and scope, but surrounded by the pressure for completion. Wagner tried out various endings — optimistic, pessimistic, 'Feuerbachian', 'Schopenhauerian' — eventually settling on an enigmatic one which seems the only fitting conclusion for the *Ring*.

Götterdämmerung is an anthology of moments twisted, bound, converted, integrated and magnified into eternity. Vibrant, intimate, moody and majestic, it steps forward by looking back, to itself and to other competing histories, filling the chasm of time with mystery, annihilation and endurance. It attests that existence is a cycle and a sequence, beginning and ending in fluctuations of contested meanings which crumble preconceptions and bid us generate anew, expanding our expectations into infinite horizons.

The final work is of the *Ring* is not, as many have claimed, an aesthetic regression, a return to the orthodoxies and operatic conventions Wagner had written so stylishly against in *Oper und Drama* and then put into practice in *Das Rheingold*, *Die Walküre* and *Siegfried*. Nor is it a regression of politics, an equivocation that denies revolution meaning or possibility. What Wagner is doing in *Götterdämmerung* is embracing the future through a more complex hybridization and acceptance of the past — both internally and externally.

By destabilizing the political allegory of the *Ring*, apparently undermining the simplicity and dignity of the three earlier works, Wagner was not lapsing into political conservatism but espousing a broader comprehension of time, art and metaphysics. By using older forms — ensembles, love duets and vengeance trios — the Wagner of *Götterdämmerung* was not tumbling into the modes and disappointments of conventional opera. He was showing how the musikdrama was now powerful and flexible enough a medium to not only adopt older forms but hijack them for its own purposes to unmask corruption and lay bare the lethargies of musical, dramatic and intellectual prejudice. Work on *Tristan*, and then *Meistersinger* and the last act of *Siegfried*, had shown Wagner that his new art had not only the potential but the duty to seize and reintegrate the past, transforming how we perceive tradition and its future application.

Such is Wagner's persuasive skill in amalgamating and repurposing older customs and principles into the 'artwork of the future' that they tend to go unnoticed, woven impeccably into *Götterdämmerung*'s fabric, until they are pointed out — and then they never go away, constantly seeming to stand out. But, again, this is to miss the point of Wagner's aims and achievement. He was trying not to hide but to expose the past, to show how not only musical but political history was fraudulent, its time finished. In *Götterdämmerung*'s prologue, the love duet between Siegfried and Brünnhilde (a continuation of *Siegfried*'s finale) is a wilfully optimistic and consciously antiquated vision of stage coupledom, prophesying the lovers' own doom. The vengeance trio which ends the first act is a deliberate and unholy alliance of corruption, delusion and deception, expressly designed to evoke operatic styles, and judicial processes, of a bygone age. The ensemble singing of the summoned vassals in act 2 is a calculatingly archaic misdirection, both internally by Hagen to his community and externally by Wagner to his audience.

It is not simply that Wagner was faced with the prospect of writing music to a libretto written quarter of a century earlier, before the world-shattering innovations of *Tristan und Isolde*. *Götterdämmerung* presented an opportunity to cultivate the principles and possibilities of the musikdrama, extending them even further, even into territory that might, to some, appear regressive.

The musico-dramatic structures and methods of the *Ring* — leitmotifs, infinite melody and so on — meant that the material was already, to an extent, preordained. Wagner could then develop and, to an astonishing degree, expand this material through an extremely sophisticated and supple musico-dramatic technique. The leitmotif system sanctioned — indeed, encouraged — Wagner to usurp and manipulate older opera forms by being itself an appropriation and exploitation of the past. This wasn't what he had planned, but Wagner was the ultimate opportunist, infinitely resourceful. He could not change the libretto he had, but he could make sure that he controlled it rather than allowing it to restrain him or retrogress the *Ring*.

Götterdämmerung's libretto, née *Siegfrieds Tod*, before its marriage to the other parts of the *Ring*, was the first of the four to be written, and before the streamlining, revolutionary principles of *Opera und Drama*. It *was* relatively old-fashioned, employing more outdated forms, but Wagner knew this was not necessarily an obstacle but an opportunity. And it was an opportunity — for immense musico-dramatic, and potentially socio-political, upheaval — made possible, in part, through the network and practice of leitmotifs.

Leitmotifs are not, contra the convenient caricature, mere musical calling cards, announcing the arrival of this character and so forth. They have an immensely complex and psychologically powerful associative integrity. They can beckon the past, make it welcome or unwanted. They can muster and manipulate the present through evoking the past or vice versa, making the past change the present or the present change the past — and allowing both to change the future. The four operas of the *Ring* thus anticipate the *Four Quartets* of T. S. Eliot in their complex comprehension and evocation of time.

Wagner had vast numbers of musico-dramatic threads in reserve and within easy reach, all thick with three long evenings' worth of enormous complementary emotional and intellectual meanings. In *Götterdämmerung*, he could spin those threads into a dense fabric of musical, dramatic, political and philosophical possibility. Not only did Wagner weave and interweave these threads with a contrapuntal dexterity to rival the finest Baroque masters, but the individual threads themselves were extended and engineered with mesmerizing proficiency. This was a truly symphonic utilization of material, constructing a vast edifice of thematic exposition, development and recapitulation, twisting and manoeuvring motifs in musically fascinating ways which not only enhanced but *created* the drama itself. In *Götterdämmerung*, the corrosion and deterioration of the musical material both mirrors and generates the corruption taking place on stage.

There is an intricacy to the counterpoint and an agility to the lyrical recklessness which make *Götterdämmerung*, even by the high standards of the *Ring* so far, a landmark and an almost unrepeatable performance. Mere chords or collections of notes are put through never-ending and uninterrupted variations and alterations, as they have been throughout the *Ring*, but now with a profusion and deftness unlike anything yet encountered. Motifs work together, joining forces to make spiteful or sympathetic arguments, showing how ideas or characters or events are interrelated or ironically linked through their mixture of connectivity and distinctiveness. Motifs can be isolated and held apart to make similar points about relative location and associative potential. Often, both the integration and separation are simultaneous, in the same passage or even the same bar.

The leitmotifs morph and evolve in dazzling, quixotic ways, changes often just flashing before our ears, never to be seen or heard again, similar to the technique Sibelius would employ in his huge symphonic score for *The Tempest*. They can emerge, conjoin and assimilate within moments, either becoming a new and influential force to the musico-dramatic course or almost immediately dispersing into obscurity. Accommodation and evaporation; building, breaking and rebuilding — these musical processes are a constant feature of the *Ring* in general and *Götterdämmerung* in particular. But whether coming or going, lingering like a stain or existing as only a transitory flicker of hope, guilt or shame, the restless leitmotifs, and their infinite interactions, have intense psychological-dramatic implications. They are never mutating for their own sake but only for the larger necessities of the overall musikdrama.

The experience of writing the first three parts of the *Ring*, as well as *Tristan* and *Meistersinger*, had led Wagner to perpetually develop (rather than simply change) the principles of *Oper und Drama*. It would be odd if such complex and innovative works as these did not cause him to develop, especially into hitherto unthinkable areas. Such are the processes, dynamics, rewards and surprises of creativity. Yet many seem still to want to judge or grade Wagner (whether up or down is often unclear) based on theoretical writings which, as in other disciplines, become swiftly out of date.

Oper und Drama (1851) had argued for the meticulous equilibrium of the arts. Music, drama, poetry, acting, dance, lighting and painting, Wagner had claimed, were all to work together, in productive harmony and majestic confederacy. It is not exactly clear either what the precise terms of unity were, given the constantly shifting nature of the works he created, which changed even — and especially — internally. His was a noble initiative, but one which could never be maintained in reality, as Wagner knew. The Gesamtkunstwerk was always an idea, a motivating creed, rather than something to be fixed or slavishly adhered to.

For Beethoven's centenary in 1870, just as he begun work on *Götterdämmerung*, Wagner had written a new theoretical essay, 'Beethoven', which proclaimed in prose — as *Tristan* had in drama — the supremacy of music as the principal vehicle of emotional-intellectual manifestation in the arts. Words, not to mention the other components of the extremely collaborative medium of opera, were now subsidiary to music. Music, indeed, was the source of drama. It is easy to see why Wagner's stage works have confused or infuriated categorization. Wagner embodied a wonderful, head-scratching incongruity: he created both the most purely symphonic/orchestral operas ever written and the ones where words, gesture, acting, lighting, and so forth matter most as well.

It is this magnificent creative paradox which helps explain the dexterity and audacity of *Götterdämmerung*. There is a confidence and abandon derived not from discarding musikdrama's values but from embracing them and their logical extension. Artistic dogmas and aesthetic principles are important in fermenting ideas, practices, boundaries. But, unlike their theological equivalents, they must have the potential to be superseded or they will cease to be truly creative.

The musikdrama, birthed and aged in Wagner's hands, had reached a level of maturity and erudition which not only encouraged but required the assertion of music — symphonic music — as the dominant force of expression and creativity. To this could be added music in vocal terms: ensemble singing, whether in pairs, trios or larger groups, could be a vital part of musikdrama's exciting new directions. Thus *Götterdämmerung* not only incorporates ostensibly older vocal forms (in reality, commandeering them for its own productive purposes) but advances them as forcefully as it does the orchestral developments below, in the pit. In *Götterdämmerung*, vocal writing, in whatever form, has a capacity and acuity, a power of expression, to match the swathes of instrumental ingenuity beneath it.

That this meant Wagner could embrace an earlier libretto is both happy coincidence and — more emphatically — the absolute result of Wagner's creative genius and artistic processes. He could not have known at the beginning of the *Ring* project where invention would take him twenty-five years hence. Creation and imagination, he knew better than anyone, have their own rulebooks. But when the time came, he was able to apply and assimilate evolving principles with his developing capabilities.

Those capacities are most clearly expressed in the astonishing symphonic drama Wagner created in *Götterdämmerung*, where the orchestra is in complete control of the drama: monitoring it, manipulating it, spawning it, with magnificently malignant resourcefulness. Baleful, malevolent motifs eat their way into the score like corrosive symphonic battery acid, scarring all in their path. But this energy is creative as well as destructive. The volcanic lava of *Götterdämmerung* consumes all before it, but the very stuff of obliteration — motifs — is also the material for new landscapes, where fresh seeds will be planted to germinate later on, in anticipation of the future, with all its ambiguity and uncertainty.

The vast orchestral score to *Götterdämmerung* has the sly sophistication and regenerative potential to match the various characters of its own plot. The possibilities of the extraordinarily flexible and subtle leitmotif process Wagner developed mean that, within the vast arc of this cosmic drama, he could create an imposing symphonic network. *Götterdämmerung* is a far-reaching, infinitely complex and exceptionally elusive orchestral labyrinth which nonetheless safely guides us, via the golden thread of the leitmotif, from entrance to exit, mountain to Rhine, dawn to dusk.

∿

Götterdämmerung asserts its corruption from its first sound. A wind chord of ominous authority and threat is heard. It is strangely familiar, curiously recognizable. But something is odd, misplaced. It is the bright major sound of Brünnhilde's awakening in *Siegfried*, but turned flat and hostile in the minor. It wears a cloaked tonality, bearing the burden of memory. The light and emancipation of *Siegfried* has wearied, sunk to the darkness and heavy constraint of *Götterdämmerung*.

The powerful E flat minor chord which opens *Götterdämmerung* reconditions reality. It is a mystical harbinger of the catastrophe to come; it is the sound of uncertainty, tragedy. It is the feeling of fate's cold hand. It is night given voice and an opaque luminosity to match the hazy stage action as the three Norns spin their rope of destiny, groping nearer and nearer to the world's end. Their scene is one of routine arachnid gloom and spindly metaphysics, infested with leitmotifs frail but still potent in their implementation, as this dubious trinity of illusory creatures tells the story of the beginning and end of the world. The Norns frame in molecular and cosmic despair all that is to come and all that went before.

One each stands for the past, present and future, and they speak in turn but out of sequence, disrupting our steady understanding of time. Like their mother, Erda, they are far-sighted but part of the realm of night, with an intuitive exploratory wisdom and instinctual prescience. We recall the events of the *Ring*, and some before it, as they sing and loop around the inscrutabilities of time. The dawn is infinitely postponed as they dream and weave, mixing our memories into the collective conscience and consciousness of the fragile globe. They probe and prod, spinning the shared history and future of the world, until their rope breaks and their prognosticating remembrance is at an end, sanctioning the chaotic sphere of humanity to replace it.

The coordinated reminiscence and snapping of the rope binds the Norns together on stage, connecting and attaching past, present and future as the music begins to shift towards the treacherous light of a new day. Downcast and dwindling cellos give way to horn salutes and other elaborations as the dun and grey colours begin to wane and the full orchestra grows. Dawn breaks into a new atmosphere of fresh, bright air as Siegfried and Brünnhilde wake to the morning of their new life together. They sing a form of duet, but their voices only overlap at the end: a crucial indicator of the new musikdrama methods Wagner develops in *Götterdämmerung*. For the first part of their scene, Brünnhilde and Siegfried sing expositions of the future: distinctive vocal lines, independently heard. By the end of the scene, however, their voices have become entwined, ensnared in the trappings of operatic past: the love duet. This old-fashioned, mawkish and habitually garrulous form is an omen of the misfortune that is to now accompany Siegfried and Brünnhilde's love. He, sent off to heroic deeds, will be duped, as will she, by the destructive powers seeking to acquire the Ring (now on Brünnhilde's finger as Siegfried's token of love).

But before the corruption, they are permitted one last (though not final) celebration of their love. As Siegfried sails away, the musikdrama develops into a festive and energetically polyphonic interlude in which a torrent of motifs relating to the hero's adventures flood and submerge the score. This is Siegfried's Rhine Journey, a symphonic tone poem of great power and adventure: it is a joyride of vim and vitality towards destruction and despair which finds a tragic parallel in Siegfried's Funeral March of the third act (just as the three wise and wizened Norns trace their smooth, oblivious sisters in the three Rhinemaidens).

The Rhine motif enters with majestic, nostalgic power, and we are reminded of where the cycle began all those days ago, the music developing swiftly, assuredly and inexorably towards the unsettling dissonance of the Gibichung court: Hagen, Gunther and Gutrune. The one is an alarmingly self-confident villain, the other two gullible utensils for Hagen/Alberich. Gunther and Gutrune are weak, desperate for prestige and recognition — but love, too, for they are deeper figures than they first might seem. They are both lonely and are two of the most 'normal' characters in the *Ring*, sharing many of our own fears and foibles: status anxiety, petty conduct, sexual jealousy and personal insecurity. Gunther, though many would find it hard to believe, is a form of hero, and his musical theme is related to the motif of heroic humanity which more obviously furnishes Siegmund, Siegfried and Brünnhilde. There is both irony and pathos in Gunther's motif, his petitions to bravery and chivalry almost satirically declared in the spineless court he thinks he rules. But those claims are there, they are real (however pathetic), and great productions do not dismiss Gunther and Gutrune as insignificant chattel for plot.

Kasper Holten's 2006 *Ring* in Copenhagen travelled through the twentieth century, reaching a cruel end in a civil war of the 1990s, recalling the Balkan conflicts. This was a brutal world less typified by the fertile humour that had pervaded Holten's *Ring* to this point. Hagen was a Goebbels lookalike, a chilling, gaunt and smirking creature, doing press-ups and weights in his T-shirt before re-donning his sinister, bland military attire. His exercise seemed an act not just of vanity but of lucidity, a regime to keep him alert: a callous and purposeful callisthenics. With him, lounging on vulgar, ostentatious sofas, the ghastly nouveau-riche duo of Gunther and Gutrune. Bored puppet leaders, Gutrune was all hair, bangles and bracelets, flipping through fashion magazines, while her brother wore a pencil moustache, a ludicrous white suit and the air of a cheap swindler. The brash stench of aftershave and perfume hung about them. But it gave them a menacing and unpredictable quality too. Their boorishness had the erratic edge of the recently rich criminal classes, plagued by the inner doubt that their power or wealth might be instantly revoked. This was why, in the atmosphere of ferocious civil war Holten fostered, they needed more power, and Hagen's help, to cement their position. As the performance wore on, Gutrune's increasing isolation, in particular, made her a sad and fraught figure, another victim of the Ring's ceaseless generation of greed and loneliness.

The music of the Gibichung court, in the first act of *Götterdämmerung*, has a disturbing playfulness. It is spiteful, glimmering, ill-disciplined, fluctuating between obedience and disobedience, ruthless order and chaotic confusion. It is Hagen manipulating his half-siblings and engineering the destiny his father, Alberich, has ordained for him from before his birth. Siegfried's arrival and the development of the plot — in which Siegfried is persuaded, under the influence of a potion, to love Gutrune and forget Brünnhilde, and which culminates in the oath of blood-brotherhood between Gunther and Siegfried — is an intricate piece of theatre, brilliantly contrived by Hagen's machinations and the credulity of everyone concerned.

We might, in the twenty-first century, laugh at notions of magic potions and magic helmets — the two strategic devices used to dupe Siegfried and Brünnhilde. But we would do well to remember that such tools persist in our own age. Internet phishing and other forms of identity fraud and theft prey on personal and sexual insecurity. Modern magic potions, in the form of the date-rape drug Rohypnol, cause severe amnesia akin to Siegfried's concerning Brünnhilde, and many a young man has wandered astray from his love at home simply by ingesting too much alcohol when away on holiday. (Kasper Holten's Gunther managed to make Siegfried forget Brünnhilde by plying him with whisky and cigarettes.)

Even if we accept these contrivances, many audiences have still found the narrative plotting of *Götterdämmerung* at best old-fashioned and at worst irksomely byzantine. However, we need to keep in mind that its complex plot is a further aspect of its intentionally retrograde anachronism. Just as with the profusion of lords, double-crossings and convoluted archaic devices Shakespeare utilizes in the *Henry VI* plays, this complexity is deliberate. Our bewilderment is part of the effect, part of the disorientation and turmoil both Shakespeare and Wagner want to create. If we are confused, we are meant to be, for *Götterdämmerung* is aiming at misunderstanding and misapprehension, just as Hagen is. In other words, the *Ring* is complex, but occasional failures in comprehension are sometimes neither Wagner's nor our own. They are the torn and frayed fabric of the drama.

As Siegfried and Gunther go off to claim Brünnhilde, the ominous interlude of Hagen's Watch manifests itself. The villain broods to the gloomy grandeur of vast, immoral strings spun from the blackest thread. The scene gradually begins to shift back to Brünnhilde, alone on her rock, where we left her in the prologue. To the sound of sparse, unadorned woodwind, we uneasily rejoin her. Treachery is on its way. But, in another masterly stroke of dramatic postponement, like those which characterized *Siegfried*, we experience first an interpolation of immense tenderness and desolate beauty: the visit of Brünnhilde's sister Waltraute. Thunder rumbles and fragments of the Valkyrie motif enter the music as Wagner condenses the texture of the score, building it up and up with increasingly dynamic motivic material.

Waltraute, a messenger from their father, Wotan, begs Brünnhilde to return the Ring to the Rhine. Brünnhilde refuses: the depth of her feeling for Siegfried means she will not relinquish his token of love. She is not interested in the Ring's power, only in its elevated status. From Waltraute, we learn of Wotan's continuing predicament: he remains caught in dread and terror, anticipating the end of the gods. Unseen until he (sometimes) appears amid the Valhalla inferno at the drama's end, the consequences of his actions dominate the music of *Götterdämmerung*. All power and agency taken from him, he would be a pitiful figure had his selfishness and arrogance not largely created the conditions which necessitate the world's destruction.

The score here is even more powerfully constructed by motifs associated with Wotan, woven and interwoven to develop a looming portrait of a god in pain. Much of the raw material is from *Rheingold*, but the texture has been thickened with suffering: layers and layers of history and woe from across the *Ring*'s events are compressed and congealed in alarming ways, motifs sounding together as the full impact of his actions hits home.

And all this is the more formidable by being narrated to us, held back in diegetic dignity, the space and detachment paradoxically making it even more present, more real to us. Motifs from the earlier works are not just reheard, which would give them a particular wistfulness at this juncture, but are expressed in new configurations and with instrumental choices yet unheard, lending a subtle uncertainty to these undying sounds, together with their obstinate rebirth. Wagner's use of perspectives and distancing here achieves a masterly effect: his two daughters converse; below them, the orchestra furiously depicts his despair amid the disintegrating futility of Valhalla. As with the Norns scene, Wotan's ruined world is shown only as an appalling reflection, a powerful, tragic echo of his former self.

Leaving in anguish, Waltraute rides back to Wotan, abandoning Brünnhilde to her own fate, which is swiftly enacted. Siegfried, disguised as Gunther, enters and steals his token of love before committing violations of a savagely indeterminate variety. The scene has a horrendous rapidity, an atrocious inevitability to it, as vicious a scene as occurs in the endlessly violent world of the *Ring*.

Act 2 of *Götterdämmerung* is short by Wagner's standards: only an hour. But it is a tightly packed hour of intrigue and conspiracy. It is dense, compressed and inscrutable, a spinning neutron star at the centre of the drama, formed from the dark and collapsing gravitational forces of the Ring, creating pockets of shifting density and clouds of ethical disarray.

It opens with a prelude of warped guilt and envy and proceeds to a scene of pronounced malice and obscurity. Alberich appears to his son Hagen as if in a dream. His father's music and behaviour are all animated agitation, but Hagen sits stationary throughout and his music is correspondingly still, with a disturbing tranquillity. Hagen's amoral strength and quiet, toxic agency are nowhere more powerfully shown than in this tense and spine-chilling scene. It ends with Alberich gradually slipping from view, his music dissolving into the texture of the score, consumed by the gloomy, heavy sounds of the lower strings and bass clarinet, the latter instrument ever the sound adjacent to doom.

In a further example of *Götterdämmerung*'s scheming and Shakespearean use of doubling, the sinister scene between Alberich and Hagen disperses into the growing light of another dawn. Like the Siegfried Rhine Journey/Funeral March and Norn/Rhinemaiden dichotomies, *Götterdämmerung*'s second dawn is quite unlike its first. The one which introduced the Siegfried/Brünnhilde scene in the prologue had a paradisiac wonder to it. It was soft, with a gently rising brightness:

a golden paean of thanksgiving. Here, in act 2, Hagen's dawn is taut, intransigent: the lugubrious march of inescapable and predestined time.

The day now appearing unmistakably belongs to Hagen, just as so much of the score does, for although Wotan is a constant presence, it is Alberich's boy who cuts through the music, defiling it with his malignant work. Conceived intentionally to govern hate and manufacture animosity, he is a frightening and magnificent dark bass, the centre of attention and attraction, especially here in the second act. Lacking morality, he is filled by a liquid intelligence to match Iago's, an audacity to mirror that of Claudius, and a ruthlessness of which Macbeth himself would be proud. His eventual demise, submerged beneath the waters of the Rhine, is fitting: it is melodramatic and unlike this low-key meandering serpent's usual presence. That Hagen is accorded the final words of the *Ring* (the caustically equivocal 'Keep away from the Ring!') would doubtless have given rise to a wry smile from this supreme and soulless villain.

As Hagen's day dawns, he sets to work, first making sure his hoodwinking is progressing smoothly and then summoning the populace — for *Götterdämmerung* is an essentially urban environment for its first two acts, as befits the corruption which occurs there, perforated by shifts to desolate pastoral scenes. As Hagen rouses the vassals of his court, we become aware of the growing presence of massed voices for the first time in the *Ring*. It is deliberately disorientating, a scene of coarse and incongruous brilliance, as Hagen dupes his men into thinking they are under attack (which, of course, they are, since Hagen cares not a jot for them). The fear of imminent incursion diffuses into the stirring C major songs of drinking and merriment — but, engineered by Iago-Hagen, it has all the threatening musical menace of its equivalent scene in act 2 of *Othello*.

It is the lively prelude to Hagen's gleefully unfolding plot. The two pairs of now asymmetric lovers arrive: Gunther and Brünnhilde, Siegfried and Gutrune. If there is a certain visual comedy to the sight of these lopsided couples, it is of the bleakest kind. Again, as in *Othello*, this act of *Götterdämmerung* proceeds in the vein of a dangerous domestic farce, the tension and darkness maintained through Wagner's sadistically persuasive music as it is in Shakespeare through his pugnaciously compelling language.

Eventually, with the crowds gone, Hagen maintains his retrogressive malevolence by organizing a splendidly old-fashioned vengeance trio, a form from a departed era given new meaning and rancour through Wagner's complex, highly involved scoring. Its vocal doublings and textual repetitions, as well as its theatrical, declamatory tone, are less subtle than we expect in Wagner. Accordingly, it stands out for its brilliantly contrived conspiratorial spite, the magnificent and heroic Brünnhilde helplessly reduced to a jealous spouse — just as Othello is, in the third act of his play, the stranded victim of Iago's venom.

❧

Wagner's third acts never fail to deliver, and the one which ends the *Ring* is an outstanding fusion of musico-dramatic time and space. A journey into despair, glory, hope and ambiguity, it opens with the distinctive sound of hunting horns, heralding the day's prey — Siegfried — then harsh chords and agitated harmonics before we slide down into the motif and realm of the Rhine. We are back where we began. The Rhinemaidens continue to lament the loss of their gold, and our sympathies grow with their woeful cries, which have been given a further pensive sonic sadness on their reappearance. Long and dreadful time has passed since we last saw them, and the musical air swirls and befuddles with pain, despondency and disappointment.

Siegfried enters, lost from the hunting party. The Rhinemaidens play in the water, teasing Siegfried and pleading for the return of their gold. He refuses to relinquish the Ring, which he still proudly wears on his finger. They depart, warning him (with the mixture of gaiety, melancholy and mockery that only the Rhinemaidens can produce) that his fate is sealed: the blind and obstinate hero is doomed. Hagen and the rest of the party appear, and Siegfried reunites with them. He tells them stories from his life and adventures, and, on cue, the score fills with reflective, celebratory musical remembrances from his escapades in *Siegfried*, before Hagen gives him another potion to restore his memory of Brünnhilde.

The very artificiality of this device — both internally and externally to *Götterdämmerung* — makes it all the more moving, as it instantly inundates the score with Siegfried's glorious memories of his beloved and her awakening. The leitmotif system is operating at its most powerful and poignant here, making the past deeply present, but stage and score tell us that Siegfried's end is fast approaching. His ecstatic recollections, and their bright C major chords, are undercut by the baleful presence of Hagen. Gunther is increasingly twitchy and appalled by Siegfried's rapturous, delighted talk of Gunther's wife. Two ravens fly out, Siegfried turns to watch them, and Hagen seizes his moment, stabbing Siegfried in the back, ostensibly to defend Gunther's honour. 'Meineid rächt' ich!' — 'I have avenged treason!', he claims and trudges off into the gathering dusk. His day is nearing its completion.

Siegfried, collapsed, calls out for Brünnhilde in an agonizing appeal to his holy bride before sinking only into the arms of death. The orchestra, which has until now been working at the furious pace only *Götterdämmerung* can offer, comes to a halt and then launches one of Wagner's most awe-inspiring and atrociously magnificent symphonic passages: Siegfried's Funeral March. (Contrary to popular belief, it was not played after the composer's own death in Venice as they transferred his coffin from the Palazzo Vendramin to the railway station to transport his body back to Bayreuth. Cosima had instructed there be no funerary music at all, and Wagner's gondola proceeded along the Grand Canal in solemn silence, aside from the occasional tolling bell.)

The Funeral March begins with the muffled stroke of a drum and a musical ornamentation of death before beginning a tragic and triumphant celebration of Siegfried's life, a dark and sombre equivalent to his merry reminiscences of only a short time before. It is, at first, an angry and violent howl of pain, the tragedy of what might have been, as this ideal and idealized hero is borne in death. We hear the strange music associated with his tragic parents, Siegmund and Sieglinde, before the music begins to move towards an aristocratic dignity and grandeur, to an unexpected but not hollow victory and an understanding that not everything might be lost in Siegfried's demise. Although Siegfried's potential — as a revolutionary hero — is now only a memory, like the memory of his love for Brünnhilde, his spirit and message can live on. Siegfried's Funeral March not only becomes a lasting memorial to this flawed and fallen hero but more vitally surges forward in time to anticipate the future of other heroes and other revolutions (just as the funeral march in Beethoven's Eroica Symphony is the second, not final, movement). The dazzling mixture of despair, glory, hope and ambiguity which will end the work has begun.

The cortège of this hero occurs, according to Wagner's stage directions, in mounting darkness, before, at the passage's climax, the moon breaks through the clouds, throwing a strange bright light on the procession as it reaches the crest of a hill. To the sound of liquefying flutes and dissolving strings, we appear back at the Gibichung court, with the moonlight reflected in the Rhine and Gutrune's sad and lonely lament for her absent husband, who she thinks is still out happy and hunting.

Hagen enters to announce their return with the spoils of the hunt, cruelly declaring to Gutrune that the mighty hero is coming home. We feel a genuine horror, straight out of Greek tragedy, at Gutrune's agony and the despicable game the heartless Hagen has played. In the resulting confusion, as they fight for the Ring over Siegfried's body, Gunther is slain, and Gutrune crumples into misery. Hagen reaches for the Ring on Siegfried's dead finger, but the corpse's arm rises in hair-raising defiance, accompanied by noble, liberating motifs released by the orchestra. Brünnhilde returns to commandeer the huge tableau of her extended final oration as she prepares to self-immolate on her true husband's funeral pyre and thus end the *Ring* — to leap into the flames on her horse, returning the Ring, finally, to its rightful place among nature in the river Rhine.

Long tampered and fiddled with, essentially fluctuating between an optimistic 'Feuerbach' ending and a pessimistic 'Schopenhauer' one, the text as we now have it is an ideally complex combination of anger, exaltation, dejection, disappointment and triumphant uncertainty. Anything simpler would not befit the *Ring*. The final minutes of stage action in *Götterdämmerung* and the *Ring*, however, are easy to relate because not only do they have a melodramatic simplicity but it is not the action which matters. It is the music.

The ending to *Götterdämmerung* is probably the most histrionic Wagner becomes — the result, it is true, of the early(ish) libretto as well as the need for a grand culmination to the *Ring*. The cycle had to go out with a (dramatic) bang. But it also needed a montage through which to present a fast array of substantial and all-encompassing symphonic music, for the conclusion to *Götterdämmerung* weaves together motifs on an immense scale, even by its own high standards. It deploys motifs from across the vast, turbulent drama. Loge makes a welcome, fiery reappearance in the score, his pyromantic skill a useful ally for the final destruction. As the Ring is finally returned to the Rhine, its maidens return one final time to hold it aloft in graceful triumph, the sinuous woodwinds flowing with their joy and the strings below conferring the elegant, fluid and rippling waters of the great river. The brass merge in the gigantic and resplendent sound of Valhalla, the mighty castle whose mortgage caused so many problems, as it begins to burn in the distance.

Motifs for the Rhine and Rhinemaidens return, but they are overcome by an ascending, elevated motif on the flutes and violins: this is the motif of Redemption, finally given its proper airing in the drama. It soars above all else, rising and rising in jubilation tinged with poignancy. Valhalla and the Power of the Gods are then heard one final time before being consumed in Loge's conflagration. The motif of Siegfried declares his celebrated memory, twinned to the Twilight of the Gods motif, which is heard again for a last time before the score develops towards its final sequence of hope and sanctification.

The *Ring* ends with the exultant motif of Redemption. Its only outing prior to the final pages of *Götterdämmerung* was in act 3 of *Die Walküre*, when Sieglinde acclaimed the marvel of Siegfried's birth as Brünnhilde prophesied it. It now rises in blissful elation from the ashes of the symbol of earthly greed and stupidity: Valhalla. Its inherent beauty as a theme needs no association to make eyes water and hearts sing. But, attached as it is to sixteen hours — and twenty-six years — of raging, violent and profoundly moving musikdrama, it can only bring rapture, sadness and a feeling of deepest fulfilment.

The *Ring* ends as it began: with some gold in a river — where it should be, not adorning the digits of villains or heroes. The rule of the gods is over — or, at least, the rule of one type of humans, since the gods of the *Ring* were only ever representative of human personalities, systems and structures. Yet the twilight of the gods is also, given the ambiguity in the German title, the dawn of the gods, the optimistic birth of a new kind of species: a freer, fairer and more equal kind of humanity.

Götterdämmerung hauls together in mystery and magnificence the vast and disparate parts of the *Ring*, daring us to challenge its supremacy and conviction. Its deceptions and mirages are multifaceted, constant and immeasurable, hovering close and shrieking far away. But it also shows us the possibility of charity amid the hopelessness of human interaction and greed, never giving up in its search for courage and emancipation.

Götterdämmerung is a musikdrama governed by time and therefore by illusion, since, as modern physics tells us, time is an essentially human construct created in order to navigate existence. Collective moments are connected into the fabric of time (past, present, future) we experience. Similarly, *Götterdämmerung* is a collection of occurrences and dense musico-dramatic associations working together to achieve an immense and animated illusion.

Götterdämmerung is therefore not just ruled but structured by time, since the leitmotif is a tool of time. It is also an expression of time, showing the relationships between events, emotions, characters and objects as they have occurred or will occur. Leitmotifs connect and merge past, present and future into a compelling mixture of certainty and chaos. Everything springs from a single source but can morph and evolve anywhere in time — into creation or corrosion, compassion or callousness. Time and leitmotifs are therefore also closely connected to ethics, and *Götterdämmerung* invites us to rehearse and examine our understanding of moral agency in relation to time. How inevitable or blameworthy, we might ask, are Hagen's actions, since they are simply the deterioration of the natural good? Does he have free will, or is he fated to do ill? Given the interconnectedness of the *Ring*'s musico-dramatic material, it is difficult and uncertain.

Götterdämmerung makes us obsess about time. It shows us time as reassurance (the sun will rise tomorrow) as well as time as bewildering bafflement (the more we think about time, the more perplexing it becomes). Time in *Götterdämmerung* comforts and confuses; it implicates, convicts and acquits. It maintains directionless, limitless and anarchic time, where the future is both unstable and peculiarly certain, managed by malign or indifferent forces (Hagen's plotting or the apathetic cosmic chitchat of the Norns). In *Götterdämmerung*, time migrates in strange ways: memory wandering and then suddenly stumbling on the pain of the past, or drifting in dread anticipation, fearing what lies in store. And all this administered via the leitmotif.

Götterdämmerung spins under the strength of its own gravity, orbiting itself in a hyperactive, furious yearning to both separate itself from and remain attached to the rest of the *Ring*. Through this, its subtle moral force emerges and glows, insinuating future realms of being and connectivity: transcendent and timeless, material and momentary. Wagner merges ethics, aesthetics and metaphysics into a continuum rather than maintaining clear-cut categories. Similarly, the associations connecting music and drama are indivisible, establishing a bond as mysterious and inseparable as that between philosophy, morality and art.

Götterdämmerung helps and hinders us as we traverse the intimidating arenas of existence: the quandaries of ethics; the unfathomable obscurity of other beings; the inscrutabilities of time, history and metaphysics. Like them, *Götterdämmerung* is daunting and profoundly unnerving. It is perhaps the most multitudinous of Wagner's works and the one where his powers are most clearly on display. The effect is extraordinary and undoubted; its meaning is less obvious, perhaps impossible to reach. And here lies some of its most important and reassuring power. The whole point about great art is that there is nothing conclusive about it. We do not need certainty, transparency or complete intelligibility. The enigma is all.

The *Ring* is an equivocation, an evasion and an illusion. It is a celebration and condemnation of human existence. It is suffering and delight; it is politics and metaphysics, love and death. It is greed, guilt and shame, a trap and a release. It is custody and freedom, landscape and portrait, atomic centre and far-flung exploding star. The *Ring* is hope and despair, fantasy and reality, time and space; the *Ring* is a message and warning, a circle and a mirror. The *Ring* is, surely, Richard Wagner's supreme achievement.

PART THREE

THE LATER WORKS

Chapter Nine

The Empty Space:
Tristan und Isolde

Firry there are the shocks — and then there are the aftershocks. The tremors and confusions from the *Tristan* earthquake are still being felt today, and the tsunamis it unleashed, first on the musical and then wider aesthetic world, continue across the artistic ocean in apparently never-ending waves of energy, creation and destruction. Its impact was immense: on composers, poets, dramatists, novelists, screenwriters, sculptors, even architects. No creative sphere was left unaffected by its raucous arrival and enormous reverberations.

Although on the surface — *Tristan*'s agonizingly slender surface — it is a conventional love-and-obstacle story, nothing else in this work is mainstream. Its music, its drama, its violent metaphysics: all rise above and far beyond any superficial conformity to produce a profound and overwhelming contemplation of the nature of human existence and the persistent confrontation between the spiritual, intellectual and material worlds.

The first voice we hear in *Tristan und Isolde*, after the extraordinary orchestral prelude (to which we will return), is that of a despondent, lovelorn young sailor:

> Westward
> wanders the eye;
> eastward
> skims the ship.

It is a remarkable way to begin an opera — or any drama, for that matter. The lines are exquisite: simple, taut, intense. An incredible tension is established very modestly with the geographic antonyms, the dynamic verbs, the stark nouns: west, east, wanders, skims, eye, ship. Everything is simultaneously acute and elusive, heightened and mysterious, the more so since it is unaccompanied by the sensuous, tumultuous orchestra which has just given us the devastating prelude.

We are on a boat, travelling between Ireland and Cornwall, and as the lonesome mariner wonders about the Irish maid he has left behind — his 'wild, lovable girl' — the orchestra suddenly returns with extreme violence and the blunt words 'Who dares to mock me?'. It is Isolde, believing the young sailor to be talking about herself. It is the first of many misunderstandings in a drama that is full of delusion, misapprehension and despair but that concurrently contains a wealth of reality, empathy and delight — indeed, rapturous bliss like no other in music. And, in *Tristan*, music is above all, for whatever its poetico-dramatic strengths, this work's supremacy and matchless ability to convey and discuss complex philosophical arguments come from its astonishing musical technique and expressive power.

Notwithstanding its superbly theatrical opening, comparable with *Hamlet*'s 'Who's there?' or *Macbeth*'s 'When shall we three meet again, in thunder, lightning or in rain?', *Tristan und Isolde* is actually a static work, dramatically speaking. Consciously following the Greeks whom he admired and built on so much, Wagner, in *Tristan* (as he had when he first envisaged the *Ring*), begins his story near its climax and gradually throughout the drama unfurls the events which have directed us here. In many ways, this is dramatically very powerful, hindsight holding sway; yet it can also, in performance, seem inert, with little of the stage action which people generally expect. It is here that Wagner's music invigorates and stimulates the story, making it truly exist theatrically. It might seem obvious when stated, but *Tristan* is an opera in which the music is executing the work, and those unable or unwilling to follow and comprehend what the music is (ceaselessly) accomplishing will be bewildered and bored in a sea of tiresome backstory and repetition (as they are in the *Ring*).

All Wagner's stage works (and, to an extent, all opera) are dominated by — made subservient to — music, and particularly the orchestra. But in *Tristan* especially the drama *is* the music, the philosophy *is* the sonic splendour. It is the presentation of human beings and human being as they most fundamentally are, without barrier or veil: interior worlds of feeling and actuality conveyed at both their subtlest and most transparent. The drama inside the characters, and hence inside us, is going on within the music, within the visibly invisible art of arranged sounds, the competing components of melody, harmony, rhythm and timbre.

(Of all Wagner operas, *Tristan und Isolde* is the one that functions most powerfully in an audio-only medium, its persuasive sound alone allowing listeners to conjure up the stage and singers for themselves, lost in the rich imaginative world the composer invokes. Although it is absolutely compelling in the theatre, with some superb stagings and exquisite, fascinating designs, it loses least when only heard. For this reason, this chapter, unlike the others, will not discuss any of the work's stage history.)

Tristan is an opera constructed from the inside, its score formed from soul states, and as a consequence, its drama merely responds to the requirements born of the fundamental essentiality of music. It is at once self-aware and oblivious, restricted and entirely free, its internal and external realms fused so that the join between them is completely undetectable. In this work, the world of reality — 'day' — is the illusion; true reality lies in the noumenal authenticity which (Wagner's) music comes closest to conveying: the unimaginably intangible empire beyond perception and the senses. Characters are not merely talking *about* their spirits, psyches, feelings or emotional states; these conditions are being actually presented to us via the music.

Wagner's *Tristan* articulates decisive and elemental philosophical insights of the most elusive and conceptual kind. Following Schopenhauer, Wagner saw human beings as the embodiment of metaphysical will: longing, thirsting for something (food, sex, career or artistic satisfaction). Although Wagner, at least at this time, would fundamentally differ with Schopenhauer on the possibilities of this will — Schopenhauer seeing love/sex as a destructive force, Wagner as a creative one — they agreed on the ultimate importance of it in human life. We do these things, but we *are* them too. And music manifests this, literally giving voice to the inexpressibly abstract. Music moves forward by creating first desire, then resolution: a simple melody needs eventually to be closed, satisfied rather than left hanging. We all know how not only frustrating but grating it is if a tune is abruptly cut off or seems to end on the 'wrong' note. We are puzzled, aggravated — and even distressed.

Music, like life, is a continuous creation and elaboration of yearnings which, once ostensibly satisfied, restart in a ceaseless cycle. It was Wagner's idea to present organic existence's interminable cravings by utilizing the medium which could most readily and vigorously convey them — music — and to stretch these desires out, not for a mere tune or song but over four hours of incredibly complex symphonic writing for a gigantic orchestra. From its fragmentation right at the beginning of the prelude, the music of *Tristan* is seeking resolution, consummation, fulfilment. Every time it seems that this fulfilment has come, it breaks again, resolving to be unresolved. The gratification is forever suspended, the tension and emotional strain ratcheted up to sometimes physically unbearable levels. It is this which makes *Tristan* the truly extraordinary work that it is. A philosophical idea — the *ultimate* philosophical idea — is communicated via music, and by music that is never less than mesmerizing, terrifying and horrendously beautiful.

It is here that the conventionality of an operatic love story metamorphoses from banality to profundity. Love and sex are our most primal urgings as well as our most fundamental desires, shaping our lives and feelings on a range of animal, personal and philosophical levels. And just about every work of art — be it poem, novel, painting or rap ballad — *is* a love song, a hymn to the most fundamental part of being human. When we want to create music, we want to use it to talk about love (and sex). When we want to talk about love (and sex), we want to use music to talk about it. To contain and realize its philosophical desires and intentions, *Tristan* had to be a love story; it could not be anything else or less.

It begins with a primary breakdown in the musical architecture. In fact, it is a twin collapse, doubly dissonant and jarring but then only half resolved. The music develops like this for the next four hours, shifting and rupturing but then obtaining only a partial resolution, constantly giving and taking, granting and removing peace. Yet this frustration is not irritating or exasperating but agonizingly beautiful. Moreover, it is always disseminating the drama it has created, journeying on until it reaches its own heat death, finally resolving at the very end of the work. This moment of fracture and destabilization which, after a few seconds of yearning cellos, sets the drama in motion has a special name, a name now full of meanings, both potential and actual, bizarre and mundane. It is the Tristan chord.

In many ways, the Tristan chord is whatever you want it to be, a sonically devastating and ambiguous space for personal wish fulfilment, an unknown instant and boundless moment to be autofilled by our own private and deepest desires, conscious or otherwise. It is everything and nothing, love and death, being and non-being. Technically, the Tristan chord is a chord made up of the notes F, B, D sharp and G sharp, and Wagner wasn't the first to use them together — composers as diverse as Bach, Mozart and Chopin had already done so. The chord lurks in musical history, occasionally troubling it. But Wagner saw the potential for this chord. He saw the musico-dramatic possibilities within it, the way it could ignite and structure not only his drama but modern music, breaking all the rules and reforging the future of sound. The arrangements and relationships of music, between keys and tonalities, were not just challenged by Wagner and the Tristan chord. They were violently destabilized, turned to musical quicksand.

Musicologists still cannot agree on how to describe the Tristan chord: analysis of it must always be fractious, vague, confusing. But what, after all, is more fractious, vague and confusing than love? Love and *Tristan* are anarchy, agony, mayhem and revolution, threatening tonal and emotional stability by escaping into a wild, free and threatening territory, full of precarious possibility as well as unanchored, alluring panic.

The *Tristan* act 1 prelude — beyond but also because of the famous chord — is an astonishing tone poem of desire and defeat, of throbbing and heartbreaking anguish. It is both pleasure and discontent, happiness and sadness, typically expressed by the same sounds; if not, they are never far apart. This is music of the staunchest, sincerest will and impulse, not merely galvanizing but actually pronouncing both its emotional states and its metaphysical worrying. *Tristan* opens in obscurity, inside darkness, advancing from but also receding back into its own silence. Cellos ache out their few notes in despair as the cosmos prepares to expand, collapse and conclude once more. These few moments of suffering on the lower strings, just prior to the Tristan chord, invite us into this profound tear in space-time that the Tristan chord will initiate, the estrangement which sparks and provokes the drama.

Tristan's prelude foreshadows and articulates the intensity and complexity that is to come by never being consummated, despite its climaxes and elations. The thematic material for the opera is developed in an astonishing arc, like the Milky Way across the night sky, plangently and passionately manifesting the sweep of infatuation and anguish which is to come. The quarrelling Tristan chord, so convincing and unsettling, is followed by torrents of ardour and crazed, conflicting delight, which thunder between heart and brain in an indeterminate riot of eroticism. But the prelude also connects with that other crucial musico-dramatic and metaphysical concern of the work: death, the clear but not always apparent converse to love and/or sex.

There is a statue of Wagner in Venice's Giardini Pubblici, that verdant civic space created by Napoleon from marshland away in the east of the city (on the kangaroo's snout or fish's tail, whichever zoic semblance of La Serenissima you prefer to keep in your mind's eye). To the composer's right stand the campaniles of San Giorgio and San Marco, plus the great dome of Santa Maria, all amid the general bustle and commotion of the basin. To our hero's left, somewhat secreted in shrubbery, is another musician, born in the same year and also petrified for posterity: Giuseppe Verdi. But Wagner looks away from both town and colleague, glowering out across the water towards the southern end of the lagoon and beyond to the Adriatic.

By late spring, the gardens fill with the heavy scent of honeysuckle, as sensual and intoxicating as the harmonic potions of *Tristan* — Wagner *puzza di sesso*, stinks of sex, as James Joyce said — and releasing the hidden energies which administer and control humanity, those venomous intricacies which encase and shroud the soul. Venice would be the city where, post-*Parsifal*, Wagner would die in 1883, an appropriately unique and hallucinogenic location, dovetailing *Tristan*'s twin concerns of love and death, since most of the heady rapture of the second act was composed in Venice in the late 1850s.

As atmospheric, stimulating locations go, Venice must be near the top, but a wealth of other elements helped create *Tristan*. Wagner's main source for his new work was Gottfried von Strassburg's thirteenth-century version of the Tristan and Iseult legend, and here, as elsewhere, the composer-librettist had an extraordinary ability to pare down and reduce vast and complex source material into a dense but efficient drama. *Tristan* has an economical and well-organized text, full of theatrical initiative and dramatic push, even in some of the longer flashbacks which are, as we have seen, nonetheless animated by their music. It also contains some excellent poetry, simple and far-reaching, carefully and scarily managing to be simultaneously ambiguous and almost embarrassingly direct, anticipating (and, to an extent, kindling, post-Baudelaire) the French symbolists Mallarmé and Verlaine, as well as a wealth of modernist poetry, perhaps most especially T. S. Eliot's.

Other influences on and origins of *Tristan* —
especially musically, in works like Berlioz's great dramatic
symphony *Romeo et Juliette* (1839), and philosophically, via
Schopenhauer — can, like the work itself, shuffle uneasily
around paradox or even contradiction, just as the opera
travels constantly between the twin poles of love and death.
On the one hand, critical history (and the gossiping classes)
have pointed to Wagner's supposed affair with his patron's
wife, Mathilde Wesendonck, as the inspiration for the drama.
(In fact, this relationship was likely neither consummated
nor anything more than platonic, however intense and real
it was.) And, on the other hand, people point to Wagner's
own assertion that *Tristan* was to be his grand monument to
love, since he himself had never, he felt, 'tasted the true joy of
love… the loveliest of dreams'.

Of course, both these elements of *Tristan*'s genesis — personal
feelings/experiences and the desire to create a testament —
combine with the range of intellectual, literary, mythic and
musical sources in the foregrounds and hinterlands of Wagner's
mind, furthered and enhanced by his own inventive and
imaginative capacity. There is also the hardly irrelevant practical
consideration that he needed to pause the composition of *Der
Ring des Nibelungen*, partly because of the urge to write *Tristan* but
also because he was not yet sure how to continue — something
the music and philosophy of *Tristan*, and then *Meistersinger*,
would help resolve. To identify, or even seek, a single creative
source for a work as rich, complex and innovative as *Tristan und
Isolde* is often misguided and almost certainly guaranteed to lead
to inconsistency and frustration. Artistic procedures, especially
Wagner's, necessitate compound roots.

The intensity of the act 1 prelude eventually abates into orchestral pitching and swelling, bleakly hypnotic and disorientating, insinuating the choppy (emotional and nautical) waters the boat-stage is traversing. Following the lonely sailor's mournful cries, we then are propelled into the drama with Isolde's fierce and impetuous reproach.

Tristan's first act (and perhaps Wagner's first acts in general) can sometimes seem to be slightly forgotten, overwhelmed by the passions of the second and transfigurations of the third. *Tristan*'s opening act is like the surface of the water on which the opera opens: all is light and movement. People and action crowd the score, if not the stage; we hear them even if we don't always see them. This seafaring act feels a little closer to Wagner's other great maritime work, *Der fliegende Holländer*, though *Tristan* is more condensed, tunes concentrated but still present, ongoing, thrusting in brightness even amid turmoil.

Daytime and gatherings recede in the second act, as the more private realm of night takes over. We seem to head underwater, the twin concealments of a protective darkness and shielding stillness, allowing different interactions between characters and the outside, surface and superficial world before its rude intrusion at the act's end.

By the third and final act, solitude is complete. In some ways, this act seems to occur beyond the divisions of night and day (the extremities which dominate the dialectics of act 2), possibly outside time, or perhaps in the dead and frightening predawn hours, caught between the dominions of night and light — both of which have failed the lovers. Yet, of course, act 3 is also the blinding return of day, a scorching sun dazzling the wounded Tristan. Here, everything seems to happen internally within the characters, divorced from outside stimulus, and the harsh sun X-rays the characters, allowing us to observe their tormented interiors. Even Tristan's experience of the shepherd's pipe is internal, wholly within himself and his memory, and doesn't truly relate to communication with the external world.

To some extent, the journey *Tristan* makes is the inverse to that of *Siegfried*. In the third part of the *Ring*, the three acts move from the obscure interiority of the cave to the confusions and contests of the forest and then arrive at the illumination of the mountain on which Brünnhilde sleeps. It is more complicated than this, of course, since Siegfried's self-awareness in the drama comes about amid the flames of light and love on Brünnhilde's distant rock, whereas Tristan's self-realizations take place in the tormenting light of his home. Both characters journey towards clarity and self-perception, but one does so in fire, the other in an internal fog weirdly shot through by blazing rays.

This is not to say, of course, that the light of *Tristan*'s first act equates with happiness or contentment. Quite the reverse. Light and daytime for Tristan and Isolde are, famously, the enemies, the adversaries to love and the rivals to true being. Daytime also represents being found out, illicit behaviour exposed by the propriety and society which the lovers seek to shun. Agony, anger and resentment flood act 1 in a series of vehement recriminations and external friction. But through this extraordinary eighty minutes of music, the hostilities between Tristan and Isolde — the result not just of previous antagonisms but of mutually unspoken love — begin to break down, before they are accelerated and finally removed by the characters' belief that they are going to die, drinking a death potion which turns out to be a love potion. (A slightly hackneyed narrative device on the surface, this yields immense riches in terms of expectation, surprise and reformulation.) In *Tristan und Isolde*, the mystical anxieties of love clash and coalesce with the physical demands of sex, weakening and eliminating the nebulous boundaries between the two, so that by the end of the first act, bodily and spiritual distinctions have ceased, merged by means of fracture, suffering and repair.

The hours of *Tristan* are anxious, idyllic. Music procrastinates polyphonically on a vast scale, relentlessly in flux, while at the same time searing ecstasy onto its fabric of pain. It is dynamically permanent and perilously approaches the threshold of clarity. In the second act, a wassail of subtle self-indulgence answers the call of self-denial before submitting to recklessness, to abandon and far-reaching impulsiveness. Captured and conveyed in music of perpetual sensual beauty, *Tristan und Isolde*'s hazardous chromaticism refutes the world's healthy diatonics. Its lurid aggrandizements transform love beyond our experience and into the abstract monarchy of idealism: impractical, seamless, absolute.

Act 2 begins in anticipation, mixed with suspense and trepidation, ahead of the illicit meeting in the castle garden. Isolde is impatient, eager. Then Tristan hurries in. A succession of symphonic detonations accompanies the lovers as they greet each other, the orchestra a ballistic riot whizzing lethal rockets across the score, apparently free-moving but subject to the forces exerted by the lovers' explosive embrace. These musico-dramatic maelstroms slowly diminish and develop into steady orchestral fires, burning on and gradually giving way to the stillness and fragrance of a summer's night: serenity, shelter, enrichment. Day has kept them apart, its hostile, conflict-ridden motifs infiltrating the score until driven out, when the music becomes calmer, kinder, mollifying itself from enmity to enchantment. The lovers try to outdo one another in their declarations of devotion and suffering, the orchestra generating euphoria and agitated relaxation before surrounding the lovers in a radiant halo, their individuality fading as they are freed from illusion, falling into a trance of tranquil rapture.

Tristan's second act is an otherworldly orgy and a sensual mass, a private liturgy of lust, transporting its lovers, and listeners, to a realm of sacrosanct sexuality and divine earthly ecstasy. So complete is their alliance that even terms like *merge* or *blend* seem inadequate, misjudged. So powerful is the music that Isolde's conversion to Tristan's dark faith appears static, eternal: their union is surely pre-existent, immutable, infinite. It is a truly holy state, but unconnected to god. It is its own religion, a creed of the night with opaque and alarming rituals. Vilification has become adulation and veneration.

Amid the holy bliss of the lovers' protracted 'duet' — the term ceases to have satisfactory meaning here, since the very notion of division between Tristan and Isolde has now broken down — comes a strangely distancing mechanism. It is the most ravishing music of the entire drama in an opera overflowing with enchanting sounds and bewitching noises. But the voice that makes it is neither Tristan's nor Isolde's. It comes from Brangäne, Isolde's maid, and lasts only a couple of brief, transitory minutes. Brangäne has been charged with keeping watch, guarding Tristan and Isolde as the lovers are lost in spiritual-sensual ecstasy, freed from the falsity of the world and the day. As they swoon, the maid begs her mistress and her lover exercise caution:

> You upon whom
> love's dream laughs,
> heed the cry of
> the voice of one
> who watches alone
> in the night,
> foresees evil
> for the sleepers
> and fearfully urges
> them to waken.
> Beware!
> Beware!
> Soon the night will slip away.

It needs a particularly stunning voice to pierce the floating beauty of Tristan and Isolde's sphere: a moonbeam through the suspended ethereal mists which the lovers and their perfumed orchestra produce. Indeed, casting directors should perhaps source their Brangäne before their Isolde...

Brangäne's Watch-song and portent is disembodied, her voice coming from an infinite distance as well as from the lookout post she occupies. She is midway between the lovers and reality, sharing their delight but also apart from it. She is, in truth, us, the listener and audience. She represents our own feelings of being simultaneously within and outside this erotic exhibition and sublime manifestation of love. Her rapturous Watch-song, 'Einsam wachend in der Nacht', is a commentary as well as a counsel, telling us what we already know — or dread — but needing to fix it in order to provide some solidity to this most unstable and unearthly of operatic love scenes.

Brangäne's extraordinary warning, honeyed and jubilant, is tinged with sadness and threat, a sorrow and menace which will all too soon be very present when King Marke and his retinue burst in, bluntly disconnecting the lovers. But between the caution and the intrusion, Tristan and Isolde bring into being the notion of death in love (Liebestod). They combine the two supposed opposites in a numinous aura, bequeathing them a correspondence, a similarity, an equality. Likewise, they eradicate their own distinct identities: the little word *and* which keeps Tristan and Isolde apart is obliterated through love and death's accord. Brangäne warns a final time of approaching day — both its diurnal manifestation and its socio-real expression in the king and his court. As the lovers celebrate the glorious triumph of night, day brutally encroaches, tedious and belligerent.

King Marke's prolonged narration (impeccably balancing the lovers' own monologue-duet), in which he despairs at his friend Tristan's betrayal, has often been disregarded. Its supplanting of the supreme musical elation of the love scene has vexed not only the lovers but audiences too. How dare he disrupt such bliss? — though both lovers and listeners are also, to an extent, relieved as well, exhausted as they are from the ecstasy. But there is nothing pathetic or petulant about Marke. He is distraught but not resentful, and his unfolding narrative plays interesting games with remorse and responsibility, interrogating guilt and shame, inviting us to query who is truly at fault. Wagner grants the cuckolded king a solo bass clarinet to attend much of his long and poignant monologue. The particularly dark and down-to-earth qualities of this instrument lend an added pathos to the scene as Marke remembers the many kindnesses Tristan performed for him, supporting his grief when his first wife died.

This sorrow yields to gentle enquiry as the king wonders why Tristan, to all intents and purposes his own foster child, deceived him. Words cannot provide the answer, but the higher woodwinds can, taking possession of the score from the bass clarinet and pronouncing the motif of longing, so familiar from the musikdrama's prelude and elsewhere, giving a Proustian rush to its reappearance. Tristan mournfully asks Isolde to accompany him back to the beginning, back to the miraculous sovereignty of night. She will, but the rhapsody of their idea withers in the orchestra, thinning out as reality takes hold: Tristan *and* Isolde, distinct beings, now exist again in dreary day. The act ends in a dwindling desperation, separation escalating, before terminating with one of the most vicious, abrupt and abrasive sounds in all music, full of hopelessness — joy punched out like a fist to the face.

The act 3 prelude to *Tristan* picks up where the second act finished: in desolation. It is a bleak and burnished bronze turning to liquid black and tortured blue. Gestures, filaments or pulses of colour briefly invade the obsidian abyss in this unyielding and lonely lament of spiritual dereliction and hellish metaphysics. It is the antechamber to death: a growing, growling echo of mortality.

Each act of *Tristan und Isolde* begins by detaching the world. The planet's reality and business are shown to exist before being questioned or rejected: the sailor's song in act 1; the hunting horns receding into the distance in act 2; the shepherd's pipe in act 3. All three are proclamations of the world beyond which Tristan and Isolde must travel, replaced by the orchestra's avowal of the lovers' kingdom, however antagonistic (act 1), impatient (act 2) or bereft (act 3) it is to be.

As the appalling wasteland of the act 3 prelude begins to subside, a shepherd is heard, playing on his pipe a refrain of immeasurable sorrow and forlorn beauty. Performed on a cor anglais, the sound is darker, riper and more nostalgic than that of an oboe but retains that instrument's elusive nasal ambiguity. It is ideal for the strange and sombre world the composer wished to evoke at the start of the third act of *Tristan*. Originally, Wagner wanted an even odder instrument: a sort of wooden trumpet that expanded further the alien, wistful sound made by the English horn (as can be heard, for example, on Georg Solti's Vienna recording). This long solo for cor anglais edges towards Tristan, now lying under a tree at his ramshackle castle in Brittany. We are in no man's land, a timeless spiritual-emotional wilderness of forgotten possibility and neglected hope.

The texture of the orchestra is rich but ragged, sumptuous but unkempt: an opulent tapestry torn, frayed, irretrievably damaged. Any flickers of optimism are swiftly silenced by the return of the prelude's raw exhalation of unrepentant regret and the melancholy cry of the shepherd's pipe. And who is this shepherd? What does he stand for? What are his messages and meanings? The perplexing sound of his peculiar pipe will negotiate its despondent way through the long and lonely third act of *Tristan*, threaded through the score until Isolde's ship is spotted (when, at Kurwenal's request, the shepherd will play a happier tune).

The shepherd's disconsolate, unfamiliar sound piques Tristan, intriguing and paining him with the burdens of memory. 'Die alte Weise', the old tune, reminds him of his mother's death while giving him birth, as well as of his father's demise. His life has been pervaded by death from its unhappy beginning, his existence suffused by aching and uproar, internal and external. Mortally wounded at the end of act 2, he drifts in and out of consciousness — day's motifs infiltrate the score and infest Tristan's scrambled brain.

Caught in the radiation of the sun, night's radiance distorted by nuclear forces, he is delirious, dejected, rambling, confused, his music switching between prolonged sorrow and bursts of frenzied anticipation: the hope of seeing his beloved once more. He longs for the protective cloak of night, shielded from both the solar glare and the social gawp, where he can gaze only into Isolde's eyes.

> Alas, now rises within me,
> pale and fearful,
> day's wild yearning;
> glaring and false,
> its star
> wakes my brain
> to deceit and delusion!

His long ravings, as he often struggles for speech and excitedly clasps Kurwenal, move towards a condition of peaceful delusion, the orchestra nursing his frantic state as Tristan hallucinates Isolde's arrival, and so bringing him the concord and resolution of death.

At last, the shepherd's tune brightens and Isolde's ship is seen approaching, then vanishing behind a rock before re-emerging, and Kurwenal and Tristan explode in joy. As Isolde draws near, the music recaps their meeting in the second act and the extinguishing of the torch. 'Do I hear the light?' says Tristan in response to his beloved's calling his name. But the light that is to be snuffed out is Tristan's: he has torn his bandages off, yearning to die into love's embrace. *Tristan*, in many ways less a celebration of love than an attempt to fend off non-being and expiry, has captured its first prize — a death. There is stagnation, disarray, malicious ennui, the descent of a thick pall of weary, obsolete decadence.

Isolde's heartbroken lament over the body of her lover, an anguished and aberrant duet for solo voice with snatches of the Liebestod music, is rudely interrupted, as had been their act 2 duet, by the arrival of Marke, now forgiving and merciful. Violent clashes and the slayings of domestic retainers frustrate the drama, and death reigns as the orchestra agitates in manic sonic apprehension before the king offers some sombre, sober reflection. At this point, as Marke and Brangäne look on, Wagner's dark wine starts to re-intoxicate the score, the lugubrious flowers beginning to bloom once again. Isolde begins her simultaneous farewell/greeting to Tristan: the climactic Liebestod, Isolde's metamorphosis into transcendent union with her beloved, where the broken first chord of the entire work will finally be repaired after its infinite dissonant ruptures.

> In the surging swell,
> in the resounding tone,
> in the infinite drift
> of the world-breath –

to drown,
to sink –
unconscious –
utmost bliss!

The music augments and undulates, the sea returning to engulf the lovers in security, not danger, before expiring into clemency, elegance and exultation. The white-hot fervour of the score has voyaged, via dangerous disorder and entropy, towards its state of harmony, its energy retained before it is released into transfiguration.

Tristan und Isolde offers numerous dialogues: on the meaning of love, the nature of death, the significance of perspective; on the structural design of sound and the shifting landscape of opera; and on the relationship between text and music. The intensity and desolation of its music, dense and symbolic, achieves a sweep over the poetry of the drama, even if the orchestra also dynamically and spontaneously engages with the text. For the most part, however, the sheer sumptuousness and prosperity of the symphonic writing habitually obscures the words — words which, in any case, are simply the materialization of musico-metaphysical states of mind into recognized linguistic ciphers.

Inside the score, motifs mingle and merge, losing their initial meanings by becoming attached to or consumed within new ones. The musikdrama and its attendant metaphysics blend, conflating themes and their connotations as the musikdrama shifts and redeploys into its various terrestrial and transcendent planes, beyond the limited intelligibility of the three-dimensional world. The fluctuating nature of the score flouts categorization, much as Wagner himself could not work out what to term his new piece, eventually settling on simply *Handlung*: drama.

With *Tristan*, Wagner opened the world to new sounds, new directions, even as he addressed the age-old, fundamental questions of human existence. Its exploratory tonal subversions and harmonic disruptions ushered in a cosmic array of musical possibilities which composers (and beyond) were consumed by: some inspired, others annihilated. None could escape it, whether they liked it or not. It helped forge and formulate the cult of Wagner and Wagnerism, a creed as distinctive, exhilarating and potentially detrimental as that which the lovers adopt. *Tristan* sent and continues to send people almost literally insane — some in pleasure, others in revulsion, still more in bafflement. It is not a work with which it is easy, even possible, to have an indifferent relationship.

The dislocations of *Tristan* — musically, dramatically, philosophically — extend meaning to its limit. Its unfinished cadences and uncertain chords stretch what music can do and say. Cross-examining its own principles and perceptions, this musikdrama asks us to enquire what love and suffering are: physically, spiritually, abstractly. *Tristan*'s nature — both pioneering and autonomous — mutually invites and repels interpretation, deflecting attempts at classification or clarification because of its inexorable instability and self-sufficient mystery. It is up to each listener to articulate their own meanings, even if these cannot be verbalized. Its dialectics of sound and text, in the best productions, are in constant communication with those of light and matter. However, even if we are merely listening to the work, it is an aural-optical hybrid, since our imaginations complete the empty spaces which the music presents, transforming ship, garden and castle into the locations of our own desires — or fears. The *Tristan* score, birthplace of modern music, is simultaneously a womb and a tomb, a cradle and a cage, a playground and a prison.

Chapter Ten

The Quiet Rebel:
Die Meistersinger von Nürnberg

I t is a common double myth that not only is *Die Meistersinger von Nürnberg* Wagner's only mature comedy but that it must consequently derive from a joyful period in his life. Lazy connections between life and art are as old as art and the lives of artists. To take one example, everyone from armchair enthusiasts to quite serious scholars has loved to argue that Shakespeare could only have written the melancholy lament for the death of a child in *King John* (*c*.1595) after the death of his own boy, Hamnet, in 1596, despite compelling evidence which proves it was written earlier. People seem to forget writers and artists have imaginations. One does not, after all, insist that Shakespeare needed to have been a Danish philosopher-prince or Scottish killer-king in order to be able to write probing dramas centred around such figures. The lives of artists, and their creative processes, are much more complicated than that, especially for long works, not only written over extended periods but often gestated for decades, internally fermenting.

Wagner's *Die Meistersinger von Nürnberg* was pondered and composed over twenty years, a long enough time in anyone's life but one of staggering emotional and intellectual change for Wagner. Although routinely adduced as a comedy, this opera is a comedy with a bleak and enigmatic core. It is also Wagner's most Shakespearean work, in terms of intricate genre mixing, and a problem play to match the Bard's own brooding masterpieces *Measure for Measure* (c.1603) and *All's Well that Ends Well* (c.1604), both complex comedies wedged into Shakespeare's tragic period. (Wagner's only other stage work that might be labelled 'comic', the urgent, orgiastic *Das Liebesverbot* of 1836, was loosely based on *Measure for Measure*.)

Although structurally a comedy, ending with conjugal prospect and containing a wealth of cheerful, upbeat music, *Die Meistersinger* is also a dark, Schopenhauer-shaped examination of human folly, human sadness, human disappointment — both personal and professional. Later, during one of the blackest episodes in human history, it would be hijacked by malevolent forces, its studious musings and communal culture twisted to promote cruelty, stupidity and the empty rhetoric of nationalism. But there again, many have quite understandably seen the seeds to that violence, sadism and jingoism in this very work, establishing an unswerving line from comic opera to concentration camp. Even its own internal history — presenting a past that never really was — is problematic. Nothing about *Die Meistersinger* is straightforward.

It begins (and ends) in strident, jovial C major fashion with music a world away from the tetchy, anguished chromatism of its predecessor, *Tristan und Isolde*. But, as we will see, *Meistersinger*'s world-weary third-act prelude is the true melancholic heart of this long and complex musikdrama. An orchestral-psychological portrait of the drama's central character, it journeys out of night-time dejection to rise in resigned hope with the morning sun, only to sink a few minutes later on stage with this same individual's paraphrasing of Schopenhauer in the pessimistic 'Wahn Monologue' on human idiocy and self-destruction. 'I laugh and I cry writing it', said Wagner of *Die Meistersinger* — and so should we, watching it.

In the mid-1840s, the composer of *Der fliegende Holländer* and *Tannhäuser* was reading Gervinus's recent *History of German Literature* in the evenings. There he discovered not only Hans Sachs, a sixteenth-century shoemaker and poet, but also the tradition of song contests and guilds of mastersingers. Wagner was especially taken with the idea of the Marker who judged the competitions and the essentially comic confrontation between the narrow custodians of tradition and a more a progressive wisdom (an allegory for anything from opera to architecture to politics). Add to this the prize of love (or, at least, some semblance of it) and much of the *Meistersinger* plot was here — and, in fact, was drafted one summer's day in 1845 as the exhausted composer took the waters at Marienbad.

Sixteen years, however, would pass before Wagner settled down to work on the project. The legends of Lohengrin and Parsifal were already gripping him, as only myth and epic could, and it was not long before the *Nibelungenlied* would further begin to occupy his time. *Meistersinger* would have to wait. But midway through the third part, *Siegfried*, of his four-drama *Der Ring des Nibelungen* cycle, Wagner broke off composing, unsure about how to continue. It was 1857. He felt he needed something simpler to further his career: a straightforward love story, *Tristan und Isolde*. As it turned out, *Tristan* would be anything but simple, either to write or perform. That work would have to wait over six years for a first performance; the *Ring* would remain unfinished. At this point, in the early 1860s, Wagner picked up his tale of town guilds and singing contests, writing to his publisher, Schott, to suggest a 'a popular comic opera... the music light in style.' *Die Meistersinger* was woken from its slumbers.

As with his other projects around saga and legend, further research allowed Wagner to assimilate history and traditions — in this case, of Nuremberg and the mastersingers — before he fashioned a drama that pierced the external material and located the ideas beneath, here concerning love, art and community. Like *Holländer*, *Tannhäuser*, *Lohengrin*, *Walküre* (and *Parsifal*, to follow in 1882), *Die Meistersinger* features an outsider entering society. But as Wagner worked on the project, it became less about the stranger-hero-knight Walther and more about the philosopher-poet Sachs. (A similar thing had happened with the *Ring*, as Wagner expanded that work from one to four dramas, principally to relocate the figure of Wotan, rather than Siegfried, at its centre.)

In Hans Sachs, Wagner, of course, saw himself. No longer quite the sprightly composer-rebel on the Dresden barricades, surely Wagner was gently deriding the flashy youth Walther, with his pop star qualities and knack for unconsciously creating popular new art. True talent was more difficult than that. But neither, too, was Wagner the rule-bound fusspot Beckmesser (the embodiment, as well, of the backward-looking music critics Wagner loathed and who had done so much to stall his career).

Wagner, by the 1860s, saw himself between these two extremes. He knew procedures, systems, regulations were vital — how could something as complex as music or opera or society proceed without them? — especially in their developing stages. But such life-giving forces could eventually constrict and suffocate. Wagner had shown over the course of several new works where he saw the future of opera, now 'musikdrama', heading. If the rules of dramatic structure or musical architecture had not been completely destroyed, they had been ruthlessly destabilized. The radical design of *Das Rheingold* and the strenuous musical language of *Tristan* had seen to that. *Die Meistersinger*, in subtler ways, would continue the upheaval Wagner had inaugurated. And Sachs was to be his quiet revolutionary.

As he worked on *Meistersinger*, Wagner's personal life disintegrated and was rebuilt: his long, difficult marriage to Minna was finally over after 'ten days in hell'; he met Cosima von Bülow, née Liszt, eventually to be his second wife and devoted companion for the rest of his life. His professional fortunes also improved. In 1864, Ludwig II, the 'Swan King' and perhaps the first true fanatical Wagnerite, ascended the Bavarian throne. He brought with him considerable money (and gullibility), both of which Wagner would exploit to realize his artistic dreams — not only to stage his unperformed masterpieces but also to build a radical new opera house for them as well. Wagner had journeyed from being a political agitator, making hand grenades and writing articles inciting the populace to bloody insurrection, to living as the fawning manipulator of monarchs. But perhaps the latter was merely a shrewder arrangement of the former, a quieter form of revolution?

Comedy, and especially comic opera, requires and must utilize traditions and conventions more than other forms, internally and externally: the aesthetic formalities but also those of the societies in and through which these comedies have evolved. A joke in one culture will not necessarily have the same import elsewhere. These comedic rules and conventions are there to be not so much broken as uncompromisingly exploited and made the most of by mischievous radicals like Wagner. Dull comedy goes through its predictable routines, lazily drawing on stereotypes, customs and expectations. Great comedy knows absolutely these hackneyed habits and can exploit them to lampoon tired comedic codes, as well as to encourage and advance its own revitalized format.

In *Meistersinger*, Wagner takes the (very Shakespearean) conventions of garment switching, mistaken identities, midsummer madness and youthful lovers and regenerates them for his own artistic goals. Wagner was a lifelong aficionado of Shakespeare, and the fizzing enchantment of *A Midsummer Night's Dream* and sardonic diversions of *Twelfth Night* pervade *Die Meistersinger*, especially in its second act. There is something, too, of *Twelfth Night*'s lovelorn puritan Malvolio in Wagner's own Beckmesser: vain and pompous, both figures are a world away from the Sir Toby Belch's high spirits or Hans Sachs' kind-heartedness, though all four share a cunning nature. In Sachs, too, the ritualized father figure, usually the butt of jokes and the primary obstacle to love, is given a rejuvenated energy, mystery and narrative responsibility.

Wagner also recultivated and manoeuvred musico-operatic conventions for his own artistic purposes. Self-sufficient songs, duets, ensembles, choruses, marches, processions, dances — all these are an integral part of the design of *Die Meistersinger*. But they are not a formal regression to the stale accoutrements of Grand Opera. Rather, just as Wagner flagrantly manipulated the Bavarian monarchy to fund and realize his art, they unapologetically — and crucially — exploit convention to forge an innovative art.

The composer-librettist had grown from the far-reaching (and quite strict) doctrines of his extended theoretical essay *Oper und Drama* (1851). Here, the principles of musikdrama, most completely fulfilled in *Das Rheingold*, were laid out: abolishing stand-alone set pieces, encouraging the organic growth of a continuous orchestral network and its associated connective motifs, etcetera. In *Meistersinger*, he was now able to seamlessly incorporate traditional forms with the architecture of the musikdrama. The tenets of *Oper und Drama* argued for change, and Wagner himself continued to be their profound, ironic and perhaps paradoxical adherent by including the forms of the past in his futuristic art. Sometimes powerful shifts can take on a more elusive, even incongruous, form than the transitory fires of revolution. (*Götterdämmerung*, finally closing the *Ring* in 1874, would be a necessary perfection of the technique of integrating tradition within musikdrama. The *Ring* project spanned over a quarter of a century, and *Götterdämmerung*'s music was written after *Tristan* to a libretto written before *Oper und Drama*. That said, all Wagner's stage works, and especially the three written immediately before *Oper und Drama* — *Der fliegende Holländer*, *Tannhäuser* and *Lohengrin* — contain pioneering developments.)

In *Die Meistersinger*, such potentially extraneous theoretical discussions form an absolutely essential part of the plot, as well as of its overall structural design. Indeed, the songmaking procedures of the mastersingers, their traditional rules and forms, drive the narrative, since it is only the realization of their technique which is to fulfil the love element of the drama. A non–Richard Wagner approach to the story might have had Eva and Walther defying the pedantic, over-elaborate and old-fashioned rules and successfully eloping into the night, the playboy free to have his girl and his tunes on his own terms. But Wagner knew this would be no true change to the conventions of opera but mere repetition of an age-old formula. Wagner the composer-librettist was also Wagner the Essayist and Wagner the Theorist, and in *Meistersinger*, all his skills were impeccably woven into the Nuremberg tapestry.

As well as an aesthetic excellence, there is a further wry comedy to this: Wagner cocking a snook to the dreary, orthodox critics, smuggling tradition not through the back door but in plain sight. Even Eduard Hanslick, Wagner's fiercest critic, liked some of *Meistersinger*. Hanslick, prince of the orthodox school in the (largely false and journalistically fostered) 'War of the Romantics', pitted composers like the 'traditional' Brahms and the 'radical' Wagner against each other — a tired dichotomy which persists to this day, in various guises. (In fact, Wagner and Brahms shared a mutual, if often circumscribed, admiration for each other's art, both seeing, for very different personal and artistic reasons, the need for tradition and innovation to merge.) Hanslick enjoyed *Meistersinger*'s 'dazzling scenes of colour and splendour', as he put it, but had his doubts about the musical qualities of the work. He seems to have been partially aware he was himself being mocked on stage in the critic-clerk Beckmesser — the artist's revenge, as Wagner craftily continued to forge the future. (In an early draft of the drama, Beckmesser was even called 'Hans Lich'.)

Among the possibly more abstruse discussions of *Die Meistersinger* are those concerning the structure of the mastersong itself, known as *Bar* form. It consists of two short identical *Stollen* followed by a longer, opposing, but eventually complementary *Abgesang*: a straightforward *AAB* form. In *Meistersinger*, this arrangement is not only continually debated by the characters but is beautifully laced into the musical fabric of the opera. Some have even argued the *AAB* form structures the entire three acts. This might be taking it a little too far, but something of that structure is certainly there, since the third act is not only very distinct from the other two in structure, tone and length but is ultimately the harmonious balancing Abgesang to the earlier acts' Stollen. (Extending the principle further, *Die Meistersinger* could be deemed the Abgesang to the earlier Stollen of, say, *Tannhäuser* and *Tristan*, a convolution

Wagner might have enjoyed. Perhaps Wagner, too, is the Abgesang to the Stollen of Italian and French opera.)

Wagner's genius, of course, is that none of the conjecturing and deliberating in *Meistersinger* is tedious or recondite. The theorizing is there in the text, and the music, but the work sweeps along and doesn't let up or sag for a moment. Comedies need drive and dynamism, and Wagner manages to sustain this one for five hours with an infectious blend of drama, debate and warm, fascinating music. There are periods of reflection and even occasional sadness, themselves vital parts of comedic procedure, but *Meistersinger* is always steering in the direction of the happy outcome, towards its mysteriously inevitable, harmonious termination. Comedies, after all, are largely deemed to be such on the basis of their amicable conclusions: change only the ending to *Othello* so that Desdemona lives, and it might well be considered a domestic farce; have a couple of deaths at the end of luminous *As You Like It*, and the whole work, without any other alterations, clouds over.

If comedy is fundamentally defined by outcome, its tone also matters: comedies tend to be funny, light, cheerful. But the inexorability and certainty of their outcomes can also sanction them to comfortably assimilate darkness. In *Die Meistersinger*, two particular characters eclipse its jovial sun: Sachs and Beckmesser. One deepens its philosophical tendencies, as well as warming its soul; the other slightly stains the work. Together, they help to illuminate this musikdrama's complex internal and external relationship with history.

Hans Sachs is probably the most appealing of all Wagner's characters, as well as perhaps the most complex. He has

the witty intelligence of Loge (*Rheingold*), the wisdom of
Gurnemanz (*Parsifal*), and the scheming guile — as well as
occasional short temper — of Wotan, on top of the amorous
spirit of heroes as diverse as Tannhäuser, Tristan and Siegfried,
though Sachs is able to control his passions for nobler ends.
In many ways, though, he has more of the discreet progressive
qualities of Wagner's female characters: Elizabeth (*Tannhäuser*),
Elsa (*Lohengrin*) and Brünnhilde (at least in *Die Walküre*) share
Sachs' desire to serve their societies while also aiding outsiders.

This cobbler-poet has seen it all, been it all, but he is not
dead or finished. If he is occasionally lonely, he is not always
alone and still forms a vital part of the community of which
he is a considerable and thoughtful member. Like the probing,
metaphysical work he increasingly begins to dominate as its
acts progress, Sachs uncovers the diligent day and muddled
night to reveal deeper meanings beneath the order and chaos
of quotidian reality. He also transcends the boundaries of the
historical time and place — sixteenth-century Nuremberg — in
which he finds himself to locate the deeper truths buried in the
layers, lies and misconceptions of history. His trade, shoemaking,
has both a practical and an aesthetic quality. Similarly, his
philosophical-historiographical enquiries are a mixture of self-
indulgent, though never self-pitying, meditation, as he tries to
understand his own place within a strange, often indifferent,
cosmos, and more pragmatic attempts at understanding his
fellow man. Sachs, and *Meistersinger*, explores a cornucopia
of everyday subjects, from the bizarre behaviour of people on
committees to their conduct when in love (or lust) and how
public holidays and public anxieties cause people to act in
imprudent or peculiar ways.

None of the music Wagner associates with Sachs is in the
prelude. Could Sachs have even (Wagner briefly glances at us)
written it himself, scribbling orchestral sketches of his town and
its folk? The prelude to *Die Meistersinger* strides self-assuredly

forward in assertive C major, that most common, fundamental of key signatures. To an extent, it returns to the designs for the overtures to *Holländer* and *Tannhäuser*, before the wholly altered preludes to *Lohengrin*, *Rheingold*, *Walküre* and *Tristan*, which operate entirely differently in relation to their own dramas. In *Meistersinger*, an ordered jumble and ragbag assembly of themes emanate from the Wagner-Sachs pen, often fraternizing via some extraordinarily skilful contrapuntal writing. We open with the opulent majesty of the mastersingers themselves — a theme in itself very noble but given a hint of pomposity when heard in relation to the others; there are ebullient marches and perky woodwind-based themes, representing some of the town guilds; more pressing, ardent refrains steal in, suggesting love or sex, and eventually evolve into the melody for the prize-winning song we'll encounter in five or so hours.

In his poignant and highly inventive production for Salzburg in 2013, Stefan Herheim staged the prelude as Sachs' dream and artistic procedure, taking the notion that the prelude is Sachs' composition a logical step further. Herheim sees the whole work as part of Hans Sachs' unconscious creative process — the subject of one of the discussions which *Meistersinger* stages when Sachs talks with Walther in act 3 about how to make use of his dream to formulate a song. Herheim has Sachs scurrying about all over the set, looking for inspiration in his own house and furiously writing things at his elegant desk. Then, in brilliant moment of theatre to match the composer's own, at the very end of the prelude, when its final chord turns into the singing congregation of St Katharine's Church which opens the opera, Herheim miraculously transforms Sachs' writing bureau into the organ of that same church. We have entered a fairy tale, a *Nutcracker*-esque world of magic, dolls and make-believe. We have entered Hans Sachs' imagination.

Beyond the obvious beauty, emotion and ingenuity of his *Konzept*, Herheim (and Wagner) were making powerful statements not only about inspiration and creativity but the past, too — whether that be our own childhoods or the wider processes of history. All our childhoods are, to an extent, an invention, fabrications of memory, misremembered truths and half-truths, untidy clutters of certainty and romanticism, and not, as a matter of fact, so outrageously different from the hectic exuberance of dreams. History, too, is a dangerous concoction of fantasy and reality, accuracy and imprecision, truth and propaganda. The picture-postcard Nuremberg beloved of 'traditional' productions of *Die Meistersinger*, such as Otto Schenk's in 1993 for the Metropolitan Opera, is as imaginary as the toy trains and soldiers of Herheim's in Salzburg. Wagner knew this — it is built into the very structure of his work — and his intention when writing *Die Meistersinger* was not the false and lazy reconstruction of a forgotten, idealized world. His art remained and always would be an artwork of the future.

Herheim's 'Hans Sachs' Dream' Konzept allowed a flood of Freud and a host of erotic and other psychoanalytic paraphernalia to inundate, but not swamp, the drama, usually with fascinating results, not least regarding Sachs and his relationship with Eva. It didn't make Sachs a pervy poet, lecherous and disloyal: his honest feelings for Eva, which contain sex as well as fondness, are clear in both Wagner's text and music. Midway through act 3, as Sachs contemplates the trap he has just laid for Beckmesser at the song contest, the orchestra floats and then hangs charming, compassionate love themes. Eva enters and shares a gaze with Sachs, the instruments in the pit telling us all we need to know about their unspoken feelings, their long-standing tenderness, whatever Eva's true passion for Walther as well. Later in the act, Wagner even dissolves the entire score of *Meistersinger* into the erotic world of his own *Tristan* when Sachs tells Eva and Walther he doesn't want to be a King Marke standing in the way of the young lovers. It is an astonishing and entirely justified musical self-quotation, displaying Sachs' self-awareness and the genuineness of his erotic drive, as well as adding a touch of sardonic mockery to the comedy — something Benjamin Britten would repeat with his *Tristan* references in *Albert Herring* (1947).

Eva herself can seem a slightly underwritten role, but she is perfectly formed and an important element both to many critical functions of the plot and to the overall character of the drama: she must be both spontaneous and sympathetic, impulsive and humane. A great Eva makes sure that however dark or introspective *Meistersinger* may become, its heart is in the right place.

This is especially so since, not long before the magnificently tender Eva–Sachs scene in act 3, *Die Meistersinger* has experienced its profoundest, most pessimistic and most explicitly philosophical passages. In the third-act prelude, we find a meticulously rendered symphonic portrait of Sachs' inner being: his searching intelligence, his cynicism, his affection, his sadness and reflective joy. Three key ideas structure this exceptional piece of emotional tone-painting: A, the Wahn motif; then B, a Lutheran chorale; and finally C, a cobbling song. Each has an abundance of extra musico-dramatic-historical meanings, packing but not burdening these seven orchestral minutes with a wealth of significant layers. Moreover, the music has a palindromic *ABCBA* structure, conveying Sachs' journey in reverie through and back across thought.

The prelude begins with a lugubrious passage for strings, with the Wahn theme entering on cellos. This, as we will see, is the lunacy and self-deception of the world, the slightly cynical lamentation of a man reconciled to displaying a smiling face to the silly world, which Sachs will shortly articulate in his Wahn Monologue. It is displaced by magnanimous horns and bassoons, which intone in the style of a Lutheran chorale the melody of the song with which the song contest will open later in the act. The song will tell of a blissful nightingale singing in the green grove, its voice ringing through hill and valley, as the ardent glow of morning penetrates the gloomy clouds. In the historical sixteenth-century Sachs poem, that nightingale is Martin Luther, composer-priest and engineer of the Reformation; in *Die Meistersinger*, the heavenly songbird is ultimately Hans Sachs himself, the overjoyed people of Nuremberg taking up the song to initiate the singing competition as well as to honour their beloved mastersinger. (This is a transferral which also encapsulates Sachs'/art's ability to simultaneously capture, abolish and transcend historical time.)

This optimistic, celebratory section yields to the third component of the act 3 prelude: the act 2 cobbling song, whose fragments the orchestra picks up and reforges. This anticipates the Eva–Sachs scene mentioned above by casting back to the scene in act 2 where the shoemaker sang as Eva and Walther tried to elope, the song also disrupting Beckmesser's attempts to woo Eva himself. Sachs' song tells of how God pitied Adam and Eve as they were expelled from Eden and sent an angel to provide them with shoes as protection from the rocky, unstable earth that was to be their new destiny. Sachs says that he would relinquish cobbling but an angel calls him to paradise: a message of patience, faith and forbearance Eva and Walther duly acknowledge. In the act 3 prelude, this music then returns to the rejuvenated version of Lutheran chorale before finally completing the *ABCBA* sequence with an abrasive reappearance of the agitated Wahn motif before the orchestra fades with benign resignation into the opening of the final act.

In the exceptional symphonic communications in the prelude to act 3 of *Die Meistersinger*, we have travelled through the mind of Hans Sachs; we have journeyed into his heart and crossed to his soul. We have found his personality and his temperament. He is kind-hearted, intelligent and humane, though far from perfect (whatever that might mean), his very imperfection simply heightening his humanity. Wagner here produces — as only musikdrama can — an intricate and extremely detailed orchestral MRI scan of the intellectual, emotional and spiritual features which comprise this character, particularizing the labyrinth of his mind and the multifaceted mechanisms of his heart. Additionally, Wagner employs motifs which stretch across the work, looking backwards as well as forwards: *Meistersinger* can be as spatially and temporally malleable a musikdrama as the *Ring*. Sachs undoubtedly ponders throughout the prelude how in his time he has himself been a form of amorous Walther, careless David and proud Beckmesser, though not so extreme as any of them. In Sachs, as perhaps in Wagner generally, we find the intellectual, the emotional and the spiritual fused, shown to be interrelated, a highly organized and symbiotic network, as impossible to separate as the orchestral system which exhibits them.

Following Schopenhauer, Wagner (the new Wagner of *Tristan*, *Meistersinger*, the later parts of the *Ring*, and *Parsifal*) asserted the superiority of music to the other arts. Both argued that music's abstractions allow it to communicate emotion in a purer and more direct fashion than the other arts. For Wagner, any notion of an unconditional parity between words and music is now a misconception, an illusion. Different words can be set to an identical tune, demonstrating that the tune has an independence, a freedom, a plasticity which words cannot have. Opera (even Wagnerian musikdrama) is regularly performed in translation. The words to songs are hardly ever spoken without the tune, yet the tune is frequently articulated without the words. And who forgets the tune to a song but remembers the words? Words and phrases can get stuck in our heads like musical earworms, especially if they have a particularly pleasing rhythm or series of sounds — i.e., their own music — but we much more frequently get catchy tunes continually running through our minds. James Joyce in *Ulysses* (1922) and *Finnegans Wake* (1939) came close to granting words the fluid freedoms of music, though he was forced to essentially make language behave *as music*. Words generally are, for most intents and purposes, much more tangible and specific than music.

Drama — stage representation — has a fluidity in visible display which approaches, if not equals, music's invisible one. Joined together in the musikdrama, the hidden metaphysical secrets of the visible, external world can be represented. A performed musikdrama is the music realized, manifested into characters and their actions. Indeed, the music in mature Wagner more often generates or anticipates the drama itself, before the action, rather than being only a commentary or accompaniment to it.

In *Meistersinger*, despite its being a very 'wordy' opera, words no longer have for Wagner the standing they were once allocated in *Oper und Drama* and *Das Rheingold*, but many of the principles of those works have now been thoroughly absorbed into his compositional practice, so that the complex relationship between text, action and music is applied unconsciously, intuitively. We cannot judge Wagner's later musikdramas according to the rulebook of *Oper und Drama*, looking for mistakes or contradictions. These principles are now one aspect of the complex fabric and features of later Wagner, but they are not its basis or objective.

Vast and highly intricate orchestral spans constitute the Wagnerian practice now, dramatically interconnected to the visual stage action they parallel (which, as we saw above, can include the internal mental and emotional states of characters). There is huge expressive potential to this symphonic network in terms of strength, variation and flexibility. It is able to progress with exceptional freedom and abstraction: portable, autonomous, metaphysical. It can ruminate and cogitate with the speed, vagueness or precision of human thought and memory, incorporating the realistic shabbiness of thinking which modernist writers like James Joyce would so enthrallingly convey in the stream of consciousness technique (a substantial enhancement of mere interior monologue). Yet, for all the communicative potential of this narrative mode, Wagner's symphonic writing — and music in general — is surely better able to express the intricate interdependence of thoughts, feelings and emotions in sound related to dramatic action. And in *Meistersinger*, the act 3 prelude is an extraordinary exhibition of this.

Such suppleness permits, encourages, the best qualities of improvisation and organization to be combined. Novelty, candour, liberty, elasticity can merge with discipline, order, harmony. This is the ultimate goal not only of Wagner's art but of the plot of *Die Meistersinger* itself, where the freshness and lithe energy of Walther's urgent, ardent innovations is to be blended with the rules of the mastersingers in order to win the contest and the girl. But before that can occur, the third act, Wagner's longest, has several depths to plumb and narrative obstructions to negotiate.

Soon after the act begins, following an amusing and touching scene with his apprentice, David, Sachs ruminates on the madness, the folly, the illusion (all three aspects captured in the single German word *Wahn*) which leads people to such injurious excesses as the riot of the night before, which ended act 2. This is the celebrated Wahn Monologue: a musico-dramatic interpretative restatement of Schopenhauer, the philosopher whose writings had so profoundly influenced Wagner's art, changing the tone, character and philosophical direction of the *Ring* as well as governing the emotional atmosphere and musical architecture of *Tristan*.

Meistersinger, influenced by Schopenhauer, re-evaluates the role of music in opera (and society), as well as absorbing many of the philosopher's discussions on ethics and metaphysics. All of these coalesce and interrelate in both Schopenhauer and Wagner: philosophy, ethics and music cannot be easily separated in either of them. 'Wahn! Wahn! Überall Wahn!' sings Sachs: 'Madness! Madness! Everywhere madness!' For Schopenhauer, this is the characteristic nature of human life, people slaves to their wills and living in a world of stupidity, foolishness, fantasy, fleshly servitude and egotistical self-deception. It is not for nothing that the disturbance of the night before has been instigated by a case of mistaken identity.

Sachs is not unaware of his role in the unrest: it was in part his plan to prevent the elopement which caused the violence, though his doing so was for the noble reason of aiding the lovers. Here, Sachs, though despondent and alone himself, is expressing his own renunciation of the (erotic) will, a musico-dramatic embodiment of Schopenhauerian humanity. Sachs frees himself, surrendering his will and, as the monologue closes in symphonic splendour, resolving to focus Wahn towards finer purposes.

As the soliloquy ends, Walther enters, and Sachs helps concentrate the knight's efforts in songmaking. Here the Prize Song is born, conceived by Walther's ecstatic dream and delivered into a mastersong via slow but steady instruction from midwife Sachs, who teaches him the rules and simultaneously secures the extemporization by putting it on paper (which will almost immediately ensnare the cheating Beckmesser).

Revolution and tradition are united in the birth of the Prize Song, and the new work of art is christened by Sachs, along with the two pairs of lovers (Eva and Walther, David and Magdalena), in the famous quintet which closes the first half of this act and leads to the second, the song contest itself. This magnificent, honourable, radiant music, in a baptism of great beauty, sanctifies the union of the lovers. Nothing can prevent Walther from winning the contest now. Not only has he a superlative mastersong but his only rival, Beckmesser, has been tricked into making both an ethical and an aesthetical mistake: appropriating the improvisation.

Beckmesser is, in most respects, merely the comic villain of *Die Meistersinger von Nürnberg*. Comedies, after all, need oppositional characters in order to hinder and drive their plots, and officious town clerk Sixtus Beckmesser succeeds brilliantly in his function. That the scheming, duplicitous scoundrel is publicly made a fool of by his own dishonest behaviour is a particularly appropriate Dantean punishment. He is hoist, very neatly, by his own petard.

And there we might have left it. To a very great degree we can, but *Meistersinger* is never straightforward. The personal attitudes of its creator, as well as the work's stage history and cultural annexation by political powers, mean some consideration, at least, should be given to this complex and unfortunate aspect of what should be treated as art — as, ultimately, the work itself argues it should. Not art in isolation, uncontaminated by the world, but working, like Sachs, towards finer purposes within it. *Meistersinger*, seen in the context of its dark history, is its own Wahn.

Beckmesser has long been regarded as, at the very least, the epitome of a certain kind of vulgar Jewish stereotype: callous, deceitful, miserly, bureaucratic, pedantic and self-important. This is the vile labelling as it is usually presented. Within *Meistersinger*, certain specific anti-Semitic elements have been unearthed, particularly in the first act, where references, both textual and dramatic, to the Brothers Grimm and their

notoriously racist folk tale *Der Jude im Dorn* ('The Jew in the
Thornbush') occur: Walther explicitly identifies Beckmesser
with the envious Jew of the story, among other disturbing
indicators.

When these specific textual-cultural references — quite
understandably missed by most listeners and audiences —
are taken together with the stereotypical characterization
of Beckmesser as a Jewish caricature, which is open to
interpretation but nevertheless a distinct possibility, the charge
of anti-Semitism becomes convincing. The work's blatant
nationalism only furthers this.

The cultural context of *Die Meistersinger von Nürnberg*'s
creation in the 1860s and birth in 1868 was dominated by
the growing movement to unite the 'German spirit' in political
terms, culminating in the unification of Germany as a nation
state in 1871. A fundamental aspect of this was the notion of
'restoration through purification', purging Germany of alien
elements. This racist component, unique neither to Germany
nor to the mid/late nineteenth century, was nonetheless
especially strong there and led directly, with other contributing
structural, economic and personal factors, to the triumph and
then atrocities of the Nazis.

When Sachs and the Nürnberg townsfolk sing proudly
at the end of *Die Meistersinger* of a Germany united, a true
German art, both potentially threatened by evil foreign
tricks, there may be a racial element to this. Still, it may be
mere patriotism, which easily and very quickly corrodes
to nationalism. If it is racist, it is disgusting. If it is simply
patriotism or nationalism, it is dull and likely contains
xenophobic elements, though patriotism and nationalism are
more understandable in the context of *Meistersinger*'s creation
amid the desire to unite the German people into a new nation
state. We need to be careful not to let both subsequent history
and Wagner's repulsive personal beliefs contaminate the entire

work or impede *Meistersinger*'s ability to utilize and overcome its own Wahn.

By the end of *Meistersinger*, Beckmesser has not been banished: in Wagner's stage direction, he merely disappears into the crowd, though productions have frequently exiled him from the stage. Perhaps he will see the error of his ways and become a kinder member of the community, his lesson learnt. Wagner's own anti-Semitism, nauseating though it was, didn't prevent him from working with Jewish musicians, and perhaps his ending to *Meistersinger* indicates that his desire to 'purge' Germany had its limitations. For Wagner, it was his art that mattered. But this is not to let either Wagner or *Meistersinger* off the hook for the way they may have helped to foster the conditions which ultimately led to the barbaric actions at Auschwitz or Buchenwald.

The Nazis certainly never understood the illusionary quality to Wagner's Nuremberg and merely wanted to commandeer it in order to promote their own false idea of an idyllic, forgotten past to which only they could return Germany. (This is something perhaps mirrored by the way many people now unconsciously, even instinctively, project the image of marching storm troopers onto the sound of the main theme of *Die Meistersinger*, which opens and closes the work.)

Wagner's Nuremberg is not an attempted recreation of a historical time and place. Wagner knew the guilds and trades did not exist in quite the way he had placed them on stage. Wagner's Nuremberg was artificial and imaginative, as imaginative as the Venusberg, Wartburg, Valhalla, Nibelheim, Kareol or Montsalvat. Throughout his work, Wagner utilized heroic legend and legendary sagas (*Der Ring*), medieval romance (*Tristan*), and blends of legend, history and organized religion (*Tannhäuser, Lohengrin, Parsifal*) as well as fantasy Renaissance history (*Meistersinger*) — whatever he needed in order to create his art. He didn't believe in the Norse gods,

Christian God, or historical existence of the Nuremberg *Die Meistersinger* presents.

Barrie Kosky's fascinating production for Bayreuth in 2017 explored some of the different Nurembergs: the one in Wagner's head; the one in the misremembered past; the one which became a site of inquiry (and retribution) after the Second World War. Nuremberg is a place for projection and reflection, both a mirror and a light — a light which, exposing, illuminating, condemns. It is a place to unmask evil as well as launch it. For Kosky, the first Jewish director at Bayreuth, it would have been too easy to make Beckmesser simply a Jew. Rather, Kosky argued, Beckmesser was a Frankenstein creature stitched together from Wagner's various hatreds — be it of the French, officials, Jews or journalists. The anti-Semitism is certainly there, for Kosky, but there are a significant number of further prejudices contained within this comic villain.

The internal and external stains on *Die Meistersinger*, as well as on the rest of Wagner's work, are problematic and troubling, so much so that many would like to imagine these problems didn't exist. Yet, rather than ignore them, we should embrace them as part of not only the work's history but also its message of overcoming Wahn. The Japanese concept of *Kintsugi* (literally 'golden repair') involves restoring broken pottery through mending areas of fracture with golden lacquer: breakage and repair are to be treated as part of the history of an object rather than something to disguise. Similarly, the Jewish caricature, the interior nationalism, the hijacking of the work for Nazi propaganda and ensuing genocide — these are part of the history of *Die Meistersinger*. They taint it. They make it imperfect. But they also communicate the way in which the drama itself has experienced processes of corruption, evil and insanity and made use of those disasters to rebuild and restore itself. In contrast with Kintsugi, the flaws don't give *Meistersinger* beauty as such, but they do add further substance, helping us better understand both the work's history and its lessons, internal and external.

When, in 1968, Wolfgang Wagner staged the centenary *Meistersinger* at the Bayreuth Festival, on the cover of the programme he added a passage from his grandfather's *Art and Revolution* (1849):

> The work of art of the future is intended to express the spirit of free people irrespective of all national boundaries; the national element in it must be no more than an ornament, an added individual charm, and not a confining boundary.

This optimistic sentence comes from the time when Wagner first drafted *Meistersinger* and is part of an actively and observably revolutionary stage in his existence. But its spirit endured through the composer's life and can still flourish. Nevertheless, only by accepting its blemishes and responsibilities can *Meistersinger* transcend the burden of its own history, as Sachs is able to do with his own, probing the deeper truths beneath the layers of its problematic past and towards the future.

At the contest, the Prize Song — which has been created by the unconscious workings of the sleeping mind becoming integrated with the conscious mechanisms of the artistic intellect — has one further trick to pull. Assessing Walther's performance, his judge becomes so transfixed by its beauty that he drops the score he is marking with. Noticing this, Walther feels inspired to take his song further, into spontaneous invention. Walther has, following his tuition from Sachs, met the demands of the contest and those of the mastersingers, while at the same time carrying them further. Sachs has contrived that tradition (history) and revolution (the future) are now working in proper creative harmony. His art has its heir and successor.

One can certainly enjoy the gorgeous Renaissance costumes and quaint timbered buildings of more 'traditional' *Meistersinger* interpretations. But we should not fetishize such productions, allowing ourselves to become seduced by an illusionary past. This would be merely capitulation to the Wahn which the whole work argues we need to overcome. 'Traditional' productions can be captivating and charming, but dangerously so — just like the past can be if we're not careful. No one should think Wagner wished his art to operate as a time-travelling device for unimaginative inhabitants of opera houses. Besides, his art is much more dynamic and powerful than mere re-creation (or recreation: it is no simple leisure activity).

In Nuremberg, Wagner saw the world entire. In Sachs, he beheld the authentic artist-revolutionary, quietly engaged in an ongoing dialectical relationship with his art, its history and the surrounding world — something ultimately to be found in all Wagner's works. Innovation by necessity requires association with the past, negotiating with it, interrogating it; but novelty need not be, cannot be, excessively obliged to convention. In the end, if art is to not only survive but thrive, revolution and tradition need to discover a mutually creative understanding — just as the Prize Song does.

Chapter Eleven

The Error of Existence:
Parsifal

To write about *Parsifal* is, in a sense, to destroy it. It is to extinguish its mystery; to undermine its immensity, its limitlessness, its incalculability. When both the medium and the message of a work of art are elusiveness and intangibility, to do anything but merely experience them is undoubtedly to sabotage their quality, their aura, their capacity.

Parsifal is an enquiry into the nature of existence: the suffering, the loneliness, the trauma, the dilemmas, the wounds. It explores the nature of the human experience, caught as it is, lost between material and abstract worlds, an animal with a sense of the divine, a fleshly mass with a complex array of emotional, intellectual and spiritual requirements which cannot be satisfied by religious belief. *Parsifal* stages the complexity not of faith but of doubt.

Part of the reason *Parsifal* has proved to be so elusive, and potentially unsatisfactory, to both believers and non-believers, Christians and sceptics, is because it refuses to give any uncomplicated answers to questions that seek unknowable responses. And this is if it gives any answers at all. Belief, existence and morality are subjected to relentless examination throughout Wagner's final musikdrama, but no outcome is conferred, no final conclusion bestowed, even in the radiance of its termination. *Parsifal* no more asserts the authenticity of the Christian heaven than *Meistersinger* presents a genuine Nuremberg or *Rheingold* an actual Valhalla. But neither does it compel us to entirely shun religion or the vital truths and symbols therein. It is a hybrid work, and every perspective which tries to claim *Parsifal* for itself will be thwarted and disenchanted. Except, perhaps, that of art.

The mystical subject of *Parsifal*, the oblique, suggestive sense of the numinous and non-human it presents and the complex, demanding relationship between this realm and our own required something far more intriguing than any simple bout between good and evil. All arrangements of morality and modes of existence are confronted, disputed, displaced. Ethical and psychological states appear and then evaporate, attempting to enforce their own stability before being undermined, dematerialized. *Parsifal* asks us to question the convenient categories which govern our existence, and it does so with a floating, weightless score and awe-inspiring, otherworldly spectacle.

Wagner's final work presents ambiguous divisions and subtle negotiations between diverse forms of being, between different categories of behaviour, atmosphere, feeling, temperament, consciousness, dimension and perspective. In consequence, musically and dramatically, *Parsifal* displays continuous adjustments, oscillations, destabilizations. Exceptionally refined but always elusive changes in the texture, tone or ambience are a constant feature of the score, as are gaps and silences which serve only to heighten the sense of flux. Its world is one of constant exquisite mutability but is always profoundly inter-reliant, offering extremely delicate and often indiscernible nuances which resist verbal interpretation or communication.

Characters and their own internal moods have a perpetually fluctuating nature, and *Parsifal's* music will not permit any easy delineation of individual being, nor the corollaries of this in terms of ethics or piety. The score, and the inhabitants of its diaphanous architecture, is fleeting, intangible, tenuous and obscure, imperceptibly variable like clouds or light. Even when it seems at its most solid and secure, when wickedness or integrity seem most apparent or self-assured, *Parsifal* disrupts and dislocates itself, eluding both us and its own equivocal presence.

Wagner's initial source for his last musikdrama — which he rather sweetly, somewhat outlandishly, but with good reason termed *Ein Bühnenweihfestspiel*, a sacred stage festival play — was the medieval epic poem *Parzival* by Wolfram von Eschenbach (*c.*1170–*c.*1220). He first encountered *Parzival* in 1845, during the fertile spa break at Marienbad which also yielded the beginnings of *Lohengrin* and *Die Meistersinger*. Twelve years later, Wagner would later claim, with some artistic licence, that on a beautiful spring morning — Good Friday, 1857 — ideas for *Parzival* began to form properly in his psyche, concurrent with his work on *Tristan und Isolde*. The one was a hymn to the erotic, the other the ascetic. Yet *Parsifal* (as he eventually called it) is not an antithesis or repudiation of *Tristan*. Rather it is, in fact, an even more radical (and complex) illustration of the same fundamental idea. But it would not be until 1877 that Wagner began serious work on *Parsifal*, other projects (*Tristan*

itself, then *Meistersinger*, *Siegfried*, *Götterdämmerung* and finally Bayreuth) intervening until he completed it in 1882.

This near forty-year span allowed — necessitated, even — a mosaic of sources to arrange and rearrange themselves in Wagner's mind, the composer-librettist taking those elements he desired for his own artistic purposes and creating the hybrid final work. In Wolfram's long Arthurian romance, the Grail is a precious stone and Amfortas is the wounded Fisher King from pagan legend, whose impotence turns his realm into a barren wasteland. The climactic Good Friday meeting in the forest that Wolfram depicted, between an exhausted, veiled Parzival and an ancient hermit, would be Wagner's culmination, too, though the composer grew a little irritated by what he saw as Wolfram's ineptitude in excluding certain useful, specifically Christian, elements. Wagner turned to narratives from other traditions, such as Robert de Boron's in the thirteenth century and Thomas Malory's fifteenth-century *Le Morte Darthur*. Both told of how Joseph of Arimathea founded the Grail community and of its custody of the chalice used at the Last Supper, which later caught Jesus's blood as he hung on the cross. Wagner was deeply moved by this brotherhood's devoted guardianship as well as by the potency of the central symbol of the Grail: the continuing presence of life and goodness in an error-strewn world.

Wagner was fascinated by the tragic, wounded figure of Amfortas but could not conceive of how to give it dramatic impetus. There was no doubt that the agonized relationship between the wounded king and the Grail, the dark links between his wounds and those of Christ, was compelling. The mixture of sex, guilt and sin had intrinsic theatrical potential — as did the vast connective span which could be centred on an object, or pair of objects. But it needed a tighter dramatic arc, a more absorbing and persuasive human journey, not least if Parsifal himself was not to simply arrive at the end as a frigidly resolving deus ex machina. Parsifal needed to be brought to the foreground, while Amfortas paradoxically would gain in power by his relegation. He would now be presented as a haunted background figure, essentially static, dominating the drama through his previous conduct rather than his stage actions.

This also allowed Wagner to better link the present with the past in the way he now preferred: musikdrama. Musikdrama, in contrast with opera, is an art of inner dialectical action, focusing on the allegorical significance of events and utilizing leitmotifs, which function to relate the present with the past. The foreground stage action is less important: it is the music, especially the instrumental music, which operates not only to bring the contextual story to life but also to make it the palpable and central element of the drama. For such a medium to work, it needed an orchestral composer capable of conceiving and sustaining highly sophisticated symphonic writing which could — for several hours at a time — explore and dramatize the past and its relationship with the present.

It has always been easy to caricature and mock Wagner's works for their interminable backstory, the characters constantly stopping to bore us with their elaborate pasts. But this is to fundamentally misunderstand the potent new genre Wagner had created. The persistent monopolization of the present by the past is not only dramatically very formidable, it also encompasses immense psychological insight. Wagner knew that it was the inner lives, the internal being, of humans which made them so special, so tragic. Actions and events come and go, but their effects linger, corrode and inspire. Music could exploit this dualism, evoking the past as well as its consequences, turning what in opera is an interruption or irrelevance — backstory — into musikdrama's governing principle and outstanding faculty. Visible stage action is a mere prop for the invisible action of music.

Appreciating how this music works is fundamental to understanding how Wagner came to develop his sources into dramas, since the choice and arrangement of his material is profoundly linked to how he would employ them in musico-dramatic terms. Hence the transfer of Amfortas to a more ostensibly ephemeral part of the drama, seldom on stage but dominating, overshadowing, the entire work: dramatically, through the consequences of his actions, as well as musically, through their assiduous evocation in the score.

For Parsifal, Wagner took from Wolfram both the essential character and biography of the hero — the name of his mother, 'Heart's Sorrow', his desertion of her and subsequent self-orphanage in the wilderness — as well as the long-suffering solitude of his mission. Although Parsifal's background is sorrowful, it is his essential ordinariness which both conceals and reveals his special status, the 'pure fool' chosen to be the redeemer. His revelatory moment, where his ignorance is turned to knowledge, comes at the instant of Kundry's kiss in act 2. Here he recognizes the kiss which had earlier ensnared Amfortas, and this connection allows him the compassion to comprehend Amfortas's suffering, where previously he had only observed it.

It is this comprehension of pain which lies at the heart of *Parsifal*, a musikdrama that explores the agony of human existence: Amfortas's misery is real but also emblematic of the permanent suffering experienced by humanity and inflicted both internally and externally. This is where, beyond Wolfram and other medieval, pagan or essentially Christian material, Schopenhauer enters into the creation of *Parsifal*, as do supplementary non-Christian religious sources such as Buddhism and Hinduism (both of which appealed to Schopenhauer and influenced his writings). Schopenhauer's own influence on the *Ring*, *Tristan*, and *Meistersinger* was profound and far-reaching. Its impact on Wagner's last work, *Parsifal*, was no different.

In an 1855 sketch of *Tristan und Isolde*, Wagner included a scene he would (rightly) later expurgate: Parzival, an errant knight lost in searching for the Grail, was to stumble across Tristan as the latter died in agony in Brittany in his own drama's third act. For Wagner it was clear, even at this stage: Amfortas was his third-act Tristan, unimaginably intensified. The parallels are evident. Tristan, like Amfortas, suffers a wound and longs for the release of death. As with Amfortas, love and sex are the origins of this injury. But Tristan's pain is personal, his love much more private. Amfortas's wound is not only an individual anguish but something which agonizes his entire community — and, therefore, by allegorical implication, the world of humanity. Amfortas's misery is the error of existence, the agony of human being.

In Schopenhauer, Wagner had found a soulmate for his increasingly dark and pessimistic view of the world, which developed during his exile in the 1850s, after the revolution failed. The philosophy of emancipation through world renunciation and final obliteration (though not, as often thought, suicide) are the essence of Schopenhauer. This was a standpoint which readily appealed to Wagner for artistic as well as personal reasons. He understood that the world was more often than not an excruciating, intolerable place, full of suffering, disappointment, neglect and fear, as well as (and not unrelatedly) irrepressible impulses, desires and instincts, especially those of the erotic will. For Schopenhauer, the sex act is the ultimate will to life, a will to life which creates — both internally and in the wider world — much suffering. Wagner was himself not in agony over fleshly guilt and was not advocating some sort of celibate society. But he recognized the destructive (as well as creative) power of sex and saw its potential for compulsion and abandonment, the torments, frenzies and mitigations of which were inherently dramatic. This, of course, was something he had known, and dramatized, since at least *Tannhäuser*, if not before. But now he had a stronger intellectual framework for what he had always felt.

Amfortas and Tristan are most usually seen as the Wagnerian characters finally granted the insight of liberation through denial. But another key figure in *Parsifal* also embodies this, as well as exhibiting Wagner's skill at compressing his vast sources not only into taut drama but into hugely profound and convincing characters. This is the extraordinary character of Kundry, one of Wagner's supreme musico-dramatic creations. She is the pin which holds the whole drama — Parsifal's redemption of Amfortas, and himself — together.

In Wolfram, Wagner was greatly taken with the potential of the first scene in the temple of the Grail. Indeed, it is likely the nut from which the vast tree of *Parsifal* sprouted. Here was a very simple dramatic confrontation. The meeting (at the end of act 1 in *Parsifal*) between the bedridden, tortured king, hemmed in by useless, helpless acolytes, and the naïve, blundering boy was dreadfully powerful, innately theatrical — and could be balanced by a mirroring one later on. Here Wagner saw again the fraught and hampered master encountering his unwitting heir — as he had when Siegfried and the Wanderer meet in act 3 of *Siegfried* or, in less emotionally loaded circumstances, Hans Sachs decides to assist Walther in *Die Meistersinger*.

Wagner's problem was how to get from the first, dumbfounded confrontation to its echo at the drama's end. Kundry was not merely this mechanism but also an instrument which overcame functionality to become one of *Parsifal*'s true centres of emotional, intellectual and spiritual being. Kundry's kiss — her attempted seduction of Parsifal in act 2 — as well as being compelling and significant in itself has a formidable and dramatically connective feature by being a repetition of her earlier seduction of Amfortas, which we learn about only in the immensely powerful musikdrama narrations. Kundry's kiss is not only the axis of the work but a reminder of its origins, motivation and misfortune. It is consequently both core and periphery, heart and margin, inside and outside the drama.

Kundry was forged from the artistic conflagration of several figures in Wolfram, as well as from a range of philosophical and religious concepts and characters. In Wolfram, Wagner found templates for her alluring beauty, her mysterious awareness of Parsifal's past, her anxious, grave and sometimes despairing enslavement and subservience to the knights of the Grail. When she bathes Parsifal's feet in act 3, she is — to certain audiences — instantly recognizable as Mary Magdalene, whom Wagner had actually drafted into an abandoned drama, *Jesus von Nazareth*, in 1848. In Kundry's dual existence as both sexual and spiritual servant, there are also echoes of Mary Magdalene's well-known conflation with Mary of Bethany and the 'sinful woman' (i.e., prostitute) who bathes Jesus's feet in the Gospel of Luke.

Kundry's originating sin, mocking the saviour at the moment of his death, for which she has been compelled to live out her wretched double life, has obvious Christian aspects. Wagner, however, also incorporated other faiths, as well as revisiting another discarded work: in his Buddhist drama *Die Sieger* ('The Victors') from 1856, the heroine was to have spurned with derisive, contemptuous laughter the love of a Brahmin's son. Other Eastern elements, ideas to which Schopenhauer's are closely related, include Kundry's agonized immortality through the transmigration of her soul. This is the Buddhist doctrine of metempsychosis, manifest in her ceaseless voyaging through time and history, in which she has — Klingsor tells us — adopted the forms of both the biblical Herodias, mother to Salome and John the Baptist's nemesis, and the Nordic Gundryggia.

The Eastern components in particular have not only frustrated those seeking a purely Christian interpretation of *Parsifal* but also confused those pursuing any intellectual unity to the work. Failing to comprehend the hybrid nature of *Parsifal*, as well as the greater potential this grants it emotionally and dramatically, critics have instead tended to narrowly argue for inconsistencies, especially to Kundry's character. But employed together in order to shape the multifaceted nature of her being, the vast range of sources that birthed Kundry help explain her depth and fascination as a character. *Parsifal* in general, and Kundry in particular, are only the final instance of the extremely skilled way Wagner amalgamated and assimilated a wealth of competing materials into extremely taut and verbally concise dramas on which he could hang the vastness of his symphonic music. The libretti for *Tristan* and *Parsifal* have an almost Eastern spareness to them, a slender austerity that belies a profound density of ideas.

We have seen how elements from two abandoned dramas — *Jesus von Nazareth* and *Die Sieger* — found their way into Kundry's character. Wagner was remarkable for finishing even those projects which he did not complete by incorporating their curtailed elements elsewhere. More fundamentally, *Parsifal* contains, as one might expect from a work which was in his mind from almost the beginning of his career to its end, allusions to a whole host of his characters. Kundry, in addition to the complex assortment of figures outlined above, shares the Dutchman's affinity with the wandering Jew, longing for death as a discharge from a damnable existence and chain of being, a delivery to be found only through another's loyalty. Her life, like Tannhäuser's, is a cycle of self-abandonment and sexual-emotional need, something Amfortas shares (and which indeed inaugurates the whole work).

Klingsor, the rejected knight turned magician, has, like Alberich, relinquished love and in the process, in his self-castration, forfeited, as with Wotan and his eye, an essential organ, which gives him a disturbing power. Amfortas, as we have seen, shares much with the third-act Tristan, though one lives and the other dies. In Gurnemanz, Wagner created something quite unique, almost a one-man Greek chorus. But the knight shares some of Wotan's impatient desire to find a hero to redeem his community/world, as well as the world-weariness Wotan assumes as the Wanderer in *Siegfried*. By the end of their dramas, both are ineffectual, if wise, spectators, bystanders to the actions of others. In the *Ring*, this other is Siegfried. In *Parsifal*, it is its eponymous hero.

Siegfried and Parsifal have much in common. Both are orphaned innocents, ignorant of the world, who achieve maturity through an encounter with desire: decisive sexual junctures which parallel earlier occasions by the discredited heroes (Siegmund and Amfortas) they have come to replace and (hopefully) supersede. Both are fond of missing mothers whose absences become alarmingly present at moments of crisis and epiphany. Both are, to begin with, blithe, happy-go-lucky huntsmen with broad fanfare-like motifs that nonetheless contain a degree of poignancy. In Siegfried's, it is the sadness of what might have been, the future disappointment of his mission. In Parsifal's, the poignancy is part of his character's history, and it also ensures the score/action can swiftly and fluently return to its forlorn mood and unhurried pace.

Both Siegfried and Parsifal stumble into a complex state of affairs they do not comprehend. Although Siegfried's entry perhaps seems less random, given his place in the context of the *Ring*, Parsifal's arrival has been prefigured not only by his special status but by the drama's music. Indeed, a moment directly before Parsifal's blundering, swan-killing entry, his imminent advent is verbally as well as musically heralded with the only leitmotif of *Parsifal* to originate in the text:

> Through compassion enlightened,
> the pure fool

Gurnemanz is relaying the past prophecy from the Grail of a forthcoming saviour, and this redeemer's immediate arrival

serves to link past, present and future and does so with the
sole leitmotif which does not derive from the orchestra. As
a unique vocally originating motif, it immaculately unites text
and music — a miniature musikdrama — at the very moment of
the titular character's entrance. This is even more conspicuous
because *Parsifal*'s art of investigating truth is primarily orchestral.
The dialectic which creates drama, including musikdrama, is,
in *Parsifal*, predominantly transferred from exterior action/
dialogue to interior conflict, an inner action which is conveyed
by a large-scale symphonic system of extraordinary subtlety
and flexibility. Before investigating the structure and narrative
of *Parsifal*, it is worth a short consideration of exactly how this
extraordinary inner action is communicated.

Parsifal's orchestral cosmos is principally one of delicate
textures and a transparent, radiant variety of infinite greys.
This refinement is unsettled by the intrusion of weightier
and more opaque sounds, such as those associated with
Klingsor's demonic self-affirmation or the harsh, anguished
cries of Kundry and Amfortas, but Wagner does not create
a sequence of symphonic tone poems in order to match the
mood of a particular scene and its occupants. His score is an
evolving series of blended developments and imperceptible
correspondences, harmony and melody continuously
interacting to produce the advancing structure of the
musikdrama. It is in this way that the complexity, subtlety,
uncertainty and beauty of the score are generated, the intricacy
of mysterious behaviour its distinguishing property. In *Parsifal*,
musical concepts such as tonality begin to lose their meaning,
as the wandering, floating score hazily and indistinctly strays

between keys: an elusive and agonizing search to match that of the stage action.

Although orchestral dialectics are a continuous, incessant and defining feature of the Wagnerian musikdrama, and *Parsifal* in particular, specific instrumental passages have a certain importance because of the exceptional way they transmit the nuance and shades of the score. We will explore just two of the most outstanding examples: the preludes to acts 1 and 3.

The work begins with silences, gaps, pauses — the empty spaces of existence, expanses of sentiment as yet without function, purpose or application. Meaning is always poignantly absent, mournfully distant, but thought begins to progress and expand through the silences, reflection and attention connecting to the stillness. Constructed in three sections, the *Parsifal* act 1 prelude is assembled from very minimal resources and presents an immediately ambiguous sound-world. It appears from the air, from silence, with an incomparable fusion of wind and strings: clarinet and bassoon, joined by a cor anglais, with violins and cellos. It suggests redemption, guilt and love, but a love dark and isolated, deprived of harmony and all rhythmic assurance. A halo of strings surrounds a trumpet as it restates its heartrending theme. This is followed by the second part of the prelude: the consoling intonation of the 'Dresden Amen', a promise of redemption, and the bold theme of faith on brass. This resolution is undermined in the third section by the return of torment and uncertainty on agonized strings: Amfortas's endless emotional distress and physical agony, unable to musically resolve themselves.

Wagner presents discernibly contrasting pairs (darkness/light, doubt/faith, pain/recovery) but with an equivocality that will come to characterize not only the work's music but its dramatic and metaphysical enigma. Although it is sometimes possible, at certain moments, to identify particular themes, part of *Parsifal's* nature is the difficulty of reaching

any certainty in regard to compelling, unambiguous labels —
something which gives the score its mysterious elation as well.
Everything is interrelated, denying and confusing the meaning
of various spheres of the music as it evolves, with intricate
ethical consequences. For instance, the Grail's remoteness
in sound only carries true significance when it is contrasted
with Klingsor's agitated harmonics — which were nearer the
musical norm of progressive music in 1882, making the Grail's
sublimity even more insulated and inaccessible. Nothing is
conveniently labelled in *Parsifal*: leitmotifs and ethical categories
are in constant flux.

Like its equivalent in *Tannhäuser*, the act 3 prelude to *Parsifal*
is a musical travelogue, a picture of Parsifal's desolate years
roaming across the earth, searching for the province of the Grail.
Like its equivalent in *Siegfried* or *Die Meistersinger*, it is also
a psychological portrait — perhaps of Parsifal, but possibly also
Kundry, a haunting presentation of the deep sleep and dreams
from which Gurnemanz will shortly wake her. Kundry has only
two words in the entire third act ('Dienen... Dienen...', 'Let me
serve, serve... ') but her music will play a crucial role in its first
part. Musikdrama, after all, is orchestrally focused: words have
become increasingly irrelevant or ineffectual. Kundry's music
permeates the score up until her blessing from Parsifal, after
which she fades from the music, a strange, altered presence,
entering a state of blissful renunciation.

The act 3 prelude begins with a languorous sigh of
resignation, a nomadic nothingness, an itinerant obfuscation
of fragments and disintegration, vaguely wandering through
the keys. Themes of servitude, laughter and awakening mingle,
evolve and regress. The motif of the Grail forlornly tries
to proclaim and establish itself, but it is weary, weakened,
powerless against the dissolving quicksand of the score. The
Grail motif, faced with this barren and threatening space,
subsides into the morass of Kundry's lust. Still identifiable,

it squirms and lurches, suffocating amid a mire of orchestral disfigurements. From this perilous warp, the motif of the pure fool begins to surface, gradually buttressed by ever more muscular ascending notes related to the spear. Escaping the quagmire, the music collapses, exhausted, into the beginning of the final act and the open meadows of Good Friday.

Such orchestral complexity necessitated simplicity in the outward framework of the drama, and the design of *Parsifal* is not only straightforward but balanced, as well as offering the structure for a compelling narrative direction. The two outer acts mirror one another with their geography: a nature scene (forest/meadow) is followed by an architectural one (Grail). These echoing acts enclose a central one where nature and architecture are combined in sinister fashion: Klingsor's castle and magic garden are a perversion of nature for nefarious ends.

But it is more complicated than this. The religious structure of the Grail temple is, in a sense, a petrified forest: both geologically, as organic matter turned to stone, and emotionally, in the frozen rituals which occur there. The static, closed-off world of the Grail is not as straightforwardly 'good' as we might believe. It is an oppressive, isolated world, judging and ostracizing outsiders — including the lustful Klingsor, whom a more merciful community might have tried to help rather than compel towards self-mutilation. Though a wizard of the dark arts, he, too, has suffered great physical and spiritual pain in his licentious will, rejection by the knights, brutal orchiectomy, and perpetual misplaced yearning for the Grail. Klingsor and the Grail, ostensibly at opposite ends of the moral spectrum, share music which has a hollow confidence, a vacant assertion of their own empty rituals.

Like the stagnant formalities of the Grail, or Klingsor, Gurnemanz's narrations are their own form of stationary ceremony but have beneath their static surface a fascinating and dynamic inner drama linking the present with the past. *Parsifal's* internal action, especially in the long first act, is principally generated by Gurnemanz, and his soft, diffused, submerged music produces a serenity not only in the surrounding score and scene but the work as a whole. Gurnemanz's narrations claim their movement, like most of *Parsifal's* music, from within, from a measured, peaceful and unhurried expansion, extemporaneously unfurling from the inside. It is a slow progression in time to match the translucent subsistence in space.

Between the simple frame and highly complex inner drama communicated through the music, Wagner gave *Parsifal* a clear-cut narrative of linear progression and gradual development. Three times, once in each act, Parsifal enters a static situation and energizes it while also growing on each occasion: intellectually, emotionally, ethically and spiritually. And the words which capture the essence of this personal journey are, of course, those which signalled his arrival: 'Through compassion enlightened, the pure fool'.

In act 1, Parsifal stumbles across the holy ground in the realm of the Grail. He has killed a swan — a particularly sacred feature of blessed nature. He is ignorant about such things, knowing about neither the sanctity of the swan nor its violation by his arrows. But, when challenged about his behaviour, the first stirring of compassion is awoken in him. If the swan is apparently incidental to the plot, a mere device to get the titular hero onstage, it is absolutely crucial in Parsifal's inner development and that of the musikdrama. Later in the first act, witnessing the Grail ceremony, Parsifal feels some pity for Amfortas when seeing him in pain but little more, not enquiring as to *why* he is in pain. He observes Amfortas as he had learnt to observe the swan: as an injured creature.

In act 2, Kundry's kiss, as we have seen, is the sudden and transcendent disclosure to Parsifal of what Amfortas has gone through: his temptation, his erotic will, his suffering, his constant agony and yearning for death. Cause and effect are made devastatingly apparent, and Parsifal experiences them in an astonishing moment of immense revelatory power which is at the structural, dramatic and ethical-metaphysical centre of the entire work. Parsifal is exposed to Schopenhauer at this moment, becoming his follower instinctively, inevitably and absolutely through his direct contact and unconditional comprehension. Parsifal sees the endless cycle of desire, self-reproach and despair which can only be destroyed through compassion and renunciation.

In the third act, that which the second promised is fulfilled. Kundry is blessed, the Grail renewed and Amfortas healed. This is the ultimate realization of Parsifal's action in regaining the spear, reconciling Amfortas with the very object which caused his pain and allowing him consequent resolution within himself. But there is more to this resolution than any mere symbolic restoration of the status quo. It is also the third and final stage of Parsifal's inner action, his journey from inarticulate feeling to knowledge/understanding and subsequently the expression of this information/compassion in a redeeming deed.

None of Wagner's vast array of sources had the simple and dramatically satisfactory pattern which the composer created for *Parsifal*. Not only does Wagner display immense skill in bringing together all the varied and incongruent elements which make up the drama but he gives it a balance and emotional arc which surpass all his sources. There had been a propensity, as the Grail legend matured over time, to focus more and more on its hero and, in so doing, make Parsifal's quest an egotistical, self-absorbed mission whose intention was less bringing assistance to a community than his own personal redemption. Wagner's Parsifal has no trace of this narcissism. He remains central to the dramatic sweep of the opera, but his vocation is more integrated than it might have been, a personal and structural humility which allows other characters scope to breathe and quietly assert their own predicaments. *Parsifal*'s final line — 'redemption to the redeemer' — asserts its hero's own deliverance, but only after he has liberated everyone else.

This is a crucial aspect to *Parsifal*, and one which also undermines attempts to claim it as a Christian work, especially one with some form of evangelical intention. The redeemer at *Parsifal*'s close is not Christ. Christ is not the one who redeems the Grail community: it is Parsifal. Moreover, the radiant, glowing conclusion to the work is not any form of assumption into heaven or any other ethereal realm. The redemption is deeply moving, deeply spiritual, but it lacks a specific soteriological agency beyond assisting the Grail community in its own renewal. The world at the opera's close is as error-strewn and empty as when it began. Dark days doubtless lie ahead. In his renunciation, Parsifal has become not a Christian but a disciple of Schopenhauer.

Of course, the immense and intense Christian hinterland to *Parsifal*, its employment of specifically Christian symbols such as the Grail and spear, naturally exhibits many features of Christian content. But, as we have seen, there are non-Christian (pagan, Buddhist) elements as well, which, though not as pervasive, deserve their place. Moreover, Wagner was clear about the Schopenhauerian philosophy behind the work: repudiating the world — but not scurrying into the arms of Christianity. Parsifal does not redeem the world. Christ might have done, but Parsifal does not.

Yet the attitude persists that *Parsifal* is a Christian opera, despite this being a total anathema to Wagner's very unequivocal stated purpose. Art, as Wagner never tired of repeating, was to salvage the beneficial, emblematic components to otherwise dead and artificial religion. The values, truths, images and symbols of religion were immensely valuable — not least for the construction of complex metaphysical musikdramas like *Parsifal*. But they were not, for Wagner, the truth in any theological sense. Wagner no more believed in Christianity and the ultimately redemptive power of Christ than he did the Norse gods or existence of magic helmets, love potions or ghostly, perpetually circumnavigating Dutch ships. As Schopenhauer knew, Christianity, like Brahmanism and Buddhism, contains great and fundamental truths regarding, say, the denial of the will. But these were messages to guide life (or opera), not a guarantee of post-mortem salvation. The faithful had made the mistake of believing in the literal truth of religious images or teachings.

For Wagner, it was essential for art to take over many of the roles (ethical, political, spiritual, aesthetic) religion had hitherto undertaken. It is for this reason that he designated *Parsifal ein Bühnenweihfestspiel*, a sacred stage festival play. Theatre, especially Wagner's theatre, was to replace Christianity as the supplier of morals and metaphysics. *Parsifal* was to consecrate his new Church and inaugurate his new religion. Given the fanaticism many feel for Wagner, and especially *Parsifal*, and their talk of pilgrimages to the temple of Bayreuth, it is hard to argue that Wagner failed, at least in some respects.

If *Parsifal* is not a Christian opera, what is it? The most straightforward answer endorses it as a tale of renunciation, a Schopenhauerian drama taking up and exploring the various

Christian, Buddhist, pagan and pessimistic concerns the German philosopher surveyed. In many respects, however, its elusive layers, its multidimensional score, its almost infinitely receding mysteries have allowed every and any interpretation to be undertaken. Just as *Tristan* resists staging, preferring the isolation of its aural kingdom, and *Meistersinger* surrenders to it, compelling decisions to be made regarding its reality and illusion, *Parsifal* hovers in between, luxuriating in obscurity but softly urging the tangibility of clarification. As with Shakespeare's endlessly posed but ultimately unanswerable questions, with *Parsifal*, meaning tends to come only with performance, with a director's (provisional and incomplete) vision of the work.

Wagner's grandson Wieland's Bayreuth production in 1951 was a poignant and epoch-making event, reopening the Festival, and Germany, to the world after the shameful twin catastrophes of global war and racial extermination. His *Parsifal* was consequently uncontaminated, chaste, minimal, reduced to its bare essentials in shape and stage architecture. Lighting, a defining feature of Wieland's spare style, worked in collaboration with the music, both floating free in a rainbow of greys and blues, turning violet for the sinister, seductive menace of Klingsor's realm. Wieland's post-war interpretations of his grandfather's works operated as timeless mystery plays or Greek dramas, and relative abstraction seemed to suit *Parsifal*, which succeeded untroubled by heavy or realistic sets. Whatever the need for post-war purification, Wieland instinctively understood the elusive, sometimes evasive, nature of the work, allowing the audience to place their own meaning upon it while also basking in the hallucinogenic beauty of his ethereal, twilit designs.

Wieland's successor at Bayreuth, his brother Wolfgang, adopted a more naturalistic approach for his mid-'70s *Parsifal*, something Otto Schenk reproduced for the New York Met in 1992. Experienced as 'authentic' productions seeking to realize the tenuous lie of the 'composer's intentions', these interpretations seem a little lacklustre. However, if they are regarded as hymns to the environment, celebrating the natural world honoured by the work's third act on the rejuvenating morning of Good Friday, they become more stimulating, more enticing. Wolfgang himself urged this interpretation and, seen thus, his 1975 *Parsifal* becomes a fascinating ecological prelude to the infamous Patrice Chéreau *Ring* production of the following year, where nature is utterly despoiled in the ruthless world of the Nibelung dramas. Wolfgang's *Parsifal* was a flourishing, vivid world of lush shrubbery and verdant colours, contrasting strongly with the solid, stark, unforgiving and empty realms of the Grail and Klingsor's castle, his magic garden a disturbing synthetic approximation of nature's wonders.

Millennial and early twenty-first-century productions have frequently asserted the essential emptiness of the *Parsifal* world, the suffering and blankness it presents, seeing the musikdrama as a Eliotian wasteland playing its despairing Beckettian endgame. Both Nikolaus Lehnhoff (Baden-Baden/London, 1999) and Dmitri Tcherniakov (Berlin, 2015) had impressively dark visions of the work, asserting its existential despair, the burden of being, but recognizing the potential freedom which such a world view both sanctions and encourages.

Between them came a production which showed the full potential of *Parsifal*, and opera, as a discursive, dialectical medium, the equal — perhaps even the superior — to academia or documentary. Stefan Herheim's 2008 *Parsifal* for Bayreuth was an intelligent, highly creative and deeply moving testimony to Wagner's vision, as well as being a warning of its limitless possibility. He staged Parsifal as a history of Germany from the time of the work's birth in 1882 to the reunification of East and West in 1990. Few centuries have been so turbulent, disgraceful, humiliating and overwhelming for a country: its own hubris and internal flaws led to violence and depravity of the most unspeakable kind, before division and the long road to recovery. Herheim's genius, his consummate skill, was to map the German century onto the existing story of *Parsifal* without any impression of contrivance but rather a feeling of common inspiration and shared influence. History became both more complex and straightforward, events more and less predictable — within and without the narrative of the drama. Time became less linear, more confusing, the past, present and future becoming mutual partners in creation and destruction, just as the weaving, elusive score of *Parsifal* invites.

Herheim engaged not only with the complications of history and historical interpretation but those inherent to *Parsifal* itself: the problems of relating the present to the past, especially a past as burdened as Amfortas's or Germany's or Bayreuth's. In this shrewd, ingenious and courageous interpretation, the narrative lines entwined so that we simultaneously saw the tale of Parsifal from boy to man, the history of *Parsifal* productions across the years, and the history of Deutschland from the Second Reich to reunification. The invasive power of Klingsor/Nazis in the second act was shocking and spellbinding theatre, but part of its power was the way Herheim (and Wagner) showed that fascism and Klingsor's malice did not come from thin air; they came from the recesses and horror of history. Herheim, via *Parsifal*, was able to show the absolute horror of Nazism while simultaneously refusing to see it as a historical aberrance.

In Herheim's production, when Parsifal destroyed Klingsor's realm with the spear at the end of the second act, this was no mere Indiana Jones–style Nazi-whipping. It was traumatizing, lacerating new cuts and lesions on an already mutilated torso. The long years of Parsifal's wandering between the second and third acts felt even longer, Herheim asking where the periphery to this internal shadow might be and what bandage he might place upon the injury for reconciliation. That resolution would come, after long years of searching, but the wounds remain, the scars painful — for Parsifal, *Parsifal*, Bayreuth, Germany and the world.

Parsifal shows the danger of closed ideologies, the danger of communities or personalities cut off, detached, isolated. It shows the corrosive power of time. It shows the absolute potential as well as the abyss of humanity and how these have similar roots, both virtuous and vile. It shows that existence exacts a demanding price for any of its goodness and meaning — the devastating penalties of suffering and desolation, the anguish caused by both physical pain and spiritual-emotional disquiet. Existence, *Parsifal* argues, is a mistake. If it is a story of hope, too, it is one restricted by the limitations of our own species: sentient, conscious, often caring beings in an ominous and indifferent universe. For Richard Wagner, art, and especially the art of *Parsifal*, was a means to correct the error of existence through examining it, understanding it. The success of this rectification is up to each individual to decide, but the world with *Parsifal* in it seems less wrong, more dynamic, more appealing, more honest and more beautiful than one without it.

APPENDIXES

Synopses

Der fliegende Holländer

A seaman, the Flying Dutchman, has been condemned for his blasphemy to rove the seas for all eternity but is sanctioned to come ashore once every seven years in search of a faithful woman whose love will release him from his curse.

Act 1 A storm has driven a Norwegian ship into a cove not far from home. Its merchant captain, Daland, encounters a mysterious stranger who offers the skipper immense riches if he will let him stay the night. When the stranger learns Daland has a daughter, he offers his entire treasure for her hand in marriage. The Norwegian greedily agrees and sets sail for port.

Act 2 The village women are at work, spinning, awaiting the return of their sailors. One of them, Senta, Daland's daughter, causes a commotion by singing a poignant, blood-curdling ballad to a portrait in which she sees the Flying Dutchman, whose tragic fate fascinates her. Erik, a hunter and her fiancé, admonishes her for her infatuation, warning of its dangers. Daland arrives with the enigmatic mariner, whom Senta immediately recognizes as the man she will redeem, and he her.

They are left alone and grow close, Senta pledging her loyalty to him, the eternal seafarer believing his suffering is now at an end.

Act 3 The people celebrate the safe homecoming of Daland's vessel, which is moored alongside the stranger's ship. The Norwegians drunkenly call out to the strange crew to join them, but their invitation is met with an eerie silence. After further boisterous songs and demands, the foreign ship suddenly pitches and tosses, as if in a tempest, and a ghostly chorus disperses the carousing Norwegians. Emerging from Daland's house, Erik reproaches Senta for breaking her vow to him, which the stranger overhears, leading him to believe Senta fickle. Senta protests her loyalty but, unconvinced, the stranger reveals himself as the Flying Dutchman and leaves on his ship. Senta pledges her devotion by leaping into the sea. The transfigured, embracing forms of the Dutchman and Senta are seen soaring heavenwards in the glow of the rising sun.

Tannhäuser

Heinrich, a singer-knight known as Tannhäuser, has left the prim and pious Wartburg court and is living as Venus's lover in the outlandish erotic cavern of the Venusberg.

Act 1 As a wild orgy takes place around him, Tannhäuser sleeps. On waking, he longs to leave the static sensuality of Venus's pleasure dome and return to the mortal world. Venus admonishes him for his ingratitude, so he sings of the enchantments of love and sex but ends each verse with an appeal for liberty: his salvation lies with the Virgin Mary, mention of whom makes the Venusberg vanish. Tannhäuser finds himself in a valley, not far from the Wartburg, as a shepherd boy greets the spring and plays on his pipe. Some pilgrims journeying to Rome pass, moving Tannhäuser deeply, followed by a courtly hunting party. Recognizing their long-lost friend, the hunters beg him to return to the Wartburg. Initially reluctant, Tannhäuser yields when one of the knights, Wolfram, mentions that Tannhäuser's singing — before he journeyed to the Venusberg — won the love of the Landgrave's niece, Elizabeth.

Act 2 Elizabeth rejoices at Tannhäuser's homecoming and jubilantly hails the great Hall of Song, which she has shunned since his disappearance. Wolfram brings in the erring knight: at first shy, Elizabeth tells how Tannhäuser's songs once moved and confused her. They praise how love has reunited them. The Landgrave enters and announces the song contest's theme: the true meaning of love. Wolfram sings of idealized love, Tannhäuser the sensual delights of Venus. The latter's scandalous paean to fleshly indulgence provokes anger and violence, but Elizabeth steps in, proclaiming that Tannhäuser must be given the chance to redeem himself via a Roman pilgrimage.

Act 3 Autumn. Wolfram attends Elizabeth as she prays, awaiting the pilgrims' return. The pilgrims arrive, but Tannhäuser is not among them. Grief-stricken, Elizabeth prays to be taken up to heaven to intercede for his soul before silently departing for the Wartburg. Tannhäuser appears, weary and in rags. His pilgrimage has failed: despite his piety and penance, the Pope refused absolution — Tannhäuser can no more be forgiven for his sexual sins than the papal staff bear green leaves. Forlorn, Tannhäuser wants only to return to Venus, who now reappears, inviting him to her carnal kingdom. Wolfram intervenes, destroying Venus by invoking Elizabeth's name. Elizabeth's prayers have been answered, and her funeral cortège now appears. Tannhäuser collapses, dead, as young pilgrims arrive from Rome bearing the Pope's staff, now covered in verdant shoots.

Lohengrin

Act 1 Heinrich, king of the Germans, has come to Antwerp to persuade the Brabantines to join him in defending Germany against Hungarian attack. Sensing internal tensions, the nobleman Telramund explains to Heinrich how the juvenile Duke Gottfried vanished one day when alone with his sister, Elsa — whom Telramund had hoped to marry, but she had spurned him. Telramund has married Ortrud instead and now accuses Elsa of murdering her own brother. Heinrich orders a trial. Elsa is dumbfounded by the charges and describes a dream in which a mysterious figure came to aid her. Heinrich decrees this person will fight Telramund to settle the matter. The herald twice sounds a summons before a swan appears on the river, drawing a boat on which stands a knight, who offers to fight for Elsa's honour. If he wins, they will wed, on condition she never ask his name or origin. He prevails in the fight, but compassionately spares Telramund's life.

    Act 2 Telramund blames Ortrud and her witchcraft for his loss and pending expulsion from Brabant. His wife retorts that the knight can be overwhelmed if the forbidden questions are asked. They vow revenge. Ortrud shrewdly manipulates Elsa, destabilizing her faith in her husband-to-be. The wedding pageant assembles and, just as Elsa is about to enter the church, Ortrud appears, mocking her liaison with the secretive knight. Telramund, too, arrives, denouncing the knight's enigmatic status. Dazed and confused, Elsa laments not knowing her bridegroom's origins, but he and King Heinrich reassure her and the pair of villains are dismissed.

Act 3 The newlyweds are in their bridal chamber, alone for the first time. Elsa is saddened when her husband uses her name, something she cannot reciprocate. She grows increasingly agitated and, fearing he will wish to return to his previous life, asks the forbidden question. Instantly, Telramund and his followers break in: her husband kills the nobleman and tells Elsa their happiness is now lost. Telramund's body is to be borne to the king; in his presence, the knight will reveal his identity. He is Lohengrin, Parsifal's son, and a guardian of the Holy Grail whose mystical powers are protected by their anonymity. The swan approaches, towing his boat. As Lohengrin bids Elsa farewell, Ortrud abruptly appears, revealing that she had turned Gottfried into the swan and, had Lohengrin stayed, he could have saved Gottfried. Lohengrin falls in prayer, a dove appears and the swan sinks below the water, remerging as Gottfried: the missing Duke of Brabant. The dove draws Lohengrin and his vessel away, and Elsa collapses lifeless to the ground.

Das Rheingold

Long ago, Wotan, chief of the gods, sinned against nature by drinking from the fountain of wisdom, losing an eye in the process, before breaking a branch from the World Ash Tree and fashioning it into a spear with which he now rules.

Scene 1 In the depths of the Rhine, three Rhinemaidens guard the Rhinegold. As they play, the dwarf Alberich tries to woo them, but they tease and rebuff him. He catches sight of the gold, and the maidens explain it gives immeasurable power to whoever can fashion it into a ring, but that person must first renounce love — surely an impossible price. Frustrated by his unsuccessful courting, Alberich curses love and steals the gold.

Scene 2 High in the mountains, Wotan is chided by his wife, Fricka, for promising Freia, goddess of love, to the giants Fasolt and Fafner as payment for building his castle, Valhalla. When the giants demand payment, fire god Loge suggests an alternative: Alberich's Ring and other treasures which the dwarf forged from the Rhinegold.

Scene 3 Wotan and Loge descend underground to Nibelheim, the dwarfs' realm, where Alberich's brother Mime has created the Tarnhelm, a magic helmet. Mime tells of how Alberich enslaved the Nibelung race to work the gold for him. Alberich arrives and mocks the gods, and Loge suggests an exhibition of the Tarnhelm's power: the dwarf agrees and transforms himself into a gigantic dragon, then an inconspicuous toad, which the gods capture and haul in chains to the surface.

Scene 4 Wotan forces Alberich to summon the Nibelungs and pile up the gold, including the Ring, which the god wrests from the dwarf's finger. Alberich curses the Ring: incessant worry and death will meet all that possess it. The giants return and accept the gold as payment, as long as it can completely hide Freia from Fasolt's adoring gaze. Even the Tarnhelm is needed to cover her, but Wotan refuses to part with the Ring. Erda, the earth goddess, appears and warns Wotan that possessing the Ring will end the gods' rule. Wotan grudgingly hands it over, and the Ring's curse immediately claims its first victim when Fafner murders Fasolt over possession of it. The gods trudge triumphantly into their new home, Valhalla — as the Rhinemaidens below mourn the theft of their precious gold.

❧

Die Walküre

To protect himself, Wotan gathers at Valhalla an army of
warriors. He also seeks to influence events so a free hero will
recapture the Ring for him and has consequently fathered the
twins Siegmund and Sieglinde, separated as children…

Act 1 Pursued by his enemies in a fierce storm, Siegmund
seeks refuge in an unfamiliar house where a woman, Sieglinde,
cares for him. They are instantly attracted, but her abusive,
controlling husband, Hunding, returns, grudgingly offering
hospitality to the guest. Siegmund tells of his tragic life and the
abduction of his twin sister. It becomes evident that Hunding
is one of his enemies. They will have to fight in the morning.
That night, Siegmund cries out for help from his father, Wälse
(Wotan), who promised him a sword in his hour of need.
Sieglinde responds that at her wedding a stranger plunged
a sword into their house's ash tree. No one has yet managed to
pull it out. Siegmund vows to liberate Sieglinde: he wrenches
the sword free, and they passionately recognize each other as
brother and sister.

Act 2 Siegmund and Sieglinde have eloped. Wotan
commands his favourite daughter, Brünnhilde, to protect
Siegmund against Hunding, but his wife, Fricka, demands
Wotan uphold the laws of marriage. His plans for a free
hero to reclaim the Ring now ruined, he reorders Brünnhilde
to fight for Hunding. Brünnhilde seeks out Siegmund and
announces his forthcoming death and eternal separation
from Sieglinde: he can go to Valhalla as a hero only without
Sieglinde. He refuses. Moved by Siegmund's love, Brünnhilde
decides to disobey her father and fight for the twins. As
Siegmund and Hunding clash, Wotan appears and shatters
his son's blade with his spear, allowing Hunding to strike
him dead. Brünnhilde flees with Sieglinde and the splintered
fragments of the sword.

Act 3 Brünnhilde begs her Valkyrie sisters for protection from their furious father. Petrified, they decline. Brünnhilde predicts the pregnant Sieglinde will give birth to a noble hero and sends her to safety in the eastern forest. Wotan arrives, scattering the Valkyries. He strips Brünnhilde of her divinity, banishing her to sleep on this remote mountaintop, the property of any man who finds her. A scene of tender recriminations follows, and Brünnhilde begs to be encircled by fire so only a fearless hero can discover her. Calmed, her father consents. Despondently renouncing his beloved daughter, Wotan solemnly plunges her into a magic sleep and, summoning the fire god Loge, surrounds her rock with flames. Brünnhilde is safe from anyone who fears Loge's fire and Wotan's spear. Wotan turns to look at her a final time and disappears through the flames.

Siegfried

Act 1 Siegfried has been raised in the forest by Mime, Alberich's brother. When Siegfried demands to know his parentage, Mime tells him how the dying Sieglinde asked the dwarf to care for her newborn son, also giving him the splinters of the dead Siegmund's sword. Siegfried dashes off into the forest and the Wanderer (Wotan in disguise) appears and challenges Mime to a riddle competition, which the dwarf loses since he cannot tell who will reforge the sword. Telling Mime that only one who knows no fear can do so, the Wanderer leaves. Siegfried returns, and Mime suggests they journey to the cave where Fafner, now transformed by the Tarnhelm into a dragon, guards the Ring and hoard of gold. Siegfried agrees and reforges Nothung, while Mime secretly prepares a potion to poison Siegfried and steal the treasure once the boy has killed Fafner for him.

Act 2 Deep in the forest, Alberich gloomily waits for Fafner to succumb to the Ring's curse so he can regain the Ring. The Wanderer enters and the two quarrel, the god warning the dwarf of his brother's greed before departing. Alberich hides when Mime and Siegfried arrive. Left alone, Siegfried reflects on his mother amid the beauties of the forest. Playing his horn, he wakes the dragon, then kills it. Pulling his sword out of Fafner's heart, he spills some blood. When he tastes it, he can now understand the song of a woodbird which had earlier captivated him. It warns him of Mime's treachery. When the dwarf returns with the poison, Siegfried kills him. The bird tells him of a woman sleeping on a mountain surrounded by fire, and Siegfried sets off to find her.

Act 3 The Wanderer questions Erda, the earth goddess, about the gods' destiny. She is evasive with him, and the Wanderer resigns himself to the gods' imminent demise. Siegfried approaches, and the Wanderer blocks his path, but his spear is shattered by the now stronger, reforged Nothung. Siegfried journeys to Brünnhilde's mountain and rouses her. She sings of her joy at the sun and light and the hero who has awoken her to life. She is initially afraid at the loss of her divinity and hesitant to meet Siegfried's ardent advances, but she soon joins him in praise of their love.

Götterdämmerung

Prologue The three Norns spin the web of destiny, weaving the strands of past, present, future. They recall Wotan's actions in cutting his spear of authority from the World Ash Tree and the tree's subsequent withering. Recently felled, its logs are ready to burn Valhalla. As they recount Alberich's theft of the gold, the rope breaks: their wisdom is ended. As the Norns vanish, the scene shifts to Brünnhilde and Siegfried. It is dawn. Brünnhilde sends Siegfried into the world to accomplish heroic deeds, bestowing on him her horse, Grane; Siegfried reciprocates her gift, giving her the Ring he took from Fafner.

Act 1 Hagen, Alberich's son and half-brother to the Gibichungs (monarchs Gunther and Gutrune), advises Gutrune marry Siegfried and Gunther, Brünnhilde to secure their rule. A magic potion will make Siegfried forget Brünnhilde and love Gutrune, Siegfried himself winning Brünnhilde for Gunther. Siegfried arrives, and the plan falls into action, Gunther and Siegfried swearing a blood-brotherhood. On Brünnhilde's rock, Waltraute visits her sister Brünnhilde and urges her to return the Ring to the Rhine. Brünnhilde refuses, since it is Siegfried's token of love. Siegfried arrives, disguised via the Tarnhelm as Gunther, and seizes both the Ring and Brünnhilde.

Act 2 Night. Hagen, half asleep, talks with his father, Alberich, who exhorts him to recapture the Ring. Dawn: Siegfried arrives to claim Gutrune. Gunther arrives with Brünnhilde, who accuses Siegfried of theft and deceit, but he is blissfully oblivious. Hagen offers to kill Siegfried for Brünnhilde, with Gunther joining their conspiracy.

Act 3 Separated from a hunting party, Siegfried encounters the three Rhinemaidens, who unsuccessfully implore him to return the Ring to them. Seeing the hunt nearby, Siegfried reunites with his comrades. Hagen asks Siegfried to recall his life, which he does. Hagen gives him an antidote to the earlier potion, and Siegfried recalls and relates how he first met Brünnhilde. Claiming perjury against Gunther and his bride, Hagen stabs Siegfried. Siegfried's solemn funeral cortège follows. Gutrune accuses Gunther of murdering her husband.

Hagen fights and kills Gunther. Hagen attempts to snatch the Ring from Siegfried's corpse, but the dead hero's arm rises in defiance. Brünnhilde orders a funeral pyre, seizing the Ring and riding into the flames on Grane. The Rhine overflows its banks. As he tries to grab the Ring, Hagen is pulled underwater by the Rhinemaidens, who joyfully reclaim their gold. The burning Valhalla is seen in the distance. The rule of the gods is at an end.

Tristan und Isolde

An unknown and gravely ill man arrived in Ireland. Isolde tended this 'Tantris' whom she recognized as Tristan, the killer of Morold, her beloved. As she raised her sword in revenge, their eyes met. This look, with its unspoken declaration of love, lies at the enigmatic heart of the drama.

Act 1 Tristan's ship is carrying the Irish princess Isolde to marry his uncle, King Marke. Isolde is edgy, infuriated, despondent, demanding where they are. Approaching the Cornish coast, says her maid Brangäne. Isolde muses on Tristan, now lost to her, and his betrayal at organizing her marriage to Marke. She asks Brangäne bid Tristan approach, but he is evasive. His servant Kurwenal jumps in, mocking Morold. Brangäne shows Isolde two concoctions her mother entrusted to her: a love and a death potion. Isolde demands the latter and that Tristan drink it with her in expiation. Tristan approaches and offers Isolde his sword to avenge Morold. She refuses and offers instead the draught of atonement. He snatches it up, believing he is drinking his own death; Isolde follows him. But Brangäne has switched the potions. Nonetheless, it is not the drug which transforms Tristan and Isolde but the belief they are about to die: they freely declare their love. The ship arrives in Cornwall, where Marke awaits his bride.

Act 2 Night. King Marke has gone hunting. Isolde is expecting Tristan in the castle garden, Brangäne warning of the risks. Determined, Isolde extinguishes the torch as a signal to Tristan, sending Brangäne to keep watch. Tristan arrives and the lovers embrace, longing for an eternity of night. Here the idea of 'death in love' (Liebestod) is born. Brangäne repeatedly warns of danger. Suddenly, Marke and his courtiers rush in, the king aghast at Tristan's betrayal. Tristan bids Isolde join him in the land of night, she asking him to show her the way. One of Marke's knights, Melot, draws his sword, and Tristan lets his former friend's blade strike him.

Act 3 The wounded Tristan lies unconscious in his native Brittany, tended by Kurwenal, who has sent for Isolde. A shepherd's sad pipe is heard. Feverish, Tristan imagines Isolde's ship approaching, then sinks back exhausted. The shepherd's tune becomes happy: Isolde's ship arrives. Tearing his bandages off, Tristan dies in her arms. A second ship — the king's — disembarks. Melot enters and is killed by Kurwenal, who is himself slain. Marke says he has learnt of the lovers' story and has come to confer forgiveness on them. Isolde, transfixed in bliss, sinks lifeless onto Tristan's body, convinced of their new life together.

Die Meistersinger von Nürnberg

Act 1 Walther, a knight visiting Nuremberg, falls in love with Eva, daughter of Pogner, the town goldsmith. However, she is set to marry the victor of a forthcoming song contest for mastersingers. To win her hand, Walther decides to become a mastersinger and enter. He is initiated into the intricate, antiquated rules governing the art of singing by David, apprentice to cobbler-poet Sachs. Walther auditions in front of the mastersingers, who cannot follow the knight's bold new song, much to the glee of town clerk Beckmesser, who wants Eva for himself. Only Sachs recognizes Walther's skills and resolves to help him.

Act 2 That evening, discouraged by the audition, Eva and Walther decide to elope, but Sachs intervenes: discounting his own feelings for her, he will surreptitiously assist the lovers. Eva switches clothes with David's betrothed, Magdalena, so she can escape with Walther. Beckmesser serenades 'Eva' but is put off by cobbler Sachs' hammering, which also prevents the lovers escaping. David is woken by the noise and attacks Beckmesser for courting his girl, sparking a riot eventually subdued by the town's night watchman.

Act 3 Dawn. The next morning, in his study, Sachs muses on the follies of the previous evening — and the world. Walther arrives, talking of a dream. Sachs teaches him the complex rules of mastersinging and how to fashion a poem from his dream. They go off to prepare, and Beckmesser enters, discovering their manuscript and thinking Sachs a rival, but Sachs assures him he is not and, indeed, can have the song. The clerk leaves, confident of victory. Eva enters in despair and Sachs comforts her, despite his own affections. At the contest on the festival meadow, Beckmesser performs Walther's poem but mangles it with an incongruous tune, to public ridicule. He accuses Sachs of tricking him, but the cobbler reveals Walther as the poem's true author. The knight himself then presents his song in the correct way, to euphoric acclaim. Walther is hailed the winner and invited to join the mastersingers. Proudly, he refuses, but Sachs reminds him of the honour due to art and tradition — which, after all, have won him Eva — to general jubilation.

Parsifal

A brotherhood of knights was founded by Titurel to guard the Grail and holy spear. Titurel's son, Amfortas, was seduced by the exiled Klingsor's temptress, Kundry, in the process both losing the spear and receiving an incurable wound from it. A prophesy states his endless torment can be healed by 'a pure fool, made wise through compassion'.

Act 1 In a forest near the castle of the Grail, the elder knight Gurnemanz and his squires awake and pray. Kundry, who serves the knights, returns from one of her long absences, bringing a healing balm to alleviate Amfortas's sufferings. Gurnemanz recalls Amfortas's sad history. A young man enters, having shot a swan. He is remorseful but can tell them nothing about himself, only vague memories of his mother, who Kundry informs him is now dead. Gurnemanz believes this is the foretold redeemer and takes him to the temple. Titurel bids his son conduct the Grail ceremony. Reluctantly, as this aggravates his mental and physical pain, Amfortas submits and begins the ritual. Parsifal understands nothing and, disappointed, Gurnemanz sends him away.

Act 2 Klingsor orders Kundry, under his spell forced to live an endless double life of holy service and sexual enticement, to seduce Parsifal. Parsifal enters Klingsor's magical garden, but the flowermaidens fail to ensnare him. However, Kundry's manipulations concerning his mother weaken him. As she kisses him, Parsifal suddenly comprehends Amfortas's suffering. Parsifal pushes Kundry away, and she tries to arouse his pity, telling of her eternal rebirth and torment for a past sin. Parsifal resists her. She summons Klingsor, who hurls the spear at

Parsifal. Seizing it, Parsifal destroys the sorcerer's realm with a sign of the cross.

Act 3 Spring. It is many years later, and Gurnemanz lives alone in the forest. Titurel is dead and the Grail locked away. Gurnemanz comes across a penitent Kundry and wakes her from a deep sleep. An unknown knight approaches. Gurnemanz recognizes him: it is Parsifal, carrying the holy spear. Parsifal tells of his long years wandering in search of Amfortas. Gurnemanz says that Parsifal is the fulfilment of the prophesy and will now lead the Grail ceremony. Kundry washes Parsifal's feet, and he baptizes her. Gazing in rapture at nature's beauty all around, Gurnemanz tells Parsifal it is the magic of Good Friday. They journey to the temple. Amfortas refuses to conduct the rite and begs for death. Parsifal arrives, closing Amfortas's wound with the spear before uncovering the Grail himself. Parsifal is the redeemer of the community. Kundry sinks lifeless to the ground, finally released.

Guide to Further Reading

Given the vast libraries of books that have been written on Richard Wagner's life, work and legacy, this guide can, of course, only hope to be a mere gesture. However, these volumes have been over the years among the most interesting and beneficial in trying to fathom the extraordinary depths of Wagner's world.

The Cambridge Companion to Wagner
ed. Thomas S. Grey
A beneficial and stimulating collection of essays covering the major issues from biography, history and compositional processes to how Wagner developed as an artist, as well as the changing ways his works have been perceived and interpreted. It also tackles the complex questions of Wagner's relationship with Nietzsche, race and politics and explores his critical, theoretical and other non-musical writings.

Bayreuth: A History of the Wagner Festival
Frederic Spotts
An extremely compelling and beautifully written account of the Bayreuth Festival, from its origins to the end of the twentieth

century; a brilliant mixture of history, biography, journalism and theatrical analysis. Spotts is a shrewd and incomparable guide, managing both to delve deep inside the festival while also remaining its detached (and wonderfully sardonic) observer. Essential reading.

Wagner and the Art of the Theatre
Patrick Carnegy

A valuable companion to Spotts. Carnegy scrutinizes how Wagner's works have been staged since the time of their conception and throughout the twentieth century — both at Bayreuth and beyond. The research is outstanding and the detail miraculous. Like that of Spotts, Carnegy's book has a wealth of beautiful illustrations and photographs, though his prose is lucid and vivid enough for them to be in many ways superfluous.

The Cambridge Companion to Wagner's *Der Ring des Nibelungen*
ed. Mark Berry and Nicholas Vazsonyi

A magnificent and absolutely indispensable collection of essays from a broad range of fantastic scholars on a vast assortment of subjects, together with an absorbing introduction from its editors. The origins and sources of the *Ring*, as well as its myriad musico-dramatic components and legacy, are given compelling space for exploration, consideration and interpretation. This is very much a Wagner for the twentieth-first century, with alert and highly intelligent new readings, but is nevertheless steeped in awareness of and fascination with scholarship from the past. A vital addition to any Wagner library.

Wagner's *Ring of the Nibelung*: A Companion
ed. Stewart Spencer and Barry Millington
Although there are some admirable short essays in this volume,
its primary interest is the exceptional English translation of the
Ring by Stewart Spencer, presented alongside the German text.
It is not only very readable but reliably captures the tenderness,
anger and spirit of Wagner's extraordinary sequence of highly
poetic libretti.

Richard Wagner: *The Ring of the Nibelung*
trans. & ed. John Deathridge
Deathridge's recent translation is a welcome and useful
contemporary supplement to Spencer's. More audacious than
Spencer in its phrase-making (occasionally perhaps a little
colloquial), it is nonetheless both great fun and extremely smart.

**Treacherous Bonds and Laughing Fire: Politics and
     Religion in Wagner's *Ring***
Mark Berry
Berry's work examines the wealth of questions Wagner's great
cycle raises, exploring with superb precision and dexterity the
way politics and religion not only inform but largely structure
the work. It is relentless and constantly profound in the way
in which it teases out the smallest musico-dramatic details
and relates them to the overall architecture and interpretative
possibilities of the *Ring*. Berry captures the almost unfathomable
reach of this enormous work across subjects, deftly and
resourcefully bringing in the relevant philosophical, religious,
socio-economic and political material but never overburdening
either the reader or his own text. Berry's unblinking eye gazes
both backwards and forwards in time but makes Wagner's *Ring*
especially pertinent to the problems which continue to plague

societies around the world today. One of the finest of all books on Wagner: eloquent, angry and very compassionate.

Drama and the World of Richard Wagner
Dieter Borchmeyer (trans. Daphne Ellis)
An excellent book which places Wagner's dramas within their literary, theatrical and cultural contexts while also exploring intricate and difficult questions of anti-Semitism, especially as they might occur in the works themselves. Borchmeyer is careful, objective and reasonable and rightly sees Wagner as a much more literary figure than the narrowly musical one we tend to know.

Richard Wagner: *Parsifal*
Lucy Beckett
A wonderful book full of enthralling contextual and background information, as well as a contentious and challenging but very engaging spiritual reading of Wagner's last work. It confronts many of our contemporary beliefs about faith, and although some of its interpretations seem untenable, especially in relation to Wagner's own views on *Parsifal*, Beckett nevertheless provokes us to re-examine this drama for ourselves, forcing us to reconsider our assumptions.

Richard Wagner: *Die Meistersinger von Nürnberg*
ed. John Warrack
A tremendous collections of essays examining pertinent topics raised by Wagner's always atypical *Meistersinger*. Not only the usual discussions of origins, sources and stage history but stimulating pieces linking Wagner with Sachs, the role of the mastersong, connections between Sachs and Schopenhauer, and the relationship between words and music which is so central to the musikdrama itself.

Death-Devoted Heart: Sex and the Sacred in Wagner's
   Tristan und Isolde
The Ring of Truth: The Wisdom of Wagner's *Ring of*
   the Nibelung
Wagner's *Parsifal*: **The Music of Redemption**
Roger Scruton
Scruton's trilogy of books on the key musikdramas consider
them from a more traditional and conservative point of view.
Although his approach is often at odds with the more radical
nature of Wagner's political and religious attitudes, Scruton
is, at the very least, thought-provoking and is often very
much more than that. A philosopher and fiercely engaged
political writer who also composed operas, Scruton is a vital
contribution to any discussion of Wagner's world.

Wagner's Women
Eva Rieger (trans. Chris Walton)
An illuminating and engaging discussion of Wagner's female
roles, examined, in part, through the women in his life and
the way they influenced his musico-dramatic methodology.
It tackles head-on and without fear of confrontation the
contradictions in Wagner's life and personality which led to
his creation of some of the most mesmerizing, paradoxical and
revolutionary characters in all dramatic art.

I Saw the World End: A Study of Wagner's *Ring*
An Introduction to Wagner's *Ring* (audio lecture)
Deryck Cooke
Two key resources. Cooke's untimely death prevented his
complete mapping of the *Ring*, which intended to chart in
detail the musical associations in the dramas. However, the
one volume we have is an irreplaceable compendium. Available

separately is Cooke's recorded lecture, with dozens of musical examples. It remains absolutely essential listening for both newcomers and seasoned operagoers, brilliantly showing how leitmotifs originate, function and interconnect throughout the *Ring*. Invaluable.

After Wagner: Histories of Modernist Music Drama from *Parsifal* to Nono
Mark Berry

A marvellous book judiciously examining Wagner's legacy in terms of composers like Strauss, Schoenberg, Nono and Hans Werner Henze, reconsidering how we think about both influence and writing about influence. Contains important sections appraising recent productions and examining the volatile, unstable and evolving nature of Wagner stagings, with an especially useful chapter on Stefan Herheim's landmark Bayreuth *Parsifal*.

Wagner Beyond Good and Evil
John Deathridge

An honest, antagonistic and remarkable book which refuses to shy away from the controversies surrounding Wagner. Indeed, it confronts them directly and argues that only through such a critical and candid appraisal can we seek to understand Wagner, his work and its meaning for us today.

History in Mighty Sounds: Musical Constructions of German National Identity, 1848–1914
Barbara Eichner

A magnificent work of scholarship which reconsiders the universal nature of the music which not only dominated the nineteenth century but remains the most popular throughout the world. With wonderfully eloquent analytical prose, Eichner investigates how music, culture, history and nationalism combined in an exhilarating but ultimately dangerous mixture, re-examining many uncomfortable assumptions about the origin, role and purpose of music in the formation and development of Germany as a nation.

Berlioz, Verdi, Wagner, Britten: Great Shakespeareans
ed. Daniel Albright

A fascinating and compelling insight into how this quartet of composers extended the critical discourse on Shakespeare to the domain of music. The section on Wagner looks beyond *Das Liebesverbot* (loosely based on *Measure for Measure*) to discuss how Shakespeare guided the German's concept of art, language and the theatre.

Wagnerism: Art and Politics in the Shadow of Music
Alex Ross

A capacious bag of ideas and influences, Ross's book charts the legacy of Wagner's philosophies and aesthetics across a vast span of history and media. Art, architecture, film, literature, politics, race, gender, sexuality — these and more are discussed with panache and insight. It is level-headed in the best sense: rational and honest.

'Nuremberg Trial: Is There Anti-Semitism in *Die Meistersinger?*'
Cambridge Opera Journal
Barry Millington

An extremely thorough essay examining the way in which nineteenth-century Jewish caricature and criticism is woven into the fabric of one of Wagner's works. A valuable and very important essay that should not be ignored, whether or not one agrees with Millington's persuasive argument. It shows not only the complexity and subtlety of great art but also its potential for disturbing ambiguity and concealment, as well as its ability to hide, change or lose its meanings through the passage of time.

The Darker Side of Genius: Richard Wagner's
Anti-Semitism
Jacob Katz

Katz asks two important questions: first about the role of anti-Semitism in Wagner's life and work and then about how far the latter contributed to Hitler's anti-Semitism/Nazism. Unlike Millington, Katz contends that little of Wagner's racism exists in his works without very strained conjecture.

Hitler 1889–1936: Hubris
Hitler 1936–1945: Nemesis
Ian Kershaw

It is impossible to leave Wagner out of a biography of Hitler, who saw his own life in Wagnerian terms and as a Wagnerian tragedy, and Kershaw's masterly two volumes show the extent to which the works dominated Hitler's mindset. A chilling study of the power of art and the abuses to which it can be put.

The Sorcerer of Bayreuth: Richard Wagner,
his Work and his World
Barry Millington

A commanding survey of Wagner's life, lavishly illustrated. Millington is a captivating and convincing biographer, and one who refuses to ignore the very dark sides to Wagner's personality. The works are given good space, too, as are appropriate and credible connections between life and art.

Wagner and Venice
John W. Barker
A fascinating account of Wagner's periodic stays in La Serenissima, including during the final few months of his life. It also gauges the legacy of Wagner's time there on the city's art and culture. Idiosyncratic but intriguing.

My Life
Richard Wagner (trans. Andrew Gray)
A riveting account of Wagner's struggles and inspirations. Needs a certain amount of circumspection, but it is an absorbing life story, entertainingly told.

Cosima Wagner's Diaries
Volume One: 1869–1877
Volume Two: 1878–1883
Cosima Wagner (trans. Geoffrey Skelton)
Not only a glimpse into the Wagners' home life, full of charming details, but containing a wealth of Wagner's own thoughts about his own works. A vast and priceless document of nineteenth-century European history.

Selected Letters of Richard Wagner
trans. & ed. Stewart Spencer and Barry Millington
Wagner was a prolific letter writer, penning tens of thousands over his life, and this selection includes many invaluable insights into his compositional processes, theories, racism and personal life.

Printed in Great Britain
by Amazon